Healing Scars

Vincent Wong

Published by W PUBLISHING, 2024.

HEALING SCARS

First edition. March 29, 2024.

ISBN: 979-8224826438

Written by Vincent Wong.

Table of Contents

DEDICATION

To my guiding lights through life's twists and turns - your presence has illuminated the pages of my story, and your influence has shaped the very essence of who I am today. Special thanks to COB and to you, the reader, for accompanying me through this narrative journey.

CHAPTER 1

"**D**o you think you'll tell him?"
Alistair ran his fingers along the thigh of his bedroom companion. It was a motion designed to tease, filled with playful desire and a reminder that there was still much of the morning left before either of them needed to be anywhere. Steven moved the hand away, slightly annoyed. In that moment, any sense of playfulness left the room.

"Stop pushing," Steven snapped.

"I'm not—"

"You are, and you know you are. And it makes you a hypocrite."

Alistair shrugged. "Lots of things make me a hypocrite. So sue me."

His smile was disarming. Steven shifted and put his hand gently on top of his boyfriend's. Despite the closed curtains, the sunlight fought its way into the room, cutting a bright line across the bed. Steven blinked. "Sorry ... I'm just ... do you think that's what he wants to talk about?"

"God, no. Pretty sure he has other things on his mind."

Steven stiffened. "I don't know how to face him."

"You do. Just look past it. Be natural and ask him for money, we could always do with more."

"We?"

"You, then. But you know what I mean; us poor students have to stick together." Alistair leaned back, grinned broadly, and settled onto the pillow. He flicked his fingers at the curtain that draped over the headboard. The tight squeeze of the double bed in Alistair's small

1

room meant sacrifices had been made with the positioning of the furniture. The window was partially blocked by the bed and caused a constant chill breeze across their faces at night.

"He's hardly rich. I'm struggling too." Steven stood up. "And when he's gone … "

Alistair slid off the bed and wrapped his arms around his lover, pulling him back onto the sheets. As a Malaysian, Steven's frame was naturally smaller than the native Scot's build. "He could get better."

"He could," Steven conceded, "but I think we both know he won't."

He settled back into Alistair's hug, closing his eyes against the world. The train to Sheffield left at a little after two in the afternoon. Six hours of quiet reading and then straight into dinner with his Dad and older sister. In truth, he was looking forward to the train journey; ever since being a child, Steven had been good at studying while commuting.

Taking the time to study was another thing that would keep his mind from his father's cancer, and coming out.

There it was.

"What're you thinking about?" Alistair broke the lengthy silence.

"Telling him," Steven admitted. "I want to, especially if he hasn't got long. I don't want him to die without me ever having had the chance. I don't want him to die thinking his only son is someone he's not."

"Then tell him."

"Oh, it's easy for you, with your Western culture and easy acceptance of all these things. In Malaysia … " Steven laughed bitterly. "Honestly, it's not just that it isn't tolerated, it's illegal. He could cut me off. Worse."

"Or he could hug you and tell you he loved you no matter what."

"Well, that shows you have never met my father."

"I haven't told mine either, remember?"

"Would he accept it?"

"Honestly, I have no idea."

"And that's why we are who we are—two queers in a closet." Steven snickered.

"Steven, your father has cancer, and it's pretty bad. If you do want to clear the air, this could be your only chance."

"Yeah. Or I could simply go on denying that his illness is terminal, keep acting like there's plenty of time for all this. I can go on thinking that they'll learn in time, that it'll come out by itself in a natural way that doesn't upset anyone. Not even my mother."

"Will he tell her?"

"Would my father tell my mother? I'd like to say he would, that their relationship is decent enough for that, but honestly? No. If he accepts it, he'd want to keep it a secret between us, and if he doesn't, then he's likely to be too ashamed and would rather deny it." Steven paused. "Of course, there's a chance he'll reject me, disown me, and call her to blame it all on her. I can't tell him."

"You need to have more trust in your parents than that."

"I do have trust in my parents—trust that they will be the people that they are. And it isn't fair of me, is it? It's meant to be a visit to him because he's ill, a visit that's about him. Isn't it selfish to take that time and make it about me?"

"Probably." Alistair reached up and yanked back a curtain, letting the morning sunlight stream in. "It's nice out, do you want to get some brunch before your train?"

"Brunch? Listen to you. You need to stop watching daytime TV. Brunch! Who says 'brunch' except wankers and well, actually just wankers?"

"Do you want food?"

"Sure."

"Then get dressed." Alistair grinned. "And pass me my clothes while you're at it."

———————

Steven put his laptop down on the floor and found himself a spot on his bed. This was it; his final moment of being at St. Andrews and the crappy flat that had he called home since he'd first arrived in Scotland. Without a sheet or any other covers, the small mattress was even more unappealing than Alistair's draughty bed, but it was the only remaining seat in a room that had been cleared of all his personal belongings.

Moving a couple of hours further north to Aberdeen for the clinical part of his medical degree was going to be a delight. More hard work, for sure, but it would be living in the same city as Alistair and, more importantly, was another step closer to his career dream. It took so long; already three years of university completed but, even with first class honours, a bachelor's degree wasn't enough.

Not enough for his father, not enough for his mother, and, of course, not enough to be able to call himself a doctor. If he was honest with himself, it wasn't enough for him, either.

But the time! Steven breathed out a disparaging breath and looked around at the last three years of his life all packed up and finished.

He looked up when Claire knocked on the door frame.

"My dad wants to go. Are you sure we got everything you need us to take?"

Steven returned the smile—he was grateful that Claire and her father were helping him move.

"Yeah, that's everything I have." Steven shrugged. "It feels pathetic now. A few books, a couple of CDs, some clothes ... They dropped into the boot of your dad's Mercedes almost unnoticed."

"Well, I'll look after it all until you make it back."

"Thanks, I really appreciate it. Tell your dad I said thanks to him, too."

"I will. Now, come here and give me a hug."

Laughing, Steven stood up and embraced her. Claire had been good friends with him since they'd stumbled into each other during Freshers' week and, of all his friends, she was the only one who would also be in Aberdeen with him. Her and Alistair, of course, but his boyfriend was different. Alistair wasn't studying to be a doctor and, though he acted as if he understood the pressures of what it was to be a foreign student desperate to become a plastic surgeon, there was still a disconnection there.

"You'll be OK?" Claire was already half out of the door.

"Yes, of course. Go, go! I'll see you in the new term."

Returning to his spot on the bare bed, Steven stared blankly at the laptop and considered the next few days while he waited for his mother to call. Despite not really wanting to speak with her, the bright alert of her Skype call was going to be the only thing to break through his dark thoughts.

There would be one last trip to Sheffield. It would be the fourth similar train journey that had happened in the recent past. Weekends had been swallowed up which, selfishly, he'd far rather have spent with Alistair. It had been weeks since he'd last seen his boyfriend and months since they'd been able to spend real time together. The brunch had been the last time that had been truly relaxing and when had that been? March? It was May now.

Each of those dutiful visits to his father had been to watch a man he didn't truly understand fall away before him, while all the time his older sister Zoe dominated with her presence. Steven wasn't sure whether she was being the caring daughter or a vulture waiting for its next meal to present itself. He couldn't get a grip on her at all, but then, that was nothing new.

One more long train ride to say goodbye to his father before flying off to Malaysia for the summer.

Was it a casual goodbye, like a hundred previous 'see you later's, or was it a true final farewell? His father had been doing his best to hide how ill he truly was. Doing his best and failing spectacularly. He just about got away with it when they spoke on Skype, but in person it was farcical. The old man was dying and he wasn't even that old.

Steven kicked out at his suitcase. He was meant to be moving across Scotland, a simple trip from one town to another, but that wasn't to be for him. No, for the good son, the ten-week gap that formed the summer break wasn't really his. After the fleeting pass-through at Sheffield, he was bound on a twelve-hour flight back to his childhood home, to visit and dote on his mother and little sister. Vivienne would provide a highlight, at least. He hadn't seen her in over a year and of all his family, he missed her the most.

But no summer of fun with Alistair. No helping Claire move in to her new place, nor finding one of his own. Instead, there was his fading father, his overbearing older sister, and nearly three months with his cloying mother. He was even going to miss his own graduation.

Steven wiped his eyes, unsure which of the conflicting emotions was the cause of the tears. "Fuck this."

A bleep drew his attention to the screen. There she was.

"Hi Mum."

"Have you got your tickets printed and your passport ready?" Immediately to business.

"I have," Steven confirmed.

"Good. Have you anything else to tell me?"

Steven shook his head. No, nothing to tell. "I'm sorry, Mum, I have to go. There's someone knocking on the door. Probably an agent coming round to check the flat. I'll call you later."

The laptop lid came down with a satisfying clunk. He'd pay for the rudeness later, no doubt, but he was in no mindset to deal with an interrogation now.

The lie made him feel strangely lonely, as if by inventing a visitor he felt there should be one. Really, there was no point sitting around any more. Time to get started on it all.

With one long look around the place that had been his home for three years, Steven folded away his laptop, grabbed the heavy backpack and equally-weighty suitcase and left without a word.

————————

His father's bedroom changed in small ways every time he visited, subtly becoming less cosy and more clinical with every passing week. Steven's eyes fell on the old alarm clock sat on the white veneer of a cheap bedside cabinet. The bright red LED lights became a haze of indistinct symbols as he stared at it. The numbers blurred until they made no sense and had instead become a bunch of small thin lines grouped in patterns that he could no longer decipher. His mind felt squeezed from the headache. Probably slightly dehydrated; it had been a while since he'd had a glass of water and sitting here just waiting for the minutes to tick by before he could reasonably and respectfully leave was becoming painful.

Zoe had left them alone for the past forty minutes; forty-three, actually, Steven reasoned as his eyes focussed properly on the clock once more. It was unusual for her as typically, she liked to hover by their father's side like a shady advisor to the king.

Zoe is Jafar. Steven chuckled to himself. Did that make him Aladdin? Jasmine? The tiger?

"Steven?" his father spoke, the first time in a quarter of an hour. The only other sound in that time had been his rasping snore.

"Sorry, did I wake you?"

"Why did you let me fall asleep? I wanted to see you before you go, and you spend that time silently sat in the chair?"

"I planned to wake you soon."

"I'm sure you did."

"I do have to go soon. The train to Heathrow is in just over an hour."

"So, you planned to wake me just in time to say goodbye."

Steven smirked. "I hadn't thought of it like that."

"I have a question to ask you."

Steven looked into the man's eyes. Much of the strength in them had gone, and with his father's strength had gone much of his own bitterness. Growing up, there had been plenty of times when Steven had wanted his father dead. Before all this. Before the UK and the cancer. Before his studies and his new life. In Malaysia. In their old life.

Now he simply pitied him. Years of medical training amplified that. Steven recognised his father's condition; he had studied it. This was no longer a vibrant man; this was something else.

Though the logistics of the trips down from Scotland had been arduous, Steven and his father had finally started to heal some of those old wounds and form a bond that had never been there before. Was it all too late?

Steven breathed out slowly through his nose.

"Ask away."

"Steven, are you gay?"

He barely held in his gasp; the question made his mind spin. What had prompted this? Had he said something to trigger it?

He held his father's gaze. Didn't even blink. And lied.

"No."

It was as simple as that. Weeks of deliberation, days of internal monologue, multiple conversations with Alistair about how much they wanted to be free, to be open and honest. All of it gone in a single word.

Steven ran his hand through his hair, surreptitiously wiping his brow that threatened to glisten with sweat. Fuck.

The quiet that followed began to stretch. Steven turned away, glanced back at the glowing clock, and then looked again at his father's face. There was room to repair it, enough silence and space to undo the lie and turn it into a truth of some kind.

Steven opened his mouth.

"Are you looking forward to going home? To seeing your mother and sister?"

And the moment passed.

"In some ways."

"And not in others." His father laughed. "Not in most, I'm sure. You'd rather get settled in Aberdeen."

Steven nodded. He answered perfunctorily and felt hollow as the conversation moved on to other things.

The clock continued its relentless updates. One minute, two, three, until ...

"Dad, I have to go. I'll see you when I get back."

And there it was; his goodbye. He did make it a 'see you later'. That was what he wanted.

"I'll look forward to it."

On the train to Heathrow, Steven replayed the moment a thousand times.

He'd said no.

He'd been frightened. Ashamed of who he was. Terrified of his father's reaction.

Could he fix it? If Dad could hold on, then when he was back in the autumn, maybe he'd bring Alistair with him. "This is my friend, Dad. You know how you asked me, and, well, I lied."

He'd lied.

Steven looked out of the window, at a greying evening that, tomorrow, would be replaced with the warmth and sunshine of home. If Dad could hold on ... please don't let that be another lie.

It had been Zoe, of course. She'd suspected Steven's sexuality for years and would have loved to stir a little, to make herself a little more perfect in Daddy's eyes. Zoe had never understood that she didn't need to step on others to make herself taller, and sadly seized every opportunity that she could to do just that. Six years older than Steven, she'd always been a bit smarter, a little more cunning, and with a cruel penchant for manipulation.

She had been there with their father, looking after him every day, just as she'd insisted. Whispering into his ear. It would have been so easy to put the suggestion into the old man's head.

"Do you think my brother is gay?" she could have said one evening. "Only we never actually see him with a girl, do we? Not seriously, anyway. He's twenty-two soon, don't you think he should at least be considering a serious relationship? Even marriage. Isn't it strange that he's never said anything about it?"

And Steven's poor excuses would have been seen for what they were. "Well, Dad," he was fond of saying, "look at you and Mum. I don't mean to be rude, but you didn't exactly show us that marriage was a perfect union."

Not when you left us alone, only to come back with your tail between your legs months later. Not when you and Mum barely speak to each other any more. Not when you live in the UK, and she stays in Malaysia.

That last one wasn't fair. Zoe had been the one to coax him to the UK with her tales of advanced medicine and a better quality of cancer care.

But his father had never argued the point. A simple nod of the head and lost expression which showed he understood and knew fully where he'd been at fault.

Until today.

"Steven, are you gay?"

And the shameful, desperate, childish "no".

Their relationship deserved better.

CHAPTER 2

Vivienne rushed him as soon as he stepped through the door at Singapore airport. At eleven, Steven's little sister was so thin that he could easily wrap his arms around her. Her ponytail bounced up and down with excitement and her brown eyes sparkled as words spilled from her mouth, a torrent of questions without any pretence of a gap of silence to enable him to answer. Him studying on the other side of the world had been wrenching for many reasons, but Viv was the main one. He adjusted his balance for the spinning hug and, three full turns later, put her down gently.

"Mum has been crazy over you coming," she said, her Cantonese a beautiful sound after months of Scottish accents at St. Andrews. "She's been cleaning and rearranging and everything."

"Is she here?"

"At the car, come on."

And that was it, he was home.

Time in Malaysia was different to the UK. That wasn't to say anything was less busy, or that more or less was done in a single day. It just felt *different*.

As the days drifted past, Steven wondered if he'd made a mistake coming back.

Away from his new life. Away from his dying father, left completely to Zoe's machinations. Away from Alistair.

The latter didn't do long-distance so well. Middle-distance, like their Aberdeen-to-St. Andrews relationship back in Scotland he just about handled, but time zone differences and that other-side-of-the-world feeling was too much for Alistair. There'd been a couple of texts the first day, a couple more the second and third, but by the end of the week, even the ritual "goodnights" had dropped away to nothingness.

The holidays constituted months. Steven wondered if his secret relationship with a man on the far side of the globe was going to survive. And if it didn't? What then? Back to lying and pretending, no doubt.

Another tension between him and Al was the latter's insistence for Steven to come out to his parents. It was somewhat hypocritical given Alistair's own family secrecy, but where Steven was genuinely frightened to broach the subject with his mother, Alistair's remaining in the closet seemed more due to laziness than real worry.

"It's different now," Alistair had said in response to Steven's reluctance to take this opportunity to speak about his sexuality to his mother face-to-face.

"Different how?"

"Because there's me."

Because there was him and surely that made it all more real, more urgent, more important that they stop hiding who they are.

Was he really that naive? Was their situation that serious?

Steven breathed in slowly. He had been thinking that Alistair was the flippant, casual one who might decide to flake out when three months apart became too much. Was it actually the other way around? Was Alistair genuinely wanting Steven to open up to his family in order to bring more security and substance to the two of them?

Steven sank back on his bed and closed his eyes. What was he supposed to feel? Wanted? Guilty? Completely freaked out? All of those or none?

But whatever change their relationship had done for Steven, it didn't change who his parents were. It wouldn't make his mother more accepting or his father suddenly lose his inbred homophobia.

Steven blinked and stared at the ceiling, forcing his thoughts in a different direction. The thrum from the ageing air conditioner denied silence, but he was used to it; he'd been doing little else but lying around for days. The flurry of excitement that came with returning home in those first few hours had drifted away rapidly, to been replaced with the rut-like monotony of homelife. Here, he was free of responsibility and didn't even have to make his own meals. Viv was still commuting off to Singapore every day for school, and their mother had to drive her, sitting in the car for six hours a day just so her precious daughter could get a decent education. For the first time, Steven had seen it from the other side, seen how much she was giving to her children, and he'd been impressed. Just not so much that he actually did anything to help.

"I'll offer to do the pick-ups in the evening," he said to the air. "It'll give me a chance to speak properly to Viv too, to find out who she really is and the things she cares about."

After his birthday. In two days he'd be twenty-two. Another step further away from childhood.

Childhood. Steven snorted to himself; his childhood had been erased a decade earlier, wiped out by reality and circumstance. The ceiling, moments before nothing more than a bland focus point in the room, suddenly came into focus. Cracks and lines that he recognised from years of lying here, hiding away and praying that he could get out, that he could get free. Yet, here he was again, willingly home for the holiday.

The light from his phone brought a welcome distraction. Steven picked it up.

Dad's in hospital. Not routine. Not simple.

Steven stared at the words, head swaying as the letters seemed to shift on the screen.

Not routine.

No, there was never a routine text message, not from Zoe.

Not simple.

He's going to die.

Steven's fingers hovered over the onscreen keyboard. Was there something he could say? Something worthwhile?

I'll tell Mum, he sent.

For fuck's sake, Steven. Pathetic!

But what were his alternatives? To write some meaningless platitude-filled response? To offer to rush back to the UK? There was nothing he could do and the logistics of getting back right now were complicated, to say the least. To call her and ask her how she was?

Steven checked the time. By the routine he'd watched for the last week, his mother would be back in less than half an hour. No point texting her, no point breaking news like this while she was busy elsewhere. It could wait.

OK.

Nothing else. What had happened to their relationship? Where was the closeness of brother and sister, consoling each other on the imminent death of their father?

Steven laughed ruefully. That had died a long time ago.

The sound of the door opening was less than ten minutes in coming. With his speech already prepared and re-prepared in his head, Steven went to meet his mother.

"Steven ..." she said.

And he knew. Zoe had already texted her. Of course she had.

————

"Happy birthday to you ..."

Steven listened to his father croak out the song. He smiled for the old man, trying to ignore the backdrop of hospital machines and clinical whiteness. Never in his twenty-two years had he ever heard his dad sing him 'Happy Birthday'.

Bittersweet that the first time was going to be the last.

"Thanks, Dad." Steven wiped his eyes. Don't fucking cry now.

"I'm sorry that I can't be there with you to share it."

There was a look of genuine honesty in those fading eyes that took Steven by surprise. Even on their best days, they'd never felt this close.

Perhaps he should tell him, right now.

A coughing fit stole the moment.

"I have to go," his dad managed eventually. "Please, do have a happy birthday. I'll talk to you, soon."

Soon would be six days later.

Death should not come by conference call.

Crowded around a laptop screen, Steven, Viv and their mother saw the faces of Zoe and their father. The latter was gaunt, struggling to speak or hold his focus on the screen. No one said anything about it, as if by remaining silent, they somehow helped the others.

"I'm sorry." The patriarch of the family opened with his apology, a need to repair some of his connection with his wife and children.

For each one of them, he'd have a different list of regrets in his head, Steven thought.

The wrongs he had done their mother would be both long and private; the wrongs he had done to each of the children were probably complicated and not easily undone. So, it was left to two weak words to convey years of regret and acceptance to four very different people.

Not good enough, thought Steven, simultaneously with 'you're forgiven, Dad.'

He stared out of the window and gazed blankly at the trimmed green grass that formed a wide, neat line between the house and the boundary wall. It hadn't always looked like that. When he'd been younger, it had been more dirt than lawn.

A stifled sob from his mother pulled his attention back to the room. Back to his family.

Tears streaked all their faces. His father's were weakest, whether from a lifetime of holding back emotion, or because the cancer had taken that from him as well as everything else. Zoe's looked oddly perfect, like fake lines that traced through the make-up on her face as if she'd planned their direction. Viv's were childlike, free of embarrassment, but also lacking experience. Steven's mother's tears were double-edged; genuine love and care that warred with a sense of finality and freedom from the lies and deceit that had riddled their marriage. And his own? Steven put a hand up to his face to wipe them away; a young man's tears, that's all, tears of loss and disappointment, of regret and personal admonishment. Tears he had never intended to show; there was little room for them now.

Dad, everyone, look, I know this isn't the best time, but I'm gay. I'm sorry, Dad, I needed to say it before you were gone. I can't live my life thinking I hid it from you, even on your deathbed.

That's what he should say, what a braver version of himself would say. In reality, Steven remained silent.

His father was going to go to his afterlife, believing his son was something he wasn't. There would never be a time to put it right.

"Zoe, you are eldest, you must look after the others."

Ah yes, the money. What did that mean? Had his father put control of their livelihoods in his sister's hands? Steven bit back the questions; again, it was inappropriate.

His mind swam as the dying man spoke to his wife and daughters. If there were words in there for him, Steven didn't hear them. He had failed his father. Failed to be there for him, failed to be honest for him, failed to be the son he wanted. Failed, even, to be the one mature enough to take on the family accounting.

Zoe was speaking about him. Promising their father that she'd help her younger brother through his degree, ensure that he would become a doctor.

Administration. That's what this had become; a business meeting about how the administration of their family would be organised upon their father's death. It was wrong. Morbid, emotionless, and not reflective of anything Steven was feeling.

But, of course, it was the only way to do things. It was what his father needed—to die believing his responsibilities were all in hand. Zoe was well prepared for the moment, and again, of course that was true. She'd been ready for months, with everything planned meticulously.

Why was no one speaking about the fun times? Why was no one sharing memories? Where had that part of being a family gone?

"It's OK, Dad," Steven heard himself say. "I'm here for everyone, too. Zoe's not the only one. I'll make sure Mum and Viv are safe and well."

"That's great, Steven," Zoe said, the sarcasm covered just enough so only Steven could be convinced it was there. "I'm sure you'll take care of everything that needs doing out there."

"Children," his mother said, her tone a warning one. Steven smiled; perhaps Zoe's snideness wasn't hidden from everyone as well as he'd thought.

And then silence took over. In the very last moments, when they should have all been together, holding his hand at his bedside, only Zoe was there when their father died. There had been no hand-holding.

Gently, Steven closed the laptop lid, banishing the image from the hospital. As his younger sister and mother cried freely, he realised his face was dry. No more tears; truly, he was now the only man left in the household.

"I'll take care of everything, Mum," he whispered, reaching across to take her hand. "I'll take care of everything."

———

"So, you're going to introduce me to your mum?" Alistair's grin was broad, filling the screen.

"Not like that, I'm not. I'm sorry, Al, but it's far too soon after everything. As far as she's concerned, we're just friends."

"Good friends, like the sort of friends where one of us sorts out where you're going to be living next week, even though it took him three days and about a hundred phone calls."

"Are you fishing for more thanks? I said thank you, more than once."

"You'll like the place, I'm just sorry it's so temporary. There's loads of room for all three of you."

"Good. And thank you again. Send me the address and I'll buy the plane tickets later today."

"Next week, yes?"

"Yes. God, it'll be good to come back. I didn't think I'd miss greyness and, well, all the Scottishness of it all, but I do."

"Don't you go dissin' Scotland!"

"Seriously? Now you're getting all patriotic."

"Nah, not at all. Is your mum sure she wants to come to the UK?"

"She's grieving and she's not coping too well. I need to stay with her and Viv to look after them and I can't just drop my degree and ruin my career to stay here, can I? It was her idea."

"It's very dutiful of you."

"It's the right thing to do. Viv is ridiculously excited. But then, she's not even twelve, and there are no responsibilities when you're just a kid."

"And Zoe?" Alistair asked.

"And Zoe what?"

"What does she think of this move to Aberdeen?"

"It's where I need to be to study. She knows that. She promised Dad that she'd keep me on that path, so she'll do it."

"Do promises mean that much?"

"Made on her father's deathbed? I don't know, but it has to stack up well enough."

"Is she going to give you money, though, Steven? It's important that you can afford to live."

Steven cringed. As much as he sometimes appreciated the bluntness to how his boyfriend could discuss finances—especially those that were not his own—it still felt invasive. He'd told Alistair how Zoe had managed to convince their father to change his life-insurance beneficiary to her, and how effective that had been at cutting money away from their mother. Alistair had been the support he needed at the time and, as a consequence, the Scot had developed a staunch dislike of Steven's older sister.

"She'll give me money," Steven assured him.

Alistair nodded, as if to say 'as long as you're sure'. He cleared his throat. "What about me? Are you looking forward to getting some more of this hotness?"

Steven laughed. "Always."

"Good, because it's been a while. I'm all for this being-together monogamy when you are in the same city, even country, but the last few months have been hard. I did think you'd come back for your St. Andrews graduation, if I'm honest. I had this whole thing planned, and then it all went to nothing."

"Dinner and flowers?"

"Something like that."

"I couldn't come. My mum just wasn't in the right place, even though she was insisting that I go back, too. In the end, it was the right decision. I still have the piece of paper, and that's what matters. Just a few more years to tick off."

"Don't rush them. Student life is better than a working one, I'm pretty sure."

"I just want to stop relying on other people and stand on my own two feet."

"Yeah, well. Just promise me you're actually coming back now."

"Yup. I've even sorted the visas for Mum and Viv. Don't worry, it's happening."

Steven looked at him, silence taking over for a few minutes. Technology was great, but it was a poor substitute for really being there. Like the final moments of his time with his father, this long-awaited conversation with Alistair was missing the physical aspects.

"You OK?" Alistair asked after a moment.

"Just thinking I want to come back. I'm pretty much done with Skype calls and organising everything. I just want it done."

"I know what you mean."

"Do you?"

Alistair shrugged. "OK, I don't. What do you want me to say? You went away for months, and I've missed you, too. Just be pleased you're coming back soon."

"You OK about me bringing my mum?"

A chuckle. "It's a bit weird, not gonna lie. But yeah, it's fine. So, you live with your mum now; just gives us more excuses for spending time at my place. I'll tidy up a bit for you and everything."

"She'll like you."

"She'll like who she thinks I am. Your *friend*. She won't like me if you tell her who I really am."

Steven sighed. "Sorry."

"It's OK, I'd do the same to you. Look, I've got stuff to do, anyway. Rather than us moaning about how we want to see each other, let's just get on with it. You do your organising and ticket buying and all that, and I'll pick up some socks."

Steven sighed again. "OK, I'll see you in a week."

The sound of the call ending annoyed him. Why was Alistair so bad at just chatting? It had to have a purpose for him or it was just a waste of time. While they were organising the living arrangements or bitching about Zoe, he was fine, happy to listen and to talk, too, but as soon as it slowed, entering that phase of just being comfortable in each other's company, Alistair was done.

It left Steven desperately lonely.

Still, there was only one more week to go. Mid-week flights would be best, both financially and in terms of travel ease. He hadn't been lying when he said he missed the colder atmosphere of Scotland; Malaysia was feeling less like home and more like somewhere he just used to live.

Viv stuck her head in through the door, a console controller in her hand. "Wanna come and play something?"

Steven stood up. One more week.

CHAPTER 3

Rain hammered at the window, wind and water creating a symphony of chaos that echoed around the small flat.

Viv ran over and pulled the curtains tight shut, putting her hands over her ears for emphasis and slumped onto the cream sofa. Beside her, the small table wobbled, the lamp that sat upon it threatening to fall. The young girl caught it quickly and breathed out in relief.

"Does is always have to rain so much here?" their Mum complained, looking up from her book with a scowl.

Steven looked at her and sighed. "You have always lived in Malaysia. It's monsoon season right now. Why are you acting like there's more rain here?"

"It's not the same. Here it is dark, and cold. The rain feels bitter."

"I like it. I think it's comfortable."

"You are a fool."

They had been in the UK for five weeks. The first three had been in a large house with a huge garden and the tail end of summer sunshine. Their temporary accommodation had needed to be replaced with something permanent and Steven had found the small two-and-a-half-bedroom flat close enough to the university campus, and close to Alistair, plus—importantly—at a price they could afford.

Steven's mother had been understanding but didn't hold back on emphasising her frustration at the comedown. It had taken her years to build her personal lifestyle up from decades of difficulty and this step backwards was obviously unwanted, even if for her, it was temporary; a break to deal with grief.

"Zoe should not be keeping us on such a short financial leash," she had complained, almost daily.

Steven felt the same way, but it would do no good for him to fan the flames of his mother's growing rage. Instead, he acted as if the miserly stipend his sister controlled and fed out to them was an acceptable amount.

"I'll get some work soon. The extra money will come in helpful."

"For Viv, yes. Does extra money stop the rain?"

Steven laughed. "No, Mum. Perhaps you can talk to it. No doubt it'll run cowering from your anger."

"I should! And don't be clever—it doesn't impress me." She put her book down. "When is Alistair here?"

"Twenty minutes." Steven didn't need to check the time.

"Good."

Alistair had quickly become a favoured guest. His offer to tutor Viv at no extra cost, to make sure that she was not only ready for a new school system, but that she'd excel had gone a long way to making a good impression on Steven's mother. A few choice gifts every now and then, in the form of tasty local delicacies he brought the older woman had cemented him as welcome at any time.

Alistair's regular presence both pleased and unnerved Steven, who worried that something would happen that would expose his sexuality to his last living parent. Alistair was less worried about the possibility, believing that his status in her eyes was good enough to survive such a shock.

"You don't know her," Steven had insisted the previous night. They were together at Alistair's flat, enjoying the privacy. Neither had really considered just how much of Steven's time his family would demand. In the couple of months since his father's death, everything had changed. Now, finding moments for just the two of them was harder than ever.

"I know her quite well," Alistair countered.

"You know her public face, her polite 'oh-I-have-a-guest' personality, but you don't know *her*."

"Fair, but I still think she'll react well, even if it's just to get me as a son-in-law."

Steven grinned. "You proposing?"

"No! You know what I mean, though."

"I do."

The conversation had gone no further, as the evening turned physical. The passionate desire stoked from months away from each other had not yet been sated, even after five weeks back. Steven had accepted the kiss and had dived into his lover's embrace.

"We should invite Alistair to stay for dinner." His mother's words pulled Steven from his recent memory. "He is very good to us. A fine friend of yours."

"He'd like that."

"Then go to the shop. There are things I will need."

"Now?"

"Of course now. I will need to start soon. It is already late."

"In the rain?"

"You grew up in the rain, Steven, don't tell me it scares you here. Or is this rain different? Too cold for you?"

"No." Steven picked up his coat. "What do you need?"

———

It took a week.

A week of Alistair's confident prodding, and hideous, embarrassed stop-starts from Steven.

"Mum, there's something you need to know," he had said, before faltering and changing the subject.

"Mum, I wanted to talk about ..."

"Mum, listen ..."

But each time, an excuse, a twist, a quick, less important lie had filled the gap.

It took a week before she stopped him.

"Sit down, Steven. Tell me whatever it is you have been trying to tell me. There is nothing you can say that we cannot solve between us."

Steven looked at her. Viv was asleep in the room they were sharing; he could hear her soft snoring through the wall.

"Have you impregnated a woman?"

"No." Steven giggled and shook his head. "No."

"Well?"

"It's the opposite, actually. I like men."

And there it was. Weeks of visiting his father, unable to share this most intimate detail of his life; more weeks in Malaysia, grieving and making arrangements for a new life; yet more weeks in Aberdeen, dealing with Zoe's tight financial control and Viv's new school. On every one of those days he had asked himself if he could possibly open up and tell someone. He'd considered his older sister, his younger sister, even family friends, but it had always been his mother who he needed to tell.

Now it was in the open.

Steven had never experienced silence so filled with rage before. He pushed himself back on the sofa, suddenly terrified of the fury that was erupting before him. Gone was the thought that there was nothing they couldn't solve. Here was a woman whose life-long understanding and beliefs had been irreversibly overturned.

"No." Just one word. It cut the stillness like a sword, honed to perfection.

Steven gasped.

"No," she said again.

And then she screamed.

Her hands flailed in uncontrolled anger, spinning fists that really had no target but found some anyway. A cushion, a knee, once or twice his head, covered over protectively with desperately crossed arms.

"Mum—"

"No! Do not call me that!"

"I—"

"You shame me! You shame your dead father!"

"But I—"

"Enough, Steven. This stops now. You take these stupid ill-thought words back."

"Take them back?"

"Yes! Take them back."

"I can't. I'm—"

"No! Don't say it again. No son of mine would ever identify themselves like that."

"Can't you even say the word?"

"You want me to say it?" she raged. "Gay, Steven, Gay. No son of mine would ever say he was *gay*."

"I am your son." Steven clenched his fists. "And I am saying it."

"No!"

"You would have accepted if I had made some woman pregnant? Some stranger?"

"Yes, of course! Some stranger, some whore? At least that is what a man does! A man sleeps with women. Stupid, uncaring, even getting diseases, but the actions of a man. What are your actions? They are not of a man. You want to lie with them? I will not accept it!"

"I—"

"You do not get to speak. You will listen."

Steven nodded. His head slumped as his eyes dropped to focus on the floor. The grey patterned carpet became momentarily important, something he could collapse on, something that might cushion him in this desolate moment. Blinking, he forced himself to look up once more as she continued.

"You are my only son. On you lies the duty to carry on the family name. Not duty just to myself or your father, but to all our ancestors. That is how you bring honour to our family. It is your responsibility so that the family line continues. Instead, you tell me this? That you are a dirty creature, looking to be with other men, instead of the true love that only can happen with a man and a woman? You bring me shame, Steven, not just in this time, in this life, but to all our family and all those who have come before us. You disgust me!"

"It's still *me*! I am still me."

"Are you? No son who I brought up would ever want to be like this. Do you not disgust yourself?"

"No! I am at peace with myself."

"Lies."

"Mum!" Steven's face was streaked with tears. Tears that had been held back after his father's death. Tears that were denied when his sister cremated their father without consultation, without him being present. Tears that were put aside so that he could be responsible and adult.

"I cannot accept it. I do not accept it."

"You must."

"Pah!"

"I am trying to do the right thing. To tell you, to talk to you. I didn't want to have this as a lie between us, as it was with Dad."

"It is good he went to the grave without hearing such things. Good for him. You allow him that peace, and then you bring this all upon me!"

"No, it isn't. I regret it every day. He died and I said nothing. I visited him in hospital and I said nothing. Every time, I wanted to. Every time we spoke about it, but I couldn't go through with it."

"*We*?"

"Yes, my boyfriend and I."

"Your *boyfriend*?" The word was spat across the room. "You have a boyfriend? This is not simply thoughts and feelings inside you? You have acted upon them, lain with men? You have a boyfriend?"

"Yes, Alistair, I—"

"Alistair!" she shrieked. "No! You have brought that filthy animal into our home. You let him teach my daughter! What is he teaching her? What disgusting thoughts is he feeding her? I have welcomed him! I have cooked for him, shared food and conversation! And this!"

"Alistair thought you would feel differently. You know him, you know he is a good man."

She spat on the floor. "He is dirt. Nothingness. You will never allow him in this house again."

"No, you can't force these things. I'm an adult, a man. This is my home."

"Your home! You think that you could afford even this alone? This flat is paid for by your father."

"Mum, please."

"When did you know?"

"What?"

"That you were against nature. When did you know you were gay?"

"When I was a kid. A long time ago. I've always really known."

"A child?"

"Yes."

"What do children know? This is a child's fantasy played out as an adult. A mental illness. You are not gay; you have just been acting out a game that went too far. Do you think you are a superhero, too? Or a wizard or dragon? Of course not. This is no different."

"Of course this is different. I am attracted to men."

"Have you even bothered to see a psychiatrist about it? It is a mental disorder."

"It is not!" Steven shouted.

"Have you even tried conversion therapy?"

"No. I—"

"I will pay for it. With my savings. You must be cured."

"Cured?"

"Yes. It is a mental illness. Did Alistair make you gay? He must have."

"I have been gay a lot longer than I have known Alistair. People don't make other people gay."

"It is coming to the UK! When you went to Brighton for the first time. Brighton! I had heard stories, but I believed it would be good for your education. That was when you were turned, isn't it?"

"What, no. Mum—"

"This cannot be! You will take the conversion therapy. We will fix you." She was crying.

"I'm not broken!"

"What will people think of me?" she said quietly, sinking to the floor. "What did I do to deserve this?"

"Mum?" Steven slid off the sofa.

"What did I do to deserve this kind of humiliation in my life?" she whimpered.

Silently, Steven stretched his hand out. Viciously, she slapped it back.

"Don't touch me."

For a long time, neither of them moved. Tears ran freely down both faces. Twice, Steven reached out to the woman who had cared for him his entire life. Twice, she rebuffed him.

"I will pray for you," she said.

"I don't need praying for."

"You don't know what you need. I will pray harder so that you can be normal."

"I am normal, Mum."

"Being homosexual is not normal, Steven."

"I'm not going to change. This is who I am."

"No, you will do the therapy. You will learn that a man belongs with a woman, and a woman with a man. This is the right way of things. You will change!" she screamed.

"Please stay calm," Steven begged. "Please."

"I will try to remain calm. You will get your phone."

"What?"

"You will call that bastard, Alistair. You will tell him that you can no longer see him, that he should not come near any of us."

"What? Don't you care about my happiness? Is it that straight couples experience love and what Alistair and I have isn't that?"

"Love?" she snarled at the word. "Men do not love other men."

"Of course, I can feel love. I love him."

"Alistair?"

"Yes!"

"You make me sick. You are twisted. Your mind is broken."

"Mum."

"No. You will do as I say. You will call him, and you will tell him it is over. He should never be seen here again, and you will not go to him."

"What happened to 'there's nothing we can't solve'?"

"We are solving it."

"No, not this way."

"There is only this way. Any other way is wrong and shameful. You will get your phone and you will tell him as I have said. I have had enough. Listen to me. I don't care if you are unhappy for the rest of your life if happiness has to mean this perversion. If you say you cannot be happy with a woman, then so be it. Be unhappy. If you can, find a girlfriend and get married like a normal person."

"And if I can't?"

"Then you stay single until the day you die. This will be our distasteful secret. I am not going to tell anyone about this, and neither will you. Don't you dare speak a word of it to anyone—especially your sisters."

She stood up, reached across the counter for the phone, and threw it into Steven's lap. "Call that bastard now."

Steven looked at the phone and listened to the sound of Viv's still-soft snoring coming through the wall. Too clear, too obvious, too fake. He said nothing as he tapped in the unlock code.

CHAPTER 4

Steven watched the sun come up with dismay. Day four. He didn't move, stuck simply staring through the gap in the curtain. Another night of fitful, restless, sleep. Another night alone.

His jeans were entangled around his ankles. Once, that would have meant he'd collapsed, laughing, mid-passion, passing out from pure joy and delight, wrapped in Alistair's arms, or just lying decadently by his side. Today, it was a very different sign; evidence that he couldn't be bothered to even disrobe before collapsing onto the bed.

That, too, was a mess. A fitting central focal point for the room as a whole. His chest of drawers open with the contents spilling onto the floor; the bedside table, usually so neat, home to a pair of cups that were days old; textbooks and the first scribbles of his new course scattered uncared-for across the carpet, threatening to trip any unwary visitor. Steven groaned.

The door opened. A short and thin body slipped in and then closed the door behind her.

"Get up, Stevie, you're a mess," Viv said. Stevie; she'd started using it as his new nickname that first morning after. It was her subtle signal to him that she knew, and she didn't care. It was the kind of cute shortening of his name that normally he'd reject, but in this new darkness represented a thin line of connection between them, and he wrapped himself around it.

"Nothing on this morning," he mumbled.

"That's hardly the point. In fact, it'll give you time to clean this pit, won't it?"

"No need. Just no need."

"God, I never knew pathetic could look so pathetic," Viv flumped onto his bed. "I can see your arse."

"Language!"

"If you don't want me saying arse, cover it up." She grinned and Steven smiled despite his sullen mood.

"I don't want to be the bad influence. You shouldn't be using words like that."

"Puh-lease, bro,."

Steven shook his head.

"Look, seriously, Mum's got me lined up to see some other tutor now that Alistair has suddenly vanished without a trace. She's taking me there in half an hour. I know it's not much, but I'll keep her out for a while and you can have the place to yourself until lunch at least. I'll text when we're on the way back, too, give you a little bit more time."

Steven turned over, pulled up his jeans and shuffled into a seating position. "Thanks."

"Yeah, well, you're welcome."

"It's a bit early for tutors, isn't it?"

"We're meeting at eight. Compared to the old days, this is pretty relaxed. I can't say I miss the Singapore commute."

Steven nodded. "I can imagine."

"Besides, we won't actually do more than meet this person and then not follow it up. I know we can't afford a tutor, really."

"Viv, that's not your concern. That's mine. Mine and Mum's. We'll make sure you've got the support you need. Your education is important."

"Sure, yeah. You and Mum. First of all, you'd need to start talking again, and second, it's neither of you, it's Zoe. Wow, you think I'm so thick sometimes, and like I can't hear anything. I know everything, Stevie, nothing is hidden."

"You'd be surprised."

"So would you."

They looked at each other for a moment, as if each were daring the other to break a confidence or spill a secret just to test. Neither did.

Eventually, Steven smiled. "You've done a good job. I'm awake, I'm up, I'm even sort of dressed. Go on and have some breakfast before you have to go out and I promise I'll clean up while you're gone."

"Good." Viv hopped back towards the door. "It's not her fault, she just wants the best for her kids, you know? All of us."

Steven looked at her, trying fruitlessly to gauge exactly what she had heard, and what she was simply fishing for. "I know. I know."

With the small flat to himself for the first time in days, Steven took a deep breath. Depression, misery, sadness; these were emotions his upbringing and personality rejected but seemed so hard to shake off. He wondered if he had wallowed enough.

In the bathroom, he stared into the mirror and despaired at the person who looked back. "A soulless outer shell," he muttered, "just a soulless shell."

Telling Alistair had been the hardest thing. Steven snorted. Telling Alistair; he hadn't even really managed to tell his boyfriend anything.

"You have to just accept it," he'd sobbed into the phone.

"Why?"

"Please, Al. Don't. Don't ask, just accept. Sometimes these things are out of our hands."

"Out of our hands? It's our relationship, Steven. The only hands it is in are ours!"

"That's not true, that's a romanticism. It's not how real life works."

"Real life? We've been living real life for months. For *years*."

Steven's tears had seemed endless. "Please don't ask me why."

"Because you don't want to say it. Your mum, is that what it is? Oh fuck, Steven, so you told her. I'm pleased. Honestly, I'm pleased and proud and—"

"And nothing! Nothing. Don't you get it?"

"I get it." Alistair was sobbing, too. "No, actually I don't get it. Explain it to me."

"I can't. My family. My culture. I'm Malaysian Chinese; do you have any idea what a Chinese upbringing is like? And my parents are far more traditional than mainland Chinese. Conservative is an understatement. I knew it was wrong to tell her. I knew it was. All those times with my dad, I was right to be scared."

"Stop this. We'll talk to her. *I* will talk to her."

"No, she won't listen. She won't even have you in the house. That's one of the things I have to tell you. No more. No tutoring Viv, none of it. No dinners. No ..." Steven had buried his face into his pillow, his voice little more than a whimper.

"Fuck this! She can't control your life like this."

"Of course she can. I have to think about her, about Viv, about what's right. I'm sorry, Al." He'd gone silent, pretending in his mind that he'd hung up the phone, but he hadn't. Instead, he stared at the screen, listening to his lover's quiet, choking cries.

"Alistair," he'd whispered.

And the phone disconnected, the contact cut off by the other man.

The face in the mirror looked at Steven.

"What're you looking at?" Angrily, he picked up the toothpaste and his brush and squeezed far too much of the former onto the latter. Bits of wasted minty stripes dropped into the basin. Steven watched as they slowly slipped towards the plug hole before coming to a stop, unable to finish the journey. He turned on the tap, wiped the mess away with a hand and scrubbed vigorously at his teeth.

In the mirror, the soulless man just watched.

"No time for this," Steven grunted, his mouth fresh. He turned on the shower and pulled his sticky clothes to the floor. However he felt inside, he had responsibilities, not the least to his little sister. Fulfil his duties as expected; it was typical Chinese culture. Do that, and be done with it.

Why should he have anything to look forward to? Why should his life be one of excitement?

"Out of the closet and into a cage." His bitter words echoed in the silence of the empty room, punctuated only by the sound of warm water hammering into his back. Only this cage was worse. At least Alistair had shared the closet with him, hiding with him as they shared their love and affection for each other.

He was stuck in this new cage with his mother. Her, desperate to hide his awful secret in case anyone ever found out the scandal, and him, bound by that duty, tied by that responsibility.

And it would be like that until she died.

Steven slipped to his knees. Part of him played with the idea, that perhaps he wanted his mother to die—dark thoughts of evil whimsey and terrible shadow that had no right to the day. No matter how badly she'd trapped him, though, he would never want that. He'd lost one parent recently; he wasn't ready to consider losing the other.

There was Viv, of course. And Zoe. Even her, clutching onto their purse-strings with almost paranoid wariness. Even Zoe was something.

By the time his sister and mother returned home, pre-empted as promised by the subtle text, the flat was bright and airy. Steven watched them come along the street through the window but ducked before he could be seen. He'd taken a step, for sure, but it was a long road, and he wasn't planning on reaching any sort of destination today. When they came in, he'd make his excuses.

"I have a headache," perhaps, or just simply "I'm busy." The latter was easily true, as well. There were studies; plenty of work to do to avoid any more drama.

"Steven," his mother said, as soon as the front door was open.

"Later," he said, already opening the opposite door to his room. "I've got some work I need to finish; deadline on Monday, and I've already spent too long cleaning up. Sorry I've been useless these past few days. Not been feeling too well, but I'm better now. I need to catch up. Maybe we can speak in the evening."

He'd shut the door before the brief monologue was even three-quarters done.

The chanting became more frequent as the days progressed. What was once a calm Buddhist ritual became almost frenzied as if somehow, by increasing the regularity and volume of her prayers, Steven's mother truly could rid him of this awful curse.

Steven cringed and lay on his bed, masochistically forcing himself to listen to the desperate pleas through the thin wall. There was little doubt in his mind that the loud clarity of the chants was for his benefit, to let him know exactly what she was praying for.

It would have been disrespectful to turn on some music, to try to drown her out. Similar with the TV, or a computer game. Disrespectful, but exactly what he wanted to do. The headphones he had been hiding behind felt like a concession to her passive aggression; she was dominating him and he had to face her in some way or it would never end.

"Enough," he swung the door open wide. "Nothing needs this much devotion."

"You do," she said quietly. With slow deliberation, she moved from the floor to the sofa. "So, you see fit to speak with me tonight? Not too busy? No headache? Not strangely exhausted?"

"None of those."

"Good."

"I have a spreadsheet," Steven darted back into his room for his laptop. "I need to speak to you about it."

His mother stared at him as he pulled open the lid of the computer and clicked on the file.

"An abrupt change of subject," she said.

"For now, yes. It has been bothering me for days."

"Then share it."

"Zoe has us on a very tight budget. I hate to say it, but it isn't enough, and if you are not going to speak to her about it—"

"It is not about not speaking to her, it is about choosing the right opportunity and moment."

"Then, if you haven't found the *right moment* to speak to her, we need to accept that we don't have enough money for all our outgoings."

The conversation about money was boring, but there was a connection in the mundanity of it all that helped to cross a bridge. Steven focussed on his ideas, coming down hard on one inescapable truth.

"I need to work. I am excellently placed as a tutor, and I know how to get the jobs. There are lots of opportunities for tutors here."

"Will it interfere with your studies?"

Steven had noticed a curl of her lip when tutors were mentioned. Alistair, of course. It had been impossible to find Viv a suitable replacement and the loss of her favoured tutor was noticeable. Steven had tried a few times to help his sister but their familiar relationship meant that the respect needed between student and teacher was impossible to maintain. The last two sessions had devolved into console gaming at staggering speed—better that than a frustrated row.

"Not at all," he said. "I am not behind at university, and a few hours a week won't have any real impact."

"I should speak to Zoe."

"And you will when the time is right, but we don't know when that will be. I'll put my name out there, let people know I'm available for tutoring. Maths, physics, chemistry, biology; all of those are subjects I'm more than adept enough for GCSE and A-Level tutoring."

"I am sorry that my praying has disturbed you," she said quietly.

"It hasn't."

The moment was gone. With a smooth movement, Steven swiped the laptop from the table and went back to his room. It wasn't long before the chanting resumed.

———

His new routine was a daze. University during the mornings and most afternoons, tutoring when there were no lectures and into the evening, often even late at night. It surprised Steven just how many teenagers were willing to keep up their studies in the hours approaching midnight; it also occurred to him that it wasn't the teenagers themselves that were so keen to add a couple of hours of mathematics to their night-time routine but their eager and driven parents.

Just as his had been.

Everything became much simpler with a hectic schedule. Like when he was a teen himself, the sheer amount of work and study did wonders in driving everything else from his mind. Of course, there were many times when thoughts of Alistair would come at him like thrown spears, piercing his flesh and threatening to make him collapse, but they were forced away. With no time allocated to self-involved misery, he simply pretended all was fine.

His mother was bent over by the sofa as he came in. She straightened and faced him. "I'm packing my bags."

Steven stared at her. He dropped his own backpack on the floor by the door and closed it quietly behind him. The flat was quiet, unusually so, with no sound of Vivienne and her music, or the beeps from her console.

"Where's Viv?"

"She was invited to a friend's for dinner. Did you not hear me?"

"I heard you."

"And you have no reaction?"

"I'm sorry, Mum; it's been a long day, very long. I'm tired. I'm hungry. I don't really want to talk."

"Just like every day, Steven, as it has been for weeks. As it has been since ... well, you know. Other than discussing money with me one day, you haven't spoken to me at all. It's 'I have a headache, Mum', or 'there's a lot of work I need to get done, Mum', 'or it's been a long day'. Always. You no longer have any respect for me. You do not want me here. I am not welcome."

"What do you expect?" Steven snapped. "You destroyed my life!"

"Ridiculous! Anything that is destroying your life is of your own making."

"Really!" He snorted and sat on the cushion with enough force to make the furniture groan.

"Please, would you pass me some water."

With a slight glare, Steven hefted himself up from the sofa and walked over into the open-plan kitchen area. The running tap provided the only sound for a while; that, and his own breathing. Steven looked to the door of his bedroom. Another excuse, perhaps? Just ignore her and go to bed early? But would she leave? Was it more than an idle threat? It must have taken her days to build up the courage to say it, and to actually do it? To leave into a foreign country, to travel where? To Sheffield? To Zoe?

"OK, Mum." He placed the glass on the small table next to her. "You want to talk, let's talk."

"Is it that you couldn't get it up?"

Steven reeled, staggered from embarrassment. He felt his cheeks flare and his back tense. Nothing was worth this. Nothing. "What?"

"Do I need to repeat myself? It is hard enough for me to ask, but we must face it. So, tell me; is it a problem with your, you know?"

"Erectile dysfunction? You think that's what I'm suffering from? No, mother, there's no biological problem with my 'you know'. I'm not interested in women."

"Have you tried it? Have you been there, with a woman, and seen what happens?"

"This is so invasive!"

"I have to know!"

"Yes, Mum, I've been with a woman. Of course I did. I forced myself to try, to go through that embarrassing moment—more than once—of standing in front of a hopeful girl, and then having to shyly apologise and slip away. To end up alone in the night, crying and shuddering. Is that enough information, or do you need to know dates and times?"

"Don't get disrespectful!"

"I'm sorry, but this is ridiculous. There's nothing you can think of that I haven't. This is my life. Mine! I have lived with this for years, and you think I haven't properly given heterosexuality the chance it deserved?"

"When you're in that dirty, disgusting relationship—when you were with him—were you the man or the woman?"

Steven laughed, part bitter, part anger, part pure disbelief. "Enough."

"Well?"

"Well what? How do you expect me to answer a question like that? And it's not how you imagine it, whatever you are imagining. Either way, you won't be happy with the answer, so why ask it?"

She turned. "I am going to take a break, Steven. From you, from this. I am taking Viv tonight and we are going to go to Zoe's. My things are already packed."

"Viv has school."

"She can miss a couple of days. She is bright, and ahead. It will just be a long weekend. But I cannot sit in this flat, in this city, thinking about you and what you have done with him, and being treated like dirt by you. You are busy; it is good. I will be back next week."

"You're really going?"

"I am a grown woman, Steven. I can make decisions and act on them. If you want to call your sister—either of them—then do. But I'd like to take my break from you until I return."

"Mum!"

"No. This tension, this atmosphere, it has gone on long enough, and I don't want to live it. Something needs to be done." She picked up a heavy bag Steven hadn't even noticed.

"Now?"

"Now."

"But the train? What time? And a taxi to the station? And picking Viv up."

"As I said, Steven, I am a grown woman. I have accounted for these things. I will see you in a week. Take the time to think."

She slammed the door. Alone in the sudden silence, Steven stared after her.

CHAPTER 5

"Good afternoon, little brother."

Steven looked out at the sunlight bouncing off the surface of the river Dee and held the phone to his ear. Around him, life went on. Other people's lives.

"Zoe," he said, simply. Acknowledgement, that was all.

"Thanks for dumping Mum on me for a weekend." Despite the words, there was a friendly laugh to her voice and Steven relaxed. "It's not like there are a thousand things I'd actually rather be doing."

"Viv OK?"

"Yeah, she's fine." Zoe and Vivienne's relationship seemed to Steven to have less connection in it than his with his older sister. Oh well, no loss for Viv, really.

"Why are you calling?" He knew why: money. It was always money. With his Mum having gone down to Sheffield, chances were that Zoe wanted to dock him some of his allowance.

'After all,' she would say, 'its not like you are paying for Mum or Viv this week, I don't see why you need that money.'

But she didn't.

"Just called for a chat, really."

"A chat?" Steven's words echoed the incredulousness in his mind.

"Rare, I give you."

"Come on, Zoe, cut the bullshit."

"She told me."

"What?" Steven's mind took a second to catch up, slow enough that it came in-line with the words from his sister's mouth.

"About your little problem regarding other men."

44

Well, that was a confidence broken. 'Little problem'—just the words that were used to hide the truth made Steven feel queasy.

"Great." What else was there to say.

"Don't be so quick to judge, Steven. I'm not some religiously and culturally-limited woman with a lack of worldly understanding. I'm a professional doctor, who has lived in the UK now for a substantial portion of my life. You won't be getting a closed-minded response from me."

"So, what am I getting?"

"Support?" Zoe's voice was genuine.

Steven fell silent. His eyes gazed out at a bird that fluttered over the water, before he blinked, twice, and brought himself back to the conversation.

"What?" he asked.

"Is it so difficult to believe? I've got your back, brother. Don't worry about Mum. She needs to cool off and understand the situation, but she will. It'll take time." She laughed. "Probably a century or two, but she will come round to the fact that you are her beloved son, and that takes precedence over your sexuality."

Steven couldn't believe what he was hearing. Unbidden, tears welled in his eyes. Was it so hard to think that his sister would be kind? That she might be understanding?

"I—"

"Yeah, look I know, OK. I get it. We've not exactly been best buddies recently. But look, I've spoken to her. It's like chipping away at a very hard, very stone, wall, but I have spoken to her. I think I got through to her that it's not a psychiatric issue, and that there's no cure. Cure." She laughed again. "Honestly, sometimes it felt like talking to someone living in the stone age. I should have asked her if she had considered trepanning."

Steven smirked. If his mother thought drilling a hole in his head would have cured him of 'the gay', she'd have already been to B&Q and come back with a shining Black and Decker.

"So yeah, look, calm down. Why don't you talk to me about it a bit. What's your boyfriend's name, anyway?"

"Alistair," Steven whispered.

"Ah yes, it did come up in conversation. Viv's tutor, right?"

"He was helping her so she didn't get such a culture shock moving schools."

"You mean Mum had to make sure she was the very top of every class?"

Steven smiled. "Yes, that."

"Introducing your boyfriend to Mum as a tutor to Viv." Zoe snorted. "Proper undercover spy stuff. Very subtle."

"She asked if I knew anyone."

"Of course that was all it was."

"Well. I wanted to see him more and honestly, I thought that if she got to know him and saw what a wonderful guy he was, that it would be easier."

"That was probably a mistake. It doesn't make it easier, just means she was betrayed by two people in one single moment."

Steven sighed. "I hadn't considered it like that."

"Well, I don't blame you for that either. So, anyway, Alistair. What did she make you do?"

"Mum?"

"Yes."

Steven took a deep breath, banished any tears. "I called him. Told him it was over. Told him I couldn't explain, but he knew it was Mum."

"Well, I assume you chose to date someone with at least half a brain, so yes, he'd know."

"Exactly, but, well, it didn't go well. He just ended up hanging up on me and we've not spoken since."

"Can you repair it?"

Thoughts swam in Steven's mind. All the dark, horrible thoughts that he'd been fighting and denying for weeks. Had Alistair found someone else? Had he gone straight from their conversation and into the arms of anyone he could, just to reject the pain, to reject Steven. Was he so angry that nothing could ever be undone? Was he lost?

"I don't know."

"Don't break up over this. You want Mum to rule your life forever? You're an adult, Steven, you have the right to choose your sexual partner."

"I—"

"Yes, I know. We had the same upbringing, remember. I know exactly how you feel and I know just how hard it is to fight. Look, I said it earlier, but I'll say it again; I have your back. Mum's here for a couple more days at least, and there's no reason you should spend that time skulking about in your flat. Find Alistair, call him, and say sorry. Tell him the truth, but don't lose him over this, that would be a tragedy."

"Thanks," Steven's eyes were wet again, but he realised, they were hopeful tears, joyful ones. For Zoe to be like this; he hadn't considered it possible.

"If you really love each other, and that was one of the things Mum said you said, so I'm going to assume it's true. If you really love each other, then you need to stay together. Don't get me wrong, I think you should keep it a secret."

"We're good at that."

"Yeah, exactly. Don't feel it's going back in the closet, or whatever. I think you can consider yourself fairly 'out' but think of it like any other sneak-around relationship. Sometimes you need to keep your private life private, you know what I mean? I've done it, we've all done it." She laughed. "Even Dad had to do it."

"Zoe!"

"Oh, come on. Adults, remember. We can talk about these things."

"Dad deserves our respect. He's gone."

"Yes, he's gone, but while he was around, he wasn't perfect, and pretending that he was doesn't solve anything or help you grow. It's OK, I understand if you're touchy about it. I'll shut up. But look, back to you and Alistair, call him. Do it when you get off the phone with me. Call him and fix all this brokenness. You have my full support."

Steven breathed out slowly.

"I'm going to have to also give Mum my full support, which means I'll be listening to her, siding with her, making her feel she has someone to talk to. It's the only way to allow her to accept this change in her life, in the way she saw her little boy. But I'm on your side, and I'll cover for you if you need me to. I'm here for you, OK?"

Steven could feel his shoulders relax, the tension in his back and neck that he didn't even realise he was holding onto. It melted. Not completely, but enough.

"Thank you," he whispered.

"Yeah, maybe I'm not just the horrible ogre you think I am."

"I don't—"

"Nah, come on. I know it. Look, I have to get on. Are you going to be OK?"

Steven nodded, even though she couldn't see. "Yes," he said. "Definitely, yes, yes. Thank you, Zoe."

"You're welcome. Speak later."

Steven stared at the phone, now back to its basic lock screen, and grinned. Of all the places he had considered that he might get help, Zoe had not been one of them. He watched as people passed on the riverbank, his thoughts swirling. It was Saturday afternoon; if Alistair hadn't changed his routine, he'd be at the gym, and coming home soon. A phone call wasn't going to do it, he had to go in person.

————————

"And then she said that I had her full support, that *we* had her full support!" Steven tugged at Alistair's t-shirt, pulling it off and over his head.

"It's great, Steve, honestly." Alistair was smiling, too, a bright and beaming curve that filled his face. "But do we have to talk about your sister? It's not making this moment quite as exciting as it could be!"

"I'm sorry, I'm sorry," Steven's words were breathless. He pushed, a little hard, and the two of them fell back onto the bed. His hands touched the sheets, a pattern of stylised leaves that he never thought he'd see again. He never thought he'd see any of the inside of this flat again and tilted his head up to take in another detail. The lampshade; round and red. He filed it into his brain, not in case it went again, but to say that it was part of his current life, that he'd see it again, that red and round lampshade.

"Then stop!"

"I will, but Al, you don't understand just—"

"I do! This is me, remember. I've been with you through all the shit with Zoe, I know how cut up you've been, how much you wished you still had a sister in there who cared about you. But shit, Steven, honestly, can we talk about her later?"

"Yes, of course," Steven planted a kiss on his lover's forehead. A silly little peck that was nothing but a precursor to what was to come. He pecked again, and a third time. The fourth found a reciprocal set of warm lips, and he closed his eyes and dived within.

An hour later, Alistair rolled off the bed and crawled on hands and knees over the floor. He put a vinyl record onto the turntable and dropped himself into the nearby chair.

Steven smiled as he immediately recognised the music from the very first sounds of the strings. As the first spoken words led into the joyful song, he breathed.

"Sammi Cheng?" he asked. "I didn't think you really liked her."

"I missed you. And maybe I like her more than I let you know, but I had to hear it. Every day. Stupid album's in danger of being worn through."

"I thought you might have moved on," Steven admitted quietly. "I worried every night."

"No," Alistair looked at him. "I loved you. I love you. I'm not the sort to immediately go out, trawling the streets, looking for an instant fuck to fix."

"I didn't mean—"

"And I'm not saying you did. Honestly, though, I thought you'd ended up with Greg at one point. I thought the whole thing about your Mum had been a lie, and that you just wanted to get rid of me so that you could be with him. It threw me into days of misery, until I realised the truth."

"Greg? Greg who?"

"Thin guy, thinks he can pull off a beard. He can't."

Steven sat up straight. "I'm tutoring his brother. A-Level physics!"

"Yes, but all I knew was you were going there every few days, late at night, staying til midnight."

Steven forced an uncomfortable laugh. "I never ... It never ..."

"I know. Although the drilling I gave Greg was kinda embarrassing." He smirked at the innuendo. "Poor choice of words."

"Come back here?" Steven smiled and stretched out his hand.

"I want something to eat. And drink. Shall we go out?"

"Oh God, yes. I've missed this life!"

"Is it a life we have back, now? Or is this just something that's happening this weekend before your mother comes home. We can't, *I* can't, live with her controlling everything."

"It'll take some time to sort it all, but we're together again, aren't we? We're used to keeping it secret."

"Yeah, OK. That's fine. It's not like I've rushed you around to meet my parents either."

"I'm sorry."

"It's fine, let's not spend our time worrying about it. There's no point in that."

"She'll be gone in a few months." The realisation only just came to him. "For a while at least."

"What do you mean?"

"Visa. She's only allowed in the country for six months and then she has to go back. She can do it again next year, of course, but there's no way for her to stay longer."

"Four months or so to go, then."

"Don't. You make it sound like forever."

"No, it isn't. It's not long at all, really." Alistair stood up and started gathering his clothes. He threw a t-shirt at Steven. "Get dressed, then. I'm really hungry."

"Me too." Steven pulled on his clothes. Because I'm happy, he realised. Because I'm happy and I've just had an hour of exquisite sex. Because I'm with Alistair again, and for the first time in months, it's actually properly sunny outside.

"You got any money?" Alistair chuckled. "Not that I'm not willing to buy you dinner—and flowers if it comes to it—but I'm not exactly the most flush I've ever been right now."

"I do have some, and I don't see Zoe complaining too much if I ask her for a little more. I didn't think I'd ever say that, but you should have heard her earlier. She was like a different person. There was none of the bitterness or confrontation she normally has in her voice."

"Ah, back to Zoe are we?"

"I'm sorry, it was just quite a shock."

"Yes, I know. Don't get too excited, though. Just because she's decided to support you in this doesn't erase all the crap. And she could just be in a good mood because she's getting some herself. All that uptightness could have been nothing more than a long span of sexual frustration."

"If it's OK with you, I'd rather not think about my sister's sex life."

"It's fine by me, but it's something you should definitely take into account when you are trying to get stuff out of her. Look at you now; one decent shag and you'll do anything for anyone. You're easy. She's probably the same."

"Al!"

"Haha, come on." Alistair gently lifted the needle arm from *Becoming Sammi* and grabbed his jacket from the back of a chair. "I'm hungry."

Walking lighter than he had in a long while, Steven followed him through the door, taking a glance around the room as he did.

I don't need to commit it all to memory, he thought, because I'll be back, again, and again, and again.

CHAPTER 6

Vivienne pulled the second jumper over her head. The grey wool snagged on the thinner black fleece that was underneath. Steven snickered at her from across the room.

"What are you doing?"

"Preparing." She turned the laptop screen around so that Steven could see it better. "Look!" She stabbed the screen with her finger.

The cheerful snow icon took up a good portion of the screen. According to the weather report she had loaded it was due in under ten minutes. Just before one p.m.

"It's not a precise timing."

"Which means it could be early," she countered, stuffing her foot into her boot.

"True."

He couldn't blame her. Though he wouldn't admit it, he had been similarly excited the first time he'd seen snow. It had been in Brighton, back in the days when he'd been doing his A-Levels. The snow had coated the beach and where he had become used to millions of tiny pebbles, instead there was a layer of crystalline white, peppered with bootprints and the tracks that had been made by running dogs. Steven had found the tiny paw prints entrancing; a fleeting record of uninhibited enjoyment.

He'd been too embarrassed to admit to his English friends that it was his first time playing with the cold frost. He had remained aloof, holding back from his real feelings. He had wanted to dive in, to roll and cover himself in the chilly ice.

Another memory of holding back. Always hiding his real feelings, always pretending to be someone he wasn't. He was tired of being too scared to be free. And it wasn't a life he wanted for his sister.

"Come on." He jumped up. "You're right—the snow is exciting. I'll see if I can find some gloves and if not ... well, I'll put socks on my hands!"

Viv hugged him and together they crashed through the flat, searching for gloves, scarves and thick socks.

"What are you doing?" Their mother looked up from her book. Reflexively, Steven stiffened but was saved from responding by his sister's quick reply:

"Snow!" she said, as if that answered all.

It seemed it did. With a slight huff, his mother returned to the pages. Steven pulled on his jacket.

It had been weeks since the long weekend. Weeks during which he and Alistair had kept their relationship secret, but it was a technical secret that Steven knew wasn't very well held. Though his mother hadn't mentioned his boyfriend to him even once, Steven was in little doubt that she knew. It was just another lie that they allowed to exist between them now, something unsaid to help maintain the front.

Either that, or his mother was particularly stupid, never wondering where Steven was when he stayed out overnight, or just accepting his increased happiness without question. In truth, Steven was beyond caring. They could argue, or they could pretend to each other. It didn't really matter which.

Viv tugged on his hand and pulled him through the door. She called goodbyes for both of them and then continued to pull until they were on the street.

"Look! It's coming."

Sure enough, the snow was falling and already settling in places, large puffs of soft white gathering on the cold surfaces. Viv turned her face towards the increasing drift and laughed as the flakes fell onto her nose and in her mouth.

"It's so cold."

"Well, it is sort of known for being cold." Steven joined her in her exuberance, collecting some of the snow on his gloved palm. "It's falling fast, but it'll still be hours before you can actually do anything with it."

"What do you mean?"

"The snow has to settle. Sometimes, if the ground isn't cold enough, it'll just melt as soon as it touches, but this looks good and it's already gathering. Still, we can't do anything like make a snowman yet."

"Oh. What shall we do while we wait?"

"We could go for something nice to eat. Inside the house is dark and boring, how about a hot chocolate?"

Viv laughed. "OK."

The cafe was busy. Steven and his sister settled themselves into a corner, hot chocolate and muffins on their tray. Steven hovered as Viv divested herself of scarf and gloves.

Viv pulled the table out of the way to give her brother more room to sit.

"Thanks." Steven squeezed himself in. He liked cafes like this; small, pokey places with plenty of warmth. The walls were bare brick, decorated with a gallery of small paintings that seemed to show nearby locations. He hadn't lived in Aberdeen long enough to recognise many but a couple were views he was sure he'd seen.

Viv played with her muffin, picking chunks out of the top while she looked out of the window. "It's so pretty in real life." She stared in genuine wonder as the flakes drifted and piled against the window frame.

"I'm glad you're enjoying it. And we haven't even started with the snowman thing."

"Have you made a snowman before? Do you know how to do it?"

Steven shook his head. "Honestly, no. But I've seen them."

"Why didn't you make one? You must have seen snow every year."

"Not every year, but yes, I suppose. I don't know. I guess I felt too old."

"That's silly. No one is too old to make snowmen."

"Well, I'll make one this year then, with you."

"If it hurries up. It's pretty heavy, look at the sky, it's all white and behind that, just dark grey."

"Just be patient."

Patience wasn't one of Viv's virtues. Steven ordered a second round of indulgent drinks and forced her to sit just a little longer. Outside, the snow piled up quickly. Once a pair of young boys started throwing snowballs at each other just on the other side of the window, Steven knew he couldn't keep his sister back. They wrapped themselves back up, left the cafe, and ran through the thick pile, adding their footprints to a growing mush. Once home, Viv squealed with delight; there, before her, lay a wide expanse of sparkling untouched stellatundra.

Steven picked up a handful, packed it adequately and threw, catching her on the back of the neck.

"Oi!" she cried, but the smile and glint in her eyes was far from annoyed.

They played for a few minutes, chasing each other around trees and low walls until Steven held up his hand in defeat. He shook the chilly flakes from his head and grinned. "OK, let's make a snowman."

Neither realised that there was a skill to building a snowman. The first couple of attempts yielded nothing more than collapsing heaps of snowflakes. Viv groaned, kicked her calf-high mound and flumped to the floor. "Can't do it."

"We're just new to it. We can keep practicing."

"You do it, I'll watch."

"You'll get wet and cold."

"I'm already wet and cold."

Steven did his best to mimic the children he had seen at other times, rolling the small sphere of snow in an attempt to have it grow. It was back-breaking work, leaning uncomfortably in the cold, but he realised he was making progress. To the delight and appreciative cheers of his little sister, he pushed on, finally creating the lower body of their snowman.

"That's perfect!" Vivienne declared.

"It's a bit small."

"It's great. I'll make a head." She jumped up and shoved him aside as she gathered more snow herself. Careful to replicate exactly what he'd done, she rolled her expanding ball until it was large enough to be the head to his body. "Oooph," she said, dumping the lump on top of its counterpart.

"Now we need a face." Steven already had two long sticks for arms. Viv dug for some stones and together they stood and admired their work.

"He's brilliant," said Viv, "but he needs a friend." She grabbed another large handful of snow and crushed it tightly. On the main snowman's shoulder, she made a second smaller figure.

"Looks like one of those little angels or demons from a cartoon, about to give him advice."

"Don't melt, that's my advice." Viv looked at the snowmen. "It's sad that they melt. Do you think they'll last long?"

"A day or so, maybe." Steven pointed to the sky. "It's still snowing, so maybe they'll be covered over before they melt."

"Like blankets, putting them to sleep."

Steven smiled. Despite the cold that had long since broken through his clothes and was now attacking him throughout, he was in no hurry to get back inside, to leave their fun afternoon and face his mother once more.

Their arguing had not stopped and the atmosphere in the flat was just getting worse. For the last couple of weeks, Steven had found himself simply counting down the days until her visa forced her to return to Malaysia for a while. Viv would stay with him, and the two of them could enjoy months of a new routine, of a peaceful life that worked for them both.

"I don't want to lose him," Viv said, breaking him from his thoughts.

"Lose who?"

"The snowman! I don't want him to melt. We're going to put him in the freezer."

"What?"

"Not the big one, the little one." She picked the miniature snowman from the sloping shoulder of its bigger counterpart.

"In the freezer?"

"Yup!"

Steven followed her back into the warm. He watched as she gingerly put the snowman on the freezer shelf. "He'll be safe there," she said, closing the door.

Their mother looked at them both grinning at each other, shook her head, and left the kitchen.

"Come on," said Steven, "still plenty of afternoon left. Let's watch a film."

Just the two of them, he thought. It'll be much better like that.

CHAPTER 7

It was as if the world moved in slow motion. The bowl hit the door frame, the side of the patterned cream dish meeting the plain white gloss in terrible horror. The spoon was still moving in the air, flying to land harmlessly on the edge of the sofa, but his focus was on the bowl.

It shattered. China pieces exploded in all directions, bouncing off door and wall alike to cascade in a shower of shards onto the carpet. In places, the salad leaves and drips of dressing still clung to the splinters, and together it all fell.

His mother had flinched, pulling herself back and reflexively throwing her hands in front of her face. She needn't have worried for her safety—the bowl missed her by more than a metre—but the effect of the violence was enough. She shrieked.

"I'm sorry," Steven said, but the words were automatic, a reaction to the shock of the event. He trembled and knew that in truth he wasn't apologetic.

In fact, he blamed her.

She looked at him, eyes burning. Though she was shorter than he was, and he was himself somewhat diminutive, she flared with a furious rage that belied her physique entirely. The words were vicious, a torrent of unbridled Cantonese that cascaded over itself in such a spew that Steven struggled to keep up. His mind raged anyway, personal thoughts overriding any vitriol that she could spit.

This moment had been building for weeks. No longer was the subject of his sexuality something that was couched in innuendo and subtly, but she had taken to simply firing insults and questions at him with painful regularity. It had been the word 'pervert', wrapped in as much disdain as it was possible to convey, that had finally sent him over the edge. Not the first use of it, to be sure, not even the hundredth, but just the wrong word at the wrong time.

The culmination of an ongoing barrage that had become a near-daily ritual of shaming.

"The lives of homosexuals are destined to fall apart," she would say, one of her often repeated refrains. "There is no way that a same-sex relationship can last. There isn't the connection, that intrinsic understanding that one of you represents the missing parts of the other. Two men are too similar, there is no room for completion, and so it will die away once animal instincts are no longer enough to keep it together."

Then, at other times, "You must make sure that you do well in life; a perfect career. You will need to afford senior care when you are older—because no one will be there to look after you. No children, you will die lonely."

And, upsettingly, "There would be no continuation of the family line. A death to everything your ancestors have striven to create. It is imperative that the male line is unbroken. It is your duty."

Steven had rebuffed that last one. "I can adopt. Or we could use a surrogate, an egg donor. There is so much that has been done in those fields. Medicine, Mother; I am here studying it. I learn more of these things every day."

"Ridiculous!" She snorted. "How would you explain that to children as they grow up? And adopted children are not genetically-related. They are not family. Not in that way!"

"Tell that to all the adopted children of the world!"

But she had no time for his arguments, his logic, his passionate pleading.

"I'm sorry," Steven said again. He looked at the fragments of the bowl on the floor. Neither of them moved.

"Can't you just find a woman, *any* woman, pretend to be in love with her and lead a normal life?" she asked.

Steven cried and sat on the carpet. "Nothing I do, nothing I have done, means anything anymore, does it? For as long as I can remember, I have always been, *always*, one of the top ten students of the year. Every year at school I'd get awards—hah, for the final two years of secondary school, I was the top student. The top! Does that mean nothing? Does it mean nothing that I made it here, across the world and into one of the most respected universities in the world? I'm studying medicine, Mum, isn't that what you always wanted for me? Or is all of that no longer relevant—was it always conditional love?"

"It is not conditional love."

"Really? Because you have a pretty strong condition placed on me here: be with a woman or be unloved. How is that not conditional?"

She ignored him, shifting uncomfortably.

"It's not conditional," she whispered.

"Yeah, right. One 'wrong step' and all the achievements, the love, the pride ... it's all been erased."

"No ... I ..."

Steven stopped listening. He stood up, walked past the pieces on the floor and slammed the door. Once alone, he began to shake. He couldn't leave her to clean up the debris. It was his mess and whatever happened, it was his to clean.

But he didn't move, and before long heard his mother on the other side of the wall, her soft movements as she picked up the shards peppered with stifled sobbing.

––––––––

"We've reached a point where I don't even want to go home." Steven sighed, holding the phone hard to his ear. He shivered, the cold wind biting the back of his fingers, and kept striding.

"It won't be that way for long," Zoe said. "Change of subject, anyway; how is Alistair?"

"He's fine. I'm going over there now. We can have dinner, watch some TV I guess. I don't know. I'm just so angry, Zoe, it's become ridiculous. I threw a bowl at her today."

"Did it hit her?"

"No! No, it wasn't like that. I said 'at her', but I didn't mean that. More just in her general direction. She wasn't in any danger of flying kitchenware." Steven chuckled. "You should have seen her face."

"I'm not going to laugh and condone you aggressively and violently throwing things at our mother." Her voice put lie to her words, a laugh obviously stifled behind them.

"I'm not proud of it."

"And now?"

"All we do is fight. Our relationship isn't going to survive this."

"I'm sorry I can't do more to help. I tried, you know, I really did, but she just sees me as an adversary every time I say anything about you."

"Well, thanks for backing me up."

"Just go and have your dinner and watch your TV and shake it off. Apologise to her when you get back."

"I don't want to. I want her to apologise to me."

Zoe laughed, a bitter and brief chuckle. "It'll never happen. You need to accept that."

"I do. I do." Steven's voice trailed off. "Look, I need to go. I'm freezing and holding the phone is giving me frostbite."

"Sure. Speak to you soon."

Steven's goodbye was quiet. He shoved the phone into his pocket and left his hand there, desperate for some warmth. In his fury, he'd left the house without a jacket and was now regretting it. He could borrow something off Alistair though, another way to subtly rub his relationship in his mother's face.

This is ridiculous, he thought, turning the corner as his feet automatically went along the familiar route. His pace increased, and as the run warmed his body, he enjoyed the feeling of his heart thumping. By the time he arrived at Alistair's door, he was panting, breathlessly leaning on the doorbell.

"What happened to you?" Alistair asked.

Steven grinned. "Nothing. I ran, that's all."

Alistair shrugged. "I'm making pasta. Sorry it's not more impressive."

In that moment, impressive was unnecessary. Steven's worries melted away as his breathing normalised. Just to be able to escape here, away from his mother and her demonising, away from those arguments and tense atmospheres.

"Pasta is perfect." He smiled up at the taller Scotsman. "What do you see in me?" he whispered to himself before following Alistair inside.

Half an hour later, Steven sank back into the sofa. "I want to do something for her to make up for it all."

"That came from nowhere," Alistair replied. "Can I assume that 'her' is your mum?"

"Yes."

"So, you come here, raging about her and everything she's put you through, upset that she pushed you to the point where you were chucking stuff at her, and now you want to do something to make up for it all."

"It's not about making up for that, it's about everything else. I haven't been considering her feelings. She's been really down since I came out."

Alistair laughed. "You have such a great perspective."

"It is my fault, Al. You can laugh, but if I had said nothing to her, none of this would have happened."

"You are not at fault for being gay. She is, for not being supportive."

Steven tensed. "Sorry, I didn't mean it like that, but maybe I shouldn't have told her. Like Dad, she didn't need to know."

"She hasn't got cancer and will probably live for decades. You want to be hiding for decades? Never living a real life?"

"No, I ..." What did he want? "I want to just do something to make up for it, in some small way."

"Like what?"

"Just a gift."

"This is great! The woman spends months grinding you into the dirt, telling you what an abomination you are, and you want to respond by buying her a present. It's not Christmas."

"It's not ever one-sided though, is it? I've given her plenty of grief for all those months, too. I haven't really thought lovingly about her or considered her difficulties one bit. Plus, at Christmas, I had no money. Look at the things I bought people, look at the things I got you."

"I liked my present."

"It was just a DVD, Al!"

"Not that one." Alistair winked. "Though I enjoyed that, too. Plus, forgive me for saying, but you still have no money."

"I have some from my savings. Enough for a present."

"What are you thinking?"

"She loves Louis Vuitton."

Alistair coughed. "From poor student to designer clothes? You really don't know how to manage money, do you? No wonder your sister parcels it out to you in such a meagre way."

"Not clothes. A bag. There's a shop in Edinburgh. We could go there, make a day of it."

"Ah, so now you're asking me to run away with you?" Alistair grinned.

"Just for the day."

"You're buying lunch."

"I'll buy your ticket, too."

"Then how can I say no? Can it wait until Saturday, though, I'm not sure there are any buses running tonight."

Steven pushed him playfully. "Yes, it can wait."

Alistair kissed him. "Just so you know, I absolutely don't support you spending all your savings on a bag. It's ridiculous. But I'd love to spend the day in Edinburgh."

––––––––––––

"Too much walking." Steven slumped onto the leather chair and put his bags by his side.

Alistair laughed. "Well, we only have one day. I'll have a latte, by the way."

"You can go and get them. If I'm paying for everything, you can be the servant."

"Is that a role-play thing?"

Steven grinned. "It can be. Only tomorrow, not tonight. Tonight, I want to give Mum this, and spend some time with her."

He opened the shopping bag and stared at its contents. The present, a Speedy 25 bag in Damien Azur Canvas, was already gift-wrapped and was beautifully presented. He had no intention of ruining that part of the effect.

"Yeah, keep staring at it. You're proper mental. All those hours spent tutoring privileged teenagers burned away to become a bag."

"It's a lovely bag."

"You're so gay."

"Admit you like the bag."

"I'll admit that I admire your desire to say sorry to your Mum. It's very sweet, though not the way I'd have done it. If I brought a bag like that back to my mother, she'd think I'd gone doolally, and not only that, but it'd be the biggest sign of coming out to her that I could ever do."

"And we'd be back here again."

"Only I don't live with my mum and wouldn't have to put up with it."

"Yeah, well, counting down the weeks now."

"I thought things were going well with the visa application thing."

Steven shook his head. "Viv staying here isn't enough to convince them, at least, I don't think so. Probably because I can look after her and provide her with a stable home environment etc. etc."

"It doesn't help that your mum doesn't speak more than two words of English and is too stubborn to learn."

"At least four words."

"Exactly."

"No, it doesn't help. They'll send her away for six months and we can be properly free. Like I've felt today. As soon as we got on that bus this morning, I relaxed. It's incredible."

"She'll come back."

"Having had months to think about it, be happy with her bag present, maybe think having a gay son isn't the living hell she thinks it is …"

"That's some wishful thinking, right there."

"Go and get the coffees."

Steven couldn't believe his nervousness. It lasted the rest of the day, driving little thoughts of despair into his mind even as he curled up with Alistair on the wide back seat of the coach. Through the window, he could see the familiar lines of Aberdeen come into focus, streetlights and buildings that marked home. Soon, the bus would come to a halt and then, just like that, his day of freedom with his boyfriend would be over.

"Planning to go straight back home?" Alistair asked.

It was the sensible thing to do; walking to Al's only to see him off and then turning back was just delaying everything.

"I don't know why I feel like this. It's like I'm a child."

"Silly boy, you are a child, to her anyway. She makes you feel that way because that's how she sees you. Maybe that's what you need to do; make her realise you're not just her little boy."

"Not sure that is how she sees it. Now I'm just an adversary."

"This really has you so twisted up, doesn't it. Look, take her her bag; she's got to appreciate that, especially considering how many hours of tutoring it took you to buy it."

"Stop going on about the money, Al, please."

"Fine, I'll stop." Alistair pushed him up a little, rearranged his seating position and then leaned over with a kiss. "We're here."

Steven stood up and picked up his shopping. "Come on then."

The bright sunshine of Edinburgh had been completely replaced with the dark chill of an Aberdeen evening. "I'll call you in the morning," he said. His hand lingered a little longer on Alistair's than might have been needed.

"Go on, tell your mum I said 'hello.'"

Steven grinned. "Don't think so."

"Tell Viv at least." Alistair waved and pulled his jacket tight around him. For the longest time, Steven watched him walk before he turned and began his own way home.

He'd had to lie to get his mother to be happy about the Edinburgh trip. To her, he'd been there as part of his course, a day with some guest lectures about other things. In his mind, Steven made up some content that could have been part of it all, just in case she asked. It was ridiculous, feeling like a small boy who had skipped school. Alistair had been right; he did need to make her realise he wasn't just her little boy.

The flat was quiet, but not silent. From Viv's room, the soft sound of a game being played seeped under the door. "I'm home," Steven called, but neither of them came to greet him.

They had obviously eaten. On the side was a bowl of rice that had been left for him and suddenly the food he had eaten in Edinburgh felt like it was many hours gone. He took the rice and stood in the kitchen while it warmed. Simple, but his favourite.

"There're some other bits in the fridge," his mum said. She stood in the doorway, watching him.

"Thanks," Steven said. Did it always have to be so awkward? "I bought you something."

He held out the package and she gingerly came forward to take it.

"Thank you," she said. "What is it?"

"Early birthday present. And an apology, for all the arguing."

She was quiet then, slowly, she unwrapped it. There was a sparkle in her eyes as she processed the contents. Steven knew his mother and knew that she was certain to understand the bag's providence. In her early life, before Zoe, before him and Viv, she had been a famous singer and actress. It was one of the many things she had given up for her family, but he didn't doubt that the yearning was still there. It hadn't been planned, but the gift of the bag was a fragment of that sort of life, the life she could have had if she hadn't become a mother.

She sacrificed, too, Steven thought. She gave up the things she really wanted in order to do what was right for her family. She stayed with Dad despite everything he did, and she went from being someone who could've had it all to living in a tiny flat on the other side of the world, unable to speak the language, without friends, without anything.

No wonder she wanted him to accept these responsibilities, too. No wonder ...

Steven looked again into her eyes. There were tears there, joining that glint. She should have been accepting awards, basking in the fame that could have been hers to keep. She shouldn't have taken on a mundane part-time job as a young mother, shouldn't have let the spotlight move away from her and onto new replacements, should never have been relegated to supporting roles on forgettable TV series. She should have had her own life.

He wasn't going to make the same mistake.

It didn't matter what pressure she would bring to bear, he was going to be the person he truly wanted to be. He wasn't going to squash his soul in the name of family. What had it brought her?

A dead husband.

A grown daughter who didn't really care.

A gay son who argued with her daily.

A younger daughter who would also move on when her time came.

It wasn't worth it. Family, commitment, bloodlines, ancestors; all strong and valuable concepts, for sure, but not at the cost of his own life.

It shouldn't have been at the cost of her life, either.

"I love the bag," she said.

Steven's mind was pulled back to the moment. His hand was still hanging in the air. He turned his focus to the rice, spooning it, now hot, into a clean bowl.

"You shouldn't have spent all that money."

"I wish people would stop going on about the cost," Steven spat, trying quickly to cover the angry snap with a chuckle.

"People?" she asked.

"Oh, just some of the other students. They were with me when I bought it for you. They couldn't believe I'd get that for my mum."

She smiled. "They are probably right, but I am grateful. Very grateful. It is beautiful. I will treasure it."

Other students. More lies. Steven smiled, an outward appearance of happiness to mask the turmoil. That's what we've become; people who lie to get along.

"I was going to watch a film. Would you like to … ?" Steven felt the offer crash even before his sentence was done.

"No, but thank you. I'm tired. I only came out to tell you about the food." She looked at the bag again, clutched it to her chest. "Thank you again for this. Enjoy your film."

And she turned. Sighing, Steven picked up his dinner.

CHAPTER 8

Steven smiled politely while his insides boiled. This, he decided, was a step too far.

But then, there had been so many steps that had all been too far.

"Fei," the girl said by way of introducing herself. She took her seat at the opposite side of the table and settled. Steven breathed; she was probably feeling somewhat embarrassed, too. It wasn't her fault, he reminded himself, she was innocent in all of this.

No, the fault lay with the woman to his left. Steven's mother had been so nice about the dinner, suggesting it a week beforehand, insisting that she'd make all the arrangements. Viv had been looking forward to it for days, eager to make it a bit of a farewell celebration.

Steven sat, and mumbled something pleasant, the words passing through his lips before he'd even processed them.

Xiu Wen was his mother's friend, the only woman in Aberdeen that had really provided any sort of companionship and support for her. Steven knew how hard it had to have been over the last six months for his mother; quite aside from their personal issues, she had been a Cantonese-speaking woman in an English-speaking city. Worse, a Scottish city where the accent was unfamiliar and the attitudes completely alien. For his mum, it had been weeks of not going out, ashamed of her lack of fluency. Finding Xiu Wen had been a lifeline, and honestly, Steven was glad she'd had it.

Of course she should invite her friend to her leaving dinner.

Fei, though. Steven sighed as he considered the situation. Xiu Wen's daughter was here because his mother still thought she could 'fix' him despite everything that had passed between them, that a beautiful woman would be able to counteract 'the gay' and turn him into a 'normal' heterosexual man.

"Hi Fei." Viv stretched over the table in an attempt to shake hands with the young woman. Objectively, Steven had to admit that she was attractive. His mother must have thought she'd hit a vein of gold when they'd first met. He could imagine the conversation with his mum, awkwardly and obviously checking whether or not Fei was single.

"It's so nice to meet you both at last," Wen said, her comments directed to both Steven and his sister. "I've heard so much about you."

Not quite everything, I hope. He shot a look to his side but was being pointedly ignored.

He could do the small talk thing. It was just one dinner.

"You too," he said, forcing the smile back. Be the dutiful son for just one more dinner, for just one more day.

On Wednesday, his mother would be returning home. Her visa was finally up, and despite significant attempts to get the government to allow her to stay, there had been no movement on any sort of permanent or long-term status. As a student, Viv was able to stay with him; it would be just the two of them in the flat while their mother made new applications at the embassy back in Malaysia.

Xiu Wen had already offered her help, too, agreeing to have Viv go over to her house on the days when Steven was busy with college or the tuition work, giving her an evening meal and making his responsibilities for his little sister a bit more reasonable. For that, he was genuinely grateful.

Just one more day.

————

Steven didn't want to appear too eager. It would do nothing but upset her for his mother to think that he was counting down the final minutes until her flight, but it was the truth. He cleaned his teeth with vigour, dressed quickly, and went to the living room where he knew she was already waiting.

"You do not need to drive me," she said immediately, "Xiu Wen said she would like to, and I have accepted her kind offer."

"To the airport?"

"Yes."

"You don't want me or Viv to come?"

"Vivienne is coming with us. Xiu Wen will drive her back, too."

"You just don't want me there?"

"Steven, let us be honest. The last few weeks, the last few months, have put a terrible, terrible strain on us. We will both appreciate our distance for a while, and perhaps when I come back in a few months, the break will have done us good."

"I'm sorry."

"Yes, I know."

No 'me, too', Steven noted bitterly.

"You understand about the companion visa?" Steven asked, turning to logistics matters as they always did when the awkwardness was too much to bear. "You will have to travel to Kuala Lumpur, to the British Embassy there, and apply in person."

"I understand."

"You will need help with the forms. Once you have them, let me know, and we can do them together. Or I can just do them if they're online."

"I understand that too, thank you."

"Mum, I'm sorry. Have a nice time at home. Really. I'll look after Viv properly, I promise, and you can have a break, see some of your friends, relax more in your own home."

"This has become my home, too, Steven. But thank you."

Viv ran into the room. "Xiu Wen is outside. I saw her car pull up."

"Then I will say my goodbyes." Steven's mother turned and hugged him. It was strange, the only physical affection they had shared in months, but it wasn't unwelcome. Softening, he hugged her in return.

"Have a good flight."

Nodding, his mother left.

Steven watched as the door closed to silence behind her. He looked around his flat for a few moments; it seemed larger now, as if there were taller ceilings and bigger windows. He didn't want to feel overjoyed by her leaving; it felt disrespectful, but he couldn't help it. Loudly, he whooped, pleased there was no one around to hear him.

It was early, Alistair would still be in bed. Nonetheless, Steven needed to speak to him. He called and sighed as it went through to voicemail. A second time yielded a similar result, but the third saw Al groggily answer.

"She's gone."

"Yes, on a very early flight, I notice. What time is it?"

Steven didn't need to check. "Five-forty. Shall I come over? No, you come over here!"

Alistair chuckled. "I will, but not yet. Please, let me sleep another couple of hours at least. Don't you have lectures?"

"Today, I have nothing. Anything I did have has been put on hold."

"I see."

"Are you coming? You are awake now, so why wait?"

"Steven, seriously. It's not even six a.m."

"Don't waste the day!"

"Fine, fine." Steven could practically hear his boyfriend's smirk. "I'll come. Don't go anywhere."

"I won't."

The phone disconnected and Steven stared at it as 5:41 ticked over to 5:42. This was it; he was free to have Alistair around, free to be a person again. Free.

————————

Weeks passed as Steven settled into his new routine, centred around Viv and making sure she was happy. Each day was similar, but enjoyable; an early rise and waking Viv up, making breakfast for them both and then leaving the laptop connected to Malaysia on Skype so that Vivienne and their mother could chat and keep in contact, then leaving—him to uni, Viv to school. The days were filled with lectures, tutoring and Alistair, and the evenings centred around dinner and an early bedtime.

"I feel like a father, you know," Steven said to Alistair one afternoon. "To Viv, I mean."

"I didn't think you meant to me, unless that's a game you'd like to play, in which case, well ..."

Steven laughed. "I'm being serious. I think I'd make a good father."

"This is because you learned to cook rice?"

"I can cook a lot more besides rice."

"Aye, you can do egg-fried rice and special-fried rice, too. It's a culinary wonder."

"Stop it Al, I'm serious."

"So am I!"

"I said it to Zoe last night and she agreed."

"She thinks you'd make a good dad?"

"Actually, she said 'a great dad'."

"Well, then that's decided. Because your bitch sister has the best perspective on everything."

"Come on, don't call her that?"

"Your sister?"

"A bitch!"

"Oh, how easily your memory fails you, Steven. It's all very nice now, isn't it? Your little morning video calls with your mum, and regular chit-chats with Zoe, but I remember what it was like before, and unlike you, I'm not so quick to forgive. Your sister is a controlling nightmare, and your mother is ... well, she's a controlling nightmare too. I suppose it runs in the family. How's Viv on that sort of thing?"

"Well, she does like to choose what we watch in the evenings."

"Yeah, controlling nightmare. No wonder you are such a wreck."

"I'm not a wreck."

Alistair laughed. "If you were a ship, you'd be lying on the bottom of the sea with the wee fishes swimming between your legs, and you know it."

Steven shrugged. "I'm getting better."

"Until your mum comes back. When's her visa appointment?"

"Next week. Thursday." Steven stared out of the window. "Then she'll be able to stay longer, no more six-month breaks."

"You're a man, Steven; don't you ever think of just telling her enough is enough?"

"While I'm studying? No, she's paying for it."

"Rubbish. You are. It's your money you make from tutoring that pays for the car, and the food."

"And the rent?"

"Parcelled to you by Zoe."

"That is my family's money."

"But it's not in your mum's control, is it? It's in your sister's control. The one you don't think is a bitch anymore, the one who thinks you'd be a great dad."

"There's Viv, though."

"Who you can look after fine. I don't know why you don't just tell your mum to stay out there. It's her home, after all, she must like it a lot more than sitting in a flat in bloody Aberdeen!"

"You know I can't do that."

"You can, and you should. You won't, though, I understand that. You like to be the victim, to be able to cry about your situation and how hard it all is, but you won't just fix it all up. You could tell her that she can't come back, and then we can just keep on going as we have been. You can't pretend the past few weeks haven't been better than the months she was here."

"Of course, but, Al, you know ..." Steven fumbled with his reasoning.

"Yeah, I know. Just don't come complaining to me once she gets her new shiny visa and comes to dominate your life here in Scotland again."

"Do we have to talk about my mother?"

"We don't have to talk at all," said Alistair with a grin. He reached over, touched Steven on the chest, and the day fell away.

————————

Steven stared at the screen, stunned by his mother's tears. "I don't understand," he said, again. But he did.

His mother's visa application had been rejected. Steven didn't know whether to cry or celebrate.

"It was horrible," she said, "horrible. They treated me like a criminal. No; worse—like a terrorist! They made me feel awful."

"But banned?" Steven tried to clarify the details.

"Oh, don't tell me you're not pleased. I know that secretly, you have been hoping this would happen."

"Mum, no, not at all."

She was still speaking: "probably made a mistake on the forms, or send the wrong documents, just to make sure."

"I did no such thing! I spent hours on those forms, longer sifting through everything and finding the right paperwork to support it. Don't accuse me of this as well."

"Does it matter? I cannot come back to my children. You are there, Zoe is there, and Vivienne; she is so young."

"We are doing fine. You know that, you've spoken to us every morning. Viv is happy. Xiu Wen has been helping, making at least two nice dinners a week. We can make it through the summer without a problem."

"The summer? Don't you understand? They banned me for a year, a full year before I can even apply again. The interviewer turned on me because I said something in English. He said I didn't need a translator, that I'd only brought one along to try to play the sympathy card. He accused me of pretending to be less fluent in English than I really was, as if I was trying to trick him in some way."

"This summer, the autumn and winter, too. Yes, Mum, we can cope. I can look after Viv."

"I felt like swearing at him, and you know I never swear, Steven."

"Yes, Mum."

"He tore the application apart. Said that there was no reason for me to reside in the UK alongside Viv. He was a horrible man, to suggest that a young daughter doesn't need her mother while living in a foreign country."

"We can put in an appeal."

"No, there is no point. Who will read that appeal? The same man? Someone who is like him? Worse? They do not want me in the country, they made that very clear. I am not welcome in the United Kingdom."

"I'm sorry."

"The translator, such a lovely young man, he said that he'd never seen anything like it, that the interviewer was being really unfair."

"Maybe you caught him on a bad day."

"If you have the kind of bad day that tears apart a family, then you don't come into work on that day. You call in sick and you stay at home. You don't go into work and interview poor women who simply want to get back to their children, and then deny them access to the country for, well, I don't even know what. Do you understand that? I don't even know why it was the application was denied."

"Did you ask?"

"Of course, I did. The woman that called said she didn't know, that they don't give out that information. She was very sorry, she kept telling me that; 'I'm very sorry', she said. Sorry! Hah! What use is that to me? I should have a visa, not a messenger's apology!"

"We'll be OK."

"Oh, I am sure you will be. You are probably holding in the glee, aren't you? Pleased that your poor mother was treated like a terrorist."

"I'm not pleased, Mum. We've had our problems over the last year, but I didn't want you not to come back."

"So now what? I stay here, alone, while my children are on the other side of the world."

"I'm sorry, Mum, truly."

"Ah, for once this isn't your fault. I hate them, those officials. I know life there in Aberdeen wasn't as enjoyable and glamorous as it could have been, but it was still *my* life that I chose. They do not have the right to take that from me."

"Sadly, they do."

"Yes, well, they shouldn't."

"Sorry."

"I don't want to tell Vivienne. I don't want to. She will think it is my fault, that the silly old woman got something wrong. Oh, don't look at me like that, we both know she thinks of me like that, the arrogance of youth. She thinks that because I am no good at her video games and all those modern things, that I am somehow lacking in intelligence. Well, let me tell you, that's not the case. Those forms were properly filled in. I checked them twice, three times, even. All the documentation was correct and up-to-date. He was just a bastard!"

"I'll talk to Viv."

"Yes, and Zoe, too. I can't face her false pitying either. Tell them both and I'll call in the morning."

"I will. I'm sorry, Mum."

"Yes, Steven, we both are. Goodbye."

As the video display shrank away, Steven felt his shoulders relax. She wouldn't be coming back, after all. Maybe, at last, he could be the adult Alistair wanted him to be, that *he* wanted himself to be.

CHAPTER 9

"You should probably answer her," Alistair said. He sat up in the bed, put his coffee cup down on the side table and threw the bright phone to Steven. "It's been three times."

"Four," Steven corrected. He didn't bother to pick up the phone. "I'll answer her later. This is our day together, and I don't want Zoe to spoil it."

"She's already spoiling it, with her constant ringing."

Steven picked up the phone and held the button down to turn it off. "There," he said, "sorted."

"And if Viv needs you?"

Steven sighed and turned the phone back on. "I'm still not answering Zoe."

"My, how you've changed." Alistair smirked. "It wasn't so long ago that you have jumped at Zoe's call, worried that she was going to cut back your money or find some other little thing to screw up your life."

"I'm older now, and she's been nicer."

"So, when people are nice, you don't answer the phone, and when they are being horrible, you do? That's backwards."

Steven shook his head. "It's not like that and you know it. Can we not, though? I thought you wanted to go out."

Alistair rolled off the bed. "Fine, fine." He yawned and then raised his eyebrows. "Or we could find something else to do."

"No, out. Your coffee is nice, but it's not food, and I would like some food."

"Let's go then." Alistair picked up a jacket, pulled on a pair of shoes and was ready with surprising speed.

Outside, the world was a mild grey. It had rained earlier, but the sky was mostly clear, and the sun was doing its best to warm the street. Steven turned as a loud call from the other side of the road drew their attention.

Ray waved briefly from the kerb, darting across through the moving traffic to meet them. Steven smiled at their friend, aware that his unexpected arrival would cause any plans they had to go awry. Ray was a good friend, happy and gregarious, but his enthusiasm and outgoing personality was often quick to dominate social situations.

"Boys!" Ray cried, "I thought you'd be around here this afternoon. I was on my way to see if ye were free."

"Aye, we're free," said Alistair, somewhat resigned. "As long as you want food; this one's starving."

Steven smiled, noting how his boyfriend's native accent strengthened around others.

"Then good, where to?"

The three of them ambled into the centre of town, walking unhurriedly past rows of semi-detached houses and small convenience shops. Steven flinched when his phone rang again.

"If that's Zoe, you should bloody answer it," said Alistair. He turned to Ray. "His sister's been calling him all day, and Steve's decided it's macho to ignore her, but honestly, it's just pissing me off now."

The light for the zebra crossing turned green. Steven gestured to it with a wave. "OK, I'll answer it. Go ahead, I'll catch you up."

Alistair shrugged and Steven dropped back, holding the phone to his ear.

"Zoe," he said, "I'm a bit busy."

"Well hello to you, too. I'm busy, too, and I don't need this. What made it so hard for you to pick up the phone?"

"I told you, I'm busy, Al and I—"

"Ah OK, with your boyfriend. Fine. Are you alone now though? We need to talk."

"Can it wait? We were going for food."

"At half past three in the afternoon?"

"Yes."

He could almost hear her shaking her head. "No, it can't wait. You need to find somewhere we can talk. Tell Alistair you'll meet him later."

"What is this about?"

"Mum. She was on the phone to me most of the night and all morning."

"Is something wrong?"

"Are you somewhere you can actually talk?"

"I'm fine, go on."

"She's decided enough is enough, and she's cutting you off."

"What?" Steven's head spun. He leaned on a cold brick wall. "I don't understand, what do you mean?"

"She's disowning you, Steven. She decided that your sexuality isn't something she can live with, and she's cutting ties with you. It's serious."

"I don't..." Steven repeated.

"She wants Viv to come and live with me."

"What?" Steven found a wall and sat on it, the chill of the stone seeping through his jeans.

"What do you really need me to explain? You can't be that surprised, the last few months with her there were horrific, weren't they? You said so yourself."

"Yes, but, well, we parted on good terms."

"Well, I don't know about that. She's been home a while now, and maybe the culture and the whole difference of being there affected her. I don't know. I do know that she was talking to me for hours this morning and there's no moving her from it. She's done with you. She said if you want to act like you are adult enough to, well, to do what you do with Alistair, then you are adult enough to stand on your own two feet."

"What's that supposed to mean?"

"Money, Steven. There's no more money."

"That's ridiculous. It's the family money. It's Dad's life insurance, his business money. You're the one in control of it, not her."

"Not exactly true. It's Mum's money. Yes, I was managing it for her and budgeting your lifestyle, as Dad had asked, but technically it is hers and she's exerting her right to choose what happens with it. If she says you can't have any of it, then, well, there's nothing I can do."

"Zoe!"

"You brought this on yourself."

"What? I thought you were on my side?" Steven was shaking.

"I was. I am. I don't know. I have to do what's right though, and she wants you to bring Viv here."

"To live with you?"

"Yes."

"When? What? She's got school."

"She'll get a new school. Tonight, Steven, you have to do it tonight. I have a life to lead, too, you know. I have work and I can't be messing about with this stretching on past the weekend. You need to bring Viv here tonight. What time's the train?"

Steven swayed, his mind struggling to process the information. "Not tonight? She's with her friend, she's not even at home. And I'm out with Al and Ray."

"You are being a baby, Steven. Snap out of it."

"I'm probably a little bit in shock."

"Yes, well, I understand that, I do, but we have to do what we have to do, right? I don't want to make this any harder on you than it already is—"

"Harder on me?"

"It's fine, though, right? I mean, you have Alistair, and you have the flat and your job."

"The flat? How am I meant to pay for the flat?"

"Honestly, Steven, that's not really my problem."

"Why are you being like this?"

"Like what? I'm trying to do the right thing, what Mum wants, what Dad wanted."

"Dad didn't want me out on the street with no money and nowhere to live."

"Well, to be fair, he didn't know about your sexuality."

"Zoe!"

"Well, he didn't. He was pretty conservative, too. The chances are he'd have been worse than Mum."

"I can't believe you are saying all this." Tears streamed down Steven's face, his voice trembling. "And telling me I have to do it today."

"Mum made me Vivienne's legal guardian. A while ago, to be honest. We didn't tell you, because, well, we just didn't, but I'm telling you now. You have to bring Viv to me tonight; that's Mum's wish, and mine, too. She's raging; you don't want her to get the authorities involved. She even said she was worried that your influence would turn Viv gay, too."

"Turn Viv gay? You don't turn people gay! This is ridiculous. And are you suggesting you'd call the police on me?"

"No, of course not. It's just that technically, if you don't bring Viv here to Sheffield tonight, you're kidnapping her, and, well ..."

"Zoe, this is insane!"

"No, this is reality. Wake up and get used to it. You need to go and get her, now, and you need to get a train ticket to Sheffield for tonight. Daniel and I will pick you up from the station. You can stay here for the weekend and go back on Monday morning, if you like."

"Daniel?"

"He's my boyfriend."

"We've not even met him. Viv hasn't met him. Does he live with you?"

"No, he doesn't live here, Steven, but he's a big part of my life and Viv and Mum have met him. They came here, remember. Look, I don't have to explain my personal situation to you. You just have to bring me my sister."

"*Our* sister."

"Yes, our sister. Like I said, I have a lot that needs to be organised, and I can't do it all if you don't get a move on. Viv has a school place for Monday and—"

"For Monday?"

"I called around, pulled some strings. I know some people in that area and, so yes, on Monday. I can hardly be expected to take time off work, so it's good I managed to get it all sorted so quickly."

"Time off? What about my missing university on Monday?"

"Well, you can rush back Sunday night if you want."

"You can't do this. You can't just call me like this and drop this all on me in the middle of the afternoon."

"I've been calling since this morning."

Steven stared, his vision blurred, his mind reeling.

"I have to get home," he whispered.

"Yes, you do. Good. Finally. Please pick up Viv, pack her things and be on the train as soon as possible. The last one is at ten to eight, it gets in really late, but I understand if that's the only one you can make."

"Four hours? You want me to do all this in four hours. Viv's been living with me for months, she has stuff all over the house."

"Sort it out, Steven. Ten to eight, I looked it up earlier. Just be on it."

She hung up. Staggered, Steven stared at the dimming display of the phone, his tears freely running down his face. Slowly, he typed a text message to Alistair, telling him that something had come up, and that he had to go to Sheffield. He didn't mention Viv or being disowned, just that something had come up. There was no reply, and Steven didn't expect one. Alistair and Ray would be sitting somewhere by now, midway through a conversation about something small and irrelevant; music, movies or sports.

He sent another text, this time to Viv. **Come home, immediately,** it said. Her response was instant.

What's wrong?

Just come home. Apologise to your friend. I'll meet you there. Please don't argue.

He knew she'd do as he asked. She was a good girl.

OK.

Steven stumbled and dragged his way back to the flat, often having to physically reach out his hand to steady himself. His life, his entire world, was crashing down around him.

The flat echoed a terrible silence. He collapsed onto the sofa, staring blankly at the door until Viv ran in moments later.

"What's wrong?" she asked.

Steven sobbed, unable to speak. Her arms wrapped around him, a small kiss on his cheek. "Tell me, big bro, what's going on?"

"You need to pack all your things. All of them. Mum and Zoe have decided that you need to go and live in Sheffield, and they want you there tonight."

"What?! Why?" Viv shot to standing.

"Mum's disowned me. She wants nothing to do with me and doesn't want me looking after you any more. And Zoe's ..." He faltered. "She's being hard about it, we just have to do what she says."

"I don't want to live with Zoe. I don't even like her."

"Shush, Viv, there's nothing we can do."

"Of course there is; I'll just stay here."

"You can't. Mum made Zoe your legal guardian here in the UK. That means she's like a parent. If we don't take you there tonight, she could call the police and say I kidnapped you."

Viv laughed. "Don't be ridiculous."

"I'm not." Steven wept. "She actually said that exact thing. That if we're not on the train before eight p.m. tonight, that she'd do that."

"I can't believe it. Why? What did you do?"

"You know what I did," Steven said, the words finally acknowledging that there had never really been a secret between them.

"Because you're gay?" Viv threw her hands into the air. "It's the twenty-first century; everyone's gay!"

Steven laughed despite himself. "That's not quite true."

"No, but what does it matter? I don't care, and Mum's a relic, she has no idea what the real world is like. Being gay is nothing, it's not like you're a serial killer."

"She sees it pretty much the same way."

"Yes, well, that's stupid."

"Viv!" Even now, Steven admonished her for the lack of parental respect.

"I'm not doing it. I'm not moving to a city I don't know, to live with someone I don't really like, and anyway, what about school?"

"Oh, she has that all sorted. You start on Monday."

"That's impossible. No one can organise a school place in a few hours on a Saturday."

"No one except Zoe."

"Have they been planning this? Plotting to send me to Sheffield? I don't want to go."

"No, but you will, and you'll be good and respectful."

"No!" Viv cried.

"I'm sorry." Steven held out his arms and they hugged again, this time with him doing the comforting. "We don't have time, you really do need to pack. Take everything, we don't know what will happen, but anything you don't take, I'll look after."

"I don't want anything, it's just stuff."

"Yes, well, right now it's stuff, but you'll want your clothes, and your cleaning stuff, and you'll want your books and music and PlayStation."

"Yes, fine, OK. We can pack."

"Good. I'll put on some music."

They danced; a strange mood of fun energy mixed with the bitterness of the situation. It didn't take long, and before six o'clock, they were packed and ready to leave. Steven had spoken briefly to Alistair, a thirty-second call of emotional tears in the middle of a whirlwind cleaning and packing, that left both of them shaken.

"We have time for food," Steven went to the kitchen. "I'll cook you a last meal."

"Just rice," said Viv, "and chicken."

He smiled; it was their favourite meal to share. Simple, but delicious, and it didn't take long to make.

There were twelve bags to take in the taxi to the station. Steven grunted as he heaved them into the boot of the large cab.

"Is there anything left?" he asked.

"Oh, yes, come!" Viv grabbed his arm and pulled him back inside. She rushed to the fridge and pulled it open.

"Remember him?" she asked. In her hand was the small snowman she had made during her first day of snow. Steven cried openly.

"It was the best day," she said, "really, the best day ever. I will never forget it, and you have to look after him, because when I come back to visit, I'll want to see him too, do you understand?"

"I do."

"I love you, big brother. Thank you for everything you have done for me."

He wrapped his arms around her. "I love you, too."

She leaned past him to put the snowman back into the freezer compartment and shut the door. For a moment, they just stood there.

"The taxi is waiting," Steven said, eventually.

"I'll be back."

"I know you will."

"You keep Mr. Snowman safe."

"I will."

Vivienne looked around the whole room before turning to the door. "Bye bye, flat," she whispered.

Steven followed her out.

———

Daniel met them at the station. He was older than Steven expected, but good-looking and fit. Vivienne had fallen asleep during the journey and was still a little groggy as she shuffled off the train, her assortment of bags surrounding her.

"Let me help." The man looked at Steven and gave a weak smile that was somewhat understanding. "I'm sorry about all this shit happening to you. It's rough."

"Thanks." Steven hefted the remaining bags. "Where shall we put these?"

"We're not parked far. Let me carry a few."

They walked in polite silence. Zoe was waiting in the car, a shining new Range Rover that probably cost as much as Steven's flat. He helped Viv in, still sleepy, and climbed in next to her.

"Steven," Zoe said curtly.

"Zoe," he replied, equally short.

The atmosphere in the car was terrible. Daniel drove through the night with his headlamps bright and the music low. No one spoke, and Viv snoozed gently, her soft snoring coming in spurts.

"I've made up the guest bed for you," Zoe said as they pulled up to the house. Steven stared. His sister had bought a huge home, a four-bedroom detached house that dwarfed anywhere he had ever lived, even their family home back in Malaysia. "Life's treating you well," he murmured.

"What? Oh, yes, I do alright. Come on."

He left Viv's bags in the car; no doubt Daniel would bring them in later, and half walked-half carried his little sister into the enormous house.

"Where do I go?"

"Viv's upstairs first on the right," Zoe said, "and you're at the far end. Bathroom is on the left at the top of the stairs."

She didn't say anything more as Steven helped their little sister to her new bedroom. Zoe remained downstairs, and he winced. It's not how he would have treated anyone, especially not a young girl having to move into a new home at no notice.

Viv's bedroom was a delight, however. Decorated in quite a girly fashion, but clean and beautiful. There was a dressing table with a mirror in one corner, and two full built-in wardrobes.

"You're going to love it here," said Steven.

"No, I'm not." Viv was far more alert than she'd pretended. "I don't want to be here, and I don't want to stay. I want to come home, with you."

"Well, you can't. Plus, tonight, at least, I'm here, too. Zoe said I had the room at the far end of the corridor."

"I'm not going to speak to her."

Steven sat her on the bed. "You are. People doing bad things to you doesn't mean you should treat them badly. Besides, she isn't really doing anything bad to you, unless giving you a beautiful

bedroom, sorting you out with a new school and feeding you is 'bad.'"
He snorted, and Viv grinned. "Be better than that, you *are* better
than that."

"We can talk about it in the morning, right, you're not going
straight back."

"I can go back tomorrow evening, or Monday morning. My
ticket is open."

"Good."

"But now, you need to go to bed. We passed the bathroom on the
way up, just at the top of the stairs."

"Thank you, night night."

Steven squeezed her tight. "Night."

He closed her door behind him and looked down the stairs. He
could go down, try to make small talk with Zoe and Daniel, be polite
... or he could just go to bed, and avoid them both until the morning.

The guest room was sparse but inviting. Steven dropped onto the
wide bed and pulled the covers over his clothes. He was too tired to
undress.

––––––––––

The breakfast atmosphere was slightly better than the previous
night in the car, but not by much. Daniel's presence made it easier,
and Steven found he liked the older man, a divorcee with two young
children of his own. As an experienced parent, he took to Viv quickly
and easily, asking her what she'd like for breakfast and preparing large
crepe pancakes with a smile.

Zoe was snappy. As Viv asked for a third crepe, she stepped in,
curtly saying that there was no need for another and that Viv had to
understand. "This is my house, you live by my rules now, and that
means no over-indulging with things like pancakes."

Steven flinched, unhappy at the sharpness of her tone, but said
nothing. He looked at Viv and shrugged with a smile, trying to signal

some sort of understanding and conspiratorial nature, an unspoken promise that there'd be plenty of treats in secret.

"When is your train back?" Zoe asked Steven.

"This afternoon." It hadn't been long before he'd made the final decision to go back as quickly as he could. As much as he wanted to stay for his little sister's sake, being around Zoe was making him feel increasingly uncomfortable.

"Good, OK. I'll drive you when you need it."

"Thanks."

"In the meantime, we need to go into town, to buy a uniform for Vivienne. There's not a lot of time, so why don't you go shower now, Viv, and get yourself ready?"

Eager to leave, Viv slipped off her seat and disappeared. As Daniel left, too, Zoe turned to Steven.

"Do you have enough money to get back?"

"Of course."

"Good, because there are no more handouts, you understand?"

"You made it pretty clear, Zoe."

"Just as long as we are clear."

"There's six months left on the flat lease, and my tuition fees are due again soon. How am I meant to pay for those things?"

"That's not my problem, Steven."

"Why are you being like this? Surely you can help."

"No, I can't. I told you, there's no money for you. Even if there were, it wouldn't be that much. With Viv living with me, I need the portion of the money that was allocated to her upbringing in order to pay for her keep and education. You are a single man, and you have a job. Sort yourself out."

"It's not as easy as that."

"Well, ask Alistair for help, then. That's what people in relationships do; they help each other out in hard times."

"Al? He's a student, too, and ten times more broke than I am. He can just about afford to pay his own way."

"But he does manage, doesn't he? So, you can, too."

"You are being unreasonable! If I can't find the money for the flat, or for my tuition, it could mean the end of my education, and the end of my career before it really begins."

"That," she said, standing and punctuating each word with a thud as she put away the breakfast things, "is not," thud, "my," thud, "fault."

"You could help me out! Look at your house, look at your life!"

"A life *I* worked for. A life I work for every single day. And yes, look at my house. I have a mortgage to pay, one that is not insubstantial. I don't have a lot of free money to pay for my loser little brother."

"What happened, Zoe? A couple of weeks ago, you were on my side, telling me how I should find love with Alistair, that you'd support me, that you understood how being gay was nothing bad. Now you are treating me just as badly as Mum."

"Maybe she has a point."

Steven pulled away from the table, shocked.

"Maybe I am being an adult and need to make sure that someone is here for Viv. You are big enough to look after yourself, but she is still a school child."

"I want to go," Steven whispered. "I just want to go. I'll walk to the station."

"Fine. Make sure you say goodbye to Vivienne before you go. I'm sure she'll miss you."

Zoe stormed out. Tears streaming and shoulders shaking, Steven picked himself up and went up to his younger sister's room. He knocked, and when Viv called out a hello, he blinked away the tears, took a deep breath, and went inside.

"I'm off now. There's an earlier train and if I get it, then I'll be able to get back in time to get a good night's sleep before uni tomorrow. I'm sorry, I know you wanted me to stay longer, but ..."

"It's OK." Viv ran up and hugged him. "I'll be OK, you'll be OK, and I'll be up to visit you really soon. Don't worry, I'm sure Zoe and I will get on fine. She's my sister, remember, not a stranger."

"Just don't get on her bad side. She can be ..." Steven thought about his sister, about how she had been when they were younger, and flinched. "She can be harsh, so be careful."

Viv planted a kiss on his cheek. "I'll be a good respectful girl. I'll study hard and do well, and everyone will be happy with me, right?"

"Right." Steven smiled.

"Bye bye, Stevie, you look after yourself."

Wiping his eyes, Steven left.

CHAPTER 10

Tearing the envelope open, Steven scrabbled at the inside, roughly pulling the folded sheet of paper out and staring at it.

"Well?" asked Alistair. The taller man lounged back on the sofa, his feet disrespectfully on the arm of the furniture.

"They said 'yes'." Steven sat on the floor and breathed out slowly, relieved.

"So, that's good then. Are you going to actually relax now?"

"You are so flippant about it all. Without this," he waved the letter, "I'd be looking at scraping food from bins in a couple of weeks."

"Don't be daft. You're a long way from bins. Besides, I support you. We practically share money, now. It's so couple-y I think it makes me feel a little sick."

"Helping me out with the occasional lunch isn't quite the same as having a solid amount in the bank. No offence."

"I paid your electricity once."

Steven raised his eyebrows, decided not to mention the number of times he'd bailed Alistair out when he couldn't cover his own expenses, and looked at the letter again to check the numbers. It was a grant; not a huge one, but enough to keep the tide at bay.

Since being cut off, his life had revolved around money. It consumed every moment of his thinking to the point of utter distraction. He and Alistair had spent one long evening going through the possible options, listing things like 'get an extra job or two' through to 'beg'. This hardship grant, one of tens he had applied to, was the first decent response out of all of them. That and the new job as a waiter that he would start tonight.

"Is it enough?" Alistair asked.

"For now. And they say it'll be in my account within three-to-five working days, so that's the end of next week, before the rent is due."

"Excellent. Dinner on you, then!"

Steven shot him a glare.

Alistair laughed. "Oh, come on, you need to lighten up."

"I can't lighten up. Paying for myself to get through this damned degree is stressful."

"But you'll do it. Did anyone get back to you about the room?"

"Lots." That had been another part of the plan; to sub-let part of the flat and effectively halve the rent. Thankfully, the landlord had seen no issue with the idea and told Steven he could do what he liked, as long as no one trashed the place and the rent kept coming in.

"But?"

"I'm just not quite ready to have someone I don't know here."

"So, you're putting it off?"

"I suppose." Steven looked at his boyfriend. He'd asked Alistair to move in with him, but the lease on his own flat was tight and the cost of breaking it a little too high. At least, that's how Alistair had framed it. Steven wondered if it was simply that the Scotsman didn't want to up their level of commitment, that they were still too young for that.

"Don't. Find three or four that you like and arrange to meet them next week. Halving the rent will surely make you feel it's all in hand."

"It would help," Steven conceded.

"See, it's all looking up. Lunch?"

Steven shook his head. "I have studying to do, and I need to get ready for tonight, and walk there." Selling the car had been another concession to his new life as a pauper. It was more than sensible, the saving on the insurance alone had been considerable.

"Wow, you're really pushing the excitement buttons today. Fine, I'll leave, do the walk of shame."

"It's not like that!"

"I know, Steve, wow, calm down."

"Sorry, it's just—"

"That you're stressed and I'm not helping. Yeah, I get it. Don't worry, I'm not offended." Alistair swung his legs around and jumped to his feet. "I'll sod off and see you later then. I was going to say Ray and I would pop in to your work tonight, but I sense you'd rather we didn't."

"It's my first night. Claire said similar and I put her off, too, even though I've not caught up with her in weeks."

"Yeah, exactly, you don't want us to. It's fine." Alistair planted a kiss on his lover's forehead. "Have a good night, and we can do stuff tomorrow."

"Thanks."

Steven listened to Alistair leaving and then went to the window to watch as the other man strode casually down the road. The flat was empty once more and the absence of Viv's presence was suddenly stark. It was a shame she'd taken her console with her; Steven felt an urge to spend an hour shooting zombies.

No, it was better to do the studying he had used as an excuse. Then he needed to shower. It was his first day as a waiter and he was keen to make a good impression.

———

Steven slumped on the bed exhausted. Three nights of seven hour shifts in a row had taken its toll, plus the university work that was layered on top of that. He stared out at the moonlit night and sighed. How long had it been since he'd seen Alistair now? A week?

He thought about calling, but it was two in the morning, and Al was never the best if he was woken up unexpectedly.

Sighing, Steven wrapped the warm duvet around himself and closed his eyes. At least the job in the restaurant came with free dinner, thanks to May's kindness. He suspected she was singling him out because he was otherwise in pretty dire straits, but it could just be because they shared a common heritage. That was something he appreciated too, being able to talk to someone about home without it being a one-sided explanation of cultural differences.

Micky was awake. The door to the bathroom closed with its distinctive click and then the whirr of the extractor fan. Steven wondered if he'd woken his new housemate when he came in, and thought about calling out an apology, but no; it was part of the deal that Micky understood and respected his landlord's overwrought schedule. The second-year maths undergraduate was a quiet man himself and hadn't shown any sign of interest in what Steven did or did not do. It had made the nervous undertaking of sub-letting his mother's old room work out fine. The rent was halved, and they hardly crossed paths.

His mother. Steven groaned to himself. There had been no real words between them since the day Zoe had dropped the bombshell on him. He'd tried with a few calls and texts, but it had all been ignored. Knowing how stubborn she was, Steven didn't hold out much hope of getting a return call any time soon.

I need to sleep, he told himself, trying to rid his brain of these wandering thoughts. Yet, one led to another and soon he was worrying about Vivienne. Despite all her assurances that she was of a younger generation, tempered by international awareness and varied culture, Zoe had shown that she had the same traditional conservatism and stubbornness that ran through their mother. She could be strict, even harsh, and Steven worried how Viv was in that environment. When it had just been the two of them here, the atmosphere had been relaxed, with Viv engaged in a happy balance between study and relaxation. He doubted she enjoyed the same freedom in Zoe's house.

And then Alistair. Al was outwardly supportive of Steven's new timetable, a wall-to-wall fest of study and work, with now three jobs vying for his time as well as the ongoing difficulty of the second half of a medical degree. Outwardly supportive, however, didn't necessarily mean that Alistair was happy with his boyfriend being so busy and unavailable. Four times, Steven had been forced to say no to proposed evenings together. How long before Alistair found someone else to be with? Someone more free?

Steven shuddered. He and Al had been together for years now, and it was a relationship he hoped would grow into something more permanent and official. They'd danced around the subject, silly jokes on drunken evenings, but had never spoken about it properly. Now, it felt so far away.

Micky walked soft footsteps from the bathroom back to his bedroom. Steven turned again, trying to get comfortable.

The new job was proving to be somewhat fun, though. In addition to tutoring and restaurant shifts, Steven had managed to secure a few jobs through a modelling agency. Not because he was particularly striking, but because suitable Asian men of his age were reasonably thin on the ground in Scotland.

Whatever the reason, it paid well and gave his ego a slight boost. There had only been two gigs so far, both a little objectifying but, he smiled to himself, beggars can't be choosers. Bare chested drink-serving hadn't been the highlight of his life so far, but it had been quite fun in the end, and it wasn't completely top-half-naked, after all—there had been that bow tie.

2:14. Steven groaned and checked that the alarm was set. Four hours and forty-five minutes of sleep, assuming he could reach unconsciousness in the next minute. He tried concentrating on his breathing, and relaxed.

———

"Tell your friend that if he isn't going to order anything more, we need the table." May's smile was friendly, but the seriousness of her tone was clear. Steven walked over to Ray.

"Time's up, sorry. May says we need the table."

"I could order another coke," Ray offered.

"You could, but even then, I don't think she'll want to let you hang around for long. It's easier for me if you go. Honestly, I don't think she likes the fact I keep coming over to chat."

"Yeah, fair enough. Keep tomorrow evening free though, don't let her talk you into another shift. Al'll kill yer fer one, and I've put a lot of thought into the movie marathon. It'll be good for ya."

"It's OK, I'll be there. And thanks for understanding."

"Aye, no problem." Ray stood up. "Here, keep the change."

He handed over a ten-pound note. Steven laughed; the change, such as it was, amounted to pennies.

"I'll see you tomorrow." He was already moving to clear the table. Ray grunted a goodbye and left.

"Good," said May as Steven deposited the crockery. "Now, go and seat that man, he's been waiting a little too long."

"Table for one?" Steven asked.

The man, a smartly dressed figure in his late 40s, nodded at him. "Thank you." Steven showed him to the seat that Ray had kept warm for well over an hour. He passed a menu, asked about any drinks, and smiled as the man ordered a whisky. People who were willing to pay the premium on drinks like that with their dinner typically tipped well.

"I'll be back with your whisky in just a moment," Steven promised.

A call from another table diverted him, and Steven hurried through a run of requests before returning with the pricy Scotch.

"Sorry it took a little while."

"That's fine. You seem busy."

"Yes. But don't worry, we're very efficient."

"Ah, I'm patient, and I understand the need to be precise with your work, so don't rush."

"What is it you do?" Steven asked conversationally, readying his pad for the meal order.

"I'm a plastic surgeon. It's definitely the kind of job where you don't want to make mistakes."

Steven straightened. "That's my dream job. I'm a medical student at the moment, but that's definitely where I'd like to end up."

"It's very rewarding." The man looked around the room. "Maybe if you get a few minutes, I could answer some of your questions."

"That'd be great." Steven did a similar visual sweep. "Though it might not be for a while."

"Indeed!"

"Can I take your order?"

The rush kept Steven busy, though twice he returned to the man's table to learn that his name was John, and that he was visiting from London for an art exhibition. All too quickly though, Steven was asked for the bill, and any opportunity he might have for getting more information was gone.

"That's a £50 tip!" Steven exclaimed, once the transaction was entered. "Are you sure?"

"Of course." John smiled. "I've enjoyed talking to you, albeit very briefly, and I know how those university expenses can add up. When you're a surgeon yourself, maybe you'll be able to do the same."

"I will, thank you!"

"Look, I appreciate that when you finish your shift, it'll be a little late, but I'm happy to keep our conversation going if you're interested. Here's my number. I'm staying in the Marriott in town and if you want to come over for a drink once you've finished here, maybe we can talk some more. Better than me watching whatever television is on."

Steven grinned. "I'd like that."

"Just give me a text later if you want to come over. I can meet you in the bar."

Clearing the table, Steven nodded. "I will." He'd be tired, but if there was an opportunity here to further his career, he'd be stupid to miss it. One drink at the bar wouldn't see him in bed too late.

Seeing his eagerness to leave, May let him go before all the cleaning was finished. Steven stepped into the cool air just before midnight and texted the number, fearing it was already too late.

Sure, come on over, came the reply. **Bar's closing, but I'm room 312 if that's OK.**

Steven stabbed at the phone keyboard. **Great. See you in a few minutes.**

Being a London plastic surgeon was his dream, and not just because of the money. Steven was all too aware how many mental health issues the patients had regarding their outward appearance. Having the ability to help them with their pain and offering a brighter life to those who had been affected by scarring or other problems would make him feel he was really achieving something. If he could impress John with his diligence and enthusiasm, perhaps he could line up some sort of opening once he completed his degree.

Steven jogged the short distance to the Marriott and into the warm lobby. As John had said, the bar staff were clearing up, the lights dim. He looked for a sign showing where the rooms were and slipped through a shutting doorway to the stairs.

Somewhat nervously, he knocked on the door of 312. "It's Steven. From the restaurant."

John opened the door with a broad smile. He had taken off his dress shirt, revealing a muscled body in a fitting white v-neck. Steven appraised him for a moment, suddenly repositioning the meeting in his mind. Had John been flirting? No, he was being silly, they had just been chatting about his career. John was just willing to help.

"Welcome. Come in." the older man beckoned him into the room with a wide sweeping arm. "Apologies about the bar, I didn't realise they shut so early. In London, many hotel bars are open past midnight."

"As long as you're sure. I don't want to intrude."

"Nonsense! Come in. I'll get you a drink. Whisky?"

"Sure." His taste for Scotch was not exactly that of a fan, but he wasn't wanting to insult his host. He stepped forward nervously into the spacious hotel room and sat on the small armchair.

John laughed, a deep rumble. "It's all on expenses, which is stretching a little, I admit, but then that's why I pay an accountant. The downside is that far too often they think they can tell you what you should spend your money on."

Steven snickered. "Sounds like my older sister, though you could say she quit recently."

"Well, that's good. Don't rely on family. It can cause issues."

Steven nodded. That was something to which he could easily agree.

The drinks were larger than he expected. Steven sipped his gingerly, noting how John didn't have the same reservation.

"So, you want to be a plastic surgeon?"

Steven relaxed and started to talk. It was easy, with John understanding every aspect of his chatter. Alistair, Ray, his other friends and family, they all listened to him with patient attention, but Steven had never really been able to speak with anyone who shared his passion. Even Claire and the other students on his course didn't quite evoke the same feeling, with their different backgrounds and end goals. With John, and the refilled glass, it was relaxing.

Suddenly, the older surgeon leaned in from his position on the edge of the bed and kissed him.

Steven froze, his words mid-flow. Obviously taking his silence as some sort of agreement, John wrapped a hand around the back of his head and pulled him closer.

Steven gasped, pulling away. "No, sorry, I, umm, I can't. I have a boyfriend."

"So you are gay, then?"

"Being gay doesn't mean being promiscuous. I'm sorry."

John laughed. "Attractive gay man comes in the middle of the night to another man's hotel room. Of course, you came for sex."

"No!" Steven's eyes flickered to the door. It seemed so far away.

John stood. He was a tall man, at least six inches taller than Steven, and far stronger. He reached forward and grasped him around the shoulders.

"Don't be coy." Roughly, he grabbed him and threw him facedown on the bed. With trembling legs, Steven could offer little physical resistance. He hit the covers with a soft thump, the mattress bouncing very slightly in response.

A large hand wrapped strongly around Steven's right thigh as the surgeon climbed across the bed. John squeezed his fingers. "Although, I'm not against playing the 'please don't' game if that's what you're into."

"It's not a game," Steven said, trying to push himself up only to find a strong, weighty hand on his back. "I'm saying 'no.'"

"Of course you are." John's voice had changed, the softer edge replaced with something more sinister. Steven struggled again and found himself shoved forcefully downward. "It's OK. I'll give you a bit towards your school bills, too." John laughed. "Paying will make it even more fun. How about two hundred quid?"

"I don't—" Steven's voice was muffled in the sheets. He found his breaths were hot and shallow.

He kicked, his heel connecting solidly with the older man's thigh. Again, he was rewarded with a heavy push. This time, a hand tugged on his trousers. Steven winced; even though they were belted, he knew they came down easily. It didn't take much effort from John to expose him, the cold breeze of the air-conditioned room chilling his buttocks.

"No," Steven tried again, his voice filled with panic, tears in his eyes.

"Just relax, and enjoy it. I know I'm going to."

He could feel John. The man's bare skin on the back of his legs. Steven trembled.

Don't let this happen.

Don't let this happen.

It didn't work the first time. John swore, angry with the resistance. He hit Steven around the back of the head, not really very hard but enough to make him cry out. The tears came easily. A second slap came for no reason Steven understood. He crumpled.

He should fight. Weakly, he tried to kick again, but he didn't have the strength for it to be more than a desperate flare. John's lips met the back of his neck as the man leaned his entire body weight onto him. There were no words, just a rush of breath and a grunting from his attacker.

On the next attempt, John managed to force his way. Steven gasped and cried, wishing he was somewhere else, wishing he was someone else, wishing it would all be over.

When was it going to all be over?

CHAPTER 11

"Don't worry, if you do what you're told, it will all be OK. You won't be hurt."

You won't be hurt.

Steven curled up in the darkness, his own bedroom an alien place, absent of the familiarity and warmth that gave him comfort. The walls moved, pressing in on him, and he cried.

"Don't worry."

He hadn't heard that voice for years, though for years before it had taunted him.

"You won't be hurt."

He'd been so young.

"I'm going to tell Mum," Steven whispered. Zoe glared at him, her hair pulled back into a ponytail that made her face stern.

"You're not. Don't be so disrespectful."

"I don't even know what that means," Steven whined.

Zoe huffed, jumped off the chair and crouched down beside him.

"It means you listen to what Dad says and do what he tells you, and if he's told you that you don't tell Mum he brought us here, then you don't tell Mum."

"But I don't like it. She doesn't like it when we come here."

Zoe snarled. "Just don't, Steven, OK? No one will believe you anyway, you're just a silly little boy and I'll tell them you're lying."

"Why?" Steven wanted to cry.

"Because it's disrespectful." She repeated the word.

"I don't understand."

"Well, I do. Just do what I say, which means doing what Dad says, and it'll be fine."

Steven shrank back, partly scared of his older sister who, at twelve, was both far stronger and more confident; partly because somewhere inside himself he knew it made no difference. Eventually, his dad would finish with whatever he did in there and he'd come out. Gambling, Mum called it, dirty gambling. Steven didn't know what gambling was, except Dad always wanted to do it, and Mum screamed about it when he did.

Here, in the small room to the side of the adult's main rooms, he and Zoe would sit and wait. There was a pile of comic books on the table. Maybe he'd look at those in a while; there might be some newer ones that he'd never seen before.

His stomach hurt. "I'm hungry."

"We're both hungry. Here." It was a small handful of peanuts, just eight, but it was nice of Zoe to let him have them. She'd probably been keeping them in her pocket for herself, for when it was even worse than this.

"He's been ages."

"I know, Steven, I know."

"I want to go home."

"Me too."

"We should tell Mum. You should let me tell her."

"No!" Zoe grabbed his face, turned it so that he looked directly into her eyes. "I don't want you to tell Mum, OK, so you don't do that. Dad won't love you for it, and neither will I."

"It's just—"

"No." She was firm.

"Will you tell me a story, then? To make the time go faster."

"I can't think of any stories. Here." She passed him one of the comics. "Read this."

Quietly, Steven opened the first page.

"I need the toilet." Zoe turned away. "I'll be back in a bit. Just stay here and keep quiet."

Steven mumbled his agreement without looking up. Already, the story had his interest.

———

Steven pulled himself onto his bed and stared at the ceiling.

Had he been to blame? Maybe John had been right. What sort of idiot comes to a man's hotel room in the middle of the night? To talk about plastic surgery? Really?

He'd gone willingly. He hadn't even stopped at reception in his eager desire to get to the hotel room on time. Walked into the room, sat down, accepted a drink.

Of course he'd looked agreeable. A fifty-pound tip. God.

He was going to have to tell Alistair, and it was going to ruin everything. What if Alistair didn't believe that he was innocent, that he'd gone there with pure intentions? He'd just wanted to help his career, to get to know someone that might be able to help him in the future. He hadn't wanted anything else.

But what if Alistair didn't understand?

———

Steven looked up from his comic book. He'd been reading for a while, surely Dad was finished now.

"Zoe?"

His sister was gone. The door to the other room was open. When had that happened? Had she not come back from the toilet? He'd read two entire comics since then.

"Zoe? Dad?"

Steven jumped down and walked to the door, peering into the other room. It was quiet, as if everyone had gone home.

"Hello?" he called.

"Oh, you're finished." A man walked over. Steven recognised him as the owner, one of Dad's friends.

"Where's my father? And my sister?"

"They've gone." The man laughed and it rang cruelly in Steven's ears.

"Gone?" He didn't understand.

"Yes, you're mine now."

Steven looked at him, into his eyes. This didn't make sense, surely the man was lying, making it up, teasing him somehow. The man was thin, his face tight, but Steven could see that he wasn't lying.

"Your father owed me a lot of money, boy, money that he couldn't pay me back. So he sold you to me. You live with me now, and you work for me."

Steven said nothing. None of this made sense.

"My sister?" Where was Zoe?

"He kept her." The owner chuckled. "A shame, because I could have found a lot more use for her than I will with you."

Steven started to cry. Swiftly, the back of the man's hand struck him across the cheek. He fell and lay, half on his knees on the floor. His face stung.

"Don't worry. If you do what you're told, it will all be OK. You won't be hurt."

The words swam in his mind, filling him with fear.

"I want my mum," Steven whimpered.

"Not going to happen." The man began to walk away. "I'll bring you some food in a while. In the meantime, wait there."

Steven looked at the door. He could run, maybe. Get outside into the street and try to get help. He stood up and turned as the owner's voice sang out.

"It's locked, you won't get anywhere. And remember, your father sold you to me. There's nothing you can do, he's not going to help you. No one is."

Steven slumped back onto the floor, his fingernails scratching on the cold tiles.

———————

5:01. Steven had been staring at the clock for more than twenty minutes, watching as each number ticked over into the next, looking for patterns in the digits. The back of his mind raged and raced, replaying the events of the night, remembering lost and buried memories.

His father had sold him to pay off gambling debts.

His mother had disowned him for being gay.

His sister was disdainful, selfish, even cruel.

By now, Viv would hate him, too. Influenced by Zoe's better life, by her money and her career and her boyfriend.

And Alistair would never speak to him again, not after this ... betrayal. That's how he'd see it. A betrayal. Going to another man's hotel room.

He'd been asking for it.

———————

Steven huddled in his corner. There was no bed; like the two dogs he was relegated to a blanket on the floor. When the light came in, he had to clean, scrub the tables and chairs, sweep the floor and clean the windows. He wasn't very good at it; there was always dirt left along the edges, and the windows smeared from his clothwork.

He was hungry. He was always hungry, and each time he ate, it made him drowsy and desperate for sleep. One afternoon, he must have fallen off the bench while he ate the bowl of noodles, because he woke up under the table with sticky congealed sauce clinging to his cheek.

So tired. So frightened.

———————

Dawn came despite Steven's clouded disdain, and with it was the need to wash and dress. He had a choice, he reasoned; to allow it to take him down a path he'd travelled before, of misery and fear. Or to try to break away and focus on the day.

One thing at a time, he told himself. Just a shower. Nothing more, no promises of action or greatness. Just the shower.

————

Steven didn't recognise her at first. His mother stormed into the building while he was fetching drinks. Four bottles of beer in his small shaking hands. She strode over to him and he shrank from this imposing woman, her face like furious thunder.

"Come with me!" she demanded.

Steven cried. His mind was foggy. Did he know her? She seemed frightening.

"You can't come in here, talking like that!" The boss stood from the table and crossed the room. "Who are you."

"That is my son," she said, suddenly calm. "And I am taking him home."

"He's mine." The man sneered. "He was sold to me."

The woman said nothing, but pulled a huge pile of banknotes from her bag. She put them down on the table.

"It's all there." She turned to her son. "Steven, come."

Steven didn't move, but as she bent on one knee and beckoned him, something snapped. He did know her. His dirty hands wrapped around her back, tears smearing down his face. Suddenly he was safe again, suddenly it was warm again.

She took him out into the daylight, carrying him in her arms.

————

"I need you." Steven didn't bother with 'hello', worried that if he did, he'd break down and not be able to say what he needed to.

"Are you OK?" Alistair was immediately alert.

"No. Can you come over?"

"I'll be fifteen minutes. Ten."

Steven let the phone drop to the bathroom floor. He'd made it to the shower, managed to wash the disgustingness from himself, but he'd got no further.

———

Micky was still up. He opened the door when Alistair knocked. From the bathroom, Steven called out and his boyfriend joined him, closing the door quietly to give them privacy.

"What happened?"

"I made a mistake." Steven's tears mingled with the water dripping from his hair. "A horrible, terrible mistake."

Alistair picked him up, holding him in his arms just like his mother had done when he'd been a child. Steven fell mute as the Scotsman wrapped a towel around him and fussed about soapsuds left in his hair. A few minutes of careful ministrations later and Alistair laid Steven gently on the bed.

"You tell me everything, leave nothing out, and start at the beginning."

Steven nodded. "It started after Ray left the restaurant last night …"

———

Alistair cried, too. Sat behind Steven, he wrapped his lover in shuddering arms. Steven listened to the soft sobs, quieter than he'd expected, and now fully replacing his own.

He'd told his story.

Throughout it all, Alistair had clutched him, promising to be there for him.

Eventually, they fell into a curled, desperate sleep.

———

Steven missed his classes, and he texted to apologise for being unable to tutor his two students in the late afternoon. As afternoon threatened evening, he turned to Alistair.

"Ray's movie marathon?"

Alistair laughed. "I thought you wouldn't be up for it. I've been thinking for the last quarter of an hour of what to tell Ray to apologise and excuse us."

"No, we should do it. We need to get out of here, anyway. It's beginning to smell."

"Do you have any idea what films he's chosen?"

"None. You?"

"Aye, I have a good idea. Might not be your thing."

"I'm open to anything. Especially today. I'm emotionally and physically exhausted." He leaned forward to hold Alistair's face in his hands. "Thank you." He swallowed hard, afraid of the next words. "I love you."

They rarely said that to each other. It had been said, of course, and was often repeated after their better physical encounters, but there was always something perfunctory about it in those times. Steven made sure to catch his boyfriend's eyes, to lock onto them and hold the gaze.

"I love you, too," Alistair equalled the sense of seriousness. Then he smiled and broke away from the embrace and the moment. "We should get some beers in, and popcorn."

"I need proper food before that."

"Aye, me too, so we need to get moving."

Steven drew back the curtains and opened the window, letting in the cool air. He gave himself one last moment of reflection, and then turned and picked up his towel.

CHAPTER 12

Steven leaned back against the soft cushions and laughed. His beer bottle had long been empty, but he clutched it in his hand anyway, occasionally putting it to his lips as if expecting it to yield more drink.

A cold draught drifted through the club. Any warmth that remained of the autumn had gone, replaced by another incoming Scottish winter. It seemed that all he had done for months was earn money and then drink the majority of it.

Ray beamed and leaned on the table. "It's a good one, isn't it? You want another drink, Stevie-boy? You've been nursing that one a while."

"Oh, umm, yeah, thanks." Steven put the bottle on to the table where it joined a growing swell of companions. Ray smiled again and left to return to the bar.

"He's a dick," said Alistair.

"You just didn't like being the centre of his little story."

"Would you?"

"I wouldn't have worn the chicken suit."

"Oh, you would. For a hundred quid you would have."

"I wouldn't have tripped up."

"It's hard to see in those things, and so hot."

"Obviously."

Alistair leaned forward and kissed him. Steven withdrew slightly; for all their many months of being together, he was still a little wary of public displays of affection.

"I have an idea." Alistair placed both his palms on the table and looked up, his serious face betrayed by the drunken glint in his eyes.

"Is it a good one, or is it along the lines of the chicken suit?"

"You tell me."

Steven waved regally, indicating his boyfriend should continue.

"We should move in together."

"Really?" Steven frowned.

"Yes. Why not? We're paying two loads of rent, your lease is up soon, and we practically live with each other anyway. It's sensible."

"So, you want to do it for logistical reasons? Not because you love me?"

"Absolutely. Love and sex are side issues."

Steven raised one eyebrow; sex was definitely not a side issue for either of them.

"OK, maybe not completely side," Alistair conceded.

They laughed and kissed again, and then Ray was back with more drinks.

"What are you two so loved up about?" he asked.

"Al wants me to move in with him."

"Fucking daft idea," said Ray. "Takes all the mystique out of the relationship."

"What mystique would that be?" Alistair turned his head to stare up at Ray.

"Ah, shit habits, picking your nose, where you dump your toenails once you've chopped 'em, that sort of thing."

"I eat mine," Alistair teased, "no use wasting such delicious crunchy treats."

"Don't be disgusting," Ray looked over to Steven for confirmation.

"He's lying," said Steven.

"I should fuckin' hope so," said Ray. "Savage."

"Oh, I don't eat them around you," Alistair continued, "but in the quiet of my own home ..."

"There you go," said Ray.

"You're right," Steven agreed. "No moving in for me."

"Ah well, fuck it," said Alistair, "if I have to give up on a short regular snack for on-tap sex and back massages, I guess it's something I'll have to live with."

"Still a daft idea," Ray argued, "but none of my business what the two of you do."

"One load of rent," Steven said.

"Yeah, there is that." He looked at Alistair with a piercing glare. "Just make sure this one pays his part."

"I always pay my part!" Alistair complained.

"Then when these are gone, it's your round." Ray swallowed a long draught of his lager.

Steven smiled. He'd long wanted Alistair to move in with him, but it had never been right. Was now right? It felt so. He'd lived with a flatmate for months now, wouldn't it have been better for Micky to have been Alistair the entire time?

There was a slight twinge. Steven realised that moving meant giving up on the home he'd had with Viv. Somewhere in the back of his mind, he'd hoped that Zoe would relent on her guardianship of their little sister and send Vivienne back to him. Instead, the communication between him and Viv had drifted, from every day to every couple of days, to once a week, and now? He counted it up; nine days since they'd spoken properly, just a couple of texts in between. Was it that she had her life now and was all happy with it, or had he been the one to ignore her, swept up in the chaos of Alistair and a summer of work, parties and fun? Every moment he had free from the ridiculous level of work that was needed to keep from spiralling debt was spent with Alistair.

All the more reason to move in together.

Steven stood up, mumbled about the toilet and crossed the floor. Viv. In truth, he had some concerns, a few little bits said here and there that perhaps he should have taken more notice of. His little sister's grades had slipped a bit, and though he hadn't wanted to put any pressure on her, certainly not the same sort of expectation that his parents had laid upon him his entire life, he did think she should pick up a bit more. Was it because he was no longer there to tutor her? Hadn't Zoe said she was getting a tutor in anyway? Steven admonished himself; in truth, he'd been so wrapped up with his own life that he'd not really considered how the months had treated Viv.

He pulled out his phone, leaned against the wall and started a slightly-drunken text message.

Hi Viv, thinking of you and realised we hadn't spoken in a while.

He looked at it, and at the time: 11:28, well past Vivienne's bedtime. With a couple of swipes, Steven deleted the short text and dropped the phone back into his pocket.

Perhaps he should be leaving Viv to lead her own life anyway.

"Life is a struggle," he said dramatically when he dropped back down onto the seat. Ray looked up at him, eyes wide.

"What the fuck?"

"These decisions," Steven said. "You know, I was meant to be my sister's big brother, looking after her and making sure she was all OK, and what am I doing?"

"Working off the horrific amount of debt she and your mother effectively put you in?" suggested Alistair. "Stop being so loyal. The fact is, your family dumped you like a ton of gay shit and left you out here to fend for yourself. You are fending, why feel guilty about it?"

"Viv didn't. She's as much a victim of my family as I am."

"Yeah, we don't pick our parents," Ray mused.

"You are just a bundle of guilt," Alistair complained. "Seriously. I ask you to move in with me, and it's not a moment of joy for you, it's filled with guilt about your little sister. Someone who doesn't even live in the same fucking country. You can move out of your flat that you had together, Steven. It's not a sin."

"I didn't say it was."

"No, but that's where your mind went. Not on picking out bedsheets or whatever, but on how you owe something to your little sister."

"Sorry for being caring, Al."

"Insinuating that I'm not? Fuck you."

Steven glanced down at the table and the empty bottles and glasses there.

"Oh, fucking get Mr. High and Mighty there," snapped Alistair. "You about to say that I'm getting agitated because I'm drunk?"

"You are a bit pissed, mate," Ray offered.

"Yeah, we all are. Maybe that's why I made the offer in the first place. Not because I actually want to see his sorry arse every morning, but because I get all lovey when I've had a few. Offer retracted, Steve. Why don't you sign up for another year in that flat of yours, just in case Viv decides to come home. Fuck it, it's about time you made up with your mother. You could spend six months dicking about fixing her visa issues and getting her back in the country to make your life great."

"Al ..." Ray said, his voice filled with diffusing calm.

"Oh what? So I'm saying stuff we all know. His mother's a bitch, who doesn't actually give two fucks about him, and his sisters are just as bad. Fuck me, Steven, I've been your family for this year. Who picked you up when your family cut you off from any money? Me. Caring, fucking stupid, non-judgemental me. Who the fuck paid for your dinner when you couldn't scrape fifty fucking pence together? Me again. Who was it that looked after you when you got summarily arse-fucked in that hotel? Oh yes, definitely me. And now instead of thinking that us actually moving forward with our lives is worthwhile, you are worried about them. Fuck's sake. Sure, give Viv a ring in the morning and ask her if she gives you her blessing. Check up with your family about whether or not you are allowed to do anything. It's so great for me to watch and live with. Christ!"

Steven stared at him. Inside he boiled, defences rushing to the fore, insults to tell Alistair what an arsehole he was being and how the things he was saying weren't true, but he stopped himself. Because the grain of truth running though his boyfriend's rant was clear. He had lived, every moment of every day, in the shadow of a family who never really showed they cared.

"What hotel?" Ray asked quietly.

Steven flushed, grabbed his jacket and stormed off to the stairs. Outside, the cool nighttime air cleared his head immediately. He wanted to cry, he wanted to rage, he wanted to scream. Instead, he just stood there, leaning pathetically against a lamppost.

The metal of the club door clanged and he spun.

Alistair looked at him from the doorway, his face guilt-ridden and remorseful. "For my part, I'm sorry. I don't think the things I said were particularly wrong, but the way I said them was. Forgive me?" He stepped forward and put his hand on Steven's shoulder, who brushed it off, but only half-heartedly.

"It's true, isn't it?" Steven avoided his boyfriend's eyes. "I've spent my whole life being ruled by them."

"Absolutely."

"Even when they're not here."

"Especially when they're not here."

Steven lifted his gaze. "Do you still want me to move in with you?"

"Of course I fucking do. Shacking up with a rich doctor type has to be good for my prospects, right?"

"Hardly a rich doctor type."

"Right now, you're not, but you will be. You'll get your dream, Steven. Plastic surgeon to the stars."

"Not the stars, the needy."

"Oh, cut the altruistic nobility. Beyoncé walks into your practice and you're bending over backwards to serve her. You can tell everyone else you know that it's about helping people with body dysmorphism that drives you, but I know you for the fame-whore you really are."

Steven laughed. "Not true."

"Whatever."

"So, do we keep your flat or what?"

"Nope. I want somewhere new, somewhere that's us, not somewhere that one of us sees as more 'theirs'. We'll need to pick out curtains and all that shit."

"We're not buying somewhere. I can't get a mortgage."

"Fine, we'll take whatever curtains they have. But bedding."

"Oh, definitely bedding."

"And I get to choose lamps. Your taste in that area is a mess."

"Lamps?"

"Exactly, you don't even see how important they are. Lighting is key to a good environment."

Steven wrapped his arms around his lover, pulling him in tight and kissing him in the moonlight.

"Get a room." Ray's voice drifted in one ear and out the other as Steven drank in his boyfriend's mellow scent. Delicate, and yet very male, it was comforting and seductive all at once.

Alistair broke off the embrace and grinned. "A room?" he said. "We're getting a whole fucking flat."

CHAPTER 13

His eyes swamping with tears, Steven stared into the freezer compartment. Now that the soggy cardboard box that had held ice lollies for months was gone, consigned like so much other stuff to one of the many black plastic sacks he'd filled in the past few days, there was only one item left.

Carefully, Steven lifted out the little snowman. "Fuck."

There was no one around to hear him. This was the clean-up day, three days until he technically needed to be out of the flat, but only one night before he was actually moving. Micky had gone the week before, two of his friends that Steven hadn't previously met helping him load his stuff into a yellow Citroen that had seen better days. They'd lived together for months, and Steven had never really bothered to get to know him.

His mind flashed back to the snowman. There had been tension in the air that day, between him and his mother, but then when hadn't that been the case? Viv, though, had been delighted, dancing in the snow with utter abandon.

Already the little figure was melting. In truth, it had long ago given up any real semblance of form. The idea of keeping it, somehow rushing it to a second freezer on the other side of town, was clearly ridiculous. Steven hurled it into the sink, watching as it skittered around the steel surface, sliding and melting until it lay, nothing more than a lump over the plug hole, and dripped slowly to oblivion.

"Fuck." He blinked away tears.

His mind was on his family now. On Zoe and Viv, and the situation he had been guiltily ignoring for weeks, and on his mother, a woman who had thrown him away as effectively as he had just despatched the snowman. Alistair was right, he was sure of that, but the Scot didn't understand the ties that kept him in his family's net. Perhaps they had treated him badly, unfairly. But they were still family and Vivienne was still his little sister. Someone he had promised to always look out for.

What had he done to look out for her recently?

"What do you want?" Zoe snapped as soon as she picked up the call.

"Nice," Steven said. "How about 'afternoon, brother, how are you?'"

"I don't have time for this, Steven. I'm a busy woman."

"I thought I'd come visit for a little. I have taken some time off work this week, and it's been a long time since I saw Viv and you."

"If you come, you're helping. I'm not hosting a guest; you're family, so you can help cook and wash up like the rest of us."

"That's fine. By the way, I'm moving in with Al tomorrow. We've managed to get a flat together."

"That's lovely, Steven, I'm sure you'll be very happy." Zoe's tone was curt, the sarcasm evident. "You can come, but I can't talk. Why don't you text me the train times and I'll make sure that Daniel's around to pick you up."

"Thanks."

Alistair was going to kill him.

———

"Seriously!? Our first week together in our new place, the first week you've arranged time off in months, fucking months, and you are going to fuck off to Sheffield? Are you fucking serious?"

Steven held up his hands, trying to calm the situation. "I know, really I do, but I had to do something. I'm worried about Viv; she's not really texted me or spoken to me properly in weeks. It's not like her. I want to just check on her."

"She's living her life, Steve, that's what people do. They move on and they live their lives without constantly clinging on to where they used to be. She probably has a boyfriend or something who is much more interesting than you!"

"Then I should be there to help her with that."

"You want to 'help her' with her new boyfriend? Bugger me, this just gets better."

"You know what I mean—brotherly advice."

Alistair laughed bitterly. "Fuck me, you are going to give relationship advice. I should call her now and tell her not to listen to it. What do you know about relationships, Steve? We're moving in together tomorrow and instead of us having a nice week relaxing in the new place, perhaps getting some furniture together or, God forbid, just lazing about and shagging, you've decided to sod off to visit your sister. She won't appreciate it either, neither of them will, Zoe doesn't want to see you for shit, and Viv will have moved on. It's a pity visit; they're going to be pitying you, not actually wanting your company."

"You don't know that."

"Of course I do, it's never been different."

"It's different with Viv."

Alistair slumped into the chair, a soft armchair Steven didn't recognise. He paused as he looked at it for the first time.

"Where's that from?" He pointed at the new furniture.

"While you've been clinging desperately to your hateful sister, I went shopping." Alistair stood proudly. "What do you think?"

"I think it looks nice, actually. Can we afford it?"

"We can't afford anything, I'm sure. It didn't cost much, it's not brand new. I found it online."

"Second hand? Did you clean it?"

"Oh yeah, because while I was out lugging this armchair about, I also took the time to buy a furniture cleaner and gave it a quick once-over. What do you think?"

"I think it's probably pretty disgusting under there."

"Then you don't have to sit in it." Alistair crossed his legs and leaned back, smiling in a half-sneer.

"I won't."

Alistair reached over and pulled, knocking Steven off balance enough that they landed back on the chair. "I don't want to argue with you," Alistair whispered into his ear, "I'm upset with you, and I'm not happy about this trip, but I know there's no point in trying to get you to see differently. They have a hold over you that's been in place since the day you were born, and I'm a fool to fight it so often. Go. Take a few days and visit and check up on your little sis and then come home."

"Home," Steven echoed, looking up at the ceiling with its ornate light fitting. "We have a home together."

"We do, and if you ever care to stay long enough, we can enjoy that fact."

Steven pushed himself up and gently disentangled himself from the embrace. "I'm sorry. It was unthinking, impulsive, but I do need to go."

"I know."

"Four days, that's all. I'll be back on Friday."

"Aye. Well, you're not going until tomorrow, are you? So let's get unboxing. I hate a half-moved-in flat."

————

Daniel was listening to Metallica, a jarring contrast to the soft tones of Sammi Cheng that had accompanied Steven on the train journey. Self-consciously, Daniel turned the volume down on the car stereo until the music was barely audible and sorted his seat belt.

"How've you been?" he asked.

Steven looked at him, appraising this man who had chosen to be with his older sister, and smiled politely. "Up and down," he said, "but good at the moment. Al and I have moved in together."

"Yeah, Zoe mentioned. Nice. I hope it works out for you."

Steven mumbled his thanks and the two of them fell into an awkward silence as the car trundled through the streets. He'd come to Sheffield many times now, but had never really taken the time to explore the city. *Something I'll change on this trip*, he promised himself, deciding that he'd suggest to Viv that she show him around.

Eventually, Daniel turned the music up a bit and Steven let the heavy drumming and energetic guitar riffs wash over him until they pulled up outside the house.

Viv was there to greet him, running from the front door with a gleeful smile. She'd responded somewhat perfunctorily to his text message and Steven had feared that she didn't really want him to come, but her welcome dismissed that worry immediately.

"Hey Bro! How long're you staying?"

"Just a few days." Steven grinned. "Long enough to spend some time, not so long as to outstay Zoe's patience."

Viv's laugh sounded strained. For a moment, Steven wondered if it was forced for his benefit. He looked down at her, but there was nothing in her expression but the welcoming smile that had been there since she saw him.

"Come on," said Viv. "I've sorted your room for you."

She led him into the house and into the spare room. With the door shut, she suddenly engulfed him in a tight hug. "I've missed you so much."

"You too."

Prying his small case from his hands, Viv pushed it under the bed before sitting down. "What's new with you?"

"Well, you know, I've moved in with Al."

"What?!"

"Yes, the other day. I texted you."

"Oh, yeah, sorry." Viv shifted uncomfortably.

"Viv?" Something was wrong. "What is it?"

"Zoe confiscated my phone. It's been a while. I'm sorry if I didn't text back."

"But you did." Steven thought of the short message and pulled out his own phone. "Look." Unlocking it, he passed it over.

Viv stared at it. "Not me."

"Zoe's texting me back pretending to be you?" Steven was incredulous.

"I don't know, but it wasn't me."

"Where is she?" Angry, Steven stood from the bed. "She should have been here to welcome me, anyway."

"Working. Don't worry about it, please, Stevie, don't make a big deal about the texts. She probably thought it was funny. I'll ask her for my phone back and it'll be fine."

At her touch, Steven calmed. He sat back on the bed and put his phone on the side. "Let's leave it, then. What do you want to do while I'm here? Shopping? I'm not rich but I've got a little saved we can use for lunch and maybe a gift. I realised as I drove in that I've never really been into Sheffield properly, you can show me around."

"I've got a bit to do."

"It's the holidays, Viv."

"Yeah, I mean, well, you know, homework and my chores around the house."

"Oh come on, there's time. I'll talk to Zoe about your chores or help you with them."

Viv visibly brightened. "Yeah, OK."

"And as for right now, we could play a game. I've been missing out ever since you left. We could have a race or something."

"I've not played in ages," Viv jumped up. "OK, yeah. Let me set it up."

Steven unpacked and quietly put his clothes in the wardrobe. He might only be here for a few days, but he hated living out of a suitcase and would always take the time to hang up his clothes. He did this even when just overnighting in a hotel, finding it grounded him and allowed him to relax and enjoy the time he was there.

His suitcase empty, he joined Viv and Daniel in the living room.

"You play?" Steven asked Daniel as the tones from Viv's games console filled the room.

"Not well."

"Join us. When's Zoe likely to be home? We can all be good boys and girls and have it packed up before she gets back."

Daniel shifted his position to make room for the three of them to sit together. "She's not that bad." His tone was light and betrayed his slight agreement. "OK. Pass me a controller."

It was evident within the first few minutes that Daniel had lied when he'd mentioned a lack of skill and experience. The first three races, he came in first while both Viv and Steven sat just outside the top three. Viv thumped him friendlily on the arm.

"You're a liar, you've done this lots before."

"Consider it a wasted childhood." Daniel wiggled his controller comically. "Come on, Viv, load up the next race."

They were still playing when the front door opened. Zoe stood behind them, her expression tight.

"What's going on?" Her lips were tight.

"Daniel's beating us both easily." Steven waved at her.

Ignoring him, Zoe picked up the remote and switched off the TV.

"I don't know where you think you are, Steven, and maybe you and Al have a different lifestyle, but in this house, we do chores and make sure everything is in order before wasting our time playing games. Vivienne, have you done the kitchen?"

Wordlessly, Viv jumped up and left the room.

"I thought not," Zoe said. "My God, Steven, you've been here for how long? Three hours? And already the place is a state."

Steven looked around at the immaculately tidy room and raised his eyebrows. "Nice to see you too, Sis. What's going on?"

"I'm tired. I've been working for over thirteen hours straight, and I come home thinking there might be dinner"—a sharp look at Daniel—"and instead find you playing kids' games. Are you ever going to grow up?"

"I'll put on some food for you, love." Rebuked, Daniel joined Viv in the kitchen.

"Unbelievable." Zoe took off her coat, walked back to the hall and hung it and her bag on a peg. "I don't know why I even said you could stay. We're far too busy at the moment."

"I'm sorry, Zoe. Honestly, we were just relaxing while we waited for you to come home. Daniel was just being a good host."

"Whatever. How was your journey?"

"Good."

"And did Viv at least sort out the room for you?"

"She did, it's lovely. I've unpacked."

"Good. Do you want a glass of wine?" Without waiting for an answer, she called out to the kitchen, asking that Daniel bring out some wine for them both. He arrived a moment later, put two glasses of Rioja on the table and dashed back to continue cooking.

"You seem really tense," Steven offered.

"I am." Zoe sipped at her wine. "You don't know what it's like, really being a doctor, having to work in the real world. You're still just a student, spending your life lazing about and turning up to the odd lecture."

"I'm a bit busier than that, Zoe. I'm not a child."

"Whatever."

"I have three jobs on top of the studying, and I've just moved house."

"Yes, you said. Congratulations or whatever."

"You should come and meet him."

"Honestly, Steven, I don't really care to. I'm sorry if that sounds nasty, but you have your life and I have mine and though we cross over at moments like this, I'm far too busy doing what I do to be able to just skip up to Scotland to meet your boyfriend. I'm sure he's really nice, and that moving in with him is a great step for you both, but personally I don't really care. It's not like it affects me."

"Wow." Steven stared at her. For a moment he considered calling her a bitch and having that argument, but he was her guest. He'd just arrived and she'd admitted she was tired and hungry. Better to leave it for another time.

"I'm not the best company, sorry." She took another gulp of wine and stood. "I'm going to have a shower before dinner. Sit, relax. I'll be back in fifteen minutes."

Once she was out of sight, Steven joined the others in the kitchen. Daniel was a good cook and was making something delicious-smelling that involved noodles and a solid amount of garlic. Viv was drying dishes and putting them away.

"Can I help?" Steven asked.

"Not really," Viv pushed a mug into the cupboard. "You don't even know where anything goes. It'll just be easier for me to do it."

"I'm the same," added Daniel, "thanks for asking though."

Steven sat at the smaller kitchen table, tucking his legs in to make sure he didn't get in anyone's way.

"She's just got a lot on at the moment," apologised Daniel, "it's been a tough few weeks. She doesn't mean to be such a cow."

"I know," Steven said.

"She'll be much more pleasant when she's clean, fed and got a glass of wine on the sofa." Daniel grinned. "The last bit is probably the most important."

Steven returned the grin, though he neither felt relaxed or relieved. Zoe was treating everyone badly, and what did that mean for Viv?

It was obvious that all was not right for his little sister. Phone confiscated, a heavy amount of chores, little to no time to relax. Steven watched her as she expertly flittered around the kitchen. There was a definite pattern to it, showing that she'd practiced and found a system that suited herself. This was far from the first time his little sister had done this particular chore. Steven kept his lips tight. He didn't like it. Viv had helped him around the flat, of course, picking up after herself and keeping things tidy. And yes, she'd cleaned up after dinner plenty of times, but there was a difference between the relaxed way he felt they had been together and whatever this was. Was he being over-sensitive, though? Viv was a technically a teenager now, and living with her sister—wasn't cleaning and keeping the house in a good state while Zoe was busy at work just something that she should do?

"Dinner," announced Daniel.

Steven looked up and saw that four plates had been dished up, each with a pile of delicious-looking stir-fry on it.

"Are you coming?" asked Viv. She grinned, hung the tea-towel on a peg and followed Daniel into the other room.

The meal tasted as good as it looked and smelled. Plus, as had been predicted, Zoe's mood lightened considerably once her hunger was sated. The time was actually quite pleasant and by the time Steven collapsed into bed, he was far more positive about the situation as a whole. He sent a quick text to Alistair, too tired to chat properly, apologising for the silence. Al's reply was short but not unfriendly and Steven slept soundly.

———

Steven passed his little sister his debit card and Viv's eyes lit up with glee. It was the least he could do, bringing a little brightness to her current life. They had been shopping for a couple of hours, Viv as eager to explore the shops and sights of the city centre as he had been. Despite her having lived in Sheffield for many months, she'd not really had the opportunity to adventure through the streets.

He paid for the few clothes, winced a little at how much the shopping excursion was costing him, and justified it to himself upon seeing her joyful face.

"Are you sure you can afford these?" Viv asked.

Steven laughed. "Those you can have thanks to my good looks." He flicked his hair with a flamboyant gesture. "I've been doing some modelling jobs and they pay quite reasonably."

Better than both tutoring and waiting, at least.

"You're a model?" Viv looked shocked.

"Actually, yes. To be fair, I think it's because there are fewer Asian men living in Aberdeen than the demand from local companies. I kind of get jobs just because I'm Chinese."

"Are you in any magazines?"

"No, not yet."

"Billboards? TV?"

"No, just small-time stuff. Catalogues, that sort of thing."

Viv smiled. "So can we afford lunch, too?"

"We can afford lunch."

They ate on a bench in a hilly park and looked out over the city. "It's quite a nice place," Steven commented.

"I'd rather be back in Aberdeen."

He looked at her. "I'm sorry."

"It's not your fault, Stevie, but it's not great here. Zoe is so strict, *so* strict. She expects me to do everything and isn't very nice if I don't jump up to do it."

"I'm going to talk to her."

"And say what? She won't listen. She talks about you sometimes, and it's always disdainful. She never says anything good about you.

She wasn't really happy you were coming, but Daniel calmed her down."

"Yeah, he seems nice."

"He is nice. He's a bit like a dad, you know? To me at least." Her words came out slightly stammered, nervous.

"It's fine, I get it. I'm glad he's there for you."

"He's not around all the time though."

Steven nodded, unsure of what to say. "What about school?"

"School is fine."

"You're not doing as well as you were." It was a statement, not a question.

"I have no one to help. In Aberdeen, I had you, and Alistair."

"Does Zoe not help you?"

Viv laughed, spluttering over her drink. "Umm, no."

"I'll talk to her about that, too."

"Oh, Stevie, just leave it. Can't we have our nice day out without talking about her?"

"That bad?"

"That bad."

Steven winced. "And Mum?"

"I don't talk to her that often anymore. There's no point, really. Once a week. She doesn't mention you, and nor do I. Sorry, that sounds bad."

"It's not bad. Go on."

"She's talking about reapplying for her visa to come over soon. At first I was trying to talk her out of it, but I think I'd like her around now. I don't know what Zoe will do if Mum does come here. She pretends to get on with her, on Skype and stuff, but you can tell she doesn't really."

"Mum is hard to get on with."

"So is Zoe!"

They laughed together, before Viv jumped to her feet and picked up her bags. "One more shop?"

————————

"Go upstairs and take it off," Zoe snapped. She spun on her brother as soon as the younger girl had left the room. "What on Earth?"

"It's fashionable," Steven sounded unsure because he was. It had been another terrible mistake; Viv running in excitedly with her bags, keen to show off her new clothes, Zoe making comments about the cost of indulgent shopping trips, and then their younger sister changing into an outfit that, even Steven could see, was a good five years too old for her.

"I'm not letting her out like that. You can take them back," Zoe snapped. "What were you thinking, allowing a young teenager to pick whatever she wants? Of course she's going to come back looking like a slut!"

"Zoe!"

"Oh, fuck off, Steven. That's what she looks like and that's what I'm calling her. What, don't you have such scary words in Scotland? Or perhaps you're just not used to them coming out of a woman."

Steven said nothing.

"I want you to go. Go back to Alistair. I'm sure he's missing you by now."

"It's been one day."

"Yes, and it was a mistake. Look, you got your time with Viv, didn't you? You checked in and made sure you looked like you cared. We get it. But she has things to do that are more important than playing computer games and going shopping with her brother."

"Does she? I thought it was the holidays."

"It is, which gives her a chance to catch up."

"Catch up?"

"Yes, Steven, when you fall behind, you have to catch up afterwards."

"Viv? Fallen behind."

"She's not the brightest spark in the box, so yes, she's a little behind."

"But that's exactly what she is. One of the brightest. How is she falling behind?"

"I don't have time to tutor her, and I don't have the money to pay for one privately. It's alright for you, single and without any sort of responsibility, flashing around your cash."

"What? You cut me off. You have no idea how hard I work for this. And I couldn't afford it, either, I was just being nice, not flash."

"I didn't cut you off. Mum did."

"Oh, and you tried *so hard* to stop her."

"What's between you and Mum has nothing to do with me."

"God, you really are such a bitch, Zoe."

"Get out."

"What?" Steven stared.

"Get the fuck out of my house. I don't know why I said you could come. Guilt, probably. That inbuilt guilt Mum and Dad instilled in me so well. But I don't need you around and neither does Viv. We do fine without you."

"No, I'm sorry. I didn't mean to call you that."

"Just like you didn't mean to buy your sister inappropriate clothing? Just like you didn't mean to upset Mum? Just like you didn't screw up her visa so she couldn't come back, and I ended up with Vivienne?"

"What? None of that was on purpose!"

"I don't know if that's worse—you being such an idiot that you just do all this crap by accident."

"I didn't mean that either. Stop twisting what I say."

"What are you saying, little brother?" Zoe stood still, her hands folded on her chest. Her anger filled the air.

"Nothing. Forget it. I'll go home; Al would like that, too. But there's no decent train until tomorrow."

"Whatever. Look Steven, you're my little brother, and somewhere in here I care and I always will, but right now I just can't connect with how your life is and the things you are doing. I think it's great you've moved in with Alistair, and I'm pleased you've sorted your money out, but this stuff with Viv we just disagree on. You're too soft, willing to allow her whatever she wants, and it's not good for a teenage girl. I think you should back off a bit where she's concerned."

"There are a few things I want to say about Viv."

"I'm sure there are. I don't want to hear them. I'm sure you disapprove, that she's painted me to be like some sort of wicked queen, but I don't think your opinion is worth shit. Yes, I get her to help around the house—she lives here and shouldn't be getting a free ride, but other than that, she gets to do what she wants."

"It looks a bit more ... oppressive than that."

"Oh, I'm sure it does. She's a good victim, and you have a hero complex where she's concerned. No, Steven, it's not more 'oppressive' than that. It's just a normal household with a teenage girl who wants to complain about doing the washing up. I'm sure I was just as bad, in fact, I know I was, but Mum made me do it, and now it's her turn."

Slowly, Steven nodded.

"Now, if you don't mind, I'm going to have a bath. You and Viv can have the living room all to yourself for the evening. Daniel's not around."

"Do you still want me gone tomorrow?"

"Do what you like, Steven, you will anyway."

Sighing, Steven slumped onto the sofa.

––––––––

Pulling out his headphones with an angry grimace, Steven leaned back in his seat and counted to ten, watching the scenery whizz past the grimy train window. It was rare that he was this frustrated, but everything seemed to be conspiring against him. Alistair had been smug with his 'I told you so's, to the extent that Steven had deleted their messages and temporarily blocked him. Viv had been despondent about his leaving, though she understood, but Zoe ... He had lost any sort of connection with his older sister, and had been desperate to leave her house. She'd gone to work that morning without any sort of goodbye and Steven had felt like a trespasser, creeping out of the house without leaving any trace he'd been there.

He picked up his phone, considered a number of nasty messages, and put it back on the seat beside him. There was no point; she'd made that clear.

What had he done to make his family dislike him so much? With his mum, the cause was plain, but Zoe? She'd flip-flopped between supportive of his sexuality and life, from indifferent through to hostile. Steven sighed; even trying to work out her motivations wasn't going to get him anywhere; there was so much about her life he didn't know. Her work, her life with Daniel, her struggles. Was this simply a situation where he needed to be more considerate and thoughtful?

He texted Alistair.

Sorry I had a hissy fit. Calm again now. Are you going to meet me at the station?

The wait wasn't too long.

Sure. You're a prick, though, remember that. Take away for dinner? I haven't properly set-up the kitchen yet.

Steven smiled.

Sounds perfect.

CHAPTER 14

Soaked, the sheets wrapped around Steven as he slept. He woke, throat dry and retching for breath and stared into the darkness. To his left, Alistair snored gently, somehow managing to sleep despite the disturbance.

Zoe.

Steven drank deeply from the room-temperature water on the bedside table. It helped calm his throat and his breathing, but not his mind.

Zoe.

———

"Steven!" At sixteen, Zoe had been quick to anger and filled with the belief that she was to be obeyed.

"Yes?"

"I'm talking to you." Zoe swiped at him, the palm of her hand connecting with the back of his head. He winced but was too used to it to cry out.

"Sorry."

"You were boring all day. I wanted to have fun with grandmother but you kept making it dull."

"Sorry."

"No, you're not."

No, he wasn't.

"You're going to have to make it up to me."

Steven groaned. Their mum had insisted he listen to Zoe in their tutoring sessions, treating her as an adult despite her being two years short. One of the powers that she had been granted was to set him extra work to do. His time was short enough without her adding hours of extra study, but she saw it as a perfect punishment whenever he did anything she didn't like.

"How about I let you off all the homework for this week?" The idea seemed to come to her from nowhere.

Steven looked at her suspiciously.

"Yeah, I know, not what you expected to hear." She sat on the long, backless bench that took up the majority of one wall. "But you need to do what you're told."

"What?"

"You have to promise. Say 'I promise I'll do whatever you tell me, Zoe,' and I'll let you off the homework for a week. If Mum asks, I'll tell her you're doing well with it.

"What are you going to tell me to do?"

"If I tell you that, it won't be fun."

Steven looked at his sister. Perhaps it would be fun, whatever silly idea she had to replace homework. No studying for a week would be amazing.

"OK."

"Say it."

"I promise."

"What do you promise?"

"I promise I'll do whatever you tell me, Zoe."

"Good. Stand still!" She jumped up and ran to the corner where the small cupboard of supplies lived. Here, she scrabbled around for a moment. "Hands please."

Steven held his hands forward and she wrapped some rope around them. It was rough, and old, having been from their garden swing. The swing had broken four years previously when, as a six-year-old boy who lost his favourite pastime, he'd cried every day and night for almost a week.

Now, the same rope that once held him up, bound his hands tightly.

"What are you doing?" he asked.

"Shush! Did I say you could speak?" Zoe asked. "No, I didn't, so don't."

Slowly, Steven nodded. He didn't particularly like what was happening, but she'd promised him a week off any sort of schoolwork.

She unbuttoned his trousers and stood back with a grin.

"Wiggle," she said.

"What?"

"Wiggle so that your trousers fall down."

"Zoe?"

"Do it!" She sounded angry.

Steven paused. "Mum!"

Like a snake, Zoe snapped forward, her hand slapping against his cheek. "What do you think you are doing? Anyway, she's not here. It's just us."

Steven whimpered. His sister had always had a tendency to be harsh and often went far with her cruelty.

"Come on," she snapped, "you promised you would do whatever I told you to do, and I've told you to wiggle your trousers off, so wiggle."

Steven shifted a bit, his wrists becoming scratched from the rough rope. "This is too tight."

She looked at him, lips tight but with no words. It was more frightening than anything she'd said. Steven closed his eyes and shook his trousers down.

"Good boy. Now ..." Zoe paused to think. "Kick them off."

It took three attempts, the hem of the leg catching on his toes, but Steven managed to do as ordered.

"Let's see it, then." Zoe giggled. She pulled at his underwear, roughly removed it and threw it to the floor. "Hello, little penis."

Steven bit his lip. Then shrieked as she grabbed at him unexpectedly. Her fingers were cold, and her nails too long to be comfortable.

"Zoe!" he said, his voice filled with a mixture of nervousness, disgust, and embarrassment.

"Oh, come on little brother, it's not like I've never seen it before. When you were little, I helped you bathe."

"Let me go."

"No! You promised."

"I'll do the homework," Steven begged.

"Oh, forget the homework, this is much more fun." She had him in her fist and began to rub. It wasn't gentle, and Steven winced on each careless tug, but his body reacted despite his will.

"Oooh, look," she said, "it works."

"Zoe," Steven pleaded.

"Fine." She dropped his erection and stamped over the other side of the room. "Why are you so boring? This, today with grandmother, and always, in fact."

"I'm ..." Steven stammered, unsure of what to say.

"Boring," Zoe finished for him.

Steven could feel tears coming. He didn't know how Zoe would react and tried to bite them back. "Can you untie me?"

She looked at him. "It looks like the horn of a unicorn. All pointing up like that."

Steven wished he could hide himself behind his hands, or move, anything to stop her staring.

"I'm going to lick it." There was a giggle behind her words, a sudden impulsive decision.

"No!" Steven cried, shifting his hips to pull away from her, but she held him firm and laughed again.

"Come on little unicorn, it'll be fun. Let's see what happens."

Steven whimpered as she put him in her mouth, his mind racing as conflicting thoughts and emotions raged within him. Physically, the feeling was intense, heating his skin and making him shift and squirm, but mentally he struggled, the sense of wrongness overwhelming him with embarrassment and shame. Suddenly, he tensed, and it was all over.

Zoe spat across the room. "Oh my god!" she shrieked, "I can't believe you did that!" She looked up at him and began to laugh again. "I didn't actually expect that, I thought you were still a bit young. Oh, little Steven, was it good for you?"

Steven began to sob.

"Come on, stop acting like it's such a big deal. It was funny. You had a nice time, don't pretend you didn't."

Steven said nothing. Still laughing, his sister pulled on the knots that held his hands, loosening them until he could move again. "Oh, little unicorn, we should do that again, sometime." She sat down on the wooden-back chair. "I tell you what, that can be our code word: 'unicorn'. You try to tell Mum anything we did here, and I'll make it so bad for you. I'll tell her you came up with it, and that you forced me. I'll tell her what a liar you are. I'll tell her you did it to get out of studying. I'll make up whatever I can, do you understand?"

Steven nodded.

"Good. Now you need to clean up, there's a mess."

———

Steven placed his palms on the cool surface of the sink and breathed. The memories were bright in his mind, and more were rising to the surface. He sobbed. He'd known they were there all along, of course, this wasn't some sort of repressed memory problem, but he'd chosen to forget. Forgive and forget, wasn't that it?

"You alright?" Alistair stood behind him. There was a click and a whirr, and the light shone brightly, accompanied by the sound of the extractor fan.

"I ..." Steven started.

"Wow, are you sick? You're glistening."

"Bad dream."

"What about?" Alistair asked, genuinely caring.

"My sister."

"Ah, I can imagine. Did she have horns and cloven hooves in it?"

Steven smiled despite himself. "Pretty much."

"Want to talk about it? Put the bath on, you can tell me while you soak because there's no way either of us is getting back into that bed now you've drenched it, and it's hard to chat if you are in the shower."

"You want me to have a bath at four a.m.?"

"If you want to talk. If not, just have a shower and I'll go strip the bed."

"I do want to talk."

"Put the plug in then. I'll get us some drinks."

His boyfriend's unprejudiced kindness moved him. Steven played with the water as it splashed into the bath and slid into the warmth just as Alistair returned.

"Go on, then." Alistair put two cups of creamy coffee on the edge of the bath.

"It was a memory, from my childhood. We'd been out all day with our grandmother and as was usual, Zoe had the task of helping me with my homework when we got back ..."

Zoe moaned as Steven followed her instructions, his fingers probing gently between her legs. He wanted to hurt her, to find something soft and pinch it out of spite, but he knew that whatever pleasure he got from such revenge, the aftermath would be terrible.

Instead, he did as she demanded, bringing her to climax as he had done now every few days for months.

Their 'study sessions' had become far less about his schooling and far more about 'unicorn'.

Zoe stiffened, shuddering happily. Steven pulled back, immediately and wordlessly walking to the door. She would always give him five minutes in the bathroom to clean himself, but then he'd have to be back in the room, ready for whatever she deigned to do next. Depending on her mood, that could mean a solid hour or two of mathematics, or another quick aside for her pleasure. Steven always prayed for hard studying.

Thankfully, today was one of those days. When he returned, she already had the textbook open.

———————

"You have to be fucking kidding me?" Alistair was incredulous.

"It went on for months," Steven's voice was stronger now than it had been when he'd started his story. Alistair's loving acceptance had gone a long way to helping him share.

"And you never told me this at all? Not once in all the years, not when she was fucking you over with the money, and not when she took Viv off you. You said nothing?"

"Honestly, it's strange. It happened, I know it happened, but I'd pushed it away. Not forgotten it, but, I don't know, written it off as something that happened when I was a kid. Something unimportant, meaningless, really. I think it came to the surface now because of being there with her, that attitude that she has, and because of Viv."

"Your sister is an abuser," Alistair said plainly.

"I'd never thought of it like that. Not those words."

"Yeah, that's how abusers get away with stuff."

Steven bowed his head. "I'm sorry."

"You're sorry?" Alistair put his coffee on the sink and stood up, striding across the tiled floor. "*You* have nothing to be sorry for. Your fucking bitch of a sister, though. My God, Steven, you said *nothing*."

"I'm sorry." Steven stopped and closed his eyes. Stop apologising. He took a breath. "About saying nothing I mean."

"What the fuck was your childhood about? It's unbelievable. No, that's not right, I'm not saying I don't believe you. I mean, it's horrific. I thought some of the stuff you've told me was bad but this is off the chart! Your own sister. She's a fucking weird freak. What stopped it?"

"She pushed it too far." Steven paused. "It was going to get ... she wanted ..."

"She wanted to fuck you?"

Steven nodded. "Yeah. She pushed for that one day and I said no. I said she could tell Mum everything, but I wasn't doing that. I thought she was going to kill me. She went so silent and so hard-faced, so I ran. I ran crying out of the house and she chased me. A couple of times, she caught up with me and hit me so hard. I kept scrambling away, but she was faster and stronger. Eventually she caught me and dragged me home.

"Our neighbour had heard, told Mum that I'd run out of the house screaming and that she'd seen Zoe chasing me. Mum spoke to us both the next day, asking us what it was about. I lied. Zoe muttered something about playing unicorns, and I knew she was going to make it so bad for me, so I lied to Mum, told her that it had been a game and that I'd got upset when Zoe didn't let me play the way I wanted. Said I'd run off and she'd had to chase me to get me to calm down and come back.

"We both got punished that night, but I couldn't bear to actually tell her what happened. Not just because of Zoe's threats, but because I was embarrassed, ashamed. I was as much part of it as Zoe, and I didn't want Mum to know. To this day, I don't think she does."

"You were not as much a part of it as Zoe!"

"But the things I had done with her ... I ..."

"No." Alistair was firm.

"I know that." Steven looked down into the cooling water. "Honestly, I know that for real, as an adult, and educated, but I was just a kid. I felt it was as much me as her."

"And that stopped it?"

"Not immediately. She tried a few times, pushed at me and threatened, but I refused. So, she made my life a living hell. She gave me homework that was impossible to complete—far beyond anything a ten-year old could do. I tried to fight back, I suppose, but every time I threatened to tell Mum, she'd whisper 'unicorn' to me. It was like we each had a nuclear button we were hovering over but both unwilling to push.

"Zoe messed up, really. Part of her vendetta against me included constantly telling Mum that I wasn't doing well with my work, that I didn't listen to her when she was tutoring me. At first this had the effect she wanted, with Mum berating me and making me do more and try harder, but eventually Mum conceded and paid for a private tutor. Just like that, Zoe's influence in that way was finished."

"She's a fucking psychopath."

"That's one way to look at it." Steven forced a laugh.

"And you've never told anyone?"

"No, like I said, I sort of forgot about it. I let it go."

"Did you ever talk about it with her?"

Steven shook his head slowly. "Not a chance."

"And you just treat her like normal? If someone had done that to me, I wouldn't go and visit them, or have anything to do with them at all."

"It's not like that. It's not as black and white as to say, 'she was bad to me as a child, so I don't speak to her,'—she's my sister and we share something. It wasn't all bad times."

"You're still defending her!"

"No, no I'm not, it's just. Maybe it's a cultural thing, but family ... loyalty is everything."

"Oh, she showed that alright. She was so keen to be loyal to her family she didn't even look outside of it for her 'needs.'" Alistair's voice was filled with disdain.

Alistair settled back, sitting on the toilet seat. "Every time I think I know you something more comes up." He sighed. "I can take it, honestly, I know who you are now. That's the person I love but still ... it's hard, hard to even imagine what you've gone through."

"Like I said, it's not that bad."

"The stuff you've told me your father did? Having your sister sexually assault you? Your family cutting you off because you are open and honest about your sexuality? Sounds pretty bad to me."

Steven pondered for a moment. "It's not that bad," he said again, quietly.

Alistair leaned forward, shaking his head. "You're mental. What the fuck have I got into?"

He slipped, a bare foot on a wet patch of the floor, and crashed forward. Seizing the opportunity, Steven wrapped his arms around him and pulled him, dressing gown and all, into the water.

Ignoring the splashes and the other's protestations, Steven locked his lips onto his boyfriend's, holding him tight and close. "Thank you," he whispered.

"Ahh, fuck ya." With just a hint of resistance, he mock-struggled for a moment before giving in. The bath wasn't really big enough for the both of them, but it would do.

CHAPTER 15

"No Al tonight?" Claire leaned on the bar and poked her head round to look Steven in the eyes. "You know, you are allowed to have fun without him."

Steven smiled at her. "I *am* having fun."

"Course you are," she said. Gently, Claire tugged on his arm, pulling him away from the safety of the polished black wood and out into the wider room. "Dance."

"I'd only show you up. Seriously, though, Claire, I'm fine."

"You're fine when you dance."

The floor was heaving with people, almost all of whom Steven knew. It was just over a week to Christmas, and it seemed every single student in the university had gathered to celebrate the end of the term and the coming holiday. It was nice of Claire to notice his solitude, and she was right—Al's strange absence was bothering him. They'd agreed to meet here at eight, and it was closer to nine. No response to texts, either, but that was hardly too unusual.

"Claire? Steven?" A voice called at them from across the crowded dance floor. Steven looked over to see an enthusiastically waving hand but little else. Then, a face popped out.

"Charles! Darling," Claire drawled. Still holding tight to Steven's hand, she pulled him over to the other man.

Charles looked good, Steven noticed with heated cheeks. Very good.

"What are you doing here?" Claire continued.

"Passing through, heard about your little party, did some blagging." Charles grinned. "OK, the last bit is a bit of a lie. Sam sent me an invite and so I came. Have you seen him?"

Claire shook her head. "Not for a while. He's about, though."

Charles smiled. "But in the meantime, I'm happy to catch up with the two of you. How have you been, Steven?"

Charles had been in his class back in St. Andrews and Steven had often admired him from afar. It was only a few years earlier, but it seemed like a lifetime. Back then, he wouldn't have dreamed of coming out as gay, and certainly would never have had the confidence to approach someone and—

"Steven?" Charles asked. "You with us?"

"Sorry, just a shock to see you," Steven winced as his words threatened to betray his long-forgotten crush. "How are you?"

"Ah, I'm good. Wishing I was qualified and able to get on with it."

"Yeah," said Claire, "I know that feeling."

"Me, too." Steven felt oddly uncomfortable. He looked back to the bar, checking if Alistair had arrived and was looking for him. Nothing.

"Come and fill me in," Charles insisted. "Unless I've broken in on your dance. Not a special moment, is it?"

"Hah, no," Claire said, "Steven was looking for a way out, I think you saved him. Right, Steve?"

"Yeah," Steven wasn't really listening. Where was Alistair? He felt himself being pulled once more, and then pushed gently onto a wide leather couch, the upholstery cracked and worn in many places.

"Come on then, what've you been up to?" Charles asked.

"Not much. Study and work, work and study."

"Don't be so ridiculous," Claire admonished. "Steven moved in with his boyfriend this year—Alistair, a big burly Scotsman. They are cute together."

"Boyfriend?" Charles eyebrow was raised. "I didn't know."

"Neither did his family," Claire was obviously enjoying her role as narrator. "They fell out hugely. His mum disowned him."

"Wow. Just because you came out as gay?"

"Yeah," Steven focussed on the conversation, aware that he was being rude. Alistair would come, or he wouldn't. He wasn't the other man's keeper.

"That must have been harsh."

"It was horrible. My father had died, my mum cut me off, and my little sister, who was living with me, got shipped off to be with my older sister in Sheffield. I don't see them much."

"People can be so reactive." Charles reached out and touched the back of Steven's fingers supportively. "Especially parents. Give it time and she'll come round—your mum I mean. Mine did."

His mum? Charles was gay? Steven stared.

"You didn't know?" Charles laughed. "Sorry, I thought my sexuality was common knowledge." He winked. "Maybe our friendship would have gone another way."

Steven grew hot once more. He hoped the lighting in the club hid the blushing.

"Ah well," continued Charles, "lost opportunities and all that."

"What about you?" Claire asked, coming swiftly to prevent any potential tension, "what have you been up to?"

"Study and work, work and study," Charles parroted Steven's earlier line. "Seriously though, it's all pretty boring, though I'm hoping that some of my patient and involved networking means that I'm lining up for a good position once all this is done. Honestly, I've just about had it all with the exams and revision. I want to be out there, doing good and saving lives."

"I just want to be paid," Claire said with a grin. "I'm bored of being poor."

"Tell me about it," said Charles, "at least you don't have to hang out with Jessica all the time. Sometimes, her generosity pushes me over the edge. Just once I'd like to buy my own Starbucks, you know what I mean?"

"Jess," Steven said. "It's been too long. I should invite her to come over. I've been so bad at keeping up with old friends."

"Well, invite her, and invite me, too. Did Claire say you were living with your boyfriend now? Do you two have a house or anything? You'll have to be quick though, she's moving back south to England for her last couple of years. Starts there in February. UCL, of all places."

Steven answered and settled into the conversation, relaxing and enjoying the nostalgic reminiscing over old friends, and places he'd once known. At some point, Claire replaced their drinks, and a little later she went off to dance.

"You won't believe it!" Alistair clapped his strong hand on Steven's shoulder. He smiled broadly at Charles and stuck out his hand. "Hi. Alistair. I'm Steven's boyfriend." There wasn't even a hint of jealousy or ownership in the tone, but it was firm and unapologetic.

Charles stood slightly and shook the proffered hand before sliding back into his seat. "Won't you join us?"

"I will, but first I need to steal Steven here for a moment." He tugged on Steven's shoulder. "We'll be back."

Shrugging to Charles by way of an apology, Steven allowed himself to be pulled once more across the dance floor, this time to one of the shadowy corners of the room.

"I know I'm stupidly late and I probably deserve to find you flirting or whatever that was, but look at this." He took a wedge of notes from his wallet and shook them.

Steven stared.

"Eight grand!" Alistair's face was a broad grin.

"What?"

"I worked out the system that the machines use in Betfred, and I took this. Combined winnings from three of them."

"You did what? Betfred?" Steven's mind swam, trying to make sense of the words. Betfred was a gambling shop, one of the ones on the high street determined to suck in unwary passers-by.

"Eight grand," Alistair repeated. "And tomorrow I can do it again—I tell you, I know the algorithm."

"Don't be stupid." Steven's voice was harsh.

"Excuse me?" Alistair took a step back.

"No one wins at gambling, you know that. You're not a kid."

"Except I have, because I worked it out."

"Well, that's great. Eight thousand pounds is a load. You don't need to go back."

"Now *you're* being stupid. I told you, I know how the machines work. I can turn this into twenty grand. Fifty! More!"

"No." Steven took his hand, looked into his eyes and was frightened. What was going on? He knew Alistair played the fruit machines occasionally; when they were in pubs, or waiting in a fast food place with one. They'd stopped in a service station once and he'd wasted twenty minutes and a solid chunk of cash on it. But going into an actual gambling shop? This was new.

"No?"

"Al, you know the house always wins. You know that's how the machines work."

"Absolutely."

"So, you won't go back. You'll be pleased with these winnings? They are great, by the way, I'm happy you won, but you know it's not going to happen twice."

"Except it will. I decoded the machines. It took a lot of time, but I'm a clever boy."

"You don't sound like one. You can't decode the machines."

"Why are you treating me like I'm thick, Steven? Is it because you're pissy at me for being late? Or has it got something to do with your new boyfriend over there?"

"Charles? He's just someone I knew from St. Andrews who happened to get an invite to this."

"And he just happened to spend most of his time here talking to you? Don't be stupid. I saw you with him, and I know what you look like when you're flirting!"

"Please, Al, don't be ridiculous. I've just been passing the time, waiting for you."

"Really? Check your phone."

"What?"

"Get it out and check it."

Steven did so. Two missed calls, and eight unanswered text messages—all from Alistair over the last hour.

"If you'd been so eagerly waiting for me then you'd've picked up the phone."

"It's loud in here. I was chatting."

"Sure."

"Oh Al, you're being even more ridiculous now."

"Am I? Ridiculous because I won eight grand or ridiculous because I caught you flirting with some guy?"

"Both, yes."

"Fuck you."

"Come on." Steven tried to diffuse the situation. "Let's get out of here. Go home."

"I want to spend some of my winnings. I wanted to have fun with you."

"And we will, but does it have to be here?"

"What's wrong with here? Are you embarrassed for your university friends to see me?"

"Of course not."

"Then we'll stay here and have a drink or ten. What are you drinking?"

"Whatever."

"Never heard of that, but I'll ask the barman. Is it a cocktail? Because I'm rich enough to afford those."

"You're being a prick, Al."

"Oh, I'm sorry." Alistair's tone was sarcastic. "Maybe because I expected a little bit of a better reaction to making eight fucking grand in an evening."

"I'm sorry. You're right. It is great, and I know it helps you a lot. Why don't we go have fun with a bit of it. A *little* bit of it. And don't you think we should go home first to put it safe? I mean, walking around with all that cash ...?"

"Home, pah. We're not going to get mugged. Who's going to mug me?"

Steven's lips took on a sardonic smile. "Anyone who has the vaguest idea you have it? Come on, taxi home, drop off the cash and then take a bit out to have fun, yeah?"

"OK." Alistair nodded, visibly cheering. "But a lot of a bit."

"A lot of a bit," Steven agreed.

It wasn't until he reached the top of the stairs that he thought to say goodbye to Claire and Charles. He turned, but there was no way to see them.

"You coming?" asked Alistair.

"Yeah, of course." Steven followed him into the cool December air.

———

Christmas Eve came suddenly. As Steven waved to Alistair, the taxi pulled away and his shoulders slumped. Zoe had made a perfunctory invitation for him to spend Christmas with her, Viv and Daniel, but everything about the email left a bitter taste in his mouth. She'd been polite, but there was no real enthusiasm in her words. He'd declined, lied and said that he was spending the holiday with Alistair in their new place but now, with Al gone to visit his family, he was alone.

It was only for a few days. Alistair planned to be back on the twenty-ninth, and they were going to Edinburgh for Hogmanay, Alistair was insisting, and insisting on paying for whatever they got up to.

His eight grand had turned into twelve. There had been dips as mistakes were made, but generally he came back with a smile on his face. Steven was beginning to hide his true feelings about the gambling from his boyfriend—perhaps he was wrong, anyway, and maybe Al really did know what he was doing.

They'd discussed it in bed on that first night, wrapped in each other's sweat and smiles.

"You don't make eight grand out of nowhere," Steven had said. "How long have you been at this?"

"A few months," Alistair giggled uncontrollably and stared at the ceiling. No doubt it was spinning as much for him as it was for Steven. "I knew what you'd say, especially since you told me about your dad."

"Exactly," Steven said quietly.

"Right, so I didn't want to bring it up. It's nothing."

"Eight thousand pounds! Did they just let you walk out of the shop?"

"Sure, what can they do? I cleaned their machines out."

"Promise me it's not going to become an addiction."

"Of course not, I promise. Easy, see."

"Because, you know."

"I know."

"You could have addiction in your blood," Steven said after a pause. He knew he was treading on dangerous territory.

"Excuse me?"

"Your dad ..."

"My dad's fucking alcoholism is his own fucking problem. And me calculating odds and beating the bookies at their own twisted game is nothing to do with it."

"I know, it's just ..."

"Just you don't trust me."

"Shush!" Steven kissed him, and for a while the conversation was forgotten.

Eventually, Alistair broke the embrace. "Then say it."

"Say what?"

"That you trust me, that you don't think I'm a fucking fool, and that you appreciate that I know what I'm doing."

"I do trust you."

"I'm not my fucking father."

"I know."

"I'm not a fucking addict."

"I know."

"I'm just good at this, it's all numbers and probabilities, for fuck's sake. They should be scared to see me coming."

"I know." Steven had kissed him again, and that time the conversation had gone away properly.

Steven looked at the bed and sighed. It was a ruffled tangle and the sheets were overdue a clean. A sudden desire to refresh the house filled him and he tore the duvet cover off. When Alistair came back, it would be to a bright and shining home, not this lived-in student mess.

By the time midnight came over, Steven was putting the finishing polish to their kitchen. The house was beautiful and the tree they had bought together (again, using some of Alistair's ill-gotten gains) was a fine centrepiece. He looked under it, took one of the many gifts that Alistair had left for him and held it in his hands. They'd arranged to call the next day and open them together.

Steven grinned to himself—it was a very cute thing to do, but he couldn't remember who'd thought of it.

For a moment, he considered tearing open the bright silver paper. Just one early present. But no, he put it back under the sparkling lights and left it there. Being alone on Christmas day would be bad enough but doing it having opened all his presents in a childish excited frenzy the night before was worse.

"Night night, Al," he said to the air. Then, with the silence echoing around him, Steven went to bed.

CHAPTER 16

The hard double doors swung closed behind him. Steven walked down the corridor with a sense of authority and confidence—he was here, and he was meant to be here. He glanced down at his white coat and smiled to himself.

He was still more than a year away from claiming this as his permanent job, but university had taken a turn away from constant lecture-based theory into placement-based work and, in addition, he'd managed to get a job as a phlebotomist. Taking bloods wasn't glamorous and he doubted he'd still be enjoying it as much a year on, but it was a solid stepping stone in his career.

He put a handful of coins into the vending machine and waited while it spat out a packet of cheese and onion crisps. The machine next to it was out of order, which meant no drink, but he didn't mind, still basking in the clinical glow of the hospital atmosphere. He sat on the small bench in the corner of the canteen and pulled open the crisps, savouring each one.

His thoughts were on Viv. The last patient had been a girl of fourteen and she'd reminded him of his little sister and how long it had been since they'd properly talked. The cold February weather had already begun to thaw as spring approached—the last time he'd spoken to Viv for any length, they'd chatted about the snow. He'd got some, she hadn't.

He pulled out his phone, knowing she wouldn't respond until the end of school anyway, but better to not forget:

Have you got any spare time this weekend? I thought I'd call for a chat sometime, let me know.

For a second, he considered texting Alistair, but he knew his comments wouldn't be wanted, not yet. Give Al a few more hours to get over his big loss of the previous night. The gambling made Steven nervous; yes, as his boyfriend kept insisting, over the time he had made a lot more than he'd lost, but the fact was he was coming back from the betting shops more upset each time. No amount of sanctimonious preaching had done anything to sway him from his current 'entertainment of choice' as Alistair liked to phrase it. Nothing Steven could say would break that chain of addiction.

Still, financially, both of them were in a reasonable place at the moment. Being a couple meant that when one of them was short the other was quick to help plug the hole, and vice versa. Steven had insisted on a strict rule that Al was not to touch their shared money to use for any of his 'entertainment' and Alistair had been firmly respectful in that regard.

Bills and rent were paid, food was in the fridge and the small amount of free time that overlapped so they could spend time together was good.

The clock ticked loudly. Steven looked up to see he had less than three minutes left. Breaks were not long.

He returned to the small room with a smile, waved genially at Sophie, his immediate superior, and took his seat.

"Little boy next," said Sophie, "let's see how you are with nervous children and their even more nervous parents."

"Like that, is it?"

"More often than not. Why don't you go get him? His name is James."

Steven picked up the clipboard, more for something to hold than because it held any information he needed, and walked to the waiting room. James was playing with a small plastic castle and a toy horse, his mother hovering nearby. They both looked up when he called the name, and Steven led them out.

Hopefully Viv would be able to find time for him this weekend.

———

The soft pillow smelled of Al. Unconsciously, Steven pulled it towards him, bunched it up and put it under his head. Lying back on the bed, he pressed the screen and waited for Viv to answer. It wasn't long.

"Hello brother, long time no chit chat," she said.

Steven smiled; it was good to hear her voice. "I'm sorry. I've been busy."

"You say that every time."

"And every time it's true."

Viv snorted. "Hang on just a second." There was a little background shuffling before she came back. "OK."

"How are you?"

She paused. Not for long, but long enough that Steven propped himself up on his elbow, shifting on the sheets.

"I'm OK."

"School?"

"School is school, Steven. It's not great, it's not awful."

"Sure." He felt stupid, like a distant parent checking up on her progress. They used to be so relaxed with each other. He wondered what had happened.

Months of distance. Over a year, now. He sighed.

"What's up?" Viv asked.

"Sorry, just thinking we never speak. I'm sorry."

"You say that every time, too."

"And every time it's true," Steven echoed his own statement from earlier. It was silent for a while, then; "Is Zoe about?"

"No. She's working today. You can chat to me for a while if you like, only I have things to do while we talk, so excuse the noises."

"What're you doing?"

"Just cleaning up."

"Oh, OK."

Again, the silence, this time punctuated by the sounds of clattering.

"Are you washing up? Sounds like washing up."

"Yup."

"I thought you had a dishwasher."

"Yup."

"So ..."

"So, Zoe doesn't like it when the dishwasher leaves stuff on the plates. She started off asking me to rinse them before hand, making sure I wasn't putting leftover food into the dishwasher. Then she wanted me to wipe them down just once. Now, I just wash everything by hand. It's quicker."

"You do all the washing up by hand even though there's a dishwasher?"

"Yup." Viv's choice of word was cheery, but her tone was not.

"How often?"

"Every day. Twice."

"Seems a bit harsh."

Viv was silent. No doubt she'd nodded. Steven breathed out. It's just the washing up, he told himself. It's normal for teenagers to pitch in cleaning the kitchen.

"Tell me about you." Viv lightened her tone.

"Me? I'm a phlebotomist." He could hear his own pride in his voice.

"A what? Is that something I don't want to know about?"

Steven laughed. "I take blood at the hospital."

"You steal blood?" She giggled.

"Haha. No, I draw blood, you know, with a needle and things. For testing."

"Is it paid?"

"Yes. Not well, but ... it's my first real job as a medical student. It's good experience."

"You seem to have so many jobs. I thought you were a model."

"I'm still doing that, too, when they call me."

"And a waiter."

"In the evenings."

"And a tutor."

"Sure, some afternoons."

"And now a plebotomist."

"Phlebotomist."

"Sounds busy."

"It is."

"No time off, then?"

"Not really." He sensed something. "Viv, are you OK?"

"Yeah ..." There was a quick trio of solid clunks while she moved around the kitchen. "I don't want to talk about me. How's Al?"

"He's good," Steven considered leaving it at that. His adult problems weren't right to share with a teenager. Yet, he had a need to talk and she had asked. "He's being a bit dumb."

"How?"

"He's started gambling. He thinks he knows how the machines work, but honestly, he doesn't. He got very lucky a few times and thinks it's more skill than luck."

Viv became stern. "You should stop him."

"He's an adult, Viv, I can't just stop him. He thinks it's all fine, and to be fair, he has plenty of winnings."

"Zoe wouldn't stand for it. If Daniel was gambling, she'd stop him."

"How?" Steven realised he was genuinely looking for some advice.

"She'd just tell him 'no'. Daniel does what he's told when she gets a certain look on her face. We all do."

"Ah, yes." Steven knew the look.

"And if he kept doing it, she'd punish him."

"Punish Daniel?"

"God yes. She'd slap him so hard he'd bounce."

"Viv!"

"It's true."

Another clatter took over the conversation for a moment. Steven listened as his little sister moved through the kitchen before it became quiet. "All done?"

"Ironing now. Hang on a minute."

Steven lay back and gazed at his own wardrobe. He'd left the door open and could see the collection of clothes hanging there. His were neatly pressed on the left while Alistair's hung slightly wrinkled bedside them. Al did manage to make himself presentable before going out but he was more last-minute while Steven preferred to be prepared.

"Ironing as well?"

"It's one of my jobs."

"How many jobs do you have?"

She ignored him. "What about when he's not gambling? Are you two still having fun?"

"Very much so," Steven said.

"That's good."

They talked more about Alistair, Steven sharing some of the weekends they had together. He left out anything personal but found quickly that he enjoyed talking to his sister about such things. Even though she was still a young teenager, she was older now and both her conversation and understanding had grown massively since they'd last spent time together. Time passed as they chatted, laughing with each other over some of the sillier stories in Steven's arsenal.

"That's me done," Viv said suddenly.

"Done?"

"With the ironing."

Steven glanced at the clock; they'd been talking for close to an hour.

"That's a lot of ironing."

Viv laughed. "Not around here it isn't. Zoe always has to look perfect."

Steven shifted uncomfortably. "Viv, how many chores does Zoe make you do?"

"It's fine. Please, I didn't want to talk about me, and I really don't want to talk about Zoe."

Steven pushed. "It just sounds like a lot."

"Don't worry."

"Viv ..."

"Fuck, Steven, can't you just leave it?"

Steven stared at the phone. Since when did his baby sister use language like that. "Viv!"

"I'm sorry, I didn't mean to swear, really, I didn't. It's just ... look, you are right. Zoe makes me do more than I want, it's true. But it's her house, and she's paying for everything and I guess it's expensive having a kid in the place."

"She's not paying for everything." Steven was sure of this. "Mum will be sending her money for you."

"Mum. Hah. She was meant to come back and never did. She hardly calls any more."

"Oh, I ..."

"Yeah, sorry. Sore subject for you, I know."

"No, it's fine. You talk, I'll listen."

"I don't have anything to say. And look, I know this probably sounds like I'm just trying to go, but I have homework to do, and we've been talking ages. It's been nice, really it has, and I'm so pleased that you and Alistair are doing well, and your phlebby thing, and all of that, but I should go."

"If you're sure."

"I'm sure. Call again soon, OK? Don't leave it weeks."

"I will. I'll text you in the week."

She was gone before he processed her final goodbye. Dropping the phone, Steven slumped back into the pillow. He could hear Alistair in his head, arguing that it wasn't his responsibility. But it was. Surely, it was.

———————

Steven's hands hurt. The day before, Mum had punished him in front of the whole school, caning him on his palms in assembly for his slipping grades and lack of motivation. It hadn't been the physical pain that had hurt as much as the embarrassment. Even the teachers had looked shocked as she dragged her poor son out in front of everyone and made an example of him.

The cream did little to help. He'd found it in the bathroom and hoped it was the right sort of cream for stinging, burning hands. All it seemed to have done was make his hands oily and slippy. He'd used a towel to wipe up the mess from the white greasy substance and then hidden it well so it wouldn't be found for weeks. Using the medicine was punishable, ruining the towel was punishable, getting cream on anything would be punishable.

Dark had fallen and the night had crept out. Steven looked out of the window at the stars, watching them flicker in the blackness. He felt so alone.

A flash in the sky drew his attention. A shooting star? The quicksilver dance of a nighttime fairy? Clenching his hands tight despite the pain, he sent out his wish. To not be alone. To have a little brother or sister to share his time with.

It was a silly wish. Childish. Zoe had told him how children were made. Shown him much of it. With all the arguing between Mum and Dad, he would never have a younger sibling.

But some months later, Vivienne was born. Had it been Steven's little wish? Was the idea that a fairy had granted him a baby sister just a romantic ideal?

From the very first days, she meant everything to him, this little bundle of soft skin and wide eyes that looked up at him and asked him, without speaking, for protection and love.

Every day, he would take time to look after her, both to take some of the burden from Mum and stop her from being so tired, but also because he enjoyed those moments so much. He would sit on the floor, with Vivienne rolling as she learned to crawl, and patiently help her.

He would always be there to protect her and keep her safe. He owed the wish fairy that much.

———————

"I need to visit Zoe and Viv again." Steven looked at the ground. He was drunk, Alistair was drunk. The two of them had just left a party, one of the slightly-experimental guy-only gay parties that Alistair had been insisting they try. It had been a failure; nice cocktails but poor company. Steven was pleased they'd got out of there when they did. His mind had been on his earlier conversation with Viv and he hadn't been in the mood for discussing anecdotal sexual stories with strangers.

"Seriously? Last time it didn't go well."

"When Vivienne was born, I made a promise to look after her, and I've been ignoring that promise."

"Yeah, how old were you? Nine? Ten?"

"That's not the point. She's my little sister and she's not doing well. And talking in there brings it back up. Zoe's not a nice person to live with."

"You're just getting there?" Alistair grinned and leaned against a lamppost.

"You could come!"

Al spluttered, slipped, and crashed onto the ground. "Shit! I'm a wee bit more tanked than I thought."

Steven helped him up, his own legs wobbly. "Would you like to come?"

"To your sister's? Fuck me, no."

"Would you, though?"

"She won't invite me, it'd be awkward, and honestly, I love you Steve, I really do, but not that much."

"She's not that bad."

"She *is* that bad. This is the whole point and yet again you refuse to see your sister in anything other than some sort of fucked-up rose-tinted light. Let's make it clear, Zoe is a bitch. She cares about one person and one person only, and honestly, I don't even know if she cares that much about herself, she's so fucking destructive. You're saying you want to go back there because you are worried about Viv. Worried what? That she's not safe? That your sister may abuse her. Your sister *is* abusing her. I fucking guarantee it."

"She's certainly giving her a lot of chores, and no real free time."

"That'll be the tip of the iceberg. Fuck me, Steven, she made you have sex with her when you were a kid, she probably has Viv tied up in a sex dungeon and only lets her answer the phone to you when she's had enough orgasms for the night."

"I think she's grown out of that."

"You *think*? Wow. Look, she manipulated your mother into disowning you, she made sure she got Viv because it means your mum sends her money."

"You think that's why?"

"Of course, that's why. You think she wants a snotty teenager around?"

"Viv isn't snotty. I think she really helps out."

"Right, so she has a slave who comes with monthly dividends. Sweet deal if you can get it."

"You see, I have to go back there."

"And what are you going to do? You'll walk in, they'll be playing happy families. A day'll go past, maybe two, and Zoe will do something horrific to you and you'll be back on the train as fast as you can."

"I'll bring Viv with me."

"Really? Kidnap your sister? You're this fucking close to finishing a medical degree, to being a fucking doctor. Do you know what having a kidnapping charge on your CV will do for you? Let's assume, for a moment, that you don't want to work for kids, because there's no way you're passing those checks as a kidnapper. Nine out of ten hospitals will reject your application out of hand, and the ten percent you get an interview with are going to ask some fucking awkward questions. Let's assume you impress half of those, you're still lowering your prospective positions to one in twenty. I wouldn't fucking bet on those odds and I like to gamble."

Steven slumped. They kept walking.

"I'm not saying you can't go," Alistair said eventually. "I'm not your keeper."

"You're right though."

"I'm just saying that you need to be realistic. Go and say 'Hi' and spend some time with her, sure, but lose this hero thing that you have going."

"I just don't understand why Zoe's not looking after her, she's her sister, too."

"Zoe is a psycho. You're her brother but nothing you have ever told me makes me think that she's looked after you. Quite the opposite. Man, she makes me fucking sick."

"I don't know, I don't feel my childhood was that strange."

"Yeah, well, it's normal for abuse victims to feel that. It was normality for you. You didn't know any better. But you do now."

"And I know that Viv's in some sort of trouble."

"If you really think that, you need to contact your mother and tell her. You should have done it for yourself when you were a kid, you should definitely do it for Viv while she still is. Or do you want her to end up telling her lover sordid stories about what her older sister made her do?"

"So, you've come around from saying I shouldn't go to saying I should?"

"What I'm saying is that yes, if you think Viv's in danger of abuse, you need to step in. Be the big man, but don't do anything that'll fuck up your own life." Alistair put the key in the lock. "Thanks for sobering me up, by the way, because it wasn't as if I wanted to get home still drunk and still slightly horny from all the talking and take you to bed, oh no. What I wanted to do is discuss your older sister and her abusive tendencies for the fifteen minute walk home."

"Sorry."

"You could make it up. Start with a cup of tea."

Steven smiled.

"But no, Steve, honestly I'm not coming with you. Go over Easter—I should go home and visit my family anyway—and sort out what you can sort. It's in a couple of weeks and she's lived this long, so she'll manage another while."

"OK." Steven sank onto the chair, pleased to finally be home. Despite Alistair's own argument that he was not sober, Steven could still feel the effects of a night of drinking. He looked at the clock and winced; 3:12. His next shift started at ten.

"Cup of tea?" Alistair prodded. He took off his shoes and kicked them to the side. "Then you can come and show me just how much you'll miss me while you are away."

CHAPTER 17

Travelling over the Easter weekend was chaotic. Steven smiled at Daniel from across the car park and slumped into the waiting vehicle with a sigh.

"Rough trip?" Daniel asked.

"No room on anything, kids running around the train, and so much noise. Not that I mind kids, but they were stuck on a train for hours and bored, and they made lots of noise entertaining themselves."

"So, a day-long journey with noisy kids and nowhere to escape to?"

"Yes."

Daniel smirked. "Well, we're looking forward to your visit. Viv's very excited."

"Zoe not so much, I assume."

"She's in a friendly enough mood. And she does care about you and looks forward to your coming, even if she has a poor way of showing it."

"Maybe one day she'll learn a better way."

"Oh, I doubt that. She's pretty stuck in her ways already."

He pushed a CD into the slot and pulled the SUV out of the car park. Steven relaxed and settled in for the short journey back to his sister's house. He realised that he had become used to Daniel and quite liked the man. Their little trips to and from the train station had become a mini-tradition, and though they had never really had a long conversation, he found the company comfortable. Plus, he knew that Daniel cared for Viv and did what he could to make her life good.

The slight bump as the car slid into the driveway made Steven blink his eyes into focus. With a mixture of excitement and tense anticipation, he climbed out of the car and retrieved his bag.

"Steven." Zoe beamed. She waved from the door and took a step towards them.

"Hey." Steven paused at her bright friendliness. "What's up with you?"

"Just pleased to see my brother."

He raised his eyebrows. "Sure."

"Oh, come in." She made an attempt at a giggle that was completely ill-fitting and strode in before him.

Viv was waiting in the hallway. Her run and hug was a lot more natural than Zoe's awkward positivity.

"Hey, what's with her?" Steven nodded his head in Zoe's direction.

"No idea. Don't really care. How are you?"

"I'm good. Ready for a weekend of chocolate?"

"Absolutely!"

Steven smiled and followed her up to the spare room. As he had done before, he unpacked and put away his things, sliding the empty bag under the bed. Viv sat silently until he was finished.

"So," he prompted, "any news?"

"Nothing much. School's closed for the holidays, of course, so I've had more time than usual. Been reading some books."

"Anything good?"

"Fantasy stuff. Vampires. I like it."

"Sounds cool."

"Oh, it is! There's one vamp, who I love, she's called Suze, and I want to be just like her. She's so great, and her fashion sense is really ...

well, the book focuses on it a lot and I can already see that I'm boring you."

"No, no," Steven hugged her again. "It sounds great, maybe I should read it."

"Oh yeah, because you really want to spend time reading a teenage girl's vampire series."

"I dunno, I might love it."

Vivienne shook her head. "You won't. Anyway, tell me about you and Al."

All too happy to bring Viv up to date on the parts of his relationship with Alistair that were suitable for her ears, Steven told her some of the stories of the things they had done recently. Sat on his bed, she laughed along as he exaggerated anecdotes and shared his recent life.

It was almost an hour later that Daniel knocked on the door, calling out that dinner was ready.

Viv shuffled uncomfortably as they approached the table, her eyes clearly on the food that had been laid out for them. There were two different dinners on the table; one, a delicate array of fresh fish and vegetables that had obviously been carefully prepared; the second, a slab of lasagne that showed signs of having been rapidly microwaved.

Zoe, sat in front of her salmon, waved Steven and Viv to their seats.

"Different food?" Steven asked.

"Oh." Zoe laughed lightly. "Viv so enjoyed the lasagne from last night that we thought she'd like it again, and I thought you would, too. Besides, there was only enough salmon for two and Daniel and I love it so much, so ..."

Steven smiled politely. It felt odd and had definitely made Viv uncomfortable, but it wasn't worth arguing about. At least they had bothered to pour him a glass of wine.

Daniel looked embarrassed, too, but that didn't stop him cutting happily into the pink fish.

"So, how have you been?" Zoe asked.

"Fine."

"And Alistair?"

"Also good." Since when did she ask about Al?

A thick silence fell and for the next few minutes, the only sound was of their eating. Steven sipped on his wine, wondered whether it was his responsibility to break the odd tension, and considered what he could say. In the end, it was Daniel who saved the situation, launching into a story of his car and how it had needed repairs at the garage. It was a dull tale, but it stopped the horrific void and for that Steven was grateful. He played his part, asking questions about clutch replacements and discussing the monthly cost of keeping a vehicle on the road with more enthusiasm than he knew possible.

Once the lasagne was over, Viv hopped down from her seat, gathered up the dirty plates and beckoned her brother to join her in the kitchen. Making polite murmurs, Steven did so, feeling his shoulders physically relax once the door was closed behind him.

"It's so tense."

"She can't keep it up for long." Viv filled the bowl with soapy water.

"I can't believe she mentioned Alistair. She never does that."

"Trying to be nice, I guess."

"What's that?" Steven pointed, eyes wide. On the side were two pots of chocolate pudding, ready to heat.

"*Their* pudding."

"Just for them?"

Viv said nothing but nodded.

"Where's ours?"

She shook her head. "I don't get pudding. I guess you're in the same boat as me, now. Same with the dinner. They eat what they eat, and I get what I get."

"Viv?" Steven watched as his little sister racked the now-clean plates.

She looked at him, eyebrows raised in question.

"They don't give you the same food as them?"

Viv snorted. "No, Stevie, they wouldn't waste their money on me."

"But she's not poor. She's happy to eat well herself."

"That's how she affords it, I suppose. Paying for me as well would be too much."

"This is wrong. It's cruel."

"Oh, it's nothing. Let it go."

Steven opened his mouth to say something more when Daniel walked in. With obvious embarrassment, he placed the plate with the two puddings into the microwave and silently, the three of them waited for the timer to run down.

"They only came as a two," Daniel said by way of explanation. "I think she got them before we knew you were coming."

The excuse was weak, and they all knew it, but Steven said nothing as the other man transferred the desserts from microwave to individual plates. Daniel added a dollop of cream from the fridge to each and shuffled out of the door.

"Seriously? Is that how you treat a guest?"

"I don't think she thinks of you as a guest."

"And you, too! I'm going to say something."

"No, you always row with her, and what's the point? Please, Stevie, just forget these little things. She's just tight and selfish, OK? We know it, so why bother trying to change her?"

"It's not right!"

"I know." Vivienne's voice was low and filled with sadness. Suddenly Steven felt he was pushing the wrong person. He gave her a hug.

"Sorry, Sis, forget it. Do you need any help doing these dishes?" She smiled. "Tea towel is over there."

———————

The next morning, Viv came into Steven's room before he was even awake. Unable to resist her emphatic excitement, he soon admitted defeat and shooed her away for long enough to have a shower and get dressed. The sky was clear and promised a pleasant, if chilly, day.

"Can we go out?" Viv asked as soon as he allowed her back into the room. She plonked herself down on his bed and grinned.

"Sure. What about Zoe?"

"She's at work. She left you a note."

A note? It seemed very old-fashioned when she could have just texted him. "Where is it?"

"Dining table."

"What does it say?"

"That she's gone to work and something about going out to dinner tonight."

The note showed her clear, crisp handwriting. For a moment, Steven shuddered—it had been years since he'd read his sister's script—but he pushed the memory down and concentrated on the words:

Morning Steven. I've booked dinner for us all tonight and I don't want to be rude, but I assume you can pay for yourself. Anyway, we're meeting my friend, Sarah, so please don't show me up and dress nicely. I'll be back by six, and we're to leave at seven. If you don't want to come, that's fine, but I told Sarah that my brother was staying so she'll be expecting to see you.

"She's so pleasant," Steven drawled sarcastically.

"Sorry."

"It's not your fault." Steven managed a smile for his youngest sister. "It just gets to me, I suppose. There's nothing wrong with me paying for my own dinner, but it's the way she asks for it. Anyway, I'll buy yours, too; it'll let you have whatever you want rather than worrying about Zoe."

"You sure?" Viv's eyes were bright.

"Of course! Just no caviar."

Viv grinned. "I don't like the sound of caviar, can't see why people eat it."

"Because they're posh and think it's impressive? I don't know either. So, what are we doing today?"

"Shopping."

"For ...?"

"Chocolate?"

"We can do that. Breakfast first though, something with fruit in it. I assume we're allowed to eat fruit?"

Viv nodded. She pushed him to sit and ran to the kitchen. "I'll do it," she said, "you just sit there."

Steven looked at the note again, twisting the paper in his hands. Zoe's handwriting was precise, one of those things that was always held up to him as an example of how it should be done. For hours he had sat alone, copying her neat script, hoping each time that she'd agree that it was done right and wouldn't punish him further with hours more of the laborious practice. As an adult, his handwriting had diverged from hers and become his own style, but the clues were still there for anyone looking.

Viv reappeared with a bowl of freshly chopped fruit and yoghurt. At least Zoe wasn't able to spoil his breakfast.

Steven stared at the display on the cash machine. There was no way the figure could be right.

"Is it not working?" asked Viv.

"Give me a minute."

He looked again. His account, that had been thousands of pounds in credit, was well into its overdraft.

"It's fine." He turned back to Viv once the card had been spat back from the slot. "But I do need to make a phone call. Do you want to go over there and get an ice cream and a drink while I do? I won't be too long. Order me a coffee."

"Are you sure it's OK."

"Yup, just something went out that I didn't think was coming out this week. It's fine, it won't affect today."

"OK." Viv took the proffered ten-pound note and skipped into the cafe. Immediately, Steven called Alistair.

"What have you done?" he asked as soon as the other man picked up.

"With what?"

"Don't be dumb, Al, my bank account."

"Ah." Alistair's voice trailed off. There was a long pause.

"Al?"

"Look, I'll put it back. Monday, OK? Well, Monday's a bank holiday, so Tuesday."

"What have you done?"

"It's fine, stop panicking."

"Panicking? Alistair, that was my money to pay my fees. It's due at the start of the term, straight after the holidays. I don't have any other money. What did you do?"

"I lost it, OK?" Alistair's voice trembled. "I fucked up."

"You *lost* it? Gambling? It was over six fucking grand, Al. What do you mean you lost it? Why did you take it in the first place? Why are you digging in my bank account?"

"I ..." Alistair faltered. "Look, I just fucked up. You don't want the details, but yes, it's all on me. I'll win it back, it's fine."

"You'll *win* it back? You mean, you don't have it?"

"No, I don't have it. I lost it."

"What about your own money?"

"That, too."

"But you told me you were fine, that you've been winning and playing it careful, putting stuff away."

"Little white lies."

Steven fell silent. "For how long."

"A few weeks, a month or so."

"And you have nothing?"

More silence. "No."

"Nothing at all?"

"Not really. I thought you'd be away until Monday. I'll have it back by then."

"How? What are you going to do? Steal from someone else and lose their money trying to get this back?"

"I'm sorry, Steve, I really am."

"Alistair, I need that money back. I can't believe you've done this."

There was no answer. Steven stared at the phone, registering the fact that his boyfriend had hung up on him. He redialed and Alistair's voicemail answered.

No fucking way.

We need to talk about this. Why have you hung up on me?

Delivered, not read.

Al. Seriously.

Delivered.

Also not read.

"Fuck." Steven looked across the road, through the cafe window where Viv sat with her ice cream and coke. His coffee cup was on the table next to her. "Fuck."

A weekend with Zoe. Chocolate eggs to buy, Viv to keep happy, a dinner to eat, and less than fifty quid for it all.

Fuck.

———

After his fifteenth text message and third voicemail, Steven gave up on Alistair. There was nothing screaming at him would fix and that's what would happen if his boyfriend did pick up now. For a while, he considered contacting Ray, but that was unfair; at least give Alistair a few days to dig himself out of the hole before involving anyone else.

But what if he doesn't?

Steven wondered about his credit. Could he get a personal loan to pay for the university fees? Had his multiple jobs and general diligence improved his standing with the bank enough for them to agree to that? Even it if did, he couldn't even discuss it with anyone until Tuesday.

And all the while, Viv chattered along.

"So, Suze had this brilliant put down. I can't repeat it, because I won't get it right, but Delver, he's one of the bad guys, had snuck into her place at night. They'd had a confrontation, and he'd started to get all in her face, and she was so harsh. It was great. Sorry, I'm not explaining it very well."

"It's fine. I think I get the idea. How many books in this series?"

"I'm on book four, but there are thirteen. She's really quick with her writing. What's that word?"

"Prolific?"

"Yeah! That's it. She's really prolific. A new one comes out every six months, and they take a while to read, so I'm going to be on it for at least a year. It's really exciting, but I have to stay away from the online stuff because it's just so full of spoilers."

"Yeah, just read it yourself. Don't worry about what other people say."

"Well, the fandom's part of it. That's what makes it so good. I'm really hoping that I can go to one of the conventions. Some of the fans meet up, and they dress up and stuff. I know it's silly, you probably think that, but they have one in Leeds in the summer and that's not far. Do you think Zoe will be OK with me going? I haven't asked her."

"Is Zoe ever all right with anything?" Steven's tone was snappy, and he knew it. "Sorry, I didn't mean to be like that."

"It's OK. Are you all right? You've been a bit off ever since you had that phone call. Who was it?"

"Just Al."

"Oh, right. Are you OK?"

Steven nodded. "I'm fine. I guess we just spend a lot of time together. It's a bit weird being here without him."

"Because of Zoe, you mean?"

"Everything, but yes, Zoe."

"Don't let her get to you. And the egg you got her is brilliant. She'll love it."

"I hope so."

"She will. I can't wait to see mine." Viv gazed at the bag by his side.

"Oi!" Steven laughed. "Come on, we have to get this lot home and then have the fun that will be dinner. Have you met Sarah before?"

"Yeah, she's really nice."

"Well that's something at least. Maybe she'll keep Zoe on good behaviour."

They grinned at each other. Viv shook her head. "Not a chance."

––––––––––

Steven's plan was simple; stay out of his sister's way until they were ready to leave. He used the main bathroom early, washing and shaving before retreating to his room to get dressed and wait.

Through the wall, he listened to Zoe's shouts of frustration. All directed at Vivienne.

"Can't you do anything right?!"

"No, not like that! Have you any idea how much this dress cost?"

"For fuck's sake Viv! I told what needed washing days ago!"

He'd promised Viv that he wouldn't intervene and potentially make things worse for her, but how could he make it worse? He hadn't realised it was like this for her.

Although he felt he should have.

Steven rocked on the bed, trying to separate the sounds of what was happening around him with his own memories. Too often, the fierce cries of his older sister felt like they were directed at him and not Viv.

"No." he slammed the door open. "This is ridiculous."

He walked down the short corridor. "Zoe? Where are you?"

"What? I'm getting ready. What do you want?"

"I want to speak to you." Steven crossed to his sister's bedroom. Thankfully, the door was open—he wasn't sure he'd have had the gall to storm in.

"Speak to me about what?"

Steven looked in. Kneeling at Zoe's feet, Vivienne was helping her sister with her shoes.

"What the fuck?"

His younger sister was in tears, wet red lines marking her face.

"What the fuck? You have her fucking putting on your shoes? Are you sick?"

"Mind your own fucking business!" Zoe snapped.

Steven stood, shock causing him to remain still.

"Sort your own fucking shoes!" he shouted. "What the hell is going on?"

"They're hard for her to do," Viv stammered, weakly defending Zoe's actions. "She needs my help."

"If she can't put on fucking shoes at her age, she does need help! For fuck's sake, Viv, get up."

"Don't you interfere," Zoe spat at him. "This has nothing to do with you."

"Nothing to do with me? You're abusing our little sister. Why is she crying? Have you hit her?"

"What I do is none of your business."

"You have, haven't you? You fucking hit her!" Steven looked at the mark on Viv's head. "Shit, you fucking hit her with your fucking shoe!"

He glanced down at Viv for confirmation. The way she bowed her head provided it. "I cannot believe this. You treat her like a fucking slave. Like an animal. I'm going to call the police. She's coming home with me."

"With you?!" Zoe cackled. "Don't think you're part of this family, Steven. Mum disowned you, remember? She didn't want anything to do with you. I am Viv's legal guardian! Me, not you. You had your chance and you'd rather shack up with Alistair than take some family responsibility. Don't fucking threaten me."

"Fuck me, you are such a bitch!"

"Please." Viv trembled, still crouched on the floor. "Both of you, please."

"You're upsetting her."

"*I* am upsetting her? What the fuck? Get up Viv, for fuck's sake. Stop crawling around her ankles. It's disgusting."

"Oh, she's disgusting now, is she?"

"I didn't say that, and you know it."

"Just get out of my bedroom. You are not welcome here." She turned to Viv. "You can go with him, I'll sort out my own shoes."

Slowly, Vivienne straightened.

"Come on, Viv."

"I ..." the girl stammered.

"Oh, go," Zoe snapped. "Go on, I need to get ready anyway. We do have a dinner to get to, after all."

Pushing Vivienne into the hallway, Zoe slammed the door.

"What's going on?" Steven slid down the wall to sit on the floor alongside his sobbing sister. He pulled her toward him, wrapped her in his arms and, together, the pair sat in silence for a while.

"We need to get ready," Viv's quiet voice banished the silence.

"You still want to go to dinner?"

"Zoe will calm down. She'll forget all this, just wipe it away to get on with life. Her friend is coming and that's what's important to her. If we get ready, meet her downstairs in twenty minutes all smiles, it'll be good."

"What?" Steven stared at her.

"Please, Stevie, please. It's easier this way."

"She's treating you like a slave, Viv. I can't just pretend it isn't happening?"

"Can't you? That's what I do. Every day. You think this is bad?" Viv pulled up her top, showing a dulled scar that crossed her back. "See this? I had to tell everyone I'd fallen from a tree, but I hadn't. She did it on a door handle. She pushed me against the door so hard one night when she was angry because I hadn't tidied up well enough."

"God, Viv, no. Why haven't you told me?"

"Because ..."

"Because I'm not here. But Mum, why haven't you told Mum?"

"Mum? What can she do? Zoe has made her think I'm a liar, a teenager acting out, and she doesn't believe anything I have to say."

"We should call someone. Social services."

"Please, Stevie, no. Please. I don't want that to happen. It won't mean I go back to live in Scotland with you and Al, will it? It'll mean I'll be put into care where something worse could happen. I don't want that."

"I have to do *something*."

"Come to dinner. Clean your face and I'll clean mine. We get ready, we smile, and we go to dinner, and we don't embarrass Zoe in front of her friend."

Steven shook his head slowly. "I can't just do that."

"Please, brother. Please."

He considered it a moment longer. "OK, I'll do it. For tonight only, but after this ... I'm not leaving this to just go on, you understand?"

"For tonight, yes. Thank you." Viv brightened.

Steven stood. "I'm already ready. A few splashes of water to get the red out of my face will do. What about you?"

"I'll be five minutes. Less. I'll meet you downstairs."

Jumping up, Viv ran off. Steven stared for a moment longer, staring at the closed door to his older sister's room, then turned and walked down the stairs.

———

The tension in the car was so thick, Steven could practically taste it. He sat in the back with Viv while Zoe drove to Sarah's house without speaking. As soon as her friend sat into the passenger seat, Zoe's expression changed, the cloud of ominous dread replaced with a bright, beaming smile. While Steven and Vivienne sat silently behind them, the two friends chatted about work and rumours. His only word the entire journey had been a polite 'hello' to Sarah.

"Just order whatever you want," he reiterated to Vivienne before they went in. "I want you to have a nice dinner, no matter what."

Internally, he screamed. Not only was he having to sit through an uncomfortable meal with his abusive older sister, but his bank account was dry. Paying for Viv's meal was going to wipe him out entirely, digging to the bottom of his overdraft limit.

"Are you sure?" she said, a bright smile crossing her face.

"Of course!"

A look from Zoe hurried them along and they filed in behind her.

"Is Daniel coming?" Steven noted that the table was for five and that Zoe's partner hadn't been mentioned.

"He's running late," his sister said sharply.

"Right."

"Have you got a problem, Steven?" Zoe turned to Sarah. "See what I have to deal with. I told you."

Sarah said nothing.

"No problem," Steven assured her. He smiled at Sarah apologetically. Did she know what her friend was like? Did she put up with that?

The restaurant was an impressive Vietnamese establishment. Steven winced as soon as he looked at the menu, quickly calculating that dinner here would be about fifty percent more than he'd expected.

"I'll just have fried rice," he said to the waitress with a friendly grin. "Nothing else for me."

Viv, responding to another emphatic nod from her brother, ordered beef pho with summer rolls starter. Steven crunched the numbers in his head with mild relief. At least his payment would go through, just.

"Fried rice?" asked Zoe, leaning across the table. "Are you trying to embarrass me?"

"What?"

"Who in their right mind comes to a Vietnamese restaurant and orders fried rice? You are uncultured. I'm ashamed to even be sat with you."

There was some shifting at the table as both Sarah and Viv reacted to Zoe's words with embarrassed looking away. Steven glared at his sister but kept his mouth shut as Daniel walked in, waving enthusiastically.

"Sorry I'm late," he panted. "Traffic. And the nearest car park is miles away."

"We parked just around the corner, on the street," said Zoe.

"Right, yeah, I didn't want to risk it." He smiled. "Has everyone ordered? I think I'll just have my usual."

"I ordered for you," said Zoe.

"Great. Thanks."

"Steven decided to just get fried rice."

"Leave it, Zoe," Steven warned.

"He's trying to embarrass me."

"I'm not."

"Either that, or he's too stupid to realise how his actions reflect on his sister. How his uncultured ways make me look like I wasn't brought up properly, either. Mum and Dad would be so disappointed."

"Zoe."

"Of course, Dad died disappointed, and Mum disowned him, so I guess a bowl of rice isn't really going to make any more of a dent."

"What the fuck is wrong with you?" Steven pushed his chair away to lean over the table. "I like fried rice, OK? It's on the menu, so plenty of people order it, and I'm paying for it, so what's your problem?"

Without hesitation, Zoe stood. In five steps, she walked around the table and slapped Steven around the face.

"You crazy fucking bitch!" Steven trembled.

Sarah, who sat next to Steven, stood, putting herself in-between the warring siblings. "Calm down."

"Me?" Steven held his hands up, gesticulating. "She's lucky I don't hit her back."

"Steven." Daniel shot his own warning glance.

"Lucky?" Zoe spat. "I'm unlucky to even know you, you bloody homo."

"I'm leaving." Steven turned and closed his eyes, taking one step before blinking them open to make his way to the door. He heard the rustle of chairs behind him but couldn't register what was happening. With each step, he just concentrated on getting outside.

"It's OK," someone said, once the cool air hit him. "I'll get a taxi. Just stay there." It was Sarah. Next to her, Viv looked up at him, one hand clinging to his shirt.

"Are you OK, Stevie?"

Steven shook his head.

"We'll go home," she said. "Sarah'll sort it."

He nodded. By 'home', though, she meant Zoe's. He didn't want to go there, but what options did he have? His return ticket wasn't valid until Tuesday, he had no money for a hotel room, and he had to protect Viv. He couldn't leave her in the house alone with the monster that Zoe had shown herself to be.

"Yes," he whispered, "we'll go back."

"Don't let her get to you," Viv pressed. "Please."

"It's OK, Viv. It's OK. I'm sorry I ruined dinner. You were looking forward to your beef pho."

She chuckled a little. "I don't mind about dinner, don't worry about it."

"Taxi's coming," interrupted Sarah. "I'll come with you, make sure you both get back OK. Do you have a key, Viv?"

Viv held up her keychain, complete with a pink fluffy pen that Steven recognised as something he'd bought her years before.

"Great. No need to talk, let's just get you back."

The taxi ride was swift and silent. Once inside the house, Viv ran to get herself ready for bed as Steven slumped on the sofa.

"It wasn't your fault," Sarah said from the kitchen. She'd already flicked the kettle on. "Zoe can be explosive at times."

"She hates me."

"I don't know that that's true."

"I fucking hate her."

"I think it's going to be OK. Look, I've texted her. She's going to stay the night at Daniel's place, so you and Viv have the house at least."

Daniel's place. Steven hadn't even registered that Daniel and Zoe didn't actually live together. But of course they didn't, Daniel just spent a lot of time here.

"Thank you."

"Oh, it's nothing. Honestly, I'd have liked fried rice, too."

Steven couldn't help but laugh.

"I'm done," said Viv, running down in her pyjamas. "Is it OK if I just go to bed?"

"You haven't eaten."

"Not really in the mood."

"Sure. Wake me in the morning, OK. Chocolate Sunday."

"Chocolate Sunday!" She hugged him. "Night, Stevie. Night, Sarah. Thanks for bringing us back."

Sarah ruffled her hair. "Night, kid."

"You alright if I leave you on your own?" Sarah asked once Viv had closed her bedroom door.

"Of course. Thank you."

"It really wasn't your fault. Honestly, I can't believe she slapped you."

"She's done worse."

"Right, yeah. Umm ..."

"Sorry, didn't mean to make you uncomfortable."

"No, you didn't. It's OK. Family stuff, right, I mean, I get it. Look, have a good day tomorrow. Eat some chocolate with Viv and have a good morning. There's no way Zoe will come back before lunchtime at the earliest. So, relax, spend some time with Viv."

"And then get out of here?"

"Well, that's up to you."

Steven accompanied her to the front door. "Night, Sarah, thanks. Good to meet you."

"Yeah, you too."

CHAPTER 18

"**I**s your mother home?"

Steven looked up at the neighbour and shook his head.

"Is she going to be long?"

He shrugged.

"What about your big sister? Is Zoe home?"

Steven shook his head again.

The neighbour smiled. "OK, love. Look, I bought some eggs round. We have some spare and I thought your mum might be able to use them. Could you let her know?"

Steven looked at the box of eggs. There were ten, in two neat rows. He nodded his head and smiled before he closed the door.

Eggs meant the rice would taste good. Plain rice was nice. Plain rice with ketchup was a bit nicer, but egg fried rice was his favourite.

He'd had nothing but rice for so long now. He was pleased that he liked it so much, pleased that Mum kept making it.

But he was looking forward to Dad coming home from his business trip. When Dad was home, there were things to put in the rice. Chicken, beef, and vegetables. Plus the sauces. Dad loved rice with flavour.

Steven put the eggs carefully on the side.

Steven stared at the ceiling. The bad dreams and associated sweats seemed more regular now. His sheets were soaking, bad enough that at first, he'd considered the horrific idea that he might have soiled himself, but a quick feel around and sniff soon disproved that theory. Not that his sweat smelled good, but at least it wasn't urine.

He wandered downstairs, naked in the dark. True to her word, Zoe hadn't come home for the night and he was alone in the big house. Everything seemed so lavish and rich, kept to a high standard of cleanliness and repair. But then, it was Viv, not Zoe, who did the hard work of keeping it in order.

Zoe couldn't even put on her own shoes without help.

Damn it, he liked fried rice.

More than once, as a child, they had been reduced to the staple food. He hadn't even recognised the irony of ordering it for himself now that all his money had been spent. Stolen, he reminded himself, by a man he trusted with everything.

Steven wanted to cry.

No wonder Zoe had reacted so badly to it. He sighed. Like him, she'd grown up with periods of abject poverty. Like him, she'd been forced to eat nothing but rice for day after day, week after week.

Month after month.

Perhaps it was only reasonable that she equated fried rice with embarrassment and shame. His father had fucked up his own childhood enough, it was understandable that he'd fucked up Zoe's, too.

Steven flicked on the kitchen light, poured himself some water, and started opening cupboards. Did Zoe even have rice in the house? Surely she did.

But no. There was none. Plenty of pasta, and a whole range of different noodles, but no rice. He laughed silently, bitterly.

Fuck me, Zoe, he thought, you're a fucking head case.

"Look at the damage you've done, Dad," he said out loud. He sat at the dining room table, illuminated by the spill of light from the kitchen door, and fiddled with his glass of water.

———

"Business trips?" Steven's mother shouted.

Steven put his hands over his ears and tried to push back her furious tirade, but the walls were far too thin to allow such release.

"I need to travel for work," his father replied at a similar volume.

"Work?" she spat the word. "If that's what you want to call what you do with the woman. Though, I suppose for her it *is* 'work', isn't it? You're just another stupid client."

"Don't be disgusting!"

"You only say that because I'm right. Don't think I don't know that this new woman in Surabaya is a prostitute. I know. I know." She was crying.

Steven really didn't want to hear it.

"Once, perhaps." His dad's voice was defensive.

Had he really decided to have an affair with a prostitute?

"Go!" his mother shrieked. "Just go. Leave your son, and your baby daughter, and me, and just go!"

"This is my home!"

"Not any longer. Go to your revolting whore, and don't turn around. I never want to see you again!"

Something was thrown. Doors slammed. Steven shuddered.

Don't break down, he thought, you're fifteen, not a child. Viv needs you. Mum needs you.

Not a child anymore.

Man of the house.

He could still hear her sobbing on the other side of the wall.

A prostitute?

Steven found he was crying, too. No. No more time for that. He wiped his eyes.

Man of the house.

Grow up.

With alien detachment, Steven visualised his thoughts. He closed his eyes and saw himself as a child; that lost, dependant boy. That child couldn't look after anyone, certainly not Viv.

Shoot him. Kill him. Kill the child. Be a man. Grow up. Man of the house, now.

In his mind, he took a gun. It felt heavy.

Shoot him. Right in the chest. No more childishness.

He levelled the gun, looked down the sights. There was little Steven.

"No room for you anymore, little boy."

He squeezed the trigger.

And he didn't cry.

_____

The water cooled his throat and he shivered. In the chill dining room, his sweat had done its job a little too well. Steven stood up.

"Seriously Dad, I can't believe I spent so long wanting to impress you. Wanting you to be proud of me. You never bothered to try to make me proud of you."

He looked up the stairs. Vivienne was sleeping there, still a little girl. Still with a childhood and a chance.

If Zoe didn't take it from her.

If he did something about it.

After all, he was the man of the house.

"Fuck."

Water wasn't strong enough. Did Zoe have anything else?

He'd forgotten that day and the strong mental image of him murdering his inner child. It had become a recurring nightmare for some years but had gone in recent times. Great to have it back.

"No room for you anymore, little boy," he whispered. "Thanks, Dad."

The glass-fronted cabinet revealed some decent-looking whisky, a half-full bottle of white rum, and some vodka, along with some liqueurs. Rum it was. And diet Coke from the fridge.

———————

"I'm sorry," she said, pushing one plate of rice toward him and another to Viv. "There's not much money at the moment."

"Where is it, Mum?" Steven asked.

"Where's what?"

"The money. We had money. The business has been doing fine." Even with Dad's indiscretion, he added silently.

She paused, her face tightening. "Your dad needed it."

You mean he stole it. It had been a joint account; no doubt his dad had drained it. After all, what was food for his wife and kids worth when there was fun to be had in Indonesia?

"Well, I love fried rice," said Steven with a smile. "So, thanks."

He gave Viv a nudge and the little girl grinned too. "Nice rice," she said.

———————

Nice rice.

Can you get food delivery at this time of night in Sheffield? What even is the time? He took out his phone.

A quarter to midnight. Earlier than he'd thought.

He was just in time. It would arrive in ten minutes, and even with the delivery charge, it was cheaper than he'd planned to pay for dinner a few hours ago.

———————

"Where's your father?" The tall man's voice was gruff.

"Excuse me?" Gently, Steven pushed Viv behind him. Ever curious, the little girl had followed him to the door.

"I said, 'where's your father?'." The man pulled a knife from his belt. "I *really* want to know."

"He's not here. He left."

"He owes us money."

"We don't have it. He left."

"We'll be back. Tell him he has until tonight." The man turned.

"How can I tell him that? He left." Steven called as the thug walked away. He closed the door.

There were four of them when they came back. Steven raced once he heard the knocking, but his mum reached the door first.

"I don't know where he is," she said. "If I did, I'd tell you. He deserves it."

"We don't believe you. Get out of the way."

"You want to come into my house?" Her voice rose. Then she calmed. "Actually, fine. You don't believe me, come in, check under the table, check in the wardrobe. You won't find him or his money. But hurt my children, and it won't be good for you."

Steven smiled. Her threat felt weighty.

The large men pushed past her without effort. Within five minutes the living room and kitchen were trashed, the men gratuitously flinging their possessions around without care.

"She's right, he's not here," one of them decided eventually. "And they really have nothing."

"Glad we're in agreement." Steven's mum ushered them to the door. "Thank you for coming."

They returned half an hour later. The knock was gentler, almost friendly.

"Yes?" Steven asked.

"Give this to your mum," the big man said. "We're sorry we made such a mess."

The bag contained vegetables, eggs, and milk. There was a packet of chicken and a bar of chocolate. Plus, a bag of rice.

Steven's mother cried.

————

Steven wiped his plate clean. He put the rice container in the bin and cleaned up any sign of it. Zoe might be aggressive and disrespectful, but he didn't have to be the same.

He finished the drink and sat, now in a loose dressing gown, on the sofa.

"I want to understand, Zoe," he said to the night. "I want to find a way to forgive you, and I keep coming up with excuses for you, but I have to look after Viv. You're an adult. You're older than me. She's just a kid. A kid you're abusing."

He breathed out slowly.

"Not that I know what to do."

————

"Thank you for seeing us," the man said. He was shorter than his wife and also—Steven thought of a polite word—stouter.

"I don't understand why you are here," Steven's mum said. The three adults sat around the dining table, each with a cup of hot tea that Steven had made at his mother's request.

"We've heard about your troubles," said the woman. "We're hoping we can help."

"What troubles? What help?"

"Now, now, we don't mean to offend or cause embarrassment," said the man, "but we'll jump straight to the point."

"We've been trying for a child for more than ten years," his wife continued, "and we have to accept it's not going to happen. Your little girl, Vivienne, would be valuable to us. A loved and welcome addition to our family. We'd treat her so well, give her everything possible—"

"And offer you a substantial amount of compensation," broke in the other.

Steven gasped. "No!"

"Excuse me, young man, we were talking to your mother."

"Get out!" He pushed at the fat man. Fat, not 'stout', he thought. He pushed at the fat man and yelled. "Get out of my house!"

He ran then, grabbed Vivienne from her room and took her to his own, which had a lock.

There was more conversation. Shaking, he couldn't hear the words.

"What is it, Steven?" Viv asked.

"Nothing, love, nothing." He cuddled her.

Eventually, it went silent outside. There was a knock at the door.

"They're gone, Steven," his mum said. "I sent them away. They won't be back. It's OK."

Steven crept to Vivienne's room and cracked open the door. She was sleeping soundly, her gentle snore filling the air.

He looked around, giving it a proper evaluation. The room wasn't filled with stuff—no doubt Zoe kept spending money to a minimum when it came to her little sister's luxuries—but it wasn't sparse either. Viv had a decent collection of books, including a number from the vampire series she'd been telling him about, and there were a few toys scattered around. There were ornaments and a poster on the wall. Signs of a normal teenage life, he thought, right down to the pile of clothes on the floor which she'd been too tired to dump in the wash basket, despite it being in the near corner.

He closed the door.

She was well looked after here. She was getting an education and she had more than many children her age have. Certainly, more than he had.

For all her meanness, Zoe wasn't relegating Vivienne to eating nothing but fried rice.

Am I over-reacting?

But then he remembered the scar. It was the length of his forearm, crossing from the base of Viv's neck to the small of her back. His studies told him that it wasn't going to fade away without some help and intervention. His little sister shouldn't need cosmetic surgery at her age, especially not surgery that was a result of Zoe's viciousness.

"I have to take you away from here. But how can I?"

Disowned. No rights. Accused of being a kidnapper.

Steven shuddered. It would destroy any chance he had of a career.

————————

He was en-route to deliver straight As. A perfect set of exam results. Revision done for the night, Steven left his bedroom and went to say goodnight to his mother.

And saw his father.

"Hello, Steven." Behind him, on the sofa, the woman he had hurt so badly wiped more tears from her eyes. Is that all he does? Cause her pain?

"What are you doing here?"

Steven's dad puffed on a cigarette, filling the air with smoke that had not been seen in the house for more than six months.

"Is that any way to greet me?"

Steven snapped. Enraged, he ran into the kitchen, searching for a weapon. His eyes fell on the meat cleaver, and he grabbed it, leaping back into the other room like a lunatic from a horror film. He screamed, a sound that echoed from his father as the other man ran.

"Steven!" his mother shouted.

He didn't listen. Here was the man who had left them, who had stolen all their money, who had left his children starving to such an extent that the loan sharks that came to collect had felt such pity that even *they* had passed on charity.

He gave chase, swinging the cleaver as he hunted his father through the house. In the long corridor, he only just missed him; a swipe that came close to the back of his dad's neck. The sounds

Steven made were deep, guttural rage. He didn't even understand them himself.

The door to the study slammed shut, the lock sliding tight. The cleaver cut into the wood deeply, gouging a gap that was almost visible through.

"Come out!" Steven screamed. "Come out and let me kill you."

His mum was shouting. Telling him to calm down, to think of his future, to think of Viv.

What did it matter?

Her hand was on his arm.

"If you kill him, you will end up in jail. You are almost an adult. Bad things will happen. Please, Steven, please."

He didn't hear it. He didn't want to hear it. The cleaver cut into the door once more.

"Steven, your sister."

His sister. The little girl who'd had nothing proper to eat for weeks, who cried herself to sleep because she was so often too hungry for words.

He hacked again. "Get out, you bastard!"

"Please, Steven, you are better than this. Don't let him do this to you."

Was he better than this?

He wanted to kill his father. No, not his father. He'd lost his father the same day that he'd murdered his inner child. Father and child, gone together. This was just an awful man, a selfish man, a betrayer, a thief, a coward.

"I will kill you!"

But it was too much. Again, his mother brushed his arm, and then Viv was there. Little Vivienne, who didn't understand, who was crying because of the shouting, because her brother, whom she loved so much, was waving a huge weapon around. He dropped it, slipped to the floor, and shook. But no tears, not for him.

———————

Of course, his dad had come crawling back. And of course, his mum had let him. As soon as his money had run dry. As soon as his mistress had become bored of him.

Steven thought of the fights they had had after that day. It took months before he stopped wanting to hit his father every time they passed. Months where, if the man ever mentioned his prostitute girlfriend, those desires manifested themselves physically and they'd brawl. Often Steven would become bruised and hurt, falling asleep with minor injuries his father had directly caused.

But then, he'd managed the same in return.

The business trips had started again but without trust. Steven offered to accompany his father, chaperoning the older man so that work could be done, and money brought in for the family without the constant worry that another fancy woman would be found and instigate a return from their recovering wealth back to devastating poverty.

Because his mum was desperate for them to be a 'complete family'.

"Doesn't feel so complete, now, does it?" Steven asked the darkness.

Mum was gone, Zoe was an abuser, Viv was in trouble, and Dad was dead, leaving just the son who was now struggling to be a man without guidance, without support.

"You were a bastard," Steven whispered, "but I could do with a little experience and wisdom right now. Things haven't been right since you died."

He needed sleep. The sheets were changed, he was no longer hungry, and, at least for the night, Viv was safe.

Tomorrow was another day.

CHAPTER 19

08:18 Steven woke up to the smell of fresh cooking coming up the stairs. Confused, he threw on the dressing gown and opened his bedroom door.

"Viv?"

There was no reply, but if she was downstairs, it would have been hard to hear him. He went out and down to the living room.

"Viv?"

"In here!" His sister's cheery voice came from the kitchen. "I've made pancakes."

She beamed as he joined her. Fresh faced and fully dressed, she had obviously been up for a while.

"They look great."

"Thanks. I thought it'd be a fun Easter morning breakfast. Happy Easter."

"Happy Easter."

She looked at him expectantly and he laughed. "I'll get your egg. Wait here."

The egg was back in the bedroom, an extravagant creation from Hotel Chocolat that had been too expensive but would be well appreciated; it straddled the line between bright children's egg with tasty extras and classy adult chocolate. She'd love it.

Next to it was the one he'd bought for Zoe. With a sigh, he slid it back under the bed.

"Have I got time for a shower before pancakes?" Steven called. "I'll be quick."

"Sure!"

"I'll be down dressed and with your egg in just a minute."

The shower took him less than ten minutes in total, a perfunctory wash rather than anything relaxing. When he returned downstairs, the table had been laid for the two of them. Chopped banana, a pot of Nutella, some halved lemons, and a bowl of sugar sat next to the small pile of expertly-made crepe-style pancakes.

"These look amazing!"

"Thanks."

"I didn't know you could cook at all. These look professional."

Vivienne flushed.

Steven reached behind his back and passed her the egg. With a squeal of delight, she turned the box around and around in her hands. "It's so posh!"

"I thought you'd like something a bit more grown-up."

"I do! Thank you." Viv jumped and threw her arms around his neck. "Now, come on, before the pancakes get cold."

09:02

"Viv, we need to talk about Zoe before she comes home."

Vivienne looked at him, the delight that had suffused the air for the last half an hour suddenly dampened.

"I know." Steven took her hand. "I'd rather we kept enjoying our day like this, but she's going to wake up and come back and we need to know what we're going to do before that."

Viv sighed. "I don't know what to do. I'd love to live with you, but I'm doing really well at school here and I have friends and I don't want to lose that. Plus, Stevie, she really will do what she threatens. She'll call the police and say you kidnapped me."

"Yes, and I will tell them about the abuse. Viv, I know there's more that you haven't told me."

His sister looked down at the table.

"It's OK, I'm not going to push that right now, but just know that I know. I've been there, too. Zoe's *my* older sister as well. Things weren't always great when we were growing up."

Viv looked up at him, surprise in her eyes.

"I just never thought she was still like that. If I had, I'd have fought harder with Mum to not let you end up here." He paused. "We could call Mum."

"What?" Viv looked incredulous. "You don't even speak to her anymore."

"I know, and she won't talk to me, but she will talk to you."

"Oh, Stevie, please. Don't make me tell her."

"It's OK. You don't have to if it's too hard, but she has to know. She'll put a stop to it, even if that means getting on a plane."

"She can't. Visa issues, remember?"

"Well, she'll do *something*, Viv. She's not stupid and she's not about to leave you in an awful position."

Viv breathed slowly. "OK"

"If you can, convince her to talk to me. Just say it's important. I can tell her, then."

09:56

Steven shook and stared at the screen. It was all too much. Zoe, his mum, Viv, and Al ... It had been a full day since he'd spoken to his boyfriend, twenty-four hours since he learned that the man he loved had stolen all his money.

If he told his mum about Zoe, where would that leave him? Assuming she believed him, assuming she even talked to him, assuming Zoe didn't manage to wiggle her way out of it, just like she always had done.

This could end as a disaster. He could be homeless, split up from his boyfriend, broke, barred from seeing Viv at all, at war with his sister and still fighting his mother. He could lose his place at university, unable to pay the remaining fees. Friendless, disowned, alone and rejected. A failure.

"Stevie?"

Viv's voice cut through the cascade in his mind.

"Yeah, sorry Viv."

"Sit out of view of the camera. I'll call first and explain you are here. Then, you can come and talk if she's OK with it."

She won't be. "Yes. Do that."

"Ready?"

"I'm ready."

The familiar tones of Skype making a video call filled the room, and then ...

"Vivienne!"

"Hi, Mum."

"Happy Easter." She paused. "Are you alone? Where is Zoe?"

"She's not here."

"Where is she?"

"Look, Mum, Steven's here. He needs to talk to you."

Their mother started to speak. Viv cut in.

"No, don't say 'no'. Just hear him out, OK? For me. It's important for me."

"I wasn't going to say 'no', Vivienne. Why would I say no?"

Steven stiffened.

"Because you're not talking to him?" Viv said, raising her intonation to make the line a question.

"That's not how it is, love. He's not speaking to me."

"What?" Steven jumped in front of the camera.

"Steven! It is so good to see you!"

"What?" he asked again, sitting down.

"I am so pleased you are willing to speak to me at last."

"Willing to speak to you?"

"Yes."

"Mum, I ..." He looked at Viv. "It's you that stopped speaking to me."

Now it was her turn to look confused. "No, Steven. I did as Zoe said and have been waiting for you to speak with me."

"What?" Steven stared at her. "You disowned me!"

There was a crunch of gravel. Both Steven and Viv turned their heads to see Zoe's car pull into the driveway.

09:59

The door to the living room swung open silently, any melodramatic impact made by the force dissolved by the smooth mechanism. Zoe strode in and scanned the room quickly. Her eyes fell on the laptop screen, bright with the image of her mother's face.

"What are they saying to you?" she roared, stepping forward and immediately pushing Steven aside.

"Zoe?" their mother asked. "What's going on?"

Zoe glared at Steven, her face flaring red.

"What have they said to you, Mum? Is he lying, again?"

"No!" Steven stood firm. "You don't get to do this. You've been lying to her the whole time."

"Me?"

"You told me she disowned me."

"Why are you making shit up, Steven? If you wanted to leave early, you could have just gone. Is Alistair lonely? Is that it? Has he been calling you, asking you to cut short your visit with Viv so that you can go back to your home with him?"

"Alistair?" his mother shrieked. "Are you still with that bastard? Is this true?"

Zoe smirked.

"Mum, that's not what this is about. My living arrangements aren't what are important right now. And why do you care? You cut ties with me. My life has nothing to do with you at all now, does it? Our interactions stopped the second you decided to stop funding my education, so really, you have no right whatsoever to tell me how I should lead my life."

"Stevie," Viv whimpered.

Zoe glared at him.

"What are you on about, Steven?" His mum's tinny voice came through the laptop speakers with surprising clarity. "I never disowned you. I have never stopped paying for your tuition."

Steven stopped. Turning from Zoe to the screen, he stared.

"What?"

"I said I never stopped paying for your tuition. And disowning you? What are you talking about? I was telling you a moment ago that I'd been waiting for you to contact me."

"What?"

"Steven, why are you saying these things? It has been very hard for me to keep it up. My savings are almost gone. Every month, I send your money to Zoe as we arranged. Money for your schooling, money for your living expenses! What are you accusing me of?"

"Fuck," Steven stammered. He looked at Zoe, at her smooth mask of condescension. "Are you fucking kidding me? Zoe?"

His sister smirked again.

"You two-faced cunt! You fucking cunt!" He'd never used that word before.

Zoe strode over. Aggressively, she pushed him, shoving him unprepared against the nearest wall.

"You deserved it, you fucking faggot."

Steven's mind raced, his thoughts cascading into each other like exploding brick work after a bomb. How long had it been? How much money had it been? Well over fifty thousand pounds in tuition fees alone, and tens of thousands more in his struggle to live. The nights trying to cope with the insecurity, the times he'd had to borrow money, the multiple simultaneous jobs driving him into the ground with stress and worry.

The night he had been raped.

He pushed her away from him. "If you lay your hands on me one more time, I *will* hit you."

Steven's focus was purely on his sister, now. Somewhere, his mind was aware of his mother calling out for them both to calm down and his little sister curled on the sofa, crying, but he couldn't pay them any attention.

10:02

Zoe pushed him again. It was a test, he could sense, to see what he would do, what he was capable of.

He slapped her hard against her face. The sting in his hand was a mere reflection of how her cheek would feel.

This was long overdue.

"Viv, call the police," Steven managed. "Do it now."

Then Zoe struck him, her hand viciously streaking through the air to bite, claw-like, into his forehead. She grabbed at his hair and forced it back, slamming his head on the wall. Steven kicked out, catching his sister in the shin with his bare foot. It wasn't well executed or particularly strong, but she stumbled and let go of her grip.

"Get away, Zoe," he warned.

"Scared of a girl, Steven?"

She launched again, attempting to pummel him across the face, but he was ready. This time he stepped aside, avoiding the first of her blows and opening her up to a punch of his own. His fist met the top of her arm, connecting with full force. Zoe gasped.

Behind her, Steven could see that Viv had reached the phone. As Zoe attacked once more, her nails catching him in his neck, Vivienne dialled.

"Hello, Police?"

10:03

Zoe moved with impressive speed. Turning her attention from her brother, she spun and snatched the handset from the younger girl. Taking a quick breath, she spoke:

"Hello, yes, please, my brother is attacking me! I need help, my younger sister is here, too. We're scared. Please come immediately."

Steven watched, open-mouthed as she gabbled out her address. When she'd hung up, she snarled at him. "Looks like you're getting arrested."

Steven leaned on his knees and breathed. His neck oozed blood from a vicious scrape and his forehead stung, the wound there probably no better. Zoe, for her part, was unharmed. Of course she was—despite his rage, he'd not really wanted to hurt her.

It hadn't been the same the other way around.

"Viv, we're leaving. Get your things."

"You stay there, Vivienne," Zoe spat. "Get up, Steven. We're not done."

"Fuck off, Zoe."

Steven glanced at the laptop. Was his mum still there? Was she witnessing everything? He couldn't see.

Zoe's kick was unexpected. With painful force, the stiletto toe of her slingback dug hard into his thigh. As he crumpled, Steven's mind jumped to thoughts of the shoe; the same ones she had hit Viv with the night before, a pair of Louboutins that cost as much as a month's rent. Paid for with money she'd stolen from him.

He groaned. "Are you fucking serious?"

Her second kick he caught, knocking her off balance. He scrambled to his feet and kicked back out at her. This time, he didn't hold back, and his sister fell from the attack.

"Stay down, Zoe. I don't want to fight you."

"I hate you!" she screamed, coming at him once more.

Stunned, Steven defended himself.

10:09

The arrival of the police put an end to the brawl. Despite his best efforts to keep his sister at bay, and with occasional breaks where the physical fighting was replaced with insults and vicious words, Zoe had done her all to excise her anger on him. Steven ached and stung, red welts and bleeding scratches a regular pattern on his bare skin.

"Sir," the police officer said. He shook his head slowly. "If you'd come into the kitchen with me, please."

Steven followed the other man. "She attacked me. I was trying to defend myself. She went mad."

"I'll take your statement, sir, and we'll make sense of it."

Spying a female officer already talking to Zoe on the sofa, Steven nodded. "Yeah, sure."

10:46

"Would you like a lift to the train station, sir?" the officer asked. Steven pushed his glass of water away and nodded silently.

Already, Viv had packed his bag for him, quietly doing as she'd been asked to ease the situation. Zoe still hovered in the dining room. She and Steven had not made eye contact once in the last half an hour.

"Yeah, thanks."

"And you're sure you don't want to press charges?"

The police had believed Steven's account more readily than he'd expected. No doubt, however, they'd asked Zoe the same. No doubt her response had been different.

"It's fine, she's my sister. It's a sibling thing, I guess."

"You're able to get home?"

"I'll sort it out."

The policeman nodded and together, Steven and the officer left the house.

"You fucking gay! I hope you get HIV and die of AIDS!" Zoe shrieked as he walked past her. Steven shuddered.

"Stevie?" Viv was at his side. "What's going to happen?"

"I don't know, but Viv, I'll sort it." He hugged her. "I'll talk to Mum, and we'll sort it. We'll sort everything, I promise. Just," Steven looked back at the house, "be safe, OK?"

"I'll be fine."

"Are you sure?"

"I'm sure."

Steven sucked in a breath. For a moment he considered telling the police about Vivienne, about the abuse. They'd act—having seen what they saw today, they'd have no choice. They'd take Viv to the station and then ...

And then she'd end up 'in the system'. Care homes. A mother on the other side of the world. Zoe with guardianship and enough money for the best lawyers.

Steven nodded slowly.

"I love you. I'll speak to you very soon."

"I love you, too."

"Happy Easter."

Viv smiled. "Happy Easter."

"Sir." The policeman gently pressed. "If you'd get into the car."

11:12

"Ray? Man, thanks for answering the phone."

"What's up?"

"I need to borrow some money. It's really important, and I have no one else I can ask. I need a hundred quid, like right now."

"What? What's going on?"

"It's for a train ticket. I'll explain later. Can you just buy me the ticket? You can do it online and I can pick it up here."

Ray paused. "Yeah, sure, man. No problem. Where'd you need to get to and where from?"

11:55

Steven found his seat. He sighed. This was to be the first of four trains and a bus. Easter Sunday was not the best day to travel.

"Happy Easter!" The woman next to him smiled brightly. "I'm off to see my grandchildren."

"Happy Easter. That's nice."

"You?"

He snorted sardonically. "Just going home after visiting family for the weekend. Need to get back to Aberdeen today."

"Oh, well, good luck. Would you like a piece of chocolate?"

12:40

His phone hadn't lit up with his mum's number for more than a year. Steven put his sandwich down on to the bench beside him and picked up.

"Mum."

"Steven, are you alright?"

"I'm fine. A little scratched, a little bruised."

"I mean about you. How you feel."

"How I feel? I don't really know. It's been a bit of a rough weekend, and I don't think you know the half of it."

"Steven, I never disowned you. I never stopped wanting to talk to you. Zoe told me you were angry, that you didn't want to speak to me because of our ... differences. She told me it was best to give you space, that once you'd sorted everything in your head, you'd call me. I've been waiting for so long."

Steven shuddered. He'd reached that conclusion an hour or so earlier, but hearing it confirmed was affecting.

"She told me the opposite. She said that you never wanted to speak to me again, that you thought I was disgusting. She told me that you'd cut me off completely and stopped paying anything towards my fees or my life."

"No! I'd never do that. You are my son."

Steven breathed deeply. "Mum, I'm sorry. I shouldn't have listened to her. I should have called you. At least asked you to say it to my face. I just never thought ..."

"I understand. I'm sorry, too. This fault is mine."

"There's worse, Mum. We need to talk about Vivienne."

"Viv? Yes, Zoe told me that you had been struggling with her being your responsibility, that it was affecting your studies. That's why I arranged for her to live with your older sister."

"What? No, that's more lies." Steven choked. "What has she done?"

"Try to remain calm, Steven. Tell me what you wanted to tell me about Viv."

"Zoe's abusing her, Mum. She's hitting her and ruling over her like an evil queen from a Disney movie. I had suspected for a while, but this weekend, I saw it. She hit Viv with a shoe."

"I ..."

"You don't need to say anything, not really. I mean, what is there to say?"

"There's lots to say, Steven. That's the whole problem. We haven't spoken in too long and now ..." He could tell she was crying in the background, even though she kept her voice firm. "I will not have Vivienne in trouble."

"Zoe's been manipulating us all. I don't understand her. She's evil."

"Steven, she's still your sister!"

"Mum, seriously? She attacked me today. You saw it. She called the police on me and tried to get me arrested."

"That doesn't make her evil. Don't go too far with the things you say."

"Fine, I'm sorry." Steven felt like a contrite child.

"And you are a big boy. Yes, there are lots of problems she has caused for you that we do need to look at, but right now, there's Viv."

"Agreed."

"Steven, I want you to get her out of there. I want you to take her away from Zoe."

Out of the window, his next train pulled into the station.

14:11

Sleeping was impossible. Bright sunlight, a packed train and the constant flood of thoughts made even the lightest rest elusive. Steven sighed and flicked his way through another level of a mindless mobile phone game.

Stevie. It's me.

Viv? It wasn't her number.

Hey. What's this phone you are texting me on?

My old phone. Zoe has taken my phone and laptop. She doesn't want me texting anyone.

What's happening?

She doesn't want me to speak to Mum. She unplugged the phone line. I don't know what she is planning. Help!

Stay calm. Just play along with her so that she treats you OK. Hide your passport and other important things you don't want her to take.

Passport? Am I going somewhere?

I'm just being careful.

OK. Gotta go.

Yes, Viv, Steven thought, you might need your passport. If going back to Mum is the only way.

15:28

Steven's phone lit up again.

It's got worse. She rang the police officer again and reported that her head was hurting so much she is going to the hospital. It's a lie so she can press charges against you. She forced me to tell the police that you hit her in the head.

Great.

It's OK. Don't worry, I'll handle it. Thanks for letting me know.

Love you.

Love you, too.

Steven stared at the phone. There was at least four hours of travel left, but he couldn't ignore it anymore. He phoned Alistair.

It went to voicemail.

Al, it's me. Look, forget the money. Other things have happened that are more important. You need to talk to me. We can worry about the money another time. Please.

The minutes ticked by. Steven watched as his phone flicked through 15:29, 15:30, 15:31. "Come on, Al," he breathed.

Then it rang.

"Alistair!" he exulted. He hadn't realised how much he missed his boyfriend.

"What's going on?"

Steven laughed nervously. "Oh, you're going to love it. So much vindication for you."

"What are you talking about?"

"Zoe went fully mental. We've had a fight. The police were called. I'm all beat up and my face stings so badly."

"What?!"

"Oh, there's more. She's stolen so much money from me." Steven chuckled. "So much more than even you."

"Steven!"

"Sorry, too soon? I've had a really fucked up weekend."

"Where are you?"

"On a train, still in England, but only just. I think we're coming up on Berwick-upon-Tweed pretty soon."

"You're coming home?"

"Yes. I was driven to the train station in a police car and 'advised' by the officer to go straight back to Aberdeen."

"Fuck!"

"Anyway, it gets worse. The reason this all happened."

"Go on."

"She's been abusing Viv. Hitting her, treating her like a slave."

"Shit! No. Is Viv with you?"

Steven smiled, suddenly aware that if he had kidnapped his little sister, Alistair wouldn't have blinked.

"No. I probably should have brought her, but the police and everything."

"Yeah, I get it."

"Mum wants me to get her, though."

"Your mum? You spoke to your mum?"

"It's a bit of a story ..." Steven began.

17:05

In Edinburgh, Steven transferred onto the replacement bus. They were due in to Dundee at 18:40, and then it was only just over an hour until he could meet Alistair at the train station. His signal had given out eventually, but the conversation with Al had been exactly what he needed. Now, the mountain he had to climb didn't feel quite so insurmountable.

At least they had an outline of a plan. A plan that had involved another conversation with his mother. It had felt strange to call her. Strange, but also right. Steven realised that even though his sister had managed to plant another larger wedge between them, probably forever destroying their relationship, she had inadvertently given him back his mother and, with that, a connection back home.

He didn't feel so lost.

Now he needed some short-term finance to resolve the situation.

"Ray," he said as soon as his friend picked up, "I'm really going to push our friendship here."

Ray didn't ask too many questions and promised to transfer the money immediately. His online banking, it seemed, didn't have the same imaginary bank holiday problems that Alistair had conjured up the day before. A thousand pounds was a lot to borrow from a friend, but with the assurance from his mother that it would be paid back within a week, Steven felt confident it wouldn't become a problem.

19:54

Alistair hugged him tightly. "You look a fucking mess."

"Thanks."

The Scot stood back. "Seriously, what did she do to you? I was expecting you to be a bit battered, but you're fucked. Have you even looked in a mirror?"

"No."

"Well, don't! Actually, I should take a few pictures, just in case." Alistair pulled out his phone and walked around Steven in a circle, preserving the evidence.

"Thanks."

"Seriously, don't look at it until tomorrow. Hopefully some of it will have gone down by then. You look like you did a couple of rounds with a tiger."

"Yeah, she was all scratching and claws."

Alistair grinned salaciously. "Mmmmm."

"Oh, you're fucking disgusting."

"It's a joke. Lighten up. I'd rather do your mum than your evil sister."

"Also nice."

"You know what I mean."

"I'm not sure I do, Al. Anyway, can you carry this? My arm fucking hurts."

20:19

His own bed seemed like a sanctuary from a lifetime ago. Steven collapsed onto the sheets and sighed.

"You don't have time to relax," Alistair said. "You need to sort tomorrow out."

"I know."

"I can be some help." He opened his laptop. "Flights?"

"Just one for Viv. She's underage for flying alone, so make sure you tick whatever boxes it needs to let them know she needs the help of a flight attendant to make the journey."

"Aye, I know what I'm doing. What time do you want it?"

"Tomorrow night, hopefully."

"No can do. But the next morning, from Manchester at 11:40."

"That'll do."

"OK, give me a moment." There was some tapping, and a little sweating. Steven stared at the ceiling.

"I'm done," Alistair announced. "That's six hundred quid we're never getting back."

"It's not your money to start with, Al."

"Yeah, I know. Let's not do that."

"Not right now, but we will when this is all done."

"Great, should I book myself a ticket to fuck off with, too."

"No."

They looked at each other for a moment. Alistair turned back to the screen.

"And you need a train ticket back to fucking Sheffield. That is bloody stupid."

"Tell me about it. I could have really done without today's journey as it was, another seven hours or so back is going to kill me."

"Buy a decent book."

"Sure."

Steven waited patiently a little longer.

"There. Train done."

"Thanks. Now the hotel. I need the one across the road from Zoe's house. You can see it from the spare bedroom window."

"What's it called?"

"I can't remember. Google it."

"I got it. Shit, that's not cheap either."

"One night, Al, that's all."

"Fine. Anything else?"

Steven sighed. "Make me dinner?"

"I'll order take out, how's that?"

"Sounds perfect." Steven paused. "Al ..."

"Yeah."

"You didn't need to ask me my bank account details for any of that. Don't think I didn't notice."

"I know, look, I'm sorry."

"I know you are. I'm sorry, too. I should have stepped in earlier. Let's leave it though."

"You're the one who keeps bringing it up. I *am* leaving it."

Steven chuckled ruefully. "Yeah, sorry."

23:32

Exhausted, Steven made his way across the room. Tonight, Alistair's snoring, often so bothersome, made him feel comfortable and secure. In the bathroom, he flicked on the light and glanced into the mirror.

He winced.

The cuts weren't really painful, nor were they particularly bad, but they were very visible, and they had been made by his sister.

"You were meant to care about me," he whispered. "You were meant to look after me."

Her words rang in his ears. *I hope you get HIV and die of AIDS.*

Weeping, he sank onto the cold hard plastic of the toilet seat.

CHAPTER 20

Called Mum and told a lie. Don't react, just play along.
Steven rolled out of bed and tiptoed into the next room,
hoping Viv's text didn't mean plans needed to change. Thankfully,
the time difference was eight hours in his favour—despite it being
just short of six a.m. for him, his mother would have been up for
many hours.

"It's fine, Steven, I'm not so old that I can't tell when my youngest
daughter is spinning lies, especially those fed to her by another."

"What did she say?"

"Oh, Zoe is apparently in a coma."

"What?"

"Her horrible brother, the one that attacked her, hit her so hard
that she suffered a serious head trauma. She's in hospital now, unable
to communicate while doctors work hard on her recovery."

"Zoe actually thought you'd believe that?"

"Viv told it quite well, to be fair. She pretended to be concerned
and scared, although I'm sure some of that was real, just not for the
reasons Zoe intended." She sighed. "I am still unsure how to react to
all of this. Part of me believes it is all a dream, some crazed imagining
that my mind has come up with. Sleep didn't help, I got very little."

"I'm sorry, Mum."

"For once, Steven, you are not the centre of my concern but,
rather, my agent in this matter. Did you manage to make the
arrangements we discussed?"

"I have a plane ticket for Viv. She will be leaving from Manchester airport tomorrow before noon. I'll make sure she's on the plane."

"Good, thank you." She thought for a moment. "Zoe is setting up the situation to drive a new wedge between us, Steven. I am not falling for it, despite her theatrics, but it means you must be open and honest with me. If something goes wrong, you must inform me right away."

"I understand."

"I pretended to believe Vivienne, for her sake. Assuming Zoe was watching the call, she will think your younger sister has convinced this addled old woman."

"A coma?"

"She understands the medical technicalities of such a thing, so I'm sure the words she gave Vivienne to say were correct and convincing."

"For a doctor, she's seen too many American movies, Mum."

"Perhaps, but these things do happen. Viv described your 'attack' on her sister and some of it was quite violent. Did you really hit her with a pan?"

"No, but I should have."

"Violence is never the answer, Steven. You do need to remember that."

"Mum, I'm not violent."

"There have been times. It is easier for men to slip like that."

"Seriously, Mum, please. Let's not start a new argument."

"Fine. I will keep my opinions to myself. Again, the chattering of an addled old woman. You will tell me when you arrive back in Sheffield?"

"I will."

"Good. Then have a safe journey."

Steven stared at his breakfast, unable to put the cold cereal into his churning stomach. What was Zoe thinking? Even if she convinced their mother that he really had attacked her so badly that it led to serious hospitalisation, there's no way that would pass with the authorities. It was unhinged.

But then, what about this situation wasn't?

"Good morning. Feeling ready for your adventure, Mister Kidnapper?" Alistair leaned on the wall.

"There's too much waiting and doing nothing."

"Ah, the stuff we never see James Bond doing."

"I won't even get to Sheffield until after five p.m. tonight. That's almost twelve hours before I can actually *do* anything."

"Relax. It's not like the enemy is aware of your coming."

"Oh, you are enjoying the drama of this a little too much. It's serious. That's my little sister we are saving."

"Your little sister has been living in these awful conditions—and they are horrific, Steve, I don't take that away—for months and months. Another day isn't going to break her."

"I should have been more aware."

"You were living a life and, thanks to Zoe, a lot of it was very hard, if I remember right. Don't beat yourself up about missing some of the clues. You're there now, right?"

"Right."

"Now, stop being a moaning bastard and make me a cup of tea while I piss."

"Lovely."

Alistair waved as he disappeared to the bathroom.

Smiling to himself, Steven got up and went to put the kettle on.

————

The train journey was as torturous as Steven had expected. Despite having a decent seat on a train with no changes, he couldn't settle. For a while he tried to study, at other times read. Even listening to music or trying to watch videos on his phone couldn't distract him. The hours passed by as if moving through treacle, each minute stretched to many times its natural length.

Sat in one of Alistair's hoodies, Steven neither looked, nor smelled, quite like himself. It was a small disguise that had come with some good-natured teasing by his boyfriend, but it would be enough that should Zoe see him at all, she'd not look twice. She didn't expect him to be in Sheffield, and she wouldn't recognise him in any case.

The hotel was very accommodating. Explaining that he wanted a view of the road, they switched his room so that he had one that could peer directly into Zoe's living room. He switched off the lights and sat by the window, watching as his two sisters moved about for the evening. Their interactions were minimal, with both doing what they could to stay out of the other's way.

Alistair had jokingly suggested he buy some cheap kids binoculars to compliment his night as a spy and Steven had dismissed the jibe. Now, however, he wished he'd taken it a little more seriously. A clear view into Zoe's house would have been valuable.

She wants me to call Mum again tonight and has briefed me on what to say. Viv texted. **What's happening?**

I'm in the hotel across the street.

What?!

I've come to get you. I'm sorry I can't tell you more, just in case something happens and Zoe ends up with your phone, but if you are worried or something happens you think is dangerous, just run across the road and come here. Come to room 19.

You're across the street?

There was a flutter of curtains and Steven saw his sister's face staring out at him. He resisted waving, just in case.

I can't see you.

I can see you. Don't worry.

She waved.

Viv, stop it!

Wow, you are actually there!

Steven wondered how it felt to be her. As a young teenager, this sort of intrigue must be exciting, but as a victim of abuse, hoping for rescue … He shuddered. He knew he'd raised her hopes; now he couldn't fail.

Pack a backpack. Make sure you have your passport and other documents. Bring the things that are important to you, but not too much.

I will.

Now, stop texting. Unless something changes, I can't get you tonight, OK? It'll be tomorrow. Just do what Zoe asks of you and then get to bed.

Really? OK. Tomorrow. I will.

She disappeared from the window and Steven could make out her moving around the room. Packing, no doubt.

He called his mum.

"Zoe plans to get Viv to call you again tonight. She said she's been prompted what to say, so expect more lies."

"Do you want to hear it?"

"What? How?"

"Steven, I am capable of using technology. I can speak to them on one thing and use my normal phone to connect to you. The quality will not be great, and you will have to stay silent, but you will be able to hear."

"Yes, do that."

"I will call you when they do, then."

It was becoming ever more clandestine. Steven tensed. He was hungry; the train station sandwich had been sorely lacking, and he'd intended to get food when he reached the hotel, but now he didn't dare to move. Would Zoe get Viv to make the call now? Soon?

His wait was not long. Again, the time difference between Malaysia and the UK worked in his favour—delay too long, and Zoe ran the risk that her mother could stay awake no longer and would have to finally go to bed.

He saw his sisters gathering in the living room a minute before his own phone rang.

"Viv sent me a message to ask if she could call. Are you listening?"

"Listening and able to see. I think what I'm seeing is Zoe arranging notes."

"Notes?"

"She's written down what she wants Viv to say."

His mother laughed. "How organised."

There was the sound of another phone ringing, and Steven flicked his own to mute.

"Has she woken from her coma?" his mum asked almost immediately. Steven applauded in his own mind; it was the convincing rushed tone of a concerned mother caring about her eldest daughter.

"No. She's still in the hospital."

"And you?"

"Daniel brought me some dinner, but he had to leave."

Daniel, Steven noted in the back of his mind, had actually been strangely absent since the restaurant dinner.

"Are you OK, Vivienne?"

"I'm fine. A little worried for Zoe."

"She'll be fine. I'm sure Steven didn't hurt her too badly."

At this, Zoe hopped up and down and began scribbling furiously. Steven saw her hold up another piece of paper.

"Oh no, you didn't see it," Viv relayed dutifully, "he was so angry."

More writing.

"It was because of Sarah. Zoe had invited Sarah to have a meal with us because she hoped that she could convince Steven to drop this silly thing about being gay and go out with Sarah. She is very beautiful, and Zoe was sure that he would fall for her."

"And?"

"Well, he was angry. Furious. He said that he didn't choose to be gay, that Sarah was a very nice woman, but he wasn't interested. He said he loved Alistair, Mum."

"Yes, well ..."

Steven tensed at the undertone in his mum's voice. How much was for show, how much was her real thought, and how much was her trying to temper because she knew he was listening?

"So, when she came back, Steven was ready for her," Viv read from another prompt. "He was waiting by the door, already angry. She hadn't come back that night because she'd been scared of him."

Ridiculous. If you are going to lie to the woman, at least make sure it lines up with the events that she witnessed herself.

"She was just defending herself from Steven's wild attack," Viv insisted. "I don't know, Mum. I just don't think I want to see Steven again."

At this, Viv glanced towards the window. Steven winced, hoping she wouldn't inadvertently provide Zoe with a clue as to what was happening.

"Well, love, families fight sometimes. Not usually with such violent passion, but as you grow up, you'll realise that there are some things that even adults struggle with."

"Right, yeah."

"It's late here for me, Vivienne, and it must be getting late there for you. Don't you have to get up early for school?"

"It's the Easter holidays."

"Well, even so, you should still get up. Don't become lazy just because you have a few days off."

"Yes, Mum."

"Go to bed now and get some good rest. Try not to worry about Zoe and Steven. I'm sure Zoe will recover overnight and she'll be home in the morning."

"I hope so."

"Just be a good girl, a good grown-up girl, and get yourself to bed now, OK?"

"Yes, Mum."

"And let me know as soon as Zoe wakes up. As soon as you know. Even if it's the middle of the night for me."

"I will."

"I love you, Vivienne. I miss you."

"You too, Mum."

Steven watched as Zoe pushed the laptop closed and took himself off mute.

"Sarah?" asked his mother.

"She's a nice woman and she deserves a better friend than Zoe. It was Sarah who did her best to calm Zoe down the previous night."

"And is she very beautiful?"

"Mum, let's not go there. If we're going to move forward with our relationship and not lose it again, you are going to have to accept me for who I am."

"And I do. But you'll excuse me if there's no love lost between me and Alistair. I don't think he's the right man for you, even if it is a 'man' you want."

"Al is a good man." Or, at least, he can be. Once more, the worry about his tuition fees rolled through his mind. Deal with it later. Once all this is done.

"Well, either way, we will let Zoe play out this ridiculous charade and tomorrow you will take Vivienne to the airport. I hope she understood my message to get sleep."

"It wasn't too subtle," Steven noted.

"To you, perhaps. To Zoe listening, it was little more than a worried mother flapping over her daughter."

"True."

"And now I will flap over my son. Get yourself some food and go to bed. You, too, have to get up at dawn."

"I will. Thanks, Mum."

"Thank you, Steven. We will talk again tomorrow."

———————

Backpack with essentials and your passport. That's all. Leave everything else behind. I will get you as soon as Zoe leaves for work.

Steven had been up for hours. He'd showered, dressed, and packed a long time earlier and was now sat in the lobby, a newspaper in front of him which, despite the time that had passed, was still largely unread.

He checked the clock on the wall. Zoe was due to leave in less than thirty minutes. If there was one thing he could trust his sister to do, it was get to work early. She'd always been a stickler for punctuality.

He'd timed the taxi to arrive just as Zoe was going to leave. He hoped the driver had the same respect for time as his sister.

OK. Viv's response came a moment later.

Steven sipped on his coffee. He really wasn't feeling like drinking it but knew he had to keep his own energy levels up.

The taxi arrived twelve minutes early. Steven swore to himself and jumped up, intercepting the driver before he reached the desk.

"I'm going to be another ten minutes or so. Are you OK to wait in the car park?"

The driver nodded and went back to his car. Steven retuned to the seat.

As the minutes ticked by, he could feel his anxiety rise. He concentrated on his breathing as the hands moved round the clock face, in for the first three seconds, out for the next three.

When Zoe's car passed the window, he leapt up, grabbed his case and ran to the taxi where he dropped it into the boot.

"Need to pick my sister up across the road," he said, pointing. "Can you pull up alongside."

"Sure." The taxi driver started to move and Steven ran.

Stop panicking. You have time. Zoe's not coming back.

And so what if she did? She couldn't physically stop him. Not this time.

Viv opened the door with a wide smile before he knocked.

"Come on, that's our taxi."

"Are we going back to Aberdeen?" Bright hope shone in her eyes.

"Talk in the car." Steven grabbed her case and moved quickly to the back of the vehicle. His heart was still pounding, even though to any outside observer it was just a brother picking up his little sister.

Once the car had properly started its way, Steven relaxed. He leaned over to his sister and wrapped her in his arms.

"I'm so sorry. Sorry that this happened to you. Sorry that I didn't get you out earlier. Just sorry."

"It's OK, Stevie. I'm not your responsibility."

"You are. You really are. You know, when you were a baby, I took on that responsibility. I was awful of me to forget it."

"Big bro, you do great."

He looked at her, admiring how she could be so positive despite the hardships she had endured. The image of Zoe hitting her with the heel of a shoe flashed before him again. He shook his head.

"So, where are we going?" she asked.

"Not Scotland, sorry. Manchester at first."

"Manchester?"

"To the airport. Viv, you have to go home."

Vivienne looked stunned. "Home to mum? To Malaysia? No!"

"I'm sorry, I know you've become used to being here, but if you stay here Zoe will do everything she can to get me arrested. Mum is going to look after you."

"But I don't want to go there. I've not lived in Malaysia for years. It won't feel like home."

He hugged her tighter. "It will. It'll take a bit of time, for sure, but you'll make new friends and trust me, the schooling is fine. If you want to come and study here like I did, then I'll help."

"When I'm eighteen? That's years away." She started to cry.

"You won't have to wait all that time, probably. But for a bit, you have to go and live with Mum. She's really looking forward to seeing you and I'm sure you want to see her."

"I do, it's not Mum, it's just ... I've got a life here. I mean, I knew I'd probably be leaving Sheffield, so I was prepared for that, but not the whole UK. I want to live with you. I'll be good."

"It's not about being good. Oh, Viv, I know you'd be good, I don't have any worries like that. But Zoe just wouldn't let it happen. She's not going to take this in a good way and she's still technically your legal guardian over here."

"No, I don't want to go."

"I'm sorry little sister, but you have to."

"No." The tears came quickly now. Steven held her close and for a while, they said nothing.

"The plane is to Singapore. Mum's going to meet you there, and I bought you a ticket with one of the stewardesses as a chaperone, so they're expecting you on the flight and will look after you all the way there."

"I don't need someone to help me on a plane."

"Probably not, but it's the rules."

Viv sniffed.

"It's a long trip, Viv. We have a little time at the airport, so I'll buy you something to keep you occupied. A book or two."

"I have my books, remember?"

"Yes, I do. I wasn't sure if you'd pack them."

"You said 'anything important'. They're important."

Steven smiled. She was, after all, still just a kid. It touched him that she considered the books an essential item.

"You *do* have your passport, don't you?" he blurted.

"Of course." She waved it at him. "I'm not dumb."

"No, no. I know."

"What will Zoe do?"

"She'll rage and rant for a while, but ultimately there's nothing she can do. She might try to send the police to me, but I'll just explain that you're with your mother. Guardianship in the UK is one thing, but it doesn't make Zoe more important than your own mum."

"She'll come after you."

"Herself? I'm not scared of Zoe, Viv."

"Are you sure?"

Steven stiffened, then smiled. "I'm sure."

Viv cried again. "It's been so long. I didn't think anyone cared about me or was coming. I couldn't tell you things. I was so frightened that it'd just make things worse."

"I know." Steven's voice was soft and understanding.

"Once she hit me with the hoover pipe, because I hadn't done the carpet right."

Steven winced.

"And there was so much washing to do. I know it was just the two of us, but she'd go to the gym and use a fresh towel every day, plus the clothes. She just didn't care that it made an extra washing load. And all her clothes were delicates that wouldn't go in the dryer. I wasn't allowed to have them hanging up, because it looked bad, even in the utility room. I had to put them up after she went out and then take them down before she got home. It was so hard."

Steven said nothing, letting it pour out of her. Not once, though, did he release her from his embrace. By the time they arrived at the airport, he'd heard much more than he ever wanted to believe.

He tipped the taxi driver well, noting to himself that the man's eyes were also lined with tears. A moment passed between them, then: "Good luck. You did the right thing."

———

Once the air stewardess led Viv away, Steven let out a breath he felt he'd kept in for days. For forty minutes, they had window-shopped and played in the small pre-customs area of the airport, squeezing every last minute with each other to add another fun memory. They didn't speak about it, but both knew it would be a long time, months at least, before they saw each other again.

There was no more talk of Zoe, nothing even remotely negative. Big bars of chocolate and a silly cuddly bear were bought, and laughter shared—the darkness firmly banished.

For Steven, it didn't quite last long enough before they were met by Millie, the tall and bright woman who would be chaperoning Viv on the flight, but nonetheless he was pleased it was all done.

He texted, rather than called his mum with the flight details and confirmation that Viv was definitely on her way. Then he headed to the adjacent train station—one change in Edinburgh and he'd be home again. Mission complete.

On my way home. See you this evening.

All successful? Alistair asked.

She's on her way.

Congratulations. See you soon.

On the train, Steven pulled out his book. With so much weight lifted, it was surprisingly easy to read.

———

"Hey Ray," Steven said, greeting his friend before hugging Alistair. "Thank you so much for the bailout. I really owe you."

"It was nothing," Ray said. "Although please do give it back when you have it, because it wasn't completely nothing."

Steven grinned. "Sure. My mum's already transferred the money, it'll just take a day or two to clear. You'll get it as soon as it does."

"Say no more." Ray led them out of the station. "And it's movie night, by the way. No complaints because I picked them all."

"All?"

"A fun, relaxing, Ray triple bill. I won't complain if you fall asleep in the last one, but give the first two some respect. Plus pizza, because I'm in the mood for pizza. You want beer?"

Steven hugged him. "Thanks, man."

"You're welcome." He turned to Al. "Did you at least clean the sheets in the spare room for me?"

"It'll only take me a few minutes. I'll do it while you order pizza. I want chicken wings as well, and garlic bread."

———

Steven stared at the note he had scribbled to himself in the middle of the night. It simply said: *Viv's tuition fees.*

The thought had come to him between movie two and movie three (which he had watched, without sleeping, all the way through). If Zoe had been stealing the money for his fees and maintenance this whole time, had she done the same for Viv? Certainly, Vivienne had been eating leftovers and scraps, but surely she'd been sent to the right school, the one Mum had picked out. Surely, her fees had been paid on time.

It took less than a minute to get the number for the school from the website. Would they be there in the middle of the Easter holidays? He had to try.

"Hi," he said when the phone was answered, "is it possible to speak to someone on your administration team? It's about my sister."

He waited while the right person was found, thankful that their training day schedule meant he'd picked the perfect time to call. It took a little work to explain that he was Viv's older brother, that he was calling on behalf of their mother who didn't speak much English, and he was checking the situation with her fees, making sure they were up to date.

"Vivienne's fees?" came the response, "your sister is on a full scholarship. There are no fees."

Steven's mind screamed. How much had Zoe stolen from their mother?

How had she had the audacity to treat their little sister the way she had.

Ten minutes later, his mother called, answering his message. Her face was smiling but tearful.

"Mum, are you OK?"

"Yes, yes. Vivienne is here with me. We've just got home. Viv, love, go sort your things and let me speak to your brother."

Steven waited, waving once to his beaming sister before she disappeared from view.

"She seems happy."

"She's so thin, Steven. You didn't mention how thin she was."

"I didn't ..." Steven stopped. He hadn't noticed, was the truth.

"You didn't what?"

"There was enough going on, Mum. I didn't want to add any complications."

"My daughter's health is not a complication, Steven." She was openly weeping.

"Yes, I'm sorry."

"Zoe already called me. Last night, before Vivienne landed."

"Oh?"

"She said, that Viv had left and that she knew it had something to do with you. She was going to the police."

"What did you say?"

"I started with 'so, you woke up from your coma.'"

Steven laughed.

"Yes, that did throw her a little. She tried to backtrack, saying it hadn't been that bad and Viv had misunderstood the seriousness of it."

"Right."

"And then she lost her mask of pretence. I worry for her."

"What do you mean?"

"She screamed at me. 'If you and Steven think you've won by doing this, you're wrong. Don't forget I am her legal guardian. I can put your precious son in jail!'"

"She said that to you?"

"Sadly, yes."

"What did you say to that?"

"I told her good luck with that. I suggested she rethink her position. I reminded her I was Vivienne's mother, and she was little more than a legal guardian that I had trusted to look after my daughter while she was in the UK. I told her as Vivienne was no longer in England, that her guardianship no longer applied."

"So, she realised the truth."

"She had worked it out, I believe, but yes, I confirmed it for her then."

"Mum, you are crying, there's more."

"Steven, I never disowned you, you know that now."

"Yes."

"But I did disown her. Last night. While she was still screaming and ranting. I said, 'Steven and I have evidence of your crimes. Let's see who ends up behind bars, I dare you.'" She stiffened. "And then I told her that I no longer considered her my daughter or part of this family. I said that I did not raise a con woman and that we were cutting her out forever."

Steven sat, stunned. "Are you OK?"

"Honestly, no. But it is not your concern. This was my decision and I had made it many hours before I said it. It was not something that just came out in the heat of the moment."

"Mum, I'm sorry."

"No, Steven, *I* am the one who is sorry. Vivienne has already mentioned enough to let me know that Zoe mistreated you too, when you were a child."

"I ..."

"No, not for now. I understand. Maybe one day, though, you will tell me."

Steven nodded.

"I need to go. I must concentrate on Vivienne. She has been through a lot, we all have, but she is not OK. She has put on a brave face to get this far, but I fear she is going to crumble."

"She'll get better with time."

"She will also need care."

Steven nodded.

"Thank you, Steven. It has been a frightening and worrying time for me, so far away and learning all this. I appreciate everything you have done."

Steven blinked away his own tears and said nothing.

"We will talk soon, son."

———

Steven looked at his phone. There had already been multiple calls from Zoe, one from Daniel and a couple from unknown numbers. He flicked the switch to silent and slid the phone into his pocket.

CHAPTER 21

Steven had arrived at the small coffee shop early. Meeting his sister's boyfriend hadn't been something he'd planned to do. Daniel had been kind on the phone though, quick to explain that he just wanted a chat. That Zoe didn't know anything about it.

Nonetheless, it had taken Al almost an hour to reassure him that nothing bad could happen.

Too late, he had realised that this was the same place that he'd come to with Viv years before. Her first snowman. Her first snow.

Nothing had really changed. Even the art on the walls was the same.

"Thank you for seeing me." Daniel put his head into his hands. "I came to tell you that I'm sorry."

Steven leaned forward. Sorry? Of all the things he had expected to hear, that wasn't one of them.

"You're sorry?"

"I cared for Viv. *Care* for her. Present tense. I should have been more aware." Daniel sat up straight and sucked in a breath. "No, I was aware. I should have been more proactive. I have children of my own, you know. I should have been more fatherly and less whatever I was."

"She's safe now."

"Yes, no thanks to me. Look, Steven, I didn't want to really bother you. I'm not here to cause any problems, but I did want to come in person to let you know not to worry. Zoe's raging, of course, but that's no concern of yours. Or mine, really."

Steven looked up, the question unspoken.

"Yes, I left her. A couple of weeks after Viv was gone. It became too much and if I'm honest, my sympathy and acceptance of Zoe's behaviour was long gone. We rowed, a lot." Daniel smirked. "Not quite as passionately as you two, perhaps, but still, it wasn't quiet."

"Oh."

"You don't have to say anything. She threatened all sorts of things. Lots of things involving you, plenty about Viv, plus your mother, and me ... I think she even ranted about Alistair for a bit. It's all just talk."

"It doesn't feel like just talk."

"Trust me, she's powerless. She's in the wrong and she knows it. Her manipulation and lies only go so far. I made it clear that if she ever actually tried to do any more harm, I'd ensure her hospital found out about it all. She shrank a little after that. It was like I'd found the right switch."

Steven sank back. He hadn't realised just how tense he'd been.

"So, like I said, I just wanted to come, have a coffee, and apologise. I hope you can accept that."

"You came all the way here to say sorry in person?"

"Oh, it's nothing. I have a friend in Edinburgh I'd been planning to see for months. I was with him last night and I'm going back there after this. It's only a couple of hours." Daniel stood. "Look, we didn't know each other too well, but I'm proud to have met you. You did something that must have been really difficult, and you saved a young girl from a shitty life. It was the right thing to do and I'm just sorry I wasn't more of a man, myself. Please, do tell Viv I'm happy for her and if she ever wants to contact me, I'll be there."

"I will." Steven took his hand. There was something oddly formal in the handshake and then, without another word, Daniel turned and left.

————

Steven's hand trembled as he took out the phone and dialled the number. He took a deep breath. Two breaths. Three.

"Hello Zoe."

"Oh, you finally decided to speak to me."

"We're done. I want you to know we're done. Viv's safe with Mum and I ... I don't even have words. I haven't had the words."

"Oh fuck off, Steven. You're so pathetic. Did you practice this little speech in front of a mirror?"

Twice. "No."

"Sure. It's fine. You can fuck off with your little life. I don't care."

"I don't think that's true, but I'll take it."

"Oh, why would I care? You've always been just my pathetic little brother. You've been a burden on me my entire life."

"Burden? Yes, that's how I feel about you, too."

"Whatever." There was a silence. "Daniel left me." Was she sobbing?

"I know. I'm—"

"Don't say you're sorry. You're not sorry. You think I am the evil bitch and I deserve everything I got, but I'm not. I wasn't. I was trying my best. Trying to look after the money, look after Mum, look after Viv. I was even trying to look after you, not that you ever appreciated it."

"I did."

"Don't fucking patronise me."

Steven didn't feel like arguing anymore; that part of their relationship was done. "If this is your way of apologising, I'm not the person you should be speaking to. Call Mum. Call Viv. Let them hear it."

"I don't have time to call them."

"Well, I'm not your messenger." His heart was thumping. He'd never have thought of talking to her like this, even just a few weeks earlier. Assertive; that had been his plan.

"Have a nice life, Steven."

The connection went dead before he could even reply. Not that it mattered; he had told Zoe everything that needed to be said.

CHAPTER 22

Bright sunshine streamed in through the tiny window. Steven turned to Alistair and grinned.

"This seat is uncomfortable." Alistair pushed on the hard yellow plastic of the headrest in front of him. "Sorry," he muttered to the woman who turned to glare at him.

"It's a cheap plane seat, Al. What are you expecting?"

"For them to take the actual size of people into account?" He glanced down at Steven's legs. "It's alright for shortarses like you. Are all planes made with Asian guys in mind?"

"Wow, racism just as we get going. This weekend's going to be incredible."

"I'm not being racist, Steve. Tell me your genetic heritage doesn't contribute to you being short, and I'll hold up my dumb Scottish hand in apology, but you know it does and so do I."

Steven shrugged. "You have the aisle seat at least."

"Aye, because tripping up anyone walking past us is high on my list of fun things to do."

"Al, are you OK? You seem edgy."

"I'm fine. Sorry, we had to get up early and I'm still coming to terms with it. A couple of coffees when we land and I'll be fine."

"Coffee in a Parisian café," Steven mused. "I'm really excited."

"Good!"

The trip had been on a somewhat-spontaneous whim from Alistair. Weeks of hard work for them both meant that time together had been short. When Alistair suggested that they fly to Paris for a weekend away, Steven had agreed immediately.

"We haven't been on holiday together since that day trip to Edinburgh when you bought your mum a bag," he had pointed out.

It seemed like a lifetime ago.

It was time to relax, to forget problems, reconnect and forgive. It had been hard for Alistair to cope with paying back the huge sum he owed Steven and then, latterly, Steven's mother who had insisted she bail out the payment for her son's tuition fees. The six thousand pound gambling debt had shrunk to a little over four, and a splurge to take Steven to Paris didn't seem too extravagant.

Extravagant, yes, just not *too* extravagant.

"I can't believe I've lived in the UK for so many years and never been to Paris," Steven looked out of the window as if he'd be able to see France already.

"You've been busy."

"I feel like life is finally opening up. Like it's mine, truly mine, for the very first time."

"Then we'd better have a bloody good weekend!" Alistair kissed him and then went back to trying to stretch his legs.

Steven smiled; at least it was only a short flight.

————

"You should teach me French." Steven watched the waiter walk away, embarrassed that he'd not understood a word. "I feel like a cheesy tourist."

"You are a cheesy tourist." Al laughed. "And I think you speak enough languages already to not worry about French."

"If you say so, Mr. Tour Guide. Where are we going after this delicious food?"

"First the Louvre. I know you want to see the Eiffel Tower, but it's so better at night so we'll do that then. It sparkles at midnight."

"OK." Steven knew he was grinning like an excited child.

Alistair smirked. He had been to Paris many times and was obviously enjoying Steven's innocent enthusiasm. "It would be nice if you turned down the overeager tourist thing a little though. Just a notch."

Steven grinned again. "Just a notch. From like a ten to a nine?"

"From like a twelve to a five."

"Seven notches?"

"Seven is a good number of notches."

Steven nodded emphatically. "Will do."

He was finished with his food in record time, failing to find a balance between savouring both the pastries and the street-side café experience with his desire to get to the gallery. Across the table, Alistair sighed as he finished his coffee.

"Come on then. But remember, level five tourist excitement."

"Got it."

The louvre was everything Steven anticipated and more. Moving through the throngs of visitors, he spent time gazing at each of the pieces of artwork, again trying to find the balance between taking in the moment and continuing with his day. At *The Coronation of Napolean*, he paused, somewhat awed by the sheer size and detail of the painting. Then, he turned to Alistair and gasped.

"What is it?" Alistair asked.

"That woman. Oh my God, Al."

Alistair turned to look, none too subtly, at the slight woman in her thirties who stood at the head of a small group.

"And she is?"

"It's Sammi Cheng!"

"Sammi Cheng, as in your favourite singer, Sammi Cheng?"

Steven surged forward, switching effortlessly between eager tourist to adoring fan. "Sammi! Sammi!"

The famed performer turned and smiled at him, lifting her face that had been lowered, presumably, to avoid too much attention.

"It's really you!" Steven blabbered, his words cascading from him. "I've been a big fan since I was a child. It's incredible to see you. Would you mind me taking a photo with you? I'm so sorry, I'm embarrassing myself and bothering you on your trip."

"It's fine," Sammi said with a slight chuckle. "Really, yes, it's fine. Are you from Hong Kong, too?"

"No, I'm from Malaysia." Steven's breaths came quickly. "But I know all your songs. I've watched all your movies!"

She laughed. "OK, where's the camera?"

"Al! Al!" Steven waved frantically.

Alistair was already prepared. With an embarrassed raise of his hand, he indicated that he was ready.

There was a click, and then another, and Steven turned back to his idol.

"Thank you. Thank you so much, I'm sorry to have interrupted your day."

"It's fine." Sammi dipped her head gracefully and then turned back to her friends.

"Sammi Cheng!" Steven murmured to Alistair as they walked away. "Sammi Cheng!"

"Really? Is that who that was? You should have said."

Steven punched him on the arm.

"Come on, there's some more stuff here to show you before we go. Or has your art and beauty capacity been reached, overfilled with the majesty of Sammi Cheng?"

"No, show me more. But Al, Sammi Cheng!"

"Yes, Steve." He laughed. "Honestly, you are like a kid today."

"It's been fantastic, and it's only lunchtime!"

"Hungry?"

"No, not yet."

"Come on then, the tour continues."

―――――――

"Wait for me here, I just need to do something," Alistair said.

"What? Where?"

He laughed. "Nothing to worry about. Just hang about here for a bit. Five minutes, that's all. I'm not dumping you in central Paris and doing a runner, I promise."

"I'll be right here when you get back."

Steven looked at his phone while he waited. It was close to three p.m.; lunch had been relatively late, but a delightful spread of *fromage* and warm freshly-baked bread that had been hard to stop eating. Now he was full and eager to send messages to his friends about his chance encounter.

Sammi Cheng! He still couldn't believe it.

"Here!" Red-faced and panting, Alistair handed him a small bag. "Sorry I didn't wrap it."

Steven looked inside. It was Sammi's latest album. He'd heard it online, but hadn't had the chance to get the CD.

"Thank you, Sweetheart!" He hugged Al tightly.

As he opened the case, a note fluttered from inside. Reaching, Al grabbed it before it was snatched by the wind. "Here!"

Steven unfolded it.

A reminder of the day you met Sammi in Paris on our first holiday. Love you always, Alistair.

His eyes wet, Steven threw himself at Alistair. "I love you, too."

"Good, because I'm exhausted. Do you mind if we go back to the hotel for a nap before dinner? I'd rather be awake for the evening."

"Sounds fantastic. Just like everything else. Thank you so much for this trip. It's been the best!"

"And it's not over, yet. Though I'm not sure what we're going to do to beat meeting Sammi Cheng."

"Sammi Cheng! I spoke to Sammi Cheng!"

"Yes." Alistair grinned. "You did say."

———

Steven found Paris in the evening entrancing. He'd always enjoyed places with a vibrant nightlife and walking around the

French capital had him gazing at many exciting-looking venues. They had a couple of drinks but kept themselves generally sober, enjoying a relaxed feeling that still allowed them to take in the sights.

"Eiffel Tower?" he pushed for the one location that his guide seemed to be avoiding. They'd passed close a couple of times, but Al had refused to stop.

"In good time. I told you that we wanted to be there for midnight."

"It's gone half past eleven, now."

"Has it?" Alistair checked his phone. "Shit, OK. Well, we're in time. Come on."

They made their way back to the tower and found a quiet corner.

"Just wait here," Alistair said, "you'll see."

Sat on the ground, Steven relaxed. He leaned into his boyfriend's embrace and stared up at the enormous structure.

As midnight came, the lights on the tower changed, turning the night into the promised glitter of sparkling stars. Alistair smiled and Steven sucked in a breath.

"It's beautiful." Steven turned to Alistair, determined to kiss him in this precious moment, and found the other man already staring at him.

Alistair fumbled, pulling something from his pocket. Steven looked down.

"Will you marry me, Steve?" the Scot asked, a wedding band in his hand.

Without a thought, Steven kissed him. "Yes."

CHAPTER 23

Rushing, Steven threw his lab coat into the locker, grabbed his bag and clicked the door shut. He had grown to hate Thursdays.

There were only twenty minutes between the end of his shift at the hospital and the beginning of his one as a waiter. He knew he should probably discuss the problem with May. She, unlike Sophie, was more forgiving with the time and if he turned up half an hour late for the restaurant, it wouldn't have too much of an impact, but then that half an hour, even literally just thirty minutes, would make enough of an dent on his weekly money to upset him. No, it was better that he arrive slightly sweaty and needing to make a quick change in the back room before smoothing his hair and appearing all sprightly for the customers.

He didn't really want half an hour, anyway. What he wanted was a week off. Two. Maybe a month.

Lunch had been short, too. A sandwich crammed into his mouth while he went back over his revision notes.

Life was definitely too busy.

What had he and Al been thinking, adding a civil partnership ceremony into the mix?

"Sorry, sorry," he said, running past May to get changed. "Thursdays are so tight!"

"It's fine, Steven, really. Please, catch your breath. Anyway, it's looking like a slow night—not too many bookings."

At least he had some understanding friends.

By the time his first break came, however, the prediction had proven false. No matter the workload, though—the tips had been good and the bump up on his pay was important. One family, two young kids, their parents and the wealthy-looking grandparents, had left him almost thirty percent. He'd been pleased that his shining personality and general good service had paid off.

How does Al have so many friends? The text was from Claire, his best woman. She'd been enthusiastic about helping him with the organisation of the ceremony, even, at one point, offering to be the person to speak to his mother about flying over with Viv. Though it was a kind offer, his sense of morality and friendship had meant that he wouldn't put her through that.

Twenty guests each, remember, we don't have too much money.

I know. I'm just trying to get him to pare his list down.

Al is gregarious and likeable, thought Steven. That's why he has so many friends, and that's why he can't choose between them.

Good luck. Can't chat, need to get back to work.

Four thousand pounds. That's what they'd agreed on as a budget. Registry office and a drinks reception afterward. No more than forty people in total. Date set for mid July, and a cheap-but-exciting honeymoon in Barcelona.

Which gave him two months to save up his half of the money for that, pay off his final tuition fees payment, complete his finals, and then get married. Or partnered—the legality of gay marriage loomed, but it could be years before it became a reality.

They had both agreed that they didn't want to wait for those politics.

Steven smiled at the couple waiting at their table. "Would you like any drinks?"

————

Alistair's heavy footsteps woke him. Slightly disoriented, Steven pushed himself up into a sitting position on the sofa. The TV must have turned itself off.

"Hey," Al said.

"Hi. You're in late."

"Yeah, sorry. Thought you'd be in bed."

"Didn't get that far."

Alistair smirked.

"Good day?"

"Yeah, it was fine."

"You sound enthusiastic."

"Just tired. Did you speak to your mum?"

"Not yet."

"Just get it out of the way."

"Sure, I will. Did you?"

"Did I what?"

"Speak to your family?"

"Oh."

"That's a no, then."

"Families are shit."

"Bed? We can deal with all this in the morning."

Alistair nodded. Forcing himself past his exhaustion, Steven got up and walked to the bathroom. Clean teeth, quick wash.

Alistair was asleep before he even got there. Steven squeezed in next to the snoring man and pulled on the covers. His mind wandered to his mother. It was easy for Alistair; his reason for not contacting his parents was more from laziness than fear. When he'd eventually come out to them, they'd acted like he'd done nothing more than told them what he had for breakfast. Within a single minute, Al's father had turned the conversation to football. It was incredible. The news of a civil partnership may be more of a shock, but if it was, it would only mean a slightly longer, two-minute pause.

Though Steven's relationship with his mother was back on good terms, she still didn't approve of his sexuality, and certainly not his partner. Alistair was always referred to—by her—as 'the bastard'.

"Mum, I'm marrying the bastard," was not a line he relished delivering.

After the visit from Daniel, the situation with Viv and Zoe had calmed down to little more than background noise. His older sister had given up trying to communicate with him completely. The first week after Viv's return to Malaysia, she'd called and texted furiously, leaving spitting voicemail messages that were filled with threats and vitriol. Occasionally, she'd tried it from a different number, but Steven had never answered and there were no instances where the petty subterfuge had worked.

Daniel had been right; it had all been talk.

At least he didn't have to use up one of his precious spaces at the ceremony for his older sister.

He yawned. He'd video call his mum tomorrow, at the beginning of his scheduled study session. He could probably afford her fifteen minutes.

Another day of hard work loomed.

————

"Steven, it is good to hear from you."

"Is Viv well? Is she there?"

"She's sleeping."

Steven looked again at the time. Sleeping? In the middle of the day.

"Mum, is she OK?"

"She's suffered, Steven. It's put a lot on her. The doctor suggested that I give her the space to relax and settle in to this life again, that I concentrate on her health rather than things like academics. It is hard for me, honestly, to think that she is wasting precious days when she could be studying, but he was insistent and I have listened."

"So, she gets to sleep into the afternoon?"

"She gets time to recover." His mum was firm. She changed the subject. "Your finals are soon, aren't they?"

"Yes."

"And you are studying hard?"

"I am. I'm very busy at the moment but yes, I'm studying all day today. I only have a short time for this call."

"Then you have a reason for it."

He breathed in. "I do."

"Well, come on. Tell me."

It should have been a joyous moment, telling his mother about his coming civil partnership—his marriage in all but a technicality. Instead, he tensed.

"Steven?"

"Mum, Alistair and I are having a civil partnership. Like a marriage. We're getting married in July."

She was silent. Steven looked at her face. She trembled. It was slight, enough that she was holding back her reaction on his behalf, but he easily saw it.

"It's OK, Mum, you don't need to say anything."

"I ..." she started.

"Please, no more."

"No, let me speak. Please."

With a sigh, Steven nodded.

"It is hard for me, Steven. Very hard. But I never disowned you over this as you thought, and I have had a very long time to think about things."

"Yes."

"You are my son. And you an admirable son, soon to become a doctor. I am proud of you."

"But ..."

"Yes, there is a but. I find this subject distasteful. It is not something I believe in and, every day, I pray and I hope that you will change your mind."

"It's not something that I can change my mind about."

"Yes, I know. I do know. I try to understand. I have been talking to Vivienne about it, too. Though she is young, she has some modern insight that I definitely lack. She speaks highly of you, and this part of your life doesn't bother her at all. She finds it slightly comical that it bothers me."

"What do you want me to say?"

"I don't want you to say anything. I want you to listen."

"Go on."

"Your sexuality, this I am coming to terms with. But Alistair himself, I do not think he is the right person for you. He has supported you, yes, I understand that, and he is not a bad man, but ... I do not feel that he has always had your best interests at heart. You are both young men, and despite what you say, it is true that you have no woman to temper you, either of you. Your relationship lacks perspective."

"Mum—"

"Please, Steven, let me finish. I know I am not sounding as supportive as you want, but I am trying. Let me be your mother."

"Fine, go on."

"I believe you should be concentrating on your studies. You should be getting yourself a good job and starting a career as a doctor. Adding a marriage, or a civil partnership to that is a lot. Regardless of who the partnership is with. Plus, you have had to come to me for financial help recently with your fees, and though you have shown honour with your desire to repay that money, it shows that you are not financially secure."

Alistair's desire to repay the money, Steven thought. Of course, his mother had no idea about Al's gambling or the real situation behind his asking for a loan.

"If I were marrying a woman, you wouldn't be so reticent. Even this close to my finals."

"Perhaps not. I do not lie and pretend I have no prejudice, Steven. But that's not the situation, and these are my feelings. Please, will you put off this event until you are properly grounded?"

Steven shook his head sadly. "I was telling you because I wanted to ask you to come."

"Steven, my son, I can't. Not in July. Even if I had no misgivings, it is too soon to sort out a visa application for both myself and Vivienne, and, in truth, I am nervous about returning to the UK with her while Zoe is still behaving as she is. She would not win in any fight between us, but she could cause problems. There have been many threats. Your older sister could make things very difficult if we came there."

"Daniel said it was all talk."

"Perhaps that's how he sees it, but I'm more cautious. My eyes are open to Zoe. She may be more vindictive than either you or Daniel believe. Especially to me."

"It sounds like you don't want to come and she's an excuse."

"I do. Honestly, I do. Even with Alistair, even like this, I do. And so would Vivienne. But I must be sensible. I cannot leave her here alone, and I cannot bring her there. Not so soon. I am sorry. Again, why not postpone? In a year, things will be different. I can plan properly to visit."

"I don't want to put things off. Nor does Al. We want to have our civil partnership."

"Rushing like the young always do."

"We *are* young, Mum."

"Yes, and so you lack wisdom. One year, Steven, that's all I suggest. You have been with Alistair for far longer than that. I am sure he will understand and wait."

"*I* don't want to wait."

"I understand. I was the same with your father. I wouldn't have waited then, either."

Steven was deflated. "I need to get on with my studies, Mum. Will you send my love to Viv?"

"I will. Good luck. Call me soon."

———————

The days had blurred, a mixture of working, studying and sleep. Finals were ever closer.

Steven made his last fees payment in person to the bursar. He'd walked home in the bright afternoon, happy to be finally clear of that financial burden.

Happiness that had been swiftly banished.

He stared at the laptop screen unmoving. He'd been looking at it for what seemed to be hours, unwilling to close the window. Twice, he'd had to click on an alert that warned him that his session was timing out.

The sound of the door opening made him let out the breath he was holding, but he didn't turn.

"Hey," Al said brightly. "How's the studying?"

"Not good. I've been distracted."

"What with?"

Steven swivelled the laptop so that his fiancé could see the screen. Alistair went quiet. "Oh."

"Yes, 'oh.'"

The computer was open on the banking for their joint account, the account they had been using to save up for the civil partnership. Of their £4,000 budget, Steven had paid in over two thousand. It wasn't that he cared about the amounts being equal—after all,

Alistair was also paying off the debt he owed to Steven's mother—but the balance of the account showed £82.14.

"I ..."

Steven stood up, pushing the laptop away. "Don't."

"It's just—"

"Look, Al, I don't know what to do. Please, don't speak for a minute because I think I'll explode if I don't say what I need to say."

Alistair nodded.

"You stole six thousand quid off me at Easter. Six grand that you fucking threw away because, whether you still want to acknowledge it or not, you have a gambling problem. I bailed you out, Ray helped bail you out and, in the end, my fucking mother bailed you out, even if she doesn't know the truth of it. Six fucking grand, Al, it's not a small amount of money. In fact, it's insane. It's enough for a deposit on a flat in some places."

"I know—"

"No, don't speak. Please, just don't speak. Listen. You think I don't know that even after Easter and all that shit, you were still gambling. I did. I've noticed, Ray's mentioned it a couple of times, Claire's seen it. Our other friends have dodged around talking to me about it. It's a problem.

"All of that though, I could overlook. But this? I've been working my fucking arse off since Paris. I haven't done anything really that's just for entertainment. I've been working, or I've been studying. I've even cut my sleep back as far as I could while still being realistic. And I don't earn a lot of money. Have you any idea how hard it has been for me to save up over two grand so far? It's been fucking terrible."

Alistair bowed his head.

"And now, it's gone. You can pretend as much as you like that you can get it back—you can't. If you could, then you'd have already made it so we reached our target. What you have done is fuck up our civil partnership. I don't even know if we should still get married. I can't trust you."

"Steve, please. Please. I'm sorry."

"Seventeen."

"What?"

"It's the seventeenth time you have had to say sorry to me for gambling reasons. Sure, most of them are small, where you've lost a little or I just caught you coming back late after you promised you wouldn't do it again, but this is number seventeen. It's a count I've been hating doing."

"I'm sorry."

"It's not fucking good enough! Don't you love me? Of course you don't. If you loved me, if you *really* wanted to have a life together, you wouldn't have taken our fucking money that was saved up so that we could have our CP and then just ... what? I mean, what have you done with it?"

"I—"

"No, don't. I don't want to know. It's horrific. It's a fucking horror story. You know, you often tell me how fucked up my childhood was, well, you know what? My father was a gambler. One of the big reasons my childhood was so fucking insane was because he was the same as you. Is that who you are, Al? Are you just my father again?"

Alistair shook his head slowly.

"How could you gamble away the funds for our fucking marriage? How? It was you who proposed to me. You made all this happen. You who took me to Paris and sat with me under the fucking stars with the lights dancing up the Eiffel Tower. Did you do it just so you could have it all crash around me? So that it could lead to this? When you took the money, did you give any of that a single thought? Did you even consider how I'd feel when I saw it gone?"

"I thought I'd be able to double it. I wanted our CP to be perfect."

"Are you fucking kidding? Did that work for you last time? You are still paying off my mum, Al. You still owe her three grand or so. We've invited people. Claire's been working her arse off, sorting out everything. We can't do it. Not now. We just can't do it."

"I'm sorry. I'll fix it."

"No! No you won't fix it because you don't know how. I will have to fix it, won't I? But I don't even know if I want to. I don't even know if I should. How can we share a life together when I'm constantly worried you are going to steal to fuel your pathetic addiction. And it is pathetic, Al, it's fucking pathetic. I'm going out."

Slamming the lid of the laptop, Steven walked to the door, biting back tears. "I can't believe you did this."

Al's weak apologies floated after him.

CHAPTER 24

Steven pushed at the balloon tied to a weight. With a small bobbing motion it floated away and hung in the air above him, the tether making sure it couldn't get too far. It was pink and had the words 'Happy Birthday' written on it in silver.

He put the two cocktails down and squeezed in with Claire at the small round table.

"Are you going to open up about Al?" she asked.

"I thought we were going to talk about your birthday and your fantastic present that I got you."

"The necklace is lovely, truly." Claire fiddled with the sparkling purple alexandrite. "But you can't avoid talking to me. And better now than when you've plied me with enough drink to try to get me to change the subject."

"It's fine, Claire."

"You changed all the arrangements, Steve. You took a four grand budget and sliced it to two. You've been cold to Al since before finals. It's been weeks."

"I had a lot of stress with the exams."

"Steven, seriously, talk to me. It's not like I don't know."

"Well, if you know, you tell me."

Claire sighed and took a long sip of her drink. "Alistair's still gambling. My guess is he drained your funds."

Steven crumpled. "Another two grand, Claire. Straight out of the savings for our CP. Our fucking marriage fund."

"Yeah. That's what I thought. Why didn't you tell me?"

"I didn't tell anyone."

"But I'm helping you organise it. You should have told me."

"Would it have made any difference. You've managed to do it on such a small budget anyway—thank you, by the way."

"It's not *that* small a budget. I've definitely heard of worse."

"It made me rethink the whole thing, I'll be honest. My brain kept coldly telling me I couldn't trust him, that I'd never be able to trust him, but my heart ..."

"You're sweet."

"Seriously, I love him. And I need to help him with this, don't I? For better or worse, that's the idea."

"Well, it's reasonable to think seriously before it becomes like that."

"But I do love him. For all my brain telling me to get out, my heart just wants to stay. That's why we're still going forward. I want to beat this, I want to put it all behind us. But he needs to do a lot of that, and I can't make him. It's not like I have any control over him, not really. I can't just lock him out from every bank account, treat him like a 1950s housewife with a small allowance and no real say in the finances."

"Maybe for a while that's exactly what you need to do."

"Well, that's what I've been doing. It's been tense. I'm also pretty sure he's not telling me everything. There might be debts I don't know about that he's secretly trying to pay off. I don't know. Sometimes I lie awake at night just imagining the worst. People knocking on the door with weapons, threatening us."

"I don't think it can possibly be that bad."

"My dad was a gambler. Trust me, I've seen it that bad, and worse."

"I didn't know. You never talk about your dad."

"He died a couple of years ago. He and I didn't really have a good relationship. I hid who I was from him and he died not even knowing I was gay."

"Oh, I'm sorry."

"He definitely wouldn't have approved of me marrying Al."

"Well, I do. Al's a good bloke, and he does love you. He's a fuck-up of course, there's no denying that, but he's a good fuck-up."

"You think it's time to forgive him and get on with it? Honestly, it's been hard keeping up the cold shoulder."

Claire leaned over to touch him on the shoulder. "You're going to forgive him eventually, and the sooner you do, the more time you can enjoy together."

"How very wise."

She laughed. "Not really!"

"Finish that drink and I'll get you another. Like you said, I need to get you drunk enough to change the subject."

———————

"May I take you out to celebrate, Doctor?" Alistair asked.

"I like that! 'Doctor.'"

"Congratulations, my love." Alistair kissed him, dispelling much of the recent tension.

"I did it! I graduated!"

"You did."

"I'm a doctor!"

"You are."

"Holy fuck, Al! I'm a doctor!"

"You really are."

"The others are having some drinks before everyone goes their own way. Are you OK coming to that rather than just you and me?"

"Sure, let's go."

Steven looked over at his peers. Almost every one of them had their family with them. Alone with Alistair, he felt small.

"I wish Mum had been able to come. And Viv."

"I know."

"Doctor Steve!" Claire waved at him breaking his melancholy. Her younger brother hovered by her side.

"Doctor Claire!" Steven called back.

Claire gestured to indicate she'd see him and Al for the drinks soon. The crowd dispersed and they were swept along in the general throng heading for the pub.

Alistair grabbed his hand. "Right, let's go and get pissed. It's still early and I intend to make you just drunk enough that you'll do whatever I suggest without passing out on the bed."

"It's a fine tightrope to walk."

"I've had practice."

They walked into the warm atmosphere of the post-graduation party and Steven relaxed. He'd done it. All the struggles and the pain, all of the money worries and arguments. He was a doctor, and no one could ever take that away from him.

———

"I've been thinking," Alistair said.

Steven turned onto his side, propping his head up on the arm. He shuffled, moving the pillow to make it more comfortable. "Sounds deep."

"I don't know about deep."

"Try me."

"You know, we've been monogamous since the day we met."

Steven shifted nervously. "Yes. That's how it is supposed to be, isn't it?"

"It is, I think. It's just there's so much out there that we haven't experienced. Either of us."

Steven was quiet.

"Would you consider an open relationship?"

Steven's mind raced. How was he supposed to answer that? Was he not enough? Was he not attractive anymore? Why was this suddenly happening?

"No." He closed his eyes, unwilling to look at his fiancé and took in a deep breath. "Our civil partnership is next week. Next week! And you are feeling like this. We shouldn't continue with it."

He pushed himself out of bed, needing to distance himself physically from the shock of what he had just heard.

"No! No! That's not what I was saying, I'm sorry. I didn't mean it."

"I'm going out. Don't follow."

He grabbed his jeans from the floor, hastily threw them on and scrambled around for socks, making sure he didn't look at Alistair the entire time. Open relationship? Had Al met someone else? Was he bored of this life?

"Fuck, where's my fucking shoe?"

It was all too much. One week before their official ceremony. It was meant to be a glorious time, a period of joy. Not this. Not tension and arguments and uncertainty.

"Steve."

"No." Steven pulled on his shoe. "Don't."

Was Alistair trying to break him? The money, the gambling, and now this. He'd had to deal with rejection from his mother, manipulation from his sister, worry over his other sister, working three jobs at a time, having thousands of pounds stolen, all the studying. He'd had his plate overfull for years and yet it had all seemed worthwhile because the end was going to be worth it. Married, and a doctor. Moving to a new life of happiness and security.

Steven stormed out of the building and into the cold night air. It was summer, but the warmth of the day had long gone.

"Fuck," he spat into the night. He leaned against a wall, letting the tears come.

A strong hand on his shoulder shocked him. Alistair pulled him into an embrace, using his bigger body to every advantage. For a moment, Steven resisted, pushing away at the man trying to ... trying to what? To comfort him? To pretend it was all OK? But there was a familiar warmth and love that ran through the arms.

"I told you not to follow me."

"Aye. I ignored that."

"Why?"

"Why did I ignore it? Because I didn't mean what you think I meant. I'm sorry. I wasn't trying to hurt you. I fucked up."

"I think you were pretty clear."

"No, not at all. I'm just scared, Steve. We've been together years and it's been fantastic. Wonderful. You are everything I ever want in a partner. But there's a niggle in my mind that taunts me. It says that I'm young, that there's lots I haven't done. It's frightened that I'll regret forever that I didn't play the field a little more."

"Play the field?"

"You know what I mean. That I didn't taste more of what was on offer."

"Fucking hell. Am I just an item on a fucking restaurant buffet menu?"

"No, no. Christ, I'm fucking this up. Not at all. You're the fucking fillet steak. And the pudding that comes after it, and the starter. You're that and fucking chips when you just feel like getting something quick and basic. You're beer and rum and champagne. Jelly babies, crisps and a fucking Snickers bar."

"Al, stop. You're just listing fucking food, now."

"OK. Well, that's how I feel. You're everything. I'm sorry. I didn't mean to hurt you or fuck up anything more. I was just bad at explaining myself."

"You know, I wonder, too. I have times when I panic and question if this is the right path. It's natural. But fuck me, it wouldn't make me think 'you know what I want? An open relationship so I can fuck who I want and still come back to Al every night without a problem'. It's relegating our partnership to what? Housewives? I don't fucking know."

"I'm sorry. I didn't think it through. Please, come back. I don't have any fucking shoes on."

Steven looked down at the other man's feet and laughed. "Can you just promise me that you're going to get through the next fucking week without more of this shit?"

"I can."

"You're a wanker, you know that?"

"Yes."

"Say it."

"I'm a wanker."

"Good." Steven hugged him. "Come on."

As Alistair climbed the stairs, Steven watched. Forgiveness wasn't that easy. Forgetting even harder. He'd had his faith in their relationship shaken and he knew it. Biting back more tears, Steven followed his husband-to-be back to bed.

———————

It was a simple but beautiful day.

Stealing a moment for himself, Steven sat on the grass, looking out at his friends. Alistair was being himself, entertaining and outgoing; it was very much his celebration. Friends and family. Al was family, now.

This was his life now. A new husband, a new lease of life.

His hand felt in his pocket for the letter he'd folded there. It had arrived that morning and he hadn't wanted to affect the day by reading it, but he knew what it was. The envelope told him that much.

"What've you got there?" asked Ray, coming from the doorway. "Big wodge of cash?"

"In a way, I hope."

"What is it?"

Steven held it up. "It's either a bitter rejection, or a job offer."

"From where?"

"London."

"Wow. And you haven't opened it?"

"Nope."

Ray passed him a glass of wine. "This'll help."

"I didn't want to taint the day. I should leave it until tomorrow."

"Fuck that!"

Steven smiled. "To be fair, that was my thought, too."

"Come on, then."

Trembling slightly, Steven tore open the envelope and read the contents.

"Well?"

He grinned. "I'm hoping Alistair wants to relocate to London."

"Relocate to where?" Alistair came out to join them. "Fuck off, is that a job offer?"

Steven nodded.

"London?"

"Yes."

"Fucking cool. Well done, Sweetheart." He crossed over and kissed him. "Do you hear that everyone?" he called. "My husband got his first choice job in London. Looks like we're moving!"

A murmur of congratulations and some cheers went up from the crowd.

"They don't want you to start right away, do they?" Alistair asked. "Only I don't want to have to cancel Barcelona."

Steven grinned. Not yet twenty-five. A London doctor. Married. Happy.

CHAPTER 25

The small London flat felt cold, empty, and not what success was meant to be. Steven looked over at the side, glanced at the picture of himself and Alistair smiling for the camera, and sighed.

His husband had gone back that morning to Aberdeen and work. The hole that he left echoed.

Steven put on the CD and tried to fill the silence with music, but it felt hollow. Two songs in, he turned it off and sat dejectedly on the bed.

Alistair had asked 'the question' again.

Despite his assurances the first time that it was just nerves, a silly thought brought on by pre-wedding jitters, he had brought it up a second time in Barcelona.

While they were on their honeymoon.

That time, Steven had allowed him to play the 'drunk' card, swallowing the sinking sensation in his heart a second time. It didn't stop him feeling awful, questioning his own life decisions, but at least he wasn't showing it. At least it didn't turn into an argument.

He'd moved to London in August. Alone. Alistair was offered a transfer, but it would take six months to organise, and so they'd agreed on a temporary long-distance relationship for the first few months of their marriage.

Moved here, to this single-man's flat. There was nothing wrong with the place; it was well furnished, didn't suffer from damp or any other real issues, and was perfectly placed for work. But it wasn't theirs. It didn't have the comfortable things that they had bought over the months to make their home a home. It was just 'the flat'.

Alistair managed to come down every second weekend. And every time he had, he'd brought up the question.

This time, to be fair, it had been phrased differently.

"Don't you think we should try this open relationship idea?"

Steven felt his stomach tighten. He'd been ready for it, but nonetheless, it stung.

"No, Al, please."

"I know, I know. I'm sorry. It's just, God, sometimes you feel so far away."

Steven had said nothing. What was there to say? 'Well, Alistair, if you had a loyal bone in your fucking body, you'd be able to deal with the fact I'm a little far away. After all, I have the same feelings and concerns. I don't know, learn to communicate over Skype a little better, maybe rearrange your work schedule so you can come for more than two days at a time.'

It would have caused a row. Not worth it. Not worth taking that precious time and destroying it.

And what about the money? Alistair had none. He was close to paying off the debt to Steven's mother, at least, with only a few hundred pounds left, but there were other debts. Things that hadn't been disclosed until later. Steven had taken on some of the responsibility; after all, they were legally partners, now, but he had to pay for a London life, and despite a general belief to the contrary, junior doctor was not a well-paid position.

So, they were perpetually broke. Time spent together was tense, relegated to a few drinks and some coffee. Steven lived in London, where he ached to see shows and go dancing. Instead, he watched the world go by from his window, hoping that soon the debts would be cleared.

The truth was, he didn't trust that Alistair wasn't just making new ones.

How long would it be before he answered the question with a 'yes'? Before he just gave up?

———

"Now that I'm here in London full-time and all moved in, we should at least get a double bed." Alistair stretched, rolled off the bed dramatically and collapsed into a heap on the floor. The duvet went with him, wrapped around his legs.

"Oh, right, yeah. Where do you intend to put it? Shall we squeeze it in between the kitchen side and the wall, or do you want to just block the front door?"

"If it was just very long instead of very wide, it'd fit in the corridor to the bathroom."

"Very long?"

"Instead of wide," Alistair confirmed.

"That's the most ridiculous thing you've said ever."

"Ever?"

"OK, well, the most ridiculous thing you've said this week."

"It is a wee bit cramped, though, don't you think?"

"I think we can afford doctor's quarters and not a lot else. I think it's two minutes from the hospital. I think I took out a lease that's not even half-way through and will have to pay for this place even if we do find somewhere better but, once you've paid off all the money you owe people, we can get whatever you like."

"I'm close to that. Paying everything off, I mean."

"Sure."

"Seriously. I know I've only been here for six weeks, but the amount we're saving not paying for our place in Aberdeen means my money is actually useful. We could move out to somewhere."

"I think you're not altogether understanding London prices, Al."

"Oh, fuck off. I'm not some thick Scot who doesn't comprehend what it's like down south. I know what London is like. And I say that in a month or so we should start looking. We could even buy somewhere. Your job has a certain level of respect, and mine's good, too. Banks would lend us money."

"Not with your record, Al, sorry. Not for a while longer."

"Well, fuck 'em then."

"Great, yeah. I think that's the attitude they like."

Alistair snorted.

"Look, I have to go to work, but we can take a proper look at bigger flats when I get back."

"Sure." Alistair stretched out on the floor and covered himself in the duvet. "I'll be here when you get back. Day off, lots of TV."

"Great, sounds fantastic. Maybe I should have a shower and get dressed first, yeah? Why don't you get off the floor and make me some breakfast?"

"Aye, I'm feeling peckish now, too."

Steven reached work with fifteen minutes to spare, his mind swimming. Alistair was right; the tiny flat was far too small for the two of them full-time. Al had done the loving thing and given up everything in Aberdeen to be with him, including a home that was comfortable and spacious, and now Steven was forcing his husband to sleep cramped together on a single bed. It was ridiculous, and far from the mature life of a couple that they had always intended. They should move, and really shouldn't wait too long to do so, but there was something about his flat that he really didn't want to lose. It was easy to blame it on the proximity to work, but it was something else. A sense of control that he lacked when Alistair was around.

During the months he'd lived alone, Steven had been lonely and often bored, but he'd also been the only one to have a say in what he did. Since Alistair had transferred to the capital, there seemed to be no space to be himself. He was consumed by his husband, by the need to please him.

Because he didn't want Alistair finding a reason to go elsewhere.

It was 'the question', the recurring worry that Al was already bored of him and now found him unattractive. Adding extra hurdles like bad sleeping arrangements just wasn't conducive to their relationship.

"Morning, Doctor," called Cherry. The administrator waved to Steven as he passed. It had almost been a year now and he still hadn't tired of being called 'doctor'. He hoped he never would.

————————

Exhausted, Steven slumped against the kitchen wall and took a quick break. As he always did, he'd rushed home to prepare dinner; Alistair's considerably-longer commute meant he was at least forty minutes later coming in the door than Steven. Summer was approaching and they'd failed to move out of the cramped flat, so Steven did what he could to make his husband as relaxed as possible. Dinner on the table when Alistair got home was a small touch, perhaps, but a significant one to him.

It was now less than a month before their first anniversary. Steven was beginning to panic that he didn't have the funds to make it truly special. He'd looked at a weekend away, but the cost of it would mean depleting his moving-out savings, and not for the first time. Was it worth it? Would Al even appreciate it?

"Hi Honey, I'm home." Alistair dropped his bag on the floor, walked into the kitchen and squeezed past Steven to pour himself a glass of water. "It's hot."

"Dinner's ten minutes away. I made us burgers."

"Sounds great." Alistair walked out to sit at the table. "Thanks. Smells good, too."

"Yeah, open the window, actually. Don't want the place to stink."

"I've been thinking," Alistair pushed open the window and stayed leaning on the sill. "Naughty thoughts."

"Oh really?" Steven poked his face around the doorway and grinned.

"Aye. It's been really distracting."

"What've you been thinking?"

"About you and strangers."

"What?"

"I've spent most of this afternoon imagining you with another man. Two or three in some versions. I'm either there watching or just coming home afterwards to hear about it. It's had me all horny."

"Seriously, Al!" Steven laughed a forced laugh.

"You can't tell me you're not into the idea."

"I can't?"

"Oh, come on. We've all imagined it, right? Either for ourselves, or the other one."

Steven's stomach sank. He knew where this was going. The smell of the cooking meat overwhelmed him for a moment and he sought the clear air of the kitchen window.

"I dunno, maybe," he managed.

Steven felt ill. His chest tightened and breathing became hard. How many more times of him saying 'no' to Alistair's request was it going to take before the man just left him? What life was Steven offering his husband? A tiny, shitty flat? Time together where whenever they spent money having fun, it came with a heavy dose of guilt? He was stifling his partner's existence, trapping him into something he didn't want. Alistair had made it really clear that he wanted to try out other men. He was young; of course he didn't want to be tied into this.

"Maybe, we really should think again about that open relationship idea," Alistair was oblivious to the panic setting in Steven's heart. "For you, as much as me. It'd be great to swap stories, don't you think?"

"OK." Steven's shoulders tensed.

"What?"

"I said 'OK'. I love you, Al, and I don't want to stop you from living the life you want to live. So, 'OK'."

"Are you serious?"

Steven closed his eyes. "Yes."

"That's cool. You know, London's great for it. There's such a busy gay scene that we haven't even touched on. We can have loads of fun."

"Sure." The waft of sizzling beef came strongly. "Shit."

"What is it?"

"Just the burgers. Stay there. I'll just be a minute."

Steven busied himself with the dinner. He'd done it. He'd said 'yes' to his husband sleeping with other men. He'd introduced chaos and uncertainty into his life. In a daze, he put the burgers on the buns, messed about with salad and sauce, and strode into the other room.

"Hope you enjoy your food." He collapsed onto the chair.

"Looks delicious."

Steven smiled thinly. The food was now completely unappetising to him. He picked up his burger and nibbled at the bread.

"Have you heard of Grindr?" Alistair pulled out his phone. "I haven't used it properly, of course, but I heard about it and downloaded it to take a look. It's an app where you can easily find gay men nearby. There's loads here, of course. You should get it, too."

The words drifted in the air. Numbly, Steven took his own phone and went to the app store. It was as if someone else had taken over, typing the letters, pressing the download button.

Alistair kept talking, excitedly chattering about bars and saunas, places where other equally-minded young guys congregated. Steven felt he could hear his mum, hovering in the background from years before.

"You know what gay relationships are like, Steven? There's no love there, not between men. Oh, you can try to show it, but there's no balance. No. What men want is sex, and they don't mind where they go to get it. There's no commitment. It'll all be seedy bars, and disgusting clubs where people meet for casual sex and orgies. Orgies, Steven! Is that a world you want to be a part of?"

"It's not like that with Alistair, Mum. You don't understand. We love each other."

"Of course, that's what you think, now. But what about when he gets bored and starts to look at other men. When you're not good enough for him. It will happen, you know. Sex. Homosexuals are just animals. There's nothing but sex."

"No, Mum. Honestly, we're no different to any other couple. Alistair wants to be with me, just like I want to be with him."

"Pah!"

Steven looked up at his husband's bright eyes as Alistair continued excitedly.

He wanted to vomit.

————

Alistair had agreed to two rules. First, always let the other person know if you meet someone for a casual hook-up (Steven didn't want to be waiting at home with dinner ready). Second, never bring anyone to the flat.

Steven hadn't bothered to emphasise any extra rules regarding safety. Either Alistair was sensible enough for that not to be relevant or there was no point telling him—it would only have been an insult that led to an argument.

Since then, Alistair had needed to 'work late' many times. Nights during which Steven had eaten alone and gone to bed early.

Staring into the darkness, Steven tried the dating app again. It felt awkward, silly even, but each time it had become easier. Closing his eyes and hearing the deafening silence of being the only person in the small flat drove his encouragement, and Steven began to enjoy himself, filtering through the swarm of graphic photos and inane chatting in the hope of finding something -someone- more connectable.

Would you like to come for dinner?

Edward only lived two streets away and over the few conversations they'd shared, he'd chatted about food rather than sex. Plus, all his pictures were more oriented around cooking than trying to impress. Steven liked him.

Tonight?

Sure. I can add to the stuff I'm making easily. Give me 40 minutes?

Alistair wouldn't be home for hours, if at all.

I'll see you then.

The shower was hot, near-scalding water that invigorated him. Steven began to relax, accepting the adventure. After all, wasn't that what his husband wanted?

He walked into the warm summer air with a sense of trepidation.

I'm on my way.

On his way. Should he text Alistair now? Let him know that he won't be home for a while?

No. See how the first half an hour goes.

"Steven?" Edward opened the door with a flourish. Steven looked right into his eyes without tilting. Unlike Alistair, Edward was of a similar height. Also, like Steven, he was from Malaysia.

Steven nodded. "Hi."

"Come in. Dinner's nearly ready. I hope you like rice dishes."

"I do."

"Great. Just sit there for a moment and I'll sort everything out. Drink? I've opened a bottle of wine."

"Wine would be nice, thanks."

It was awkward, but Steven tried to relax. Edward's home was larger than his and warmly furnished, with more material and soft coverings in reds and orange than the starker decor of the flat. Steven realised with sudden shame that neither he nor Alistair had really brought their own mark into their London flat. Each so desperate to move to somewhere new, despite never managing to do so, they had never bothered to make it homely where they lived. A few framed photographs of their special day were the only real indications that they lived there at all, and Steven had put those up as soon as he'd moved in.

"I wondered if you wanted to watch a movie or something," Edward offered. "Probably not, though, right?"

"Actually, that'd be nice."

"Then that's the plan. Dinner first, though, right?"

"Absolutely."

Edward was a good cook, his touches to the meal were delicate, reminding Steven immediately of some of the tastes of his home. It was like being in a different world, and Steven opened up easily.

"I have to text my husband," he said at one point. He'd already mentioned his situation with Edward during their text conversations, but it hadn't come up yet during the evening. Edward didn't flinch, instead he laughed and waved to indicate immediate acceptance.

I might not be home tonight. Met someone and gone to their place for dinner.

Alistair's text was unusually quick in response. **Sure. Have a good night. See you tomorrow.**

Steven flinched. He'd expected something more, some sign that Alistair didn't like the idea. But nothing.

"Are you OK?"

Steven looked up. "Yeah, sorry, just. No, it's fine. What did you want to watch?"

Watching the film was easy. Steven settled back into the soft cushions and allowed himself to be distracted. Alistair's lack of care in his response had thrown him, but he was determined that it wouldn't show. Not to Edward, at least.

They were both laughing by the end of the movie.

"This is your first Grindr meet-up, isn't it?" asked Edward.

"Did I do something that gives it away?"

"You've been very nervous and you overshare a little."

"I'm sorry."

"No." Edward reached out a hand to calm him, touching his arm. Steven looked at it; it was the first physical contact they'd had. "No, there's nothing wrong with it. Actually I like it, it's nice to actually speak to someone, not just get sent a dick pic and request for an hour of my free time."

"Yeah, I've seen more dicks in the last few weeks than in my life beforehand." Steven grinned.

"Right. So, yeah, I like this. Plus, you enjoyed my cooking which is a big plus."

"I did! It's really good."

"So, what's put you on Grindr?"

"My husband. Our civil partnership was almost a year ago—next week, in fact—and ever since then he's spoken about having an open relationship. Eventually, I said yes."

"But you don't really want it?"

"I haven't. Today's been nice though. I'm relaxed, it's good to talk to someone."

"You'd be equally happy if it remained just talk, though, right?"

Steven said nothing.

"Oh, Steven, that's fine with me. I'm pleased to have the company. Who knows, you may warm up to the idea later on, but I'm certainly not the pushy type. Far too much of that in this community as it is."

"Thanks."

"You know, the open relationship thing is quite common in the gay world. Especially in London; it's like bringing a child into a candy store. There are so many options and nothing is ever enough."

Steven nodded. Gay men were everywhere; why would anyone settle for just one? Why had he expected Alistair to?

"Forget your idea of a fairy tale. The sooner you get over it, the better you'll feel."

"Maybe."

"No maybes, definitely. Anyway, more drink and more movies—the night is still young. What do you think?"

"That'd be great."

"How was it?" Alistair glanced over the food that Steven had made and instead dropped onto the sofa.

"How was what?"

"Last night, with the guy you met."

"It was great." Steven paused. "Genuinely, it was great."

"Was he good in bed?"

Steven flinched. Was Alistair really turned on by the idea of his husband having sex with a stranger? There had been no bed, not in the way Alistair meant. Edward and Steven had watched a couple more films and talked until the early hours of the morning. Finally, tired but happy, Steven had fallen asleep on the bed next to his new friend. So, there had been bed, but no sex. It had been the best night's sleep he'd managed in months.

"He was," Steven said, a smile on his face.

Alistair grinned. "I told you this would be good. Honestly, it makes me feel much better. The last few weeks have been tense between us, right?" He jumped up and kissed Steven on the top of his head. "So, what delights have you made us for dinner?"

Steven felt almost shy as he passed the envelope over to Alistair. He'd been up for a couple of hours already, despite it still being before eight, and the flat was sparkling. Today, of all days, he wanted it to be good.

"What's this?" Alistair asked.

"It's a present. Happy anniversary." Steven leaned over and kissed his husband. There was a second's hesitation before Alistair responded.

"Are you OK?" Steven asked.

"I feel shit, I'm so sorry. I'm a right wanker. I forgot it was today. I haven't got you anything."

"Well, that's OK. What I got is for us both." Steven turned away, allowing his disappointment to flash on his face unnoticed.

"Let me see, then." Alistair tore open the envelope. "Tickets to a show. Thanks."

"It's in Paris," Steven explained. "The show tickets come with a full weekend away. I've booked us a hotel and the train. It's not until September, but I'm really looking forward to it."

"Paris? Why did you get tickets for Paris? We live in London. Wouldn't it be much cheaper to pick a show that's more local?"

Steven staggered. He didn't know if Alistair was deliberately trying to hurt him, casually dismissing the location as irrelevant, or if he was genuinely unthinking.

"I thought you loved Paris. I thought it'd be a nicer thing." The words sounded weak even to his ears.

"I do! No, seriously, it's great, Sweetheart. It's perfect."

"You haven't called me that in a while."

"Of course, I have."

"No, Al, you haven't."

"Well, I've been distracted, I suppose."

"Distracted? Fucking other people, you mean. Yes, I can see how that might *distract* you."

"What?"

"You heard me."

"It's got nothing to do with that. Work's been hell."

"Has it? I wouldn't know because you never talk to me anymore. No doubt you've told great stories about your work and everything going on there with other people."

"Christ, Steve, what's up?"

"What?"

"I said 'what's up?'"

"Are you fucking insane? Maybe the fact that my husband would rather spend his nights away from me than remember about our anniversary. Our *first* anniversary."

"Like I said, work—"

"Don't fucking use that excuse. What the fuck is going on?"

"Nothing! I mean, you said the open relationship thing was a good idea. You said it'd be fun."

"No, Al, I just agreed to what you wanted. When did I say it would be fun? Never. You wanted it and I love you, so I said 'yes.'"

"Fucking hell. Look, I'm sorry I forgot our anniversary. You're right, it's totally out of fucking order. It won't happen again."

Again. Would they even reach their second year?

"No, I'm sorry. I wanted this to be nice. I bought some fresh orange juice for breakfast and was going to cook you sausages and bacon. Let's not have this row. The open relationship thing is just taking me a little getting used to."

"You had fun with it too though, right? I mean, you had a good night the other day with that bloke. You said he was great."

"He was great."

"Right, so, that's OK, then. Look, I'm sorry I fucked up by forgetting what day today is. I'll fix it. I'll go out before I come home, and I'll get you something fabulous. I already have a good idea; I know exactly what I want to get you. I just didn't remember the date and it passed me by."

"OK."

"And Paris sounds brilliant. You're right—I do love it there."

"OK."

"So, what about this breakfast you just promised?"

"It won't take long." Steven walked to the kitchen. "Why don't you have a shower?"

CHAPTER 26

The doors of Heaven were open. Edward laughed, tightened his grip on Steven's hand, and pulled him in. "Finally, we've got you in here."

Steven looked around. "This place is huge."

"Yeah, stick with me. First—the bar."

"Ed ..." Steven realised he was shouting.

"Relax! Fun, remember."

It had taken them an hour of queueing to get in. Before that, however, had been weeks of cajoling and begging by Edward. Though he'd always accepted Steven's 'no's, he was open about how he'd try again the next time they met. Finally, Steven had relented, but rather than immediately rushing, Ed had delayed the night out for a full week.

Heaven was only one location on Steven's new friend's list; a fairly comprehensive-looking compilation of the best places to spend time while gay and in the country's capital. Some of the places Alistair had mentioned too, though he'd never been as enticing in his invitations. Somehow, Alistair made everywhere sound sleazy, while Ed framed the same locations as fun and vibrant.

Steven pulled at his wedding ring. If he was out here being gay and available, then surely his wedding ring sent all the wrong signals.

"What're you doing? Keep it on." Edward grinned.

"What? I just thought ..."

"You're thinking wrong. Guys want what other guys have. You'll pull more with it on than with it off."

His relationship with Edward had remained platonic, a meeting of friendly minds rather than bodies, but Ed was eager that Steven fix his 'uptight un-gay attitude'. A diet of casual sex and random contact was his immediate solution. In many ways, Ed shared some of Alistair's beliefs.

It took ten minutes before they were served. Edward saved time by ordering them two drinks each and then took Steven on a tour. "Lots of rooms, plenty of different music," he hollered. "Drink one quickly, you don't want to be carrying two."

Steven downed the drink and then started on the other. They weren't his first drinks of the night; the route to Heaven had been a line of smaller bars and pubs dotted across Soho.

Each one he'd walked in, he'd looked around nervously, expecting to see his husband similarly out. There had been no sign of Alistair.

"I'm going to get lost," he complained.

"If you do, you know where you live!" Edward chuckled. "It's not a problem, is it? We'll try to stick together but when the night gets going, who knows what's going to happen."

It was an attitude Steven wasn't used it. Whenever he'd been out with Alistair, it had been an unspoken assumption that they'd aim to remain with each other for the entire time, sharing the enjoyment and going home as a couple. In Edward, Steven had a guide, but not a partner. As far as the other man was concerned, he was a free agent.

It was equal parts liberating and terrifying. Again, Steven found himself wishing he was here with his husband and not with his over-relaxed newer friend.

But Alistair had made that choice for him.

"Come on." Ed pulled him towards the dancefloor. "Let's get into it!"

Drink and excitement mixed to make his inhibitions low. Steven shook off his worries and allowed the beat of the music to overtake him. Time became irrelevant, worries became little more than background noise, the turmoil of his life was put aside.

His lips found another's almost as a surprise. Arms wrapped around a strong frame, Steven kissed the stranger who had cut into his personal space with such confidence. He closed his eyes and let the moment consume him, pulling back eventually and grinning wildly.

And then his new partner was gone, sliding away to disappear into the throng.

"Hah! I can't believe you did that," Ed shouted into his ear. "That's more the sort of thing you need!"

"It was fantastic!" Steven's grin seemed fixed to his face. He lifted his head to the ceiling, letting the thrum of the beat suffuse him. "Can you get me another drink?"

Edward made a line for the bar. Alone in the midst of a crowd of energetic, enthusiastic and, most importantly, gay men, Steven howled. He thrust his hands into the air and giggled.

Another kiss came, joined with hands that ran appreciatively along his side and wrapped him. Steven fell into the embrace with abandon, throwing a fleeting thought of Alistair far from his mind before it was able to take hold. This time, his unnamed partner stayed with him for a while, pressing close and delivering positive comments in a flood. Steven kissed him again, and then pushed him away with a flirtatious shove.

"God, you're pissed." Ed passed him another cocktail. "And next round's on you, these aren't cheap."

"I'm having fun! Isn't that what you wanted?"

"It is!"

"Then stop commenting on how drunk I am, because, trust me, I really know it."

"Just don't throw up on me."

"Never!"

"I told you this place was good, and there's loads more to see. Do you want to go to a different room? Change the music up a bit."

"I can do that."

"Come on, then."

"I don't even know the names of those guys." Steven grabbed the bannister as they took to the stairs. "I kissed two men, really properly kissed them, and I don't even know their names."

"Wonderful, isn't it?"

"It's definitely something."

"I told you, there's plenty of fun to be had out here. I can't believe you've been spending your evenings in your tiny flat until now. You haven't been living."

The unexpected reminder of his flat and his life with Alistair caused Steven to sway. He gripped hard onto the wooden bar and took another step up the stairs.

"Well, it's time for a new Steven today."

"I'm pleased." Edward ran past him and waited at the bottom.

"How are you not drunk?"

"Oh, I'm completely fucked." Ed laughed. "I'm just better at staying upright. Are you coming or what?"

"I'm coming."

The next room was even more vibrant than the last. Steven met it with abandon, once more concentrating on the music rather than his thoughts.

———

Alistair leaped out of the bed and up onto his feet without pausing. Steven stared at him. "What is it?"

"Nothing." Alistair breathed deeply. "Nothing."

"Nothing you're going to tell me, you mean."

"No, nothing to tell."

"Is it me? Am I just not interesting enough for you any more?"

Alistair glanced at him with a slight sneer. Steven winced at the look. "Don't be stupid."

"This was the first time we've had sex in a month, Al, and when you're done you jump out of bed like I stabbed you."

"Are you wanting an argument, Steve? It sounds like you want an argument."

"Fuck, no. I'm just asking if you're OK."

"And I've said it was nothing. I'm fine."

Steven closed his eyes. How had it come to this?

The beginning of the night had been fun. Exciting, even. He'd been pleased that for the first time in weeks, Alistair had been home on time. They'd had dinner, chatted, and it had felt like old times. When they ended up in bed together, it had felt natural, and though there was still the issue of the stupidly small bed, they'd laughed about it, made it part of the play. For a while, Steven had thought it was all going to be OK.

He looked at the clock. For a while—it had been less than twenty minutes.

"Do you want to do anything else?"

"Not really." Alistair pushed himself out of the chair and wandered into the kitchen. "Have we got anything good to just eat?"

"Sorry, don't think so."

"I want a fucking Mars bar. And I don't want to get dressed."

"I'll get one for you." Steven pushed himself up and swung his legs off the side of the bed. "The shop's not far."

"Fuck me, you would, wouldn't you?"

"What?"

"You'd go and get me a bar of chocolate at two a.m., just because I mention it."

"Yes, Al, it's called 'love.'"

"It's called being a fucking walkover."

Steven shrank. "I offered to get you chocolate. I don't see that you need to insult me because of it."

"No, I don't, I suppose. Sorry." Alistair returned to the room and sat back down in the chair. He was naked, and Steven could see scratches and other marks that he knew he hadn't made. He turned away.

"I'm sorry it was shit," Al continued. "I'm just tired, I guess. I'd planned to sleep tonight."

"You can have the bed." Steven stood up and stepped out of the way. "I'll crash on the floor."

"Do you see how fucking stupid this is? We're a married couple in our twenties. You're a fucking doctor and my job isn't bad, and yet we're living like teenage students in fucking squalor. Why?"

"I don't know. You're never around long enough to talk to about it. We never sit and plan to move on. Money gets spent."

"Oh, it's my fault. Should have guessed."

"No, I wasn't saying that. But it's hard. Getting a decent flat, we'd need at least two grand. More. And we'd have to prove your credit rating. I'm sorry, Al, I know you've been working hard and doing well, but it's still not great, is it?"

"I don't fucking know how good or bad it is."

"Have you been gambling?" Steven couldn't remember the last time he'd asked.

"What? No."

"Then how much do you have saved? You've paid off all the debt, right?"

"Most of it. It takes years."

"You can speed it up. Pay back more."

"Yes, Steve, I know how loans work."

"Well, what then? Because you're the one complaining about this flat and yet I don't see you doing much to sort it."

"You're right. I don't. I'll look at my accounts in the morning. See if I can afford a deposit."

"Fine. Do you want the bed?"

"Yes." Alistair moved over to get in. "I do want some sleep."

Steven went into the kitchen, flicking off the main light. He leaned against the side and sighed.

He was living three lives. In one, he was a married man living with his husband and struggling with just about everything. In the second, he was a doctor, working hard to impress those around him. In the third, he was with Edward, spending weekends drinking and clubbing, snogging random strangers and, a couple of times, a little bit more. Steven could still claim that Alistair was the only lover he'd ever had, but the line was getting thinner.

And Edward was becoming more and more enthusiastic with their weekends. What had simply been visiting gay bars and clubs, places where Steven was happy drinking and flirting, had become pointed talk about gay saunas. When Ed explained them, he was always exuberant.

"It's an absolute free-for-all. You find the right one, of course, and then you let all your inhibitions go. You're completely free. They have different rooms for whatever you're into. Dark rooms where you can go and just explore each other, or whoever's already there. There are rooms for the shy, with glory holes in the wall. It's exciting and feels dangerous even though it's perfectly safe. Imagine it, Steven, that freedom to just let it all go. Where you can touch and be touched and just dive into it."

For a while, Steven had been enticed. For a minute, he'd been horny and imaginative, dreaming up what it would be like to lose himself like that, enjoying the unfamiliar unfettered contact of strangers. It didn't last long; his doctor's training started screaming inside him about germs and the illusion shattered abruptly.

"Not for me," he'd told Edward.

His friend had backed down, but it felt like 'the question' all over again. A different one, from a different person, but the same slow persistence. Would he be worn down again?

"Alistair?" he whispered, coming out of the kitchen to join his husband.

From the bed came the steady sound of the big man's snoring. Steven crept over, took the spare covers and curled up on the floor. It was cold, hard and uncomfortable, but somehow felt infinitely better than being alone in the bed while Alistair slept somewhere else, out there in the city.

————

Steven glanced up at the clock displayed in the corner of his laptop screen. It had changed by a minute since he'd last looked but he'd expected more. Alistair had promised to be home tonight, on time. Dinner was already going cold and Steven was losing patience.

When the door opened, he forced a smile for his husband.

"So, what was it you wanted to talk to me about?" asked Alistair as an opener to the conversation. No 'Hi honey, I'm home', no small talk.

"Christmas."

"That's not for a while. It's still October."

"I know, but we've been invited somewhere, and I wanted to talk to you about it."

"We have, have we?"

"Malaysia. My mum wants me to come home for the holiday."

Alistair cackled. "You're serious? She invited me?"

"She did."

"Oh, that must have broken her to do. Did you get a video of it?"

Steven smiled. "No to the video, and yes, she looked a little strained."

"Well, she doesn't need to worry, I don't want to go."

"What?"

"I don't want to go."

"Al!"

"What? It's not because I'm being a wanker. I'm saving your mum the horror of having to put up with 'the bastard'."

Steven dropped his gaze, staring at the floor.

"Oh, you didn't know that I know that she calls me that, right?"

"No."

"I've known forever. Anyway, it doesn't bother me, but no. I don't want to go. How long for, anyway?"

"Three weeks."

"I couldn't even anyway. Work wouldn't give me that sort of time of, certainly not around Christmas."

"You could make it work. Maybe we could go for only two weeks."

"No, Steve. Look, you go. You haven't seen your mum and Viv in over a year. You can go, and I'll just stay here."

"So you can do what you like?" Steven snapped.

"Do what I like? What do you mean by that?"

"Have you got a boyfriend?"

"What?"

"It's a simple question, Al. Is there someone you'd rather be spending Christmas with?"

"No, you fuck. I was actually being nice. You obviously want to go and I'm not about to stop you. Like I said, it'd be good for you to see your sister. But no, I don't want to go. Your mum doesn't really want me there—she invited me for your benefit and to show how grown up she is now, but let's not be stupid. You will all have a better time without me. And I really can't take the days off work, it's not the right time to drop a solid three-week holiday on them."

"So there's no one?"

"Christ. No, Steve, there's no one. You know, the idea of an open relationship is just to allow us to explore some of our sexual desires outside of our committed relationship, but you are still my husband and this is still my marriage. Is that not how it is for you? Are you seeing someone?"

"No!"

"Well then, why the fuck would you think I was?"

"Sorry."

"Yeah, whatever."

"Look, Al, I'm sorry. I was just hoping you'd come. Viv would love to see you."

"Yeah, and if it wasn't the holiday season, and wasn't with your mum, maybe Malaysia would be cool. I know I've thought about going, but those things aren't changing, right? Christmas with your mum just isn't my thing." Alistair sighed. "Look, you go. Seriously. Tell her you are coming. Can you even afford it?"

"She's paying. She offered to pay for you, too."

"Well, that helps."

"Does it make a difference? Will you come?"

Alistair shook his head. "It's still a hard 'no' from me. Still, thank her for the offer."

"Are you sure. Because I need to tell her soon so she can book everything. I don't want to go back on it once she has."

"Yes, I'm sure. Go, have fun. Bring me back something great."

"Oh, I will. It'll be strange though—the first Christmas we'll have spent completely apart since we first got together."

"Well, that had to happen at some point."

"Did it?" Steven was quiet.

"Aye, it did. And Malaysia's about the best reason I can think of. It'll do you good."

"Maybe when I get back in the new year we can properly look for a new flat."

"Fuck yes, anything to get out of this hole. Now, what have you made me for dinner? Smells great."

———

The hug his little sister wrapped around him was the tightest and most enthusiastic he'd had in months. He squeezed her back before disentangling himself from her grip. "You look good."

"I'm feeling good. I've been so excited to actually see you."

Steven's mother took his hand. "I am pleased to see you, too, Steven."

He smiled at her and followed the two of them out to the car. The heat once they left the air-conditioned terminal was both familiar and utterly strange; London had been cold and raining.

"Is it good to be home?" asked his mother.

"It is."

"Such a shame Alistair couldn't join us."

Steven smiled. "Thank you for inviting him." He'd already made Al's excuses weeks earlier via Skype and had seen the poorly-hidden relief in his mother's eyes. Still, she kept up the pretence of his husband's welcome and he appreciated it.

"I've got loads of stuff to tell you," said Viv.

"Are you still reading those vampire books?"

"Which ones?"

"The ones with," he strained his memory, "Suze in them."

"Oh, yes!" Viv giggled. "They're a guilty pleasure. I didn't realise I'd ever spoken to you about them."

"You did. You were a big fan."

"Well, I still am."

Steven relaxed into the seat. "It is good to be back."

———

It was good to be back. The days passed in easy relaxation. Though his mother had to work, Viv was free to spend her time with him. Brother and sister took turns in showing each other the city; her from her current perspective as a teenager, him with his point of view of having been a teenager a decade earlier. Many things had

changed; Johor Bahru didn't sit still for long, but there was enough
that had lasted the decade that Steven was able to educate his sister
on some of his favourite places.

He couldn't help but compare the place to London and the
dizzying nights he'd spent in Soho over the past year. The atmosphere
there was completely different, despite it also being a thriving city.
Now that he knew what to look for, Steven noticed a spread of gay
couples. Despite being in a country where being gay was illegal, it
was obvious to him that the law wasn't stopping many people from
embracing their sexuality. Still, there was no overt affection between
gay partners, not where he could see it. He wondered what it would
be like to live in daily fear like this, something he hadn't thought
about twice while in London.

"What's it like living in London?" asked Viv one evening.

"Our flat is tiny and we've been meaning to move out all year,
my work is exhausting but fun, and the evenings and weekends are
..." Steven paused. "They're complicated."

"Complicated?

"Alistair and I don't always want to do the same thing. He has his
friends, I have mine. There are some weeks where we don't see each
other much."

"Oh, that must be hard."

"It's not great. It isn't what I wanted for our life together."

"Why don't you move?"

"Out of London?"

"No. Just out of your flat."

"We're going to. We needed to save money a bit, but we have it
now. I think we'll move when I get home."

Viv smiled. "Looking up for next year."

There was a silence for a while and then:

"Steve, do you ever hear from Zoe?"

Steven shook his head. Zoe hadn't been far from his thoughts lately, especially as it came closer to the flight out. Seeing his mother and his sister had brought it all to the surface. "No."

"Me neither. Mum cut her off, or at least she says she did, but I think she still hears from her sometimes. She'd lie if you asked her, say she doesn't. But she knew that Zoe and Daniel had split up and I don't know how she'd know that."

"I told her that. Daniel came to see me soon after it all happened. To say sorry. I thought she'd have told you."

"She didn't."

"I'm sorry. I should have talked to you directly, but talking about all that wasn't a conversation I felt was right to have with you over Skype. Maybe I should have treated you less as a child."

"It's OK. I appreciate you talking to me now."

Steven breathed in slowly. "Well, Daniel and I met up. Just once. He said he wished he'd looked out for you more. He was a nice man."

"Yes. He was."

"And she wasn't, and isn't, a nice woman, Viv. I had a very short conversation on the phone with her back then, too. You don't need to feel bad for anything that happened back there."

"I don't," Viv pursed her lips. "Really I don't. But sometimes I feel it wasn't all her fault."

"How can it not be her fault?"

"Just that maybe she had her problems, too. Maybe we should have spent more time listening to her."

"All she ever did was make us listen to her."

Viv laughed lightly. "Yes, I suppose that's true. What did she say?"

"What? When?"

"Zoe. When you spoke to her afterwards. What did she say?"

"Just more of the same. Nothing worth repeating." Steven hugged his little sister; his *only* sister. "Anyway. What are we going to be doing over Christmas itself?"

———————

Lying on his bed, Steven reached for his phone. It would be late in England, but not so late that Alistair wouldn't answer. Communication between them had suffered since he'd gone away, as it always did with Al, but tonight his husband had promised to pick up when he rang. Steven settled himself in comfortably and initiated the call.

Alistair picked up right away. His background was unfamiliar.

"Where are you?" Steven peered at the painting half-obscured by Alistair's head.

"Sally's. From work." Al moved the camera around so that Steven could see. The room looked warm and soft. The painting was an abstract piece of deep reds and orange.

"Looks nice."

"Aye, spent last night here with a couple of work friends. Sally insisted that I stick around rather than go back to an empty flat."

"Nice of her."

Alistair smiled. "How are things with you?"

"Honestly? I want to come home. I was thinking of flying back early so I could spend New Year's Eve with you. It was weird enough missing Christmas Day. What do you think?"

"I think that sounds expensive. Can you move your flight?"

"There's a fee, I think, but it won't kill me."

"I dunno, Steve. It's a nice idea but doesn't seem worth the money for a couple of days. I mean, you're flying back on the second anyway."

"I want to spend New Year with you, though."

Alistair shrugged. "If you really want. I can't see us doing anything special though."

"Come on, it's London on New Year's Eve. It's going to be epic."

"I just don't think it's worth the money. We wanted to move when you get back. I'd rather save the money for some furniture."

Steven was crestfallen. "Don't you want me there?"

"Of course, I want you here. It's just I don't see the point of wasting hundreds of pounds for two days."

"You would have, once."

"Once when?"

"Oh you know, Al. Before all this."

"Before what?"

Steven sighed. "Forget it."

"No, come on. You have something to say, say it."

"Before all this open relationship crap."

Alistair stared at him. "What are you talking about?"

"Seriously? You don't even bother to spend time with me anymore. Not like it used to be. You'd rather be off with whoever you've found on Grindr. It's like we're not together."

"That's bullshit, Steve. You're my fucking husband."

"Am I? Because it doesn't feel like that. You didn't want to come here for Christmas, and you don't want me to be with you for New Year's Eve. I thought you'd be pleased."

"I just think it's a waste of money."

"God, have you got someone there you are planning on being with?"

"What? No. Sally and the others were thinking of having a wee party, that's all."

"That's all? No hook-up."

"No, Steve, I'm not as fucking shallow as you think. And I didn't want to come there because your mum thinks I'm fucking scum."

"She doesn't."

Alistair raised an eyebrow. "Really?"

"It's hard for her, sure, but ..."

"But nothing. Look, why are we doing this? It's late, I should go to bed."

"No, I ... We haven't chatted in ages."

"We're not chatting now. You are arguing with me. You know, this open relationship stuff was your idea, too. You said you were excited by the idea."

"I never said anything like that! I agreed because—"

"Oh, come on. Because what?"

"Nothing."

"No, come on," the Scot pressed. "Why did you agree?"

"Because you made me feel that if I didn't, you were going to leave anyway. Like you were bored of me and that was that."

"What the fuck?"

"Ever since our ceremony. Even before it, you've been on about sleeping with other guys. And ever since I let you 'experiment around', you've not bothered with me. We hardly ever have sex anymore and when we do, you're not into it."

"Fuck this. I'm sorry Steve, but I'm not fighting with you from the other side of the fucking world. I'll see you on January 2nd."

The phone went dead. Steven looked at it and shook with rage and tears.

CHAPTER 27

With a solid thump, Steven threw the bag onto Edward's old armchair. Then, with equal melodrama, he dropped onto the adjacent sofa and sighed.

"Something wrong?" Edward prised the top off a bottle of lager and passed it over.

"He's fucking gambling again. I finally managed to get him to sit down and discuss moving to a new place, and he admitted that he'd lost his half of the deposit. He just expected me to put up the whole thing myself and I swear, I'm not going to do it."

"Oh."

"Yeah, 'Oh'. After that cold shoulder shit when I got home, I don't need this right now. Fuck Alistair, I tell you."

"May I? I know I've never actually met him, but I've seen pictures and he looks like he could be good."

Steven threw a cushion at his friend but smiled despite himself.

"What you need is a night out." Edward had the same answer to all problems.

"No, I need an early night so I can get to work tomorrow on time. I'm on a six a.m. shift."

Edward beamed. "Then we have almost ten hours to kill."

"Oh fuck, no."

"Come on. Grab your jacket." The other Malaysian was already moving to the door. With an exaggerated huff, Steven joined him.

The first three bars passed fairly swiftly, a single drink in each. As was becoming a regular occurrence, the two men found their way into Heaven almost without thinking. Steven went to the bar to get drinks while Edward relaxed.

"Let me buy those," said a voice. Steven looked up into a face he vaguely recognised. A hand on his arm and a gentle squeeze helped refresh his memory.

"Gary, thanks."

Gary smiled. The first time they'd met, Gary had been keen to boast about his affluence and insisted on buying drinks. That night had included a number of impressive kisses and some dancing that could have featured on late night TV channels. Gary had invited Steven back to his flat and Steven had politely declined. He liked to keep all his extra-marital affections in public and restrained.

"Where's Ed?" the tall man asked. "Tell him to come over."

Steven looked around for his friend, but Edward had disappeared into the general crowd. "He's probably dancing. He'll come over when he realises I haven't found him with his drink."

"Then stay here and chat."

Two more drinks in and the chat became physical. They laughed as a bar stool fell and Steven bent over to pick it up. Gary slapped him solidly on the arse.

"Come back with me and fuck."

Steven looked up at the other man, leaning the bar stool back onto its legs. Gary was not unattractive; subtly muscular and well groomed, he also smelled expensive and enticing. Steven grinned.

"Is that a yes?"

"Sure," Steven grabbed the other man's hand tightly. "Why the fuck not?"

The voice that always warned him against such things began to babble incoherently. Steven silenced it.

Gary didn't need to be told twice. He dropped some notes onto the bar for payment and a tip and pulled Steven up the nearby staircase. Too drunk to drive, he flagged down a taxi and kissed

Steven again as they climbed in. The address wasn't far, but of course not; a man of Gary's standing would have a flat in Belgravia.

Steven immediately determined that he would never invite anyone back to his lowly home. Gary's place was palatial, filled with exquisite art and expensive technology. Steven accepted another drink from a well-stocked cabinet and allowed himself to be led into a sumptuous bedroom with a bed larger than his living room.

"I've been wanting to do this with you for months," Gary growled. "You were always so coy."

"I've had a change of heart." Steven lay back and spread his arms out wide. "Do to me what you will."

Gary willed with delightful imagination.

———

"Mind if I sit here?" Doctor Eric slid his tray of mundane canteen food across the table and pulled up a plastic chair.

"How are you?" Steven asked.

He and Eric had been friends for a while, though their conversation time was usually limited to a crossover of lunch breaks. Eric tore open the sandwich packet and began to eat, speaking while chewing.

"I'm good," he said through muffled chomping. "Actually, I meant to ask you something."

"Professional?"

"No, personal."

Steven looked quizzical.

"Are you and Alistair in an open relationship?"

Steven was shocked. It was a strange question to come to him while at work, and it wasn't a proposition; Eric was straight and engaged to a lovely woman Steven had met at a couple of gatherings.

"How did you hear that?"

"Word gets around, but it's not just that. Is it true?"

"Yes." Steven's shoulders slumped. "It's true."

What have I done? Is this where Eric tells me he's friends with Rudy, or Gary, or ... Steven searched through his mind for the names of the other men he'd slept with over the past two months. Since Gary there had been few. Never the same man twice, despite Rudy's repeated persistence.

Or is this where he tells me I've been with someone with an STD. Shit!

"It's just that a friend of mine, Jamie, told me that he'd met someone over Christmas and when he described him, it made me think of Alistair. I mean, there aren't that many big gay Scots living around here, are there?"

Met someone? Steven tried to mask his shock. Then the other words filtered through. 'Over Christmas'.

"We're ..." Steven couldn't find any words, not any that would cover his shock and embarrassment. "We're working through it."

"Right, yeah. Sorry, none of my business really," Eric shoved the rest of his sandwich into his mouth, obviously wanting to get out of there as soon as possible.

"It's fine, Eric, really." Steven's own lunch was depleted. "Look, sorry, I have to get back to work."

"Yeah, of course."

Steven staggered past the bin, slid the remnants of his meal into the receptacle, and put the tray in the shelf runners. He left the room and went into the bright corridor.

Met Alistair over Christmas? Eric hadn't said it in a way that meant 'bumped into'. He meant 'boyfriend'. While Steven was in Malaysia.

He'd asked Alistair bluntly. And he'd been lied to.

Sally! Was there even a Sally? Was she just someone who was friends with them both, covering for them?

Back then, Alistair had erupted on the phone. Accused Steven of being the jealous one. Treated him like he was in the wrong.

And then hung up on him and not spoken to him for days.

Steven stumbled into the toilet and locked the door.

It was all coming crashing down.

But was Alistair any worse than he was? What about that night with Gary? Or Rudy's passionate lust? It was true that every time he was with someone that wasn't his husband, Steven hadn't really felt as into it as he thought he would. Recently he'd taken to swallowing viagra just before going out, just to help him sustain an erection, because the sex itself wasn't actually as exciting as he pretended it was.

Not like it had been with Al.

Wasn't he as deceitful?

Wasn't he worse?

Steven looked at his phone. If he made the call, what then? If Alistair denied it? If he didn't? If he said it was all true and that Jamie and he were a couple?

Oh God. He wanted to be sick.

It was probably just a one-night thing. Eric had misinterpreted his friend, or Steven had misinterpreted Eric. It was just a one-night thing, and they were allowed. That's what the open relationship was, right? That's what Alistair had wanted.

He had to know.

"Steve? What's up?" Alistair's voice was calm. Steven had caught him on his lunch break.

"I just spoke to Eric." He forced the words out. "A friend here at work. You met once or twice."

"Yeah, I remember him."

"He was telling me about a friend of his. Jamie."

Alistair was silent.

"Al? Do you know Jamie?"

"I ... yeah."

"Were you with him over Christmas?"

"What?"

"You heard."

"I ..." Alistair was quiet.

"Fuck, you were. All that bullshit about me not coming back early. Did you spend New Year's Eve with him?"

"It's not like that."

"You did? What is it like, then?"

"He came over a couple of times, that's all."

"Came over? To our flat? To my home?" Steven shook. "Oh fuck, did you screw him in our bed?"

More silence. "I can explain."

"Explain? What is there to explain? No. This is it. I want you out by the time I get home. I want you gone." Steven let go of the phone. With a clatter it knocked against the edge of the toilet before falling in entirely. He stared at it, lying on the bottom of the bowl under water, still shining brightly despite now being convincingly useless and destroyed. Closing his eyes, Steven flushed.

———

Alistair was lying on the bed when Steven got home, curled up and crying.

Steven stormed to the stereo, put in Beyoncé and selected the track: *Irreplaceable*. He ramped up the volume and picked up a photo. There they both were, smiling as if everything was perfect. Perfect then, and perfect forever. He smashed it, pulled the photo from the frame and tore it in half. Striding over to the wordless Alistair, he threw the pieces at him.

"Get out! Now!"

"Let me explain—"

"Now!"

Moving slowly, Alistair stood. He made his way to the door with deliberate footsteps, glancing back at Steven who turned away. The door opened and he was gone.

Steven collapsed to the floor. His own tears coming freely now, drowned out by the sound of Beyoncé's singing.

He remained there for fifteen minutes. Eventually, his body calmed, the shaking subsided and the tears dried. Moving in a haze, he cleaned up the mess and began separating Alistair's things from his own, putting the former into a bag.

There was a knock on the door half an hour later.

"I have nowhere to go," Alistair gazed at the floor. "Nowhere at all."

"Jamie's not interested then?"

Alistair didn't look up.

Steven considered pushing him away. Much of his anger had gone, but he still seethed. What about Sally, can't you stay with her? But he didn't say it.

"Come in, you might as well."

"I can explain."

"No. I don't want your explanations. This has gone on for too long, and you have hurt me too much. I want a divorce, a dissolution, whatever you call it. I want an end to this. There's no chance of us getting back together. You took my love and my happiness, and you tore it apart bit by bit. As soon as we can, I want us legally separated."

Alistair nodded mutely.

"You can stay here until you find somewhere else, or until June when the lease here ends. I'm not renewing it. You can sleep on the floor, I don't care where."

Neither of them said any more. Steven went into the kitchen and began to prepare a dinner for one.

———

Steven looked out of the small airplane window. Despite the weeks, he was still numb. Travelling back to Scotland felt like an insult to add to the injuries, but Ray had convinced him it was the right thing to do. The conference would be good for his career and Ray agreed to travel down to Glasgow to meet him for the two days.

His old friend, *their* old friend, had been a pillar of support. Once the shock had subsided, he'd propped Steven up with genuine care.

"I'm so sorry, Steve. I really thought he would be the one for you. But don't be too harsh on yourself; tears, heartache and heartbreaks are all part of love. There will be unbearable moments, but you'd want it all over again. You will love again, with the right person."

They had been good words, loving words, but also just words.

The clouds drifted past. So fluffy. He sighed. Love is like a cloud; it looks fluffy and comfortable, but if you lie or lean on it, you fall right through and, even if you survive, you hurt yourself.

Steven imagined the fall and closed his eyes.

CHAPTER 28

Sweating, Steven put the two dumbbells down on the mat and sat on the bench. He grabbed the bottle of water from beside him and took a mouthful. A quick glance at his phone told him that he still had two more sets to do, and he drew in a breath and readied himself again. It felt good to be this fit and he had no intention of giving up. Two more sets wouldn't kill him.

"How's the training going?"

Steven scoured his mind for the name of the man making small talk. He'd crossed paths with him almost weekly for three months but could never remember his name.

He smiled politely. "It's good."

"You're doing some sort of dancing thing, aren't you?"

"Yeah, that's right, for London Pride later this year."

London Pride. Steven was gleeful that he'd been invited to take part at such a level. Three years of long hours and hard work had pushed his career to exactly the place he wanted it to be. It had been the right thing to focus on and was paying dividends now with some of his celebrity clients becoming friends. The life of a respected plastic surgeon had many perks.

"Sounds fun." Grabbing his small towel, the man was obviously done and planning to leave. "Hope to catch a glimpse of your thing there."

"Thanks."

Steven checked the next exercise on his list. Just a couple more sets to go and then he could get to the shower. The dance training started in forty minutes and was ten minutes drive away; he was cutting things tight, but turning up sweaty wouldn't be nice.

In the changing room, he leaned back on the bench. His chest tightened and he struggled to breathe. Closing his eyes, he concentrated on the air going in and out to his lungs, wishing it didn't hurt quite so much. Perhaps he was pushing himself too far. He'd been at the gym at least once each day for the past twenty—it was becoming an obsession. Joey had told him that five days a week was plenty, but he'd chosen to squeeze in the weekends, too. Besides, what did a personal trainer know anyway?

Steven winced. A personal trainer knew to take a break to allow your body to recover from the exertion. He coughed, clutched his chest and gasped for breath. Maybe tomorrow would be a day too long.

Blinking, he looked up to see if anyone was staring at him, but no; the few other people here were all too busy with their own lives to bother with the half-naked choking guy on the bench. Steven would have smiled if it didn't hurt so much.

He was glad it was one of Joey's days off. The last thing he needed on top of the crushing tension was one of her lectures.

Giving himself five minutes that he could ill afford, Steven calmed his heart rate and regained control of his breathing. He hadn't felt quite this bad in ages, though a few days in the past week his exercise had led to some shortness of breath.

He remained motionless for a while, his eyes on the clock as his five minute break became ten. The dance session was in twenty minutes. By now, the Uber would be waiting outside. Skipping his shower, Steven pulled on his trousers and did up the belt. He stuffed what was left into his bag and left the gym.

From one high-energy session to another. If the gym had been tough, then the dance practice was going to really press on him.

Steven left the car with a few minutes to spare and ran into the studio to get changed.

"You OK, Steve?" Simon's brow furrowed in concern.

Steven leaned against the wall and nodded. "I'm fine, really. Overdoing it a bit at the gym this morning is all. Then I rushed here and didn't really give myself time to rest."

"Well, rest now. Take ten minutes. Join us before we finish stretching."

"Yeah, I will."

The others filed through. All friends he had made over the past few months. His decision to become an activist for the LGBTQ+ community hadn't been undertaken lightly. Edward had been a major advocate, talking at length about how his new influence and growing celebrity would be good, while also mentioning how much more alluring it would make him to other men. It hadn't been about that, though, not for Steven. His mind kept going back to the early days of hiding his sexuality, being too scared to tell his father and missing the opportunity altogether, and then the fracture with his mother.

Now, she was all too proud of her son, the gay rights activist. Nothing like regular conversation and growing understanding to get her to reassess.

Splitting up with Alistair had helped. The breakup had sent Steven into a spiral of darkness that had lasted months, but it had strengthened his relationship with his mother hugely. She'd long suspected that Alistair was at the root of Steven's financial struggles, had blamed the Scotsman for holding her brilliant son back, and had been all too happy to see the civil partnership dissolved.

Not that it was legally finished yet. Alistair's excuses for not filing the appropriate paperwork had been a constant grind for years, but that, too, was coming to an end now that Steven had competent solicitors on his side.

The relationships he'd had since, though all relatively short, had all been much more to his mother's liking. When he'd split up with Harry, a totally amicable separation, she had even cried. It hadn't been a total surprise, however; Harry had probably spent more time and attention courting Steven's family than he had on Steven himself.

"Feeling better?" Simon opened the door to check on him.

"I'll be one more minute," Steven pulled his shoes on and waved the choreographer away.

His breath was coming easily again. Writing off the incident as a blip of over-exertion, Steven joined his fellow dancers as they continued to polish and improve their routine. Whatever happened, he wanted to dazzle.

———————

"Hey Steven, how are you?" Ray opened.

"I'm fine. You?"

"Yeah. Look, about Alistair."

Steven groaned.

"I'm sorry. I should probably call you sometimes to just chat to you and not immediately mention Al."

"It's fine. Is he OK?"

"Honestly, no, but I've managed to convince him he has to turn up to your meeting and sign the papers."

"Finally."

"Well, yeah, he's going to come now. I wanted to give you a head's up about it. You haven't seen him in a while, and I don't want you getting a shock."

"What sort of shock?"

"He's just a wee bit wasted looking. Oh, he'll probably scrub himself up, but he's broke, and it shows."

"Broke?"

"Some days he doesn't even have the money to get to work. He's been scrounging off me and others for months."

"Because of gambling?"

"I assume so. I don't even bother to ask any more, but when your friend comes to you desperate for a fiver, you just hand it over, don't you?"

"You're a good friend."

"Yeah, well, that's debatable. What are you up to anyway?"

"Lots. Did you hear that I've been asked to judge the Miss Universe competition?"

"Oh, that's hilarious. Do you know how many straight guys would love that gig?"

"Which is why they ask people like me. You know, professional beauty experts, not leering leeches."

"I wouldn't leer."

Steven laughed.

"I should take you up on one of your offers to come down and stay. It's dumb that I never do."

"Yes, you definitely should. We could do a movie marathon."

"Hah! Those were the days."

Steven didn't want to be drawn into a nostalgia conversation, certainly not one about a period about which was filled with hurt. Alistair's life may have gone downhill, and Ray seemed to be the same old Ray, but his new life was considerably better than the 'good old days'. He didn't want or need to go back there.

"They were something," he conceded.

"You're in the news too, Mr. Plastic Surgeon to the Stars."

"Hardly page one."

"But if you know where to look when you're off googling a friend, you can find stuff. What else is coming up?"

"London Pride is my next big thing. There'll be loads of celebrities there, people I actually know. It's crazy to think that people I looked up to and adored from afar when I was younger are now people I get to party with."

"Ah, name dropping. Classy."

"I'm not naming names, Ray!"

"Not yet."

"Fine, no names. But it *is* cool. Sometimes I can't quite believe it."

"So, what are you doing at the Pride thing?"

"Dancing. I've become quite good at that. It's fucking hard work, but it's good fun. I have abs now. I'm ripped."

Ray laughed. "Little man did good."

"Plus I have a doctor's conference in Shanghai coming up. That's exciting, too."

"Seriously? The furthest I ever get to go is Edinburgh. Fucking Shanghai."

"It's a medical conference, Ray, not exciting."

"You'll spend time before and afterwards in Shanghai, right? So, you have to talk and then shop for a few days, so what? Shit, man, I envy your life."

"Don't."

"Why not? It's great. I'm going to definitely come and visit then. How about over the Pride festival thing? Have you got space to crash at yours? I've never been to a gay parade."

"I'd love to have you. And of course, I have space. I'm going to be busy in the run up to it, though."

"That's fine by me. Any man who can't find stuff to do in London for a few days doesn't deserve to be there."

"That's true enough."

"OK, it's a plan, then. I'm glad I called now."

"Yes, me too, I'm looking forward to seeing you. I'll introduce you to all the unnamed celebrities."

"Sounds good. Before me, though, there's Alistair. Don't forget. I'll put him on the train myself. Plus, I'll probably have to pay for the ticket."

"Thanks Ray."

"Anytime, man. Speak soon."

Steven breathed out slowly and looked around his flat. It was so far removed from the months he'd spent squeezed with Alistair in the single-bed nightmare that had been the doctors' accommodation in his first year. He sat in a living room that was larger than that entire flat had been, with glorious windows that looked out over Kensington. He had two double bedrooms, though he lived alone, the second always set up for any guests to use. There was a luxurious multi-head shower, a private office space, and a polished kitchen that was the envy of everyone who visited. It was rented but the deal he had was reasonable and there was little chance he'd ever be asked to leave. Not until he was ready.

It was a bachelor pad of dreams and came with all the lack of responsibility that slightly show-off rented spaces were meant to. There were days he was lonely, of course, but a crazy schedule and plenty of people keen for his attention made times of actual solitude a true rarity. He even had a personal assistant; the kind of man who genuinely believed everything was his responsibility. Sometimes, Steven had to schedule in time to pee.

He'd dived into work once Alistair went home to Scotland. It was a blur of condensed memories that he found hard to untangle. He'd lived like a real life montage, concentrating on attaining career goals like they were the only thing in his life and, in truth, they had been.

It seemed Alistair had been less focussed. Steven had known that Al was in trouble, depressed and struggling. He still had enough friends in Aberdeen to keep an eye on his ex-husband and report in every now and then. Ray might be the most overt of those, but he certainly wasn't alone in suggesting that Al had gone back to heavy gambling.

It would be effortless to put his hand into his pocket and bail Alistair out again.

Steven shook his head, admonishing himself. No, that door was firmly closed and opening it again would invite the flood. He couldn't really help Alistair anyway—any money he sent would just feed the man's vice. To get out of his troubles, Alistair had to make the decisions himself.

Steven couldn't help feeling that it would never happen.

"So, you're finally coming to sign the paperwork," he said to the empty room.

He would be legally single again.

———————

Ray hadn't been lying. Sat across the empty table from Alistair, Steven felt his emotions warring. He had expected this to be easier.

"If we could just have your signature here." Mariah, Steven's solicitor, wasn't wasting time, and why would she? This wasn't a reconciliation or a court hearing, it was just the last-ditch attempt to get Alistair to actually sign the papers. She handed the big Scot a pen.

Alistair said nothing as he scratched his name onto the paper. Once, twice, three times as the woman at his shoulder pointed. He hadn't said anything of note since he'd arrived, and nothing at all to his ex-husband. Steven had remained quiet as well. What was there to say?

"That's excellent, thank you." Mariah accepted the pen back.

Al's clothes were smart but old, clean but worn. Steven knew the man well, knew that he didn't want to be like this. Alistair had been stylish and well-dressed. He enjoyed luxuries like good shirts and quality products. Sitting there, slightly dishevelled, and obviously lacking sleep, he seemed a shell of the man he'd once been.

"Am I done?" he asked.

"Yes, that's everything. Thank you."

He didn't speak another word as he stood and left the room. Steven watched him go, but Alistair didn't even glance in his direction.

"Steven, it's done." Mariah passed him the papers. "You are officially a single man."

Steven didn't glance at the envelope as he put it into his bag. "Thanks."

"Are you OK?"

"I'm fine. A little emotional as to be expected. I thought he might say something to me."

"They often don't. I wouldn't take it personally. I'm sure in the future, you'll be able to talk again, if that's what you want."

Working with Mariah for months meant they had built up a small friendship. Steven felt relieved that she was there now.

"Do you have somewhere to go?" she asked.

He looked at his phone. "Actually, I need to rush. I'm meant to be meeting my personal trainer soon."

"Sounds good. I'll be in touch."

Steven pushed himself up and out. He sent for an Uber and made his way down the stairs to meet the car. As he exited into the street, he coughed hard. As had happened a few times, his chest felt tight and it was hard to breathe. Steven leaned on a wall and steadied himself as the Uber pulled up.

"Are you alright, sir?" One of the perks of the luxury service was a driver who pretended to care.

"I'm fine." Steven slipped in through the proffered door. "I'll be fine."

It wasn't far to the gym. As they drove, Steven tried to shake off the turmoil in his mind. Should he have offered something to Alistair? He hadn't even invited him for lunch.

Lunch with Al. He shook his head. How long had it been since he'd enjoyed lunch with Al? Well, it would never be again.

Joey met him in reception. "You look like a man in need of a workout."

"I do." The focus and distraction would set him right.

"Then let's get to it. Get changed and I'll meet you in the gym in five minutes."

Alone in the gym except for his personal trainer, Steven's mind whirled. Alistair had aged more than the few years it had been. What troubles was he having? Hadn't Steven agreed to be with him through thick and thin? Had he abandoned his husband when he had been needed the most?

That damned open relationship. Why had Alistair been so keen to fuck other men? Why had he taken everything they'd had and ruined it? Had Steven really not been enough? Had he been too fat? Too unattractive? Too boring?

These were thoughts that had plagued him for months following the initial breakup. Thoughts that had been purged and were meant to be gone forever.

Gone forever. Like Alistair.

Steven cried. He stepped off the elliptical machine and sunk to the floor.

"Steven?" Joey asked.

Unable to control himself, he sobbed.

"Shit, Steven, what happened?"

"I'm divorced. After three years, I finally managed to get Alistair to sign the papers. He was here, he came and did it, and now it's done. I should feel free and instead ..."

He looked at the floor. "He was supposed to be my fairy tale. My happily ever after. He was my everything. Through all the troubles I had, he was there. We were inseparable and our civil partnership ceremony was our big day. It was meant to be the happiest day of my life. *He* was meant to be the love of my life. And it's all been erased. Officially removed as if it never happened in the first place."

"I'm sorry."

"It's not your fault. It's mine. Mine and his. We didn't know what we were doing and we couldn't make it work. No fairy tale. No happily ever after. Just a piece of paper that says we are no longer legally tied."

He stood up. "I'm sorry, Joey, look at me being a wanker."

"It's fine. If you want to stop for today, go out and get drunk or something ..."

"At three in the afternoon?"

"Many people have done far worse."

Steven laughed ruefully. "Me included. But not today. Today I'm going to get buff."

He stepped back on the elliptical. "Push me harder and further than we've been doing. I'll sweat him out of my system."

Or, at least, he thought, I'll try.

CHAPTER 29

The bubbles in the champagne clung to the side of the glass. Steven watched them rise, pop, and disappear with distracted interest.

"Steven?" The voice made him turn. It was repeated, louder. "Steven!"

Waving at him was a familiar face, though one he'd not seen in years. Charles had his hand high in the air and a broad smile on his face.

Christ. Steven stared. You haven't stopped being fucking handsome, have you?

Charles had obviously dressed up for the event. They all had—there was something about a gay networking event that brought out the shiniest version of each attendee. With Charles, though, the effect was both stunning and seemingly effortless. He wore the tailored jacket with a comfortable ease as if it was little more than casual wear, and his neatly pressed shirt perfectly offset both the cool mahogany of his hair and the blue tone of his jacket and trousers.

Steven realised with a start that he was analysing the man's look in a little too much detail and took a step forward instead.

"I can't believe it's you!" Charles said. "After you disappeared with your boyfriend at that party in Aberdeen, I never heard back from you."

Steven was stunned that the other man remembered.

"I'm so sorry about that! But Charles, how have you been?" He embraced the other man tightly.

"I'm well." Charles grabbed Steven's hand and pulled him. "Come on, there's someone I want to introduce you to."

Steven breathed in his old friend's scent as he followed him across the room. Feelings he had long forgotten flooded him such that his heart skipped.

Calm down, Steven.

"This is my friend, Josh."

Josh was slight and Asian. Steven took him in a single glance, noting immediately the similarities in their look and build. Immediately, a wave of jealousy took him. He gulped.

"Pleased to meet you."

"Josh, this is Steven." Charles beamed. "We went to St. Andrews together. I had the biggest crush on him back then!"

"What?" Steven stared. "No way! I had the biggest crush on *you*, Charles."

Suddenly, Steven felt mortified. To have blurted that out in front of Charles' boyfriend was horrific. He felt his face flush, turned to Josh and apologised. "That was a long time ago. All in the past. I'm really happy to meet you Josh, it looks like you are keeping Charles happy."

Josh laughed. "Me? No! No! It's not like that. I mean, I'm sure I do keep Charles happy but we're not together like that. You can have nostalgic crushes all you like, they don't bother me. I'm a colleague, a paediatrician."

"Wow, a gathering of doctors!" Steven was painfully aware that everything he said was vapid.

"What about you, Steve? Happily married?" Charles asked.

Steven held up his left hand, the mark that had remained for so long after he'd taken off his ring now faded to nothing. "Happily divorced."

"What?" Charles reached out to Steven's hand, his finger touching where the ring had once been. "How did that happen?"

"I know, right? Who'd be stupid enough to let all this go?" Steven took a small step back and gestured at his body. Internally, he winced again.

Charles and Josh both smiled.

"Hey, Steven." Edward tapped him on the shoulder. Steven breathed out, relieved to be saved by his friend.

"Hey, Ed. Charles, Josh, this is my good friend, Edward."

They exchanged greetings. Edward looked at him. "I promised to drag you over to talk to some friends."

"Sure." Steven turned back to Charles. "Let's not lose touch this time. Why don't you take my number?"

It took less than half a minute to add Charles to his contact list. Steven excused himself and allowed Edward to lead him away.

"He's not bad on the eye," Ed opined.

"No one is bad on the eye to you." Steven laughed. "But I do agree. I've always had a thing for Charles."

"No shit, I could feel you babbling from across the room."

"It hadn't quite got that bad."

"It was about to!"

Steven grinned. "You're right."

"And you have his number."

"I do."

"And he has a boyfriend."

"No, just a friend."

"Oh, that's a good, then. You should follow it up, but not now. The dragging you away excuse wasn't a lie. There are people who'd love to meet Mr. Famous Doctor."

Are you free today? Would love to meet up. C.

Steven and Charles had been texting each other for a few days. Steven had left it a full twenty-four hours after the party but didn't really know why. The first simple 'hello' message had led to a relaxed three-hour text conversation that had been far more entertaining than the documentary he'd had on in the background. But neither of them had previously broached the subject of a date.

Was this a date?

Steven had met Charles at St. Andrews, his first medical university before he moved to specialise in Aberdeen. Charles had been someone he had lusted over from afar, unsure of the other man's sexual leaning and unwilling to declare as being gay himself. A little experience would have told him Charles was into men, though; looking back at his behaviour, it was obvious.

Obvious to everyone except the nervous Malaysian guy who wanted it to be that way the most.

There had been a crossroads moment where perhaps Steven's life could have gone differently. The second-year medical students had all been split into groups of four for a rural placement in the Scottish countryside. Two of the girls, plus Charles and himself, were sent away to see what it was like being doctors in the real world.

The girls had shared accommodation, naturally, and he and Charles had been given a room between them. The journey there had been great, filled with getting-to-know-you chatter and budding friendships. Charles had smiled at Steven constantly, but the tall man's confidence had been intimidating rather than enticing.

Because I was so nervous. Because I was such a fool.

Being intimidated meant he never kept the gaze, never smiled back. Instead, he'd avoided looking at Charles as much as possible.

The place they had been allocated had three rooms; a small kitchen, quaint and dated living room, and a bedroom with two small separate beds. Of course, there was no problem for the young men to take one of the beds each and spend the week chatting through the nights, but again, Steven's nerves had got the better of him.

He'd lied to avoid the awkward room sharing. "I've been a bit ill and my cough hasn't gone. How about I sleep in the living room so that I don't disturb you at night?"

How about I sleep in the living room because your very presence excites and unnerves me?

"The living room?" Charles asked. "On the sofa? In case you wake me up?"

"Yeah, it's fine. I'll be comfortable. Honestly, I'm waking up throughout the night and sneezing a lot at the moment. I know this placement is important to you. I don't want to affect your time here because I'm stopping you from getting a good night's sleep."

Charles raised an eyebrow. "If that's what you want, I suppose."

It's not what I want.

"Yes. I'll just feel a lot less guilty."

He took the duvet and pillow and placed it at the end of the sofa. "There, sorted."

Charles shrugged.

In the morning Steven washed quickly and knocked on the bedroom door. He'd unpacked into there and if he wanted to get dressed, he needed to go in.

"Come in."

"Hey, did you sleep well? I just need to get dressed."

Charles was lying on the cold floor, doing sit-ups in his underwear. His chest was smooth and toned. Steven watched as the other man pulled himself up, lay down, pulled up again, each time with a slight grunt of effort.

"I see you're into your fitness."

Charles wiped the sweat from his forehead. "Gotta keep myself in shape."

It was the same each morning. A gentle knock from Steven, a welcome greeting from the other side, and then Charles exercising, never wearing more than a pair of boxer shorts.

320 **VINCENT WONG**

It was everything Steven could do to keep his overwhelming crush a secret, but the week went past and nothing was ever said. Nothing was ever done.

Had that been his opportunity? Had that been the time he should have come out to someone?

He'd have said 'no', anyway. The handsome and well-dressed medical student was leagues away from anything Steven could hope to touch.

Meet? Of course. Lunch?

12:30?

Steven grinned as his younger heart fluttered.

I'll get Martin to make us a reservation.

Charles had teased him relentlessly about his personal assistant in an earlier exchange. Having Martin organise their little lunch date would be a sort of inside joke that Charles would enjoy.

Oh yes, get Martin to. Far be it for you to pick up a phone yourself.

Well, I have to phone Martin, so...

Charles sent a crying laughing emoji. Steven breathed deeply and switched to messaging his PA. All of a sudden, lunchtime seemed impossibly far away and desperately soon all at once.

Hi Martin, can you arrange a lunch appt. for Charles and myself for 12:30. Somewhere nice and central.

A single thumbs-up was Martin's typical efficient acknowledgement. Why waste time typing a sentence when you can use a simple picture?

It wasn't a date, though. Just lunch.

———

Charles was there first. He stood as Steven approached and pulled out a chair.

"Really?" Steven settled himself into the seat.

"Sorry, I don't know why I did that. Over polite upbringing, I suppose."

"It's nice. Very different from some of the ways I've been treated."

"I aim to please."

Steven beamed at him. Charles had always been very easy to like. "Are you hungry?"

"Not hugely." Steven's appetite had been diminished lately. "But this place is delicious, so I'll eat, even if it's just a salad. I'm trying to be healthy, too. I have ..."

Charles raised an eyebrow. "Are you going to share?"

Steven giggled. "Oh, it's silly, really, but important to me. London Pride is coming up and I'm part of a dance troupe. We're performing on the stage there. It's harder than it looks and the training is really intense. I've been hitting the gym constantly."

"It's not silly, it sounds great."

"Yeah it is. Geri—she's the singer—she's really fantastic. Such a vibrant person to be around and ..."

Steven became lost in his own enthusiasm, his words tumbling over each other in a flood. It had been so long since someone had just sat and listened to him like that, with no poorly-disguised impatience on their face. Charles genuinely seemed to enjoy the story, laughing in all the right places.

The food came and they ate and a slot in Steven's schedule that had meant to be no more than an hour became an uncharacteristic afternoon of selfish pleasure. He texted Martin as they left the restaurant, telling his assistant to put off everything for the rest of the day as something had come up.

As they walked through St. James' Park, Steven realised Charles had taken his hand. When had that happened? It felt so natural, so comfortable.

"No open relationships." Steven blurted out the sentence in the middle of Charles' unabashed amusement regarding a squirrel.

"What?"

"This." Steven indicated their joined hands. "This is something great. Something that I think I've wanted ever since I first met you, and certainly something I never thought I'd have, but I need to be honest with you from the outset if it is going to become anything, and honest means we cover this right now. No open relationships. No secret liaisons. No fucking Grindr."

"I ..." Charles eyes were wide. Then Steven was unexpectedly wrapped in a tight embrace. "I don't know what happened with you and Alistair, and I'm not about to ask. Not yet. But if you need the assurance that I won't go off fucking other men, then you can have that right now. I feel the same way. Why even be in a relationship if it's not going to be monogamous. You might as well just not bother with it. No open relationship."

Steven shook. His eyes were wet.

"Come on, let's not worry about this. I'm not about to hurt you, and you interrupted me telling you about the time a squirrel got tangled in my hair. I'll finish my story and then, if you want to share what happened to you, I'll listen. And if not, then we can go and just have an ice cream."

"I'm not eating an ice cream. Do you have any idea how hard I've worked on these abs?"

"No ice cream? OK. And I've not actually seen the abs, yet. I've been imagining them for a while, though." Charles' eyes sparkled.

"On our first date?!" Steven's mock offence came with fluttering eyelashes.

"Imagining is definitely allowed, right?"

"Oh, more than imagining is allowed."

———

Charles' work schedule meant he left a little after five o'clock. Steven packed his gym kit and made his way to meet Joey. Tonight's workout was going to be fantastic. A great end to a perfect day.

CHAPTER 30

Shoot him. Kill him. Kill the child. Be a man. Grow up. Man of the house, now.

The gun felt heavy.

Shoot him. Right in the chest. No more childishness.

Down the sights was little Steven.

"No room for you anymore, little boy."

He squeezed the trigger.

Steven woke up with a strangled breath. His chest was tight, the air struggling to reach his lungs. Trembling, he leaned over the side of the bed and clawed at the air, desperate for oxygen. He coughed, spat sticky mucus into the glass on his bedside table and drew in a painful breath. With a strange instinct, he looked to his side, expecting to see Charles sleeping there, hoping that he could curl in the other man's calm arms for comfort.

It was ridiculous; they'd been on one date.

One joyful date.

He peeled himself out of the sheets. It had been years since he'd had that dream, the one where he killed his inner child. What had once become a nightly fear had faded into nothingness.

Why was it back?

His life was different now. He was successful, he was healthy and fit, he had new friends and a career that he'd always dreamed of. He had Charles. Nightmares of his childhood from half a world and half a lifetime away were no longer relevant.

He looked at the clock. Five a.m. If he had a longish shower and a small breakfast, the gym would open and he could shake off the unpleasantness there.

The hot water relaxed his muscles and brought a smile to his lips. The shower in this place was one of the indulgences he truly relished.

The rail had warmed the towel to a pleasant temperature. Wrapped in the soft fabric, Steven made himself a breakfast of fruit and yoghurt. He dressed, ate, and called an Uber.

The gym would clear his head.

———

"Is lunch together going to become a thing?" Steven pulled out his own seat, noting that Charles had not stood to do so this time.

"If you want it to be. Good day? I ordered you a salad, as this is going to be fleeting. I have a horrific work schedule today."

"Work's been OK. I need to make up for yesterday."

"Sorry."

Steven chuckled. "I'm not complaining."

"I spoke to Claire." Charles took a sip of his water. "I just had to share with someone we both knew. She said to say hi, and that she was pleased, and that you owe her a phone call."

Steven looked up as the waiter put his plate in front of him. Charles had called Claire? This was moving forward far quicker than he imagined it would. Telling their friends was ...

Was what? Why was he so worried?

"Steven?" Charles gently poked the back of his hand with his fork. "Still with me?"

"Yes, sorry! I was just thinking." Be honest. "I was thinking how nice it was that you told Claire. Does this make you my boyfriend?"

"No. Yesterday made you my boyfriend. Telling Claire was just icing on the cake." Charles leaned forward and kissed him across the table. There was a clatter as a glass tipped and water spilled onto the cloth. Steven felt it drip onto his thigh.

He didn't care. He wrapped his arms around Charles' neck and pulled him in tight. He wanted this. He wanted all of this.

———

Geri hugged Steven tightly. "That was brilliant," she said, referring to the latest run through of the routine. There were less than two weeks before their performance at London Pride. Two weeks and it was already looking polished.

The others gathered around. It had been Steven's idea to add the death drop to the choreography, much to Geri's delight and Simon's slightly nervous acceptance. That he was now able to pull it off every time had everyone smiling.

"I'm so hyped." Steven's life was back on the path that he wanted. Sure, the gym regime, now up to twice a day, was punishing, but his spare time was spent with Charles and his friendships with all his dance troop had gone from strength to strength. He felt on top of the world and had no intention of coming down.

"I wish you weren't going away," Geri said, not for the first time.

It had become an almost-farcical conversation between them. The singer would push on him to cancel his trip to Shanghai, and Steven would impress on her about what an honour it was for him at this stage of his career, and how it could mean so much for the future. She'd relent, he'd feel relieved, and they'd do it all again tomorrow.

"It's late." Simon held up his hand. "You lot all need to go home. We're back here tomorrow at seven."

Steven looked at the clock. Quarter past eleven. He'd hoped to spend another couple of hours with Charles after practice, but it had gone long. If he was to be up in the morning, he needed his beauty sleep.

A few moments later and the Uber had been summoned.

"Get some rest." Geri met him on his way to the door.

Wearily, Steven nodded back.

The next two weeks were going to be some of the busiest of his life. The flight to Shanghai was in three days and he'd not be home for another six. Ray's visit began the day afterwards, and London Pride came three days after that. It was only a single day after the dust had settled on their dance routine before he was due in Cardiff for the Miss Universe competition. There was a motivational speech for children with learning difficulties a couple of days after that, and he had a lecture to give on the same day. It was too much, he knew; in truth both his mind and body were beginning to build to a crescendo, but with the right amount of focus, he could achieve it all.

He forced himself to shower before collapsing and looked at the bedsheets with pure exhaustion; last night's fever dream meant he had to strip the linen. With a sigh, he pulled the covers away from the bed and replaced them with clean, soft, cotton. His body ached everywhere, but the memories of the evening's perfect practiced death drops had been worth it.

Despite his aching tiredness, sleep didn't come easily. It was hot, even with the indulgent air conditioning, and he was sweating more than was comfortable.

By the time his eyes closed for the last time that night, the morning alarm was looming. Sleep was going to be short.

————

Be a man.

Kill the child.

Steven looked down the sights at the small boy, shivering from fear.

"No room for you."

No room for you.

"No room for you anymore, little boy."

He squeezed the trigger.

And woke in agonising pain.

Steven gasped, but the breath didn't come. Crunched up foetal, he felt every muscle in his body tense. The pain ran through him like fire, but worse was the lack of oxygen. Desperate, he blinked and grabbed for his phone. It lit the night, but anything more was impossible as his fingers fumbled with the controls.

With a rasping gasp, warm air sucked into his throat. It filled his lungs but felt as if it did nothing when there. He coughed, still doubled over, and his eyes filled with tears.

Slowly, it subsided a little. Steven forced himself out of bed, ignoring the moisture that made the sheets stick to him. He grabbed the glass of water, forced some inside him and scrambled for ibuprofen. They went into his mouth like tiny white saviours, and he fell back onto the bed.

The pain didn't go away. It drove down his right-hand side like he'd been harpooned in the chest. Years of medical training and knowledge swam in his mind as he diagnosed himself. Not the left-hand side, he reasoned, all concentrated in the right, so not too serious.

Not too serious? He couldn't speak. Breathing had become something that required his full concentration.

He propped himself up with pillows and tried to relax, counting each breath. One ... two ... three ...

He drifted back to sleep in the low two-hundreds.

Waking hours later, the pain had dimmed but not stopped. He pushed himself to his feet and took another two painkillers. He was due at the gym. His stomach was toned, and he looked good but he couldn't let the regime slip. The pain would go. It wasn't serious. Just a reaction to all the intense exercise. Just a couple more weeks, that's all he needed to push for. He'd have a proper break when the performance was done.

By the time the car picked him up, he'd regained control over his body. The pain had dropped back to being a dull ache—either that, or he'd become used to the stabbing sensation. It was fine. Daylight and cool air were all that had been needed, something to shake off the nightmare.

"No," said Joey, fifteen minutes later. "Don't be fucking ridiculous."

"I just need to do the toning exercises."

"You need to let your body rest. You're a fucking doctor, Steven. What would be your professional opinion? What advice would you give someone coming to you in your condition? Would it be a hard hour's workout at the gym? Two hours?"

Steven looked at the floor. "The pain's gone."

"Bullshit." Joey picked up a dumbbell, a small one; eight kilos. Steven had outgrown those a year before. "Catch."

His hand gripped the bar and the pain ripped through him. The dumbbell hit the padded floor with a thud.

"Yeah, I thought as much."

"Fuck."

"Go home. Rest."

"The performance is in two weeks. I'm not going to be training for almost a week of that because I'm in Shanghai. I need to be shredded."

"You are shredded. Have you looked in a mirror recently?" She shook her head. "You will also find a gym in Shanghai, idiot. You won't even need to leave the hotel for that. Don't lie to me. Today is your day off. Go home, watch some fucking TV."

"I have work."

"No, you don't. Call in sick."

"You're not my boss."

"Who is, Steven? Who is going to call this if it isn't your personal trainer? You're not seeing a doctor today, are you? You're not calling your mum. No, I'm what you have, so I'm what you get. As your *professional* personal trainer, I know more about your body and its limits than you do. I am telling you that you hit a limit. You know this. Waking up with stabbing pain in the middle of the night and being barely able to stand? That's a limit. Go home. Go to bed."

Steven smirked. "You're cute when you are all stern."

"You're flirting with me, now? It's not going to work in any way. Home. Now. Do you want me to call you a cab?"

"No, I got it. I'll just go get changed."

"Change at home."

"Are you serious?"

"Very. Go." Joey pointed to the door.

Steven grinned. For all his resistance, he knew she was right, and more than that, he very much appreciated her caring.

He instructed the driver to stop at a chemist. He needed a pharmacy if he was going to stock up on enough painkillers to keep whatever this was at bay. In the car the pain had built up again, and it took everything he had just to walk to the counter.

He didn't expect to fall.

He didn't expect to pass out.

————————

The ambulance monitor showed an O2 stat under 85%.

They'd put him on high-flowing oxygen.

Pneumothorax, thought Steven, self-diagnosing.

Not a big deal. A little too much time at the gym.

Just a little too much time at the gym.

————————

Coming out of the x-ray, the radiologist ran over and pushed one of the porters out of the way.

"Are you wearing a chain?"

"What?" Steven felt around his neck. "No."

"Let me see."

She pulled down his hospital gown to check.

Steven stared. Weirdo.

———————

"Oh fuck!"

Whose voice was that?

Steven looked around him. Medical emergency unit. UCLH. He recognised it.

———————

"Have you had any exposure to asbestos?"

"What? No. Not that I know of."

"Do you smoke?"

"No."

"Weed? Recreationally?"

"No."

"Any other drugs?"

"No, they're not my thing."

"Have you noticed any weight loss?"

Steven shook his head. "I'm in a dance group for London Pride coming up. I've been training hard. Of course, I've had weight loss, I've been working for it. Abs like this don't make themselves! I'm happy with the results."

"Night sweats?"

"I've had a few nightmares. And it's warm outside. I've had to have the air conditioning on."

Steven paused, his mind alert and working.

"What's wrong? I'm a doctor. I've been where you are, asking the questions. Just tell me what you're thinking."

He wasn't going to do that. Training dictated that he wouldn't speculate. Analyse the data, look at the evidence. No guesswork. Not out loud, anyway.

"Just cut to the point," he insisted.

"We found a slight shadow on the x-ray of your right lung. We need to do further tests. I'll prepare your admission now."

––––––––––

"I'm sorry, Steven. I told your mum." Martin hovered over his bed. His face was contrite and worried.

"My mum?"

"Everyone is worried."

"That's taking it a bit far."

"It isn't and you know it. I know I overstepped. I hadn't meant to, but she's on your WhatsApp group and I was telling your friends. Some of them are here to see you."

"Some of them?"

"Geri's here. Charles is on his way. Joey's been on the phone to me all day. She can't come for a while, but she'll be here this evening."

"I need to get out of here."

"Not going to happen. Stop pretending this isn't what it is."

"We don't know what it is. They need to do more scans."

"I know." Martin's phone bleeped. "I need to go. I'll tell Geri to come in."

––––––––––

"I'll be up and about in time for the performance," Steven promised.

"Stop it. That's not important. You are." Geri waved aside his worry.

"It is important."

"It will be fine, and no, it isn't important, Steven. Trust me. I've been around a little longer than you, and I've seen a lot more. You learn what is important and what isn't when your friends are lying in hospital beds. Now, stop talking about the performance and tell me if there's anything you need."

––––––––––

"We're coming to London." The voice was cracked and filled with tears.

"Mum, what?"

"Vivienne agrees. She's arranged everything."

"I'm fine, you don't need to come here."

"Don't you tell me what I need and don't need. We're coming."

"Mum."

"I won't have any of it, Steven. Just accept that your mother is visiting London for a while, and don't worry about our accommodation. It is already sorted. Your singer friend, Geri, has offered her spare apartment. Honestly, that you have friends who own 'spare' apartments now is very strange to me, but it is what it is. She seems very kind."

"She's lovely, Mum."

"Good. That's all settled then. I have to get off the phone now, but we will see you soon."

"Thanks, Mum."

"I love you, my son."

"I love you, too."

"They're letting me stay overnight." Charles took Steven's hand.

An afternoon of insistence meant that Steven no longer had the energy to argue. In truth, he wanted his new boyfriend there. "Thank you."

"I never thought I'd actually end up with you, you know. I remember that first week we spent together. Rural placement out in the middle of nowhere north of Perth. Do you remember that?"

Steven smiled. "Of course."

"You did that weird thing where you fucked off to sleep in the living room. I was so upset. I figured you were rejecting me. Push away the gay guy, was what I thought. One of those 'I'm not staying in the same room as the gay man'. But, then, I was also sure you were gay then, too. It was all a bit confusing."

"I wasn't—"

Charles cut him off. "So, I ... God, it's so embarrassing now that I think about it. I would listen out for you waking up, and then I'd start exercising. I knew you'd come in for your clothes, so I made sure I was just wearing underwear to get your attention. I was relatively proud of my looks, I admit. I thought you'd see me all sweaty and naked and not be able to resist. But you did. Every day for a fucking week. I did my little semi-nude performance for you; sit ups, press ups, those fucking chin up bastard things on that bar that I broke half way through the week. None of it made a difference to you. You kept fucking off, saying you had a cough. You know, I lay awake all night one night and you didn't cough once. You liar."

Steven laughed. It caught his breath and made him wince, the air suddenly vanishing. In pain, he squeezed his eyes closed and regained control.

"I was definitely a liar. Not lying now, though."

———

"I'm arranging for an MRI and a CT scan." The doctor walked around the bed, took a look at the flowers distractedly, and then met Steven's eyes. "Don't expect to be going anywhere."

———

"You need a biopsy. It'll happen later today."

"Later today?" Steven cringed. "I need to get out of here. It's been two nights. This is day three. I can't just stay here."

"Get up and run off then, if you like. Don't come crying to me if you collapse in the corridor, though."

Steven smirked. He liked the man's direct manner and sense of humour.

"Oh good, I can see we're done being pathetic then. You have a PA. Nice man, Martin, I've spoken to him. He assures me that all will be fine."

"I'm meant to be flying to Shanghai."

"You're not flying anywhere. He's doubtless sorted that out by now. Fly and die, that's my professional opinion. I suggest that you stay in the bed instead."

"And I have a performance in just over a week. I need to be there for it. I need to get fit for it."

"Very nice. I'll look forward to seeing it on the TV."

Steven gave in. "What time is the biopsy?"

"It'll happen when it happens. Not in a rush, are you?" The consultant smiled and left the room.

Steven gazed at the ceiling. With the doctor gone, the humour had gone too. A biopsy. It could be for a few reasons, technically, but he knew that only one of them was relevant. Data gathering. Checking. Ruling it out or ruling it in.

Steven felt the tears run down his face. A biopsy was so they could confirm that he had cancer.

CHAPTER 31

Ray sat slowly onto the plush armchair. He exhaled and leaned forward, putting his palms on his knees.

"Cancer?"

Steven smiled weakly from the other chair.

"Your fucking life, Steven, I swear."

"Yeah, I know."

"I don't think you do. Have you any idea how many times I nearly backtracked on this visit, thinking I should just leave it, let you do whatever you needed in peace?"

"But then you remembered I'd got you tickets for Miss Universe and everything else became irrelevant?"

Ray grinned. "Something like that. Plus, you know, I thought it might be the last time I ever fucking see you."

Steven looked at the floor. "It's not like that."

"It could be, couldn't it? I mean, you're the fucking doctor, you tell me."

"It could be."

"What're the results. Is it cancer? I mean, what are they saying?"

"They sent me home early. That's why I can be here to meet you. They sent me home because there were too many emergency cases that needed seeing to. They needed my bed. They didn't even get around to doing the biopsy."

"Fuck, that's cold."

"Yeah, I'm waiting to hear when I should go in for it."

"So, now what? We just sit around and watch movies until the doctor phones?"

"Pretty much. My mum might pop over. Her and Viv are staying at Geri's place, and it took me all the convincing I had to get her to let me sleep here rather than there. You coming has been my lifeline to a bit of privacy."

"Glad I could help."

"You always do."

"I didn't tell Al. I felt I should; hell, I even picked up the phone a couple of times with the intention of doing so, but I thought you wouldn't want me to. Old life intruding on the new one and all that."

"Thanks. I don't want him to know. I don't want to see him. That part of my life is over. It's bad enough that Zoe found out."

"Your sister?"

"One of the people I work with knows her. They've been at a few conferences together. Emma didn't really understand how deep the split between us went and thought that Zoe should know, so she called and reported it in like a good little spy."

Ray snorted. "What did the bitch say?"

"I think her exact comment was that I deserved it. Emma was shocked. She said Zoe had no soul."

"Are you OK about it?"

"About Zoe? Or about probably having cancer?"

"Either. Both."

"Zoe's part of that old life. Very much gone. No, I don't care what she thinks, not really. Sure, there's a part of me that wishes I'd had a sister who loved me and tries to make sense of it, but I've had therapy for that now. Honestly, I don't let it bother me."

"And the cancer?"

Steven looked up. "I'm scared shitless."

"Sorry, man."

"It's OK, Ray. It's just part of it all. I'm beginning to think I did something fucking horrific in a past life."

"Like I said earlier, your life ... fuck me."

"My life is pretty sweet now though, except for the cancer, and fuck that shit. I have Charles and that's fucking wonderful. I have Geri and the dancing. I'm so ripped." Steven tapped his stomach. "I'm not allowed to exercise until we know what's going on, so I'll just run with not eating in order to stay in shape for the performance."

"Are you still doing that?"

"Absolutely. It's been months of training and I'm not about to let a little shortness of breath get in the way."

"You're a machine. The rest of us would just fucking lie back and hammer the shit out of Netflix, trying to take our mind off it. You're wondering how you can squeeze a bit more training into the week."

"I was meant to go to Shanghai, too. Remember that?"

"Conference thing?"

"Yup. Only no Shanghai. I missed out on something that could have been really influential for my career."

"Good. Shows you have enough sense to listen a little."

Steven snorted. "Whatever."

"Anyway, I'm here now, so what's the plan?"

"I have to stay in. You can go explore the sights if you like—I can make a few calls and get you in places and stuff, or sort you out for some decent food, whatever. I'm stuck here, though. Hopefully that call will come soon or, like I said, we might get an impromptu visit from my mum and little sister. Charles is coming over to make us dinner once he's finished at work. He's a great cook. You'll love him."

"All sounds good. I'm staying with you all day, don't think I need to go out. I can see London any time."

"Are you sure? I'm not going to be very exciting."

"We haven't had a proper conversation in ages. I've got my own news, too, so I'll catch you up on that and you know what, if you become horribly boring, then I see a really big TV screen over on that wall." Ray chuckled. "I bet your busy lifestyle means you've missed tons of great shit to watch."

———————

From the sofa, Steven listened to the chatter of his family and friends. Geri had brought his mother and Viv around late in the afternoon, Charles had surprised them all by having Claire with him when he arrived at six, and Ray had been there the whole day, waiting on Steven as if he was a prince.

The seven of them gathered in the living room and spilled into the kitchen regularly to check on their affable chef as Charles worked on conjuring a gastronomic masterpiece for the impromptu dinner party.

Ray sat down next to Steven.

"Your mum seems quite taken with Charles. I didn't expect that."

"Yeah, it's been a minor shock to me, too. I'm just pleased there's no drama. This could have all gone very wrong."

"Oh, Steve, it's early yet. Give it time and a little more booze."

Steven grinned.

"Anyway. I'm meant to be helping in the kitchen. Back in a wee while. Shout if you need anything."

Viv took Ray's place by Steven's side. "Your place is crazy. I just went and poked in the shower. How many heads do you need?"

Steven smiled. "All of them."

Viv pulled a face. "I don't think I want to know." She laughed and Steven smiled. He hadn't heard his little sister so joyful in such a long time. The years had passed since her ordeal and now she was almost considered an adult. Her childhood was being left behind where it belonged.

"How's life at Geri's?"

"Oh God, Stevie, that's dumb, too. Honestly, the woman has a second four-bedroom apartment that backs on to her own. There's an adjoining door and you can go from one luxurious home into another without stepping outside. And it's huge. I mean, your place is sick, but hers is on another scale. I'd feel squashed staying here with you and Ray by comparison."

"I'm glad you are enjoying your stay."

"It's great that all your work paid off, though. Do you remember when we used to worry if we could afford a coffee? You seem rich enough now to buy Starbucks. And I mean the company, not just one cup."

"I'm a bit off Starbucks. In fact, I think I'm a bit off even one small branch of Starbucks."

"Well, whatever. It's still a different world from how it used to be. Do you remember the little flat in Aberdeen where you, me and Mum used to live? I used to think that place was pretty cool, and you could fit all of it in your bedroom here."

"I liked living with you there. I'm surprised you remember."

"It was the first place I ever saw snow. I'll never forget it. I made that little snowman and put him in the freezer, do you remember?"

"I do."

"What happened to him?"

"He lived in the freezer a long time. Until I moved out, and then, sadly, he had to go."

"Was it a humane death?"

"I think he melted into the sink."

"It's the best way for a snowman." Viv chuckled.

"What are you two talking about?" Claire interjected. "Sorry, being nosy. Came over to say 'hi' and heard something about a snowman."

"Viv made a little one the first time she saw snow in Scotland. We kept it in the freezer for months."

"Aww, that's sweet. And what do you mean the first time you saw snow?"

"We don't get a lot in Malaysia," Viv said.

"Wow, I've never thought of that. Imagine growing up not seeing snow. That's crazy."

"My first time was in Brighton," said Steven. "I was even older. Seventeen."

"I think it loses its excitement. A few too many winters where it gets inside your clothes and runs down your back. You can have too much snow."

"Never!" cried both Steven and Viv together.

Claire laughed. "OK, I'm outvoted. Fair enough."

They continued discussing the differences between Malaysia and Britain for a while. Steven drifted off gently as the voices of his friend and his little sister passed over him. He winced; he needed his painkillers. With a gentle cough, he interrupted their conversation to ask if Claire would get the pills for him.

It was like he'd poured cold water over the atmosphere. Immediately, heads turned towards him, sympathy evident on them all.

"Oh come on, you can't all be like that." He swallowed the pills and drank deeply from his glass of water. "Yes, I have a tumour, but we don't even know if it's malignant. You are all doing well not mentioning it, and I appreciate it, but there's no point pretending it's not happening."

"Sorry," mumbled Geri from the kitchen door.

"You all have nothing to be sorry about. I tell you what, let's make it easy. We're going to give it a name." He thought for a moment. "Tristan. My tumour is called Tristan. Tristan, the tumour."

Ray snorted.

"And if you want to talk to me about it, do. You can ask me how he is. 'How's Tristan?', you can say, and I can answer 'oh, he's doing well, thanks for asking. I'll pass on your best wishes.'"

"That's a bit ambiguous," said Ray. "Is Tristan doing well mean it's good for you, or good for Tristan? Because I think you have opposing intentions."

"Hmm." Steven put his finger on his lip as if deep in thought. "Good for Tristan means good for me. When Tristan's doing badly, it's because I'm in pain." He gritted his teeth. "Which is the case now, actually, so if you'll all let me shut up for a bit and just talk over the top, that'd be great. I like listening to you all chat."

The room fell silent for a moment and then Charles called out for the table to be cleared. "Dinner's almost done."

Steven closed his eyes and let the pain wash over him. It was a regular dullness, something he was used to, as well as the shortness of breath that had now become part of his regular day. All those times at the gym and before ... He should have recognised the signs earlier.

"Come on, son," his mother was suddenly next to him. "Can you make it to the table to eat, or would you like us to bring your food to you here?"

"I'll come." He pushed himself up a little and then sank back down. "Though Charles may have to help me."

"Nonsense. I don't need a man to help me help my son, though he is a good man. I think I approve of him." With a strong arm and ignoring his protestations, Steven's mother lifted him to his feet.

————————

The biopsy was finally scheduled for the day before the London Pride festival.

"It's just in and out," Steven had assured Simon and Geri. "I'll be there on stage tomorrow. It'll be fantastic."

"We took out the death drop, Steven," said Simon. "We talked about it and we both know you worked so hard on it, but Geri and I agreed it was best not to push you too far. Especially the day after your biopsy."

"It's routine, the worst that happens is that I feel a bit giddy for a few hours afterwards. They said it was normal if I coughed up a bit of blood, that's all."

"Nonetheless, considering everything ... The rest of the routine is the same, and we're looking forward to having you up there, but let's not be stupid, OK?"

Steven nodded. In truth, he was relieved; the move was hard to get right and messing it up hurt. He knew that from the practice sessions.

"Be well. We'll see you tomorrow."

Outside UCLH, Claire held his hand. "It's going to be fine."

"Thanks for coming with me."

"Honestly, I'm pleased and surprised you picked me. I expected your mum or sister would want to be here instead."

"Mum would stress me out, Viv covers everything over with chatter and can get too much. You're my oldest friend."

"Wow, am I now? I suppose I am. We've known each other for so long. But what about Charles?"

"He's in there." Steven pointed to the hospital. "But he has a shift. He'll check on me as soon as he can."

"Well, come on then. Don't want to be late."

"Claire, I'm scared."

"I know, love. I am too. In fact, I'm fucking petrified and it's not something that's happening to me. But this is just a test. They're just wanting to see the situation."

"It is."

"And tests are easy. We've done a million ourselves."

"This is one of the less easy ones, but yes."

"Right, so come on, Doctor Steven."

"Lead on, Doctor Claire."

The hospital seemed more clinical than usual. Steven felt he was on the wrong side of every short conversation and the smells and sounds of the familiar environment were suddenly alien. He sat in the waiting room and glanced up at the reception desk every time there was a noise.

"You need to relax," said Claire.

"I'll get right on that."

The wait wasn't long. Soon, Steven was lying on a bed, looking up at the bright lights and trying to keep his mind off the proceedings. There was every chance they'd find it was benign.

The sedative took him off into a peaceful sleep ...

... And then Claire was holding his hand.

"Wake up, Mr. Sleepy Head. You're all done."

Steven tried to sit up and winced.

"Take it slow."

Steven pushed himself up and propped against a pillow.

"You feeling OK?" Claire asked. "Remember, you might cough up a bit of blood."

Steven nodded and then clutched his nose. A gush of blood poured into his hand.

"Fuck."

A nurse rushed over. She caught the blood in a bowl. "Unusual, but not totally unexpected. You'll be fine."

Steven looked up at her and tried to force a grin. "Sure, I'll just bleed to death here, save everyone some time."

He allowed the nurse to clean him up and lay back down.

"Just rest for an hour or so. Then you can go home."

"Just like that," said Claire.

"How's Tristan?" Steven asked.

"Big, like an orange. That's all they know. They'll phone you the results in a day or two."

"And until then?"

Claire twirled on the spot. "Don't you have a dance you want to get to?"

CHAPTER 32

The crowd jumped and danced in the sunlight. From his position on stage, a few steps from Geri's right side, Steven followed the practiced routine. His friend's singing boomed out into the audience and buoyed him. All the work, all the early mornings and late nights, all had come to this.

Forty minutes earlier, he had taken a full dose of painkillers and then more, determined that Tristan wouldn't spoil the event. So far it was working, pushing the pain from a debilitating roar to a dull ache that he was aware of but could ignore. The song was less than five minutes in total.

He could do this.

Around him, the other dancers moved in sequence, an array of colour and happiness of which he was thrilled to be a part. His own costume was flamboyant; a piece he'd designed himself to show off who he was, to make a statement. It was London Pride—it was a time to be honest, to be true to himself, to celebrate his life.

Looking out over the heads of the revellers, Steven wondered if his mother could see him. She'd said that she would come along in support but was this one step too far for her?

Geri caught his eye and beamed. The centre of everyone's attention, she was radiant on the stage. Steven smiled and pumped his hands in the air. He didn't need to concentrate on the dance, not anymore; the weeks and months had drilled it into him.

Hot.

Sweaty.

Breathless.

Perfect.

Then it was over, and he was being hugged, hustled off the stage with his fellow dancers, each one chattering about the experience, each one high on the delight.

"Fantastic," said Geri. She ran to him, looked him in the eyes. "Are you OK?"

"I'm good," promised Steven. "I'm better than good."

"How's Tristan?"

"Tristan can fuck off!" he howled.

They laughed together.

"I have to go," she apologised, "they want me to go straight into an interview. Are you sure you're OK?"

"Ray's here." Steven pointed down the ramp. "He'll look after me."

"Enjoy the party, but don't be irresponsible."

"Oh, I'm going to be irresponsible!" Steven flung his hands into the air dramatically. "I'm going to have the time of my life! Tristan's not getting in the way of anything today."

Geri hugged him. "Good for you." Then she was gone, pulled along by the rush of the afternoon.

Steven locked eyes with Ray and made a line for him. He had friends, good friends; he was going to be OK.

————

"You looked the part!" Edward grinned at him and knocked back his drink. "I don't think there was even space for you to be more gay than you were up there."

"Thanks." Steven accepted the compliment for what it was.

"You're welcome."

"I didn't want to say anything," Ray added, "but he's right. That pink shit was very gay."

"It's Pride, Ray, it's meant to be."

"Yeah, I get it. It's not like you've not been outdone, though, there are some people walking the streets like fucking peacocks."

"Your friend is being homophobic." Ed flicked his hair flamboyantly.

"Am I fuck!" Ray pushed him gently on the shoulder.

Steven laughed. "He's teasing you, Ray. And Edward, seriously, give the man a break. It's his first Pride."

"Where's Charlie, anyway?" asked Edward. "Isn't he meant to be meeting us?"

Steven looked at his phone. "Fifteen minutes. He'll be here."

"Time for a couple more then," said Edward.

"I'm up for that."

Ray caught the attention of the barman.

By the time Charles caught up with them, the three men were already feeling light. Steven grabbed his lover before he sat down and kissed him full on the mouth.

"Did you see me at all?"

"Sorry. I did ask for them to have the live stream on in the hospital, but it didn't fly with management. The news was on and we saw the odd bit, including some segments with Geri, but I couldn't quite see you. At one point, I thought I saw your arm, if that helps."

"Awww, Steve, didn't make the news." Ray patted him on the back. Steven noticed how gentle his friend had made the gesture. How gentle Tristan had forced the gesture to be.

"There's always YouTube." Steven grinned.

"Fame at last!"

"More drinks?" asked Charles. "I assume it's my round."

"I should probably slow down," said Steven. "Too much alcohol is not advised."

"Fuck that," said Ed. "Get him another, Charlie, and damn the Tristan problem."

"Just for a day," said Steven.

"Just for a day."

Steven leaned back into the chair. His back stung, the dressing that covered up the site of the biopsy was coming away under his t-shirt. Charles would fix it for him when he got back if he asked him to, but he wouldn't ask. Today was a day of celebration, a day of parties and delight, a day of friends and lovers.

It wasn't a day for Tristan. Steven was going to have fun.

————

The alarm beeped incessantly. Steven swore and forced his eyes open. Next to him, Charles stirred but remained asleep despite the noise. Reaching out an arm, Steven stabbed at his phone to be quiet and slowly sat up. He took the glass and the pills that he'd laid out the night before and swallowed. The painkillers would deal with Tristan and the hangover in equal measure; or at least he hoped that would be the case.

Ray was already up and eating breakfast.

"Fuck me, you're keen," Steven said.

"It's a four-hour drive and we're meant to be there for three. You actually need to get a fucking move on. I know how long it takes you to pamper yourself when you are being seen by people."

"Ray, it's eight in the morning. Even if I were to languish in the shower for an hour, we have time."

"It's ten past nine, and I want to stop for lunch."

Steven checked his phone. "Shit, how many times did I hit 'snooze'?"

Ray laughed. "More than once, it seems."

Charles was awake by the time Steven finished his shower. The three of them chatted as he got ready, comments shouted through doorways and across rooms. Each time the pain got too much, Steven pulled back from the conversation, but Ray was in full flow and neither of them noticed his silence.

More painkillers, an internal mask to add to the external one he was preparing. He had to look good today; after all, he was judging a beauty contest.

The car arrived all too soon. Charles kissed him goodbye at the door and Steven walked with Ray to the waiting Mercedes.

"You're one posh twat now, you know this, right?" Ray grinned once they were sat in the car.

Steven smiled. "We can drop you at Paddington and you can take the train, if you'd prefer."

"Yeah, fuck off."

"Honestly, Ray." Steven kept his voice low. "I'm quite pleased of the comfort. I don't think I'd feel a hundred percent doing this in some squashed train carriage."

"Tristan doing badly?"

Steven nodded. "Let's just have fun."

They relaxed into the drive and Steven drifted in and out of sleep. He was pleased to not be going to Cardiff alone.

The buzzing from his phone woke him sometime later. Looking out of the window, Steven saw the wide lanes of the M4 motorway. He breathed in and answered.

"Hello."

As the person on the other end of the line spoke, Steven nodded, quietly responding with murmurs of understand and assent. When it was done, he dropped the device onto his lap and his eyes filled with tears.

"Steve?"

"It's malignant. I have stage three lung cancer."

The operation was booked for four days later. Steven lived in a haze, relying on his friends more than he really wanted to. Once Ray went home to Scotland, Martin moved with impressive efficiency, taking every thread of Steven's life and controlling them like a master puppeteer. From an outside perspective, the Miss Universe GB judging night was an absolute triumph, and Steven was back the next day and straight into his other duties. Tristan, now growing dangerously, was not going to win.

In the bathroom, Steven coughed blood into the sink. It had gone from being a one-off event a few days earlier, to once a day, to today. He watched the red spittle swirl away down the plug hole and gritted his teeth. That was the fifth time since he'd struggled out of bed.

"Stevie?" Viv poked her head around the door. "You've been a while. Mum's worried."

"It's OK. I'm coming out."

They had all insisted that he move temporarily in with his Mum and little sister. Viv had been right; Geri's spare apartment was beautiful and spacious. He felt guilty tainting it with Tristan's foulness.

He squirted the spray cleaner and wiped around the sink.

"Hey, stop that, I'll sort it," Viv insisted. "Go and lie down."

He didn't want to lie down. He wanted to work.

But he couldn't. With one day left before the operation, he knew that was truly impossible.

"I want to talk to you and Viv, Mum," Steven chose to sit on one of the sumptuous settees rather than return to his bedroom.

"About what?"

"About what happens if I die tomorrow."

His mother stared at him. "Don't you say that!"

"I have to, Mum. I'm sorry, I know it's not what you want to hear, but there's only a fifty-fifty chance that I'll make it. This is cancer, not some scuffed knee."

"Steven, you are not going to die."

"Hopefully not, but we should be prepared. I've had Martin sort out some paperwork and I'll be signing it tonight when he brings it over. It gives you and Viv equal shares in everything if I don't make it."

"I don't want your money, Steven."

"No, maybe not, but I want you to have it. Both of you."

"We're not talking about this now." Her eyes were wet with tears.

"No? Then when are we going to talk about it?" He glanced up at the large clock hanging on the wall. "From what I can see, we're short on hours."

"Mum," Viv put her hand out onto her mother's arm. "He's right."

Their mother shook her head. "No."

"I'm sorry, Mum. I really am. All I seem to have been for you is a sequence of difficulties and conversations you don't want to have."

"What's that supposed to mean?" she snapped.

"It's OK."

"No, no it isn't. What are you saying, Steven?"

"Let's just say you didn't react particularly well when I came out to you as gay."

"No." She fell quiet. "No, I didn't."

"I'm sorry. I wish I'd been more, well ... I wish I'd been the son you wanted."

His mother stood and, with rapid steps, crossed the room to him. She knelt on the floor at his feet and took both his hands in hers.

"Steven, stop."

"Stop what?"

"Stop speaking. You do not need to say 'sorry' to me. Far from it."

"I feel I do." He coughed again, spitting more blood onto the tissue he held. His eyes dripped tears, his body bent in pain and struggles.

"No, you listen to me. You are my son, and if there has been any conflict between us, it is my fault, not yours." She looked up at his face.

"I reacted badly. Homosexuality wasn't something that my generation discussed openly. We didn't mention it at all and we all heard about AIDS. When that came to the world, it came with a lot of hatred for gay people and I was as swept along with that as anyone else. Hearing that from you, it cut me. It tore into me. You are my perfect boy and I had to ask myself what had happened. What had I done wrong? I had to find something or someone to blame, and so I blamed you. You and Alistair. And your father. I didn't speak much about that, but it was inside me."

Steven nodded mutely.

"That first year after you told me was a struggle. Your sister was there in my ear, twisting my thoughts with her own prejudice and hatred. I was cast away, sent back to Malaysia and unable to get back to my children in Britain. Your father had died, and yes, we'd had our problems, but that affected me, too. I was alone for the first time and it was so difficult for me.

"Now, your happiness is my priority. Whatever makes you happy makes me happy. My journey of acceptance isn't complete yet. I have been back here in England for some time. I have met your friends and your boyfriend. I have spoken with some wise and intelligent people, like Geri, Claire, and Charles himself. I have listened to my other daughter. Vivienne speaks very highly of you." She smiled at Viv.

"I admit, I still wouldn't want my friends or relatives at home to know, yet. I still keep it from them. And sometimes, I find it uncomfortable seeing you promote your work within your community, but I tried, and I try. I saw you on stage that day with Geri and I was proud. I am proud. Of course, I am proud. I'm not quite there yet, you will have to bear with me. I want you to see my progress, though, so you must survive tomorrow to witness it. You *must*. I'm really trying."

Through his tears, Steven looked down at his mother's earnest face. She had come a long way, such a long way.

"I want to see your progress. I want to survive."

"I love you, son."

Steven coughed again. His own, similar affirmation lost in the blood-spitting spasm.

"It's a major operation." The surgeon stood on one side of the room, one of four men. Steven's family, Martin, and Claire on the other. "I want you to understand that there's a good chance that you don't survive the surgery." He held up the x-ray. "It is our intention to remove the tumour in its entirety. We are going to be cutting out your entire right upper lobe, some lymph nodes and part of your bronchus. Externally, you will have a significant scar on your side, plus you will be in ICU for a couple of days, with a chest drain."

He was holding a thin stack of papers. "These are the consent forms. Are you happy to sign them now or do you need time to discuss this with your family?"

"It's all been discussed." Steven held out his hand. "Do you have a pen?"

Once the surgery team left the room, Steven's mother released a low wail.

"It's OK, Mum, it'll be OK."

Steven accepted his mother's embrace and then, one by one, hugged each of the others. Only Charles was noticeable by his absence; his doctor's life forcing him to be absent at this precious time. He and Steven had said their words earlier, spending a heartfelt hour in the morning before dawn. Charles would come as soon as he could, crossing the very hospital he worked in to be there when the man he loved came out of his operation.

The anaesthetist came next and, once his part was explained, had Steven wheeled out into the corridor.

There was no more space for words. Steven looked around him as he travelled, becoming steadily more disoriented from room to room.

The anaesthetist chatted away as he worked.

"Enjoy the sleep," he looked down into Steven's face.

Who says that? Steven was bemused by the man's morbid humour. He was unconscious before the thought was done.

The rainclouds were thick. Steven held up his umbrella and noted absently how it matched his black suit. Here, in the graveyard, it felt fitting.

"What are you doing here?" Zoe sneered. She was dressed well, also all black. Steven noted her shoes; inappropriate for the weather, but probably quite good for hitting people with.

"I think someone died.".

"Well, obviously." His sister walked over to look at the gravestone, pushing a mourner out of the way to do so. "Oh, good, it's you."

"Me?"

"That's what it says here."

"Oh yes, it was you." The man turned to look at him. Dad.

"I died?"

"Good, isn't it?" Zoe clapped her hands. "Can't say you didn't deserve it."

Steven looked around. Other people were dotted around, coming closer now to look at the grave. His grave.

"John." The man he noticed smirked at him. Steven's mind flashed to a hotel room, after work. *Just relax and enjoy it. I know I'm going to.* Steven shuddered.

"Who's that guy?" Zoe asked.

"No one." Steven looked at the ground.

"Oh!" Zoe brightened. "I know this man, though. Do you remember him, Steven? He hasn't aged a day!"

Steven followed her gaze. Another man, another time. Of course, he remembered him. Remembered hiding under a table. Remembered having to scrub the floor. Remembered the fear that his dad and his sister had just left him there.

Old memories, unwanted memories.

What was going on?

"Why are these people here?" Steven asked.

He scanned the faces as people approached. A man he was sure was a waiter, a boy who had bullied him at school, a fat man and woman come to buy his little sister, the prostitute who had stolen his father from his family.

"Nice company you like to keep." His father put his arm around his old mistress and pulled her in tight.

The rain came down, hard droplets hammering on the umbrella.

"All here to see you die," said Zoe.

Another man stood behind her. Steven looked into his face and recognised him immediately. It was like staring into a mirror.

"Tristan," said the newcomer. He held out his hand to shake.

The storm increased around him.

"No!" Steven pushed at Tristan, tripping him up. His doppelgänger slipped, falling and flailing in the mud.

Steven turned to Zoe. "You're not here to see me die. None of you. You are here because I am done with you. I am done with all of you!" He pointed to the gravestone. "This isn't my funeral. It's yours."

Ignoring the rain, Steven strode away from the gathering.

A tall man leaned against a tree. Steven walked past him, not caring to see any more.

His voice was immediately familiar. "Don't look back at all of this, don't ever look back at it again. Go forward and breathe."

Steven turned. "Al?"

Alistair smiled and walked away.

Steven opened his eyes and immediately closed them again from the brightness of the room. Charles held his hand.

"Hey," Steven said.

"Afternoon. Have a good sleep?"

Steven trembled.

Charles leaned in and kissed him on his forehead. "I knew you'd make it."

THE END